THE ARTERIAN SERIES: BOOK ONE

OF FLAMES & FALLACIES

COURTNEY WHIMS

To you.
"We either outgrow our grief, or our grief outgrows us."
You can do the hard things.
I believe in you.
♥

PRONUNCIATION GUIDE

ARTERIAS: *Ar-tear-ee-us*
ARTERIAN: *Ar-tear-ee-uhn*

KATERINA: *Kat-er-eena*
DAEJA: *Day-shuh*
COLE: *Coal*
LELAND: *Lee-land*
DARIAN: *Dare-ian*
ARCHIE: *Arch-ee*
MARGE: *Mar-juh*
CARLISLE: *Car-lie-ul*
MELAINA: *Mel-ain-uhh*
GAVIN: *Gav-in*
NOLAN: *No-lan*
CELESTE: *Suh-lest*
TAWNY: *Taw-knee*
SETHAN: *Seth-uhn*

Of Flames and Fallacies is a fast-paced fantasy romance
that takes place in a kingdom where dragons are forbidden.
This is an adult series which contains elements that might
not be suitable for some readers.

For the most updated list of elements,
please refer to the URL below:
courtneywhims.com/book

Readers who may be sensitive to these elements, please take note.
Your mental health matters. ♥

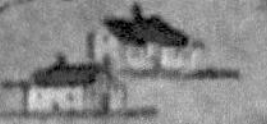

DRAGON'S
NORTHERN
FOREST
THE
OUTPOST
KAT'S HOME
HORNWOOD
PADMOOR
SPILLBURG
GROVEDEN
BROOKVALE
OF FLAMES &
FALLACIES

BACK RIDGE
SKYLARK
MISTWOOD
STONE SHIRE
WINDMERE
BLACKFELL
WYNNBAN
ARTERIAS
SILVERPEAK
HELMBROOK
SHADSTEAD

ONE

THE CARNYX

I don't know a lot of things. But one thing I do know, is that once you hear it, you fucking run.

The distant cry of it splits the air. A deep, haunting bray. An alarm as hollow as any nightmare could conjure.

The Carnyx.

They couldn't have picked something a little less menacing to alert the towns? Maybe a regular fucking bell instead?

"Take cover!" a voice shouts over the frantic screams exploding around me.

Men and women dash left and right. Shoulders and elbows jab into me as we scatter separate directions in the cobblestone street. A woman stumbles. She collapses to the ground, and the crowd tramples over her. My breath catches and I freeze, the seconds ticking by painfully slow as I wait for her to resurface. Despite my instincts screaming at me to run for my life, I push against the urge and race toward the woman. Shoving my way through the crowd, I find her on her hands and knees, struggling to get up. I hook my arm through hers, pulling her to her feet with all of my strength. She finds her footing, and her wide brown eyes meet mine.

"Come on!" I tug her arm and push through the crowd.

We break away from the main street and skirt down a shadowed alley ending in a dead end. I turn toward a familiar door on my left and slam a fist against the wood.

"Willard! Willard, please! Let us in!" With each slam of my fist, my knuckles scream in pain. The main street falls eerily silent. I whip my head over my shoulder to scan the now empty road, then turn back to the door and ram my body against it. Pleading with everything I am for the man inside to open it.

"Stop," the woman whispers and pulls me from the door.

A screeching roar thunders nearby.

I freeze. *Shit.*

The woman yanks me down to a crouch, and we fumble backwards, tucking into a corner behind a stack of wooden crates. My strained breath rattles in my chest, my heart pounding in my ears. I peek around the edge of a crate toward the main street, but the woman's shaky hand grasps my shoulder, pulling me back.

But not before I see it.

With a terrified scream, a man races down the main street, followed immediately by an explosion of fire. Within seconds, he's engulfed in flames. His cries are cut short by the roaring inferno.

Even from this distance, the heat radiates over me. I turn, tucking my face into my shoulder. A heavy beat of wings approaches as loud as distant thunder.

Against my better judgment, I dare one more peek. A dark shadow looms over the flame-filled street. The silhouette disappears as quickly as it appeared, its fiery breath the only evidence in its wake.

Dragons.

"What are we going to do?" the woman whispers.

"I have to go."

She grabs my arm. "Absolutely not! You'll attract its attention!"

I rip away from her grasp. "And you'll be trapped if you stay."

"It's a risk I'm willing to take."

"But not a risk I can take." I slink out into the alley.

I have to get to my mother.

The woman doesn't follow as I edge closer to the flames. The heat of it warms my skin as I approach, and sweat trickles down the nape of my neck. I pause at the corner where the alley meets the main street, searching the skies for the dragon, but it's nowhere in sight. I shift my focus back to the street. My breath catches in my throat at the heap of ash where the man had been moments earlier.

After a few heartbeats, I slip between the dying flames lining the street and race for the northwestern border of town. A few townspeople peek out from behind merchant carts and from windows carved into the sides of stone buildings. Their wide stares hook into me, begging me to hide.

"Katerina!" a voice hisses at me.

Ignoring it, I pass the last few buildings of Padmoor and reach the town's outskirts. The land gives way to the familiar rolling hills that stretch from here to the distant Northern Forest. Tucked into those hills is the faint roof of my home, a speck against the landscape this far out.

A dark figure glides in and out of the clouds above the Northern Forest. I stiffen as it turns back toward Padmoor and grows larger.

And larger.

Closer and closer.

Close enough that I note it's a red dragon, with scales shimmering blood-red in the sunlight. Monstrous twisted black horns crown its head, with smaller spikes outlining its face. The creature parts its jaws, and daylight gleams against rows of black daggered teeth the length of my forearm. The thick scales armoring its chest glow a soft orange, its black talons flexing open and closed as it gathers its strength.

Shit.

Shit, shit, shit.

My legs freeze in position, my mind screaming at me to run. I glance left then right, but the vast open space leaves me no place to hide. The red dragon releases a high-pitched roar, a cacophony more terrifying than any beast known to humans. My ears ring, and my blood shudders in my veins.

The beast's molten yellow eyes lock with mine.

My breath is stuck in my throat.

I'm as dead as the man in the street.

I drag my gaze away, looking down at my feet and accepting my fate. A wall of solid wind hits me, knocking me off balance. I fall backwards, landing on the ground with a splitting ache in my head. Blinking open my eyes, the scaled underbelly of the beast bullets past me. The air around me stills.

I shift up to my elbows and toss a glance over my shoulder.

The dragon dips low and glides toward Padmoor again.

Steel javelins from the Padmoor outpost's ballista rocket toward the creature. From this distance, the sharp slivers of metal are no bigger than the size of a child's arm. But up close, they're as tall as a doorframe, with multiple sets of metal barbs lining its column.

Several of the javelins sink into the red webbing of the dragon's wings. The beast screeches, and I clap my hands over my ears as its high-pitched cries reverberate within me. The dragon falters mid-flight, the flap of its wings becoming erratic as it careens toward the ground. It slams into the earth, rocks and dirt bursting into the air on contact, and the ground shudders underneath my feet. The dragon attempts to rise, its thick talons sinking into the ground for leverage, but with its wings punctured, it's unable to maintain balance.

Soldiers close in, swarming around the beast, their weapons raised and aimed on their target. I look away as a strained roar dies, and triumphant cheers ring out across the land—confirmation of the soldiers' success.

I've always wondered what they do with the bodies. It would take at least two dozen men to drag something of that size, but to where? By the next day, there will be no trace of the animal. It will be as though it never existed. The only remaining evidence will be the crater left behind where it landed, and the char marks in the streets of Padmoor.

And the empty bed where the dead man used to lay.

My heart sinks. He was probably someone's father, brother, husband, or friend. *He could have been me.*

Or Cole.

My heart tumbles at the thought of Cole. Memories crash and swarm around me, drowning every other thought aside from him. I force my steps forward, walking west toward home, one foot in front of the other.

It's been months since I've seen or heard from Cole—the longest we've ever gone without speaking. Knowing we may never speak again pains me. The military doesn't allow correspondence except from family members or spouses. Had I agreed to his proposal, I would have fit in that latter category.

I shove the thought away. I have too much to do and too many worries to spend additional time or energy thinking about Cole or what could've been. In fact, I'm more pissed off than sad— at least that's what I tell myself.

The ground beneath my feet rises and falls as I trek through the hills. The sun warms my back, and the wind picks up, brushing against my clothes. As I near the familiar angled roof of my home, free of any flames or scorch marks, I loose a shaky breath. The doorknob squeaks in my hand as I twist it and open the front door.

"Mother?" I call out as I enter. My gaze sweeps across the kitchen with our rickety wooden table and chairs, to the makeshift fireplace in the opposite corner of the room. Despite the season nearing fall, the room is uncomfortably warm. Flecks of dust fall like snow in the rays of light streaking through the windows across the room. I walk toward the windows, cracking them open to admit fresh air. My gaze catches on the distant speck of the dragon and the swarm of soldiers. I glance toward the sky and breathe out a sigh of relief. No trails of smoke nor flares of orange block out the sky. The city Padmoor will survive another day.

I set my satchel down in my room then walk across the hallway to my mother's bedroom. I stare at the doorknob, debating whether to disturb her. I turn the knob, achingly slow, hoping she might be asleep. The door squeaks open, and I peer through the few inches of space.

Mother sits on the edge of her bed, back facing me, and her attention focused out the window at the forest behind our house. She's still, animated only by the gentle rise and fall of her shoulders.

I wait a second, maybe two, then walk toward her as she lifts a hand and points one finger toward the window. As I turn the corner of the bed I scan her face. Her skin is pale, the sockets of her eyes deepening with each passing day. Even her long, blonde hair has lost its luster. But what haunts me most is the glazed vacancy in her eyes and the way she fixes her gaze at the window. The first time I discovered her this way was terrifying, her body so eerily still and quiet, yet somehow a warning.

I lay my hand on her outstretched one, then crouch in front of her. "Mother." My voice is only a hair louder than a breath.

Her gaze remains focused on an invisible something in the distance, and her hand trembles, the shaking rising up her arm.

"The one son," she murmurs.

I shake my head and brush my fingertips over the back of her hand, hoping the sensation will break her concentration. "Mother, I'm here. It's me. It's Katerina."

"The one son." Her voice grows louder. "Chosen to lead them all. Wasn't a son but a maid."

I cradle her face in my hands and stare into her blue eyes as I brush my thumb over her right cheek. "It's okay, it's just a dream. I can get your medicine. Did you take it this morning?"

"Until binds of death did that grave deed bade…" With each word, her tone tips toward hysteria.

I turn toward her nightstand and pull open the top drawer and retrieve her bottle of medicine. The cork is missing and nothing but droplets are left inside.

"In death blood is shed!" she screams.

I bolt for my room, bursting through my door and dropping to my knees near the bed. My chest tightens as I rip out the wooden crate stashed under my bed. I rake through other empty vials until I find a full one. Swiping it, I race back to my mother.

Standing near the window, now she splays her open palms

to the window, her forehead pressed against the pane. Her wide blue eyes stare outside.

"But from blood there is life!" She explodes into maniacal laughter then rears back and slams her head against the glass.

"Mother!" I jolt forward, grabbing her shirt.

Once again she rears back, slamming her head into the window a second time before I can stop her.

Wrapping one hand over her forehead, I pull her back toward me. A warm, sticky substance drips down my forearm.

"No!" She thrashes against me.

Bracing the back of her head against my chest with one hand, I clench her cheeks between the fingers of my free hand, forcing her mouth open and pouring the liquid inside. I hold my grip until she swallows.

"Restored by air and night to end allll ssstrifee." Her words slow and morph into a slur.

Her body slackens, and relief floods me. I shift my attention to my forearm where blood—my mother's blood— stains my skin crimson.

Mother's eyes flutter closed, her jaw relaxing into a lazy grin as a trickle of blood drips down her forehead toward her chin.

I grab a handkerchief from her nightstand and press it to the wound on her forehead. Swaying her back and forth, tears well in my eyes. My gaze moves to the cracked window and the dark green pine trees of the Northern Forest it frames. It's over—for now, at least. Though she'd begun pounding her fists with her last few episodes, she'd never done this kind of damage. A shiver shoots down my spine at the realization of how her episodes have escalated and how much more she might still spiral.

When I was a kid, her episodes consisted of her singing as she watched the distant clouds roll by, swaying to whatever had entranced her. At the time, I thought it was an exaggerated song of the sun and night. My older brother told me to ignore it and not to interrupt. But then I got older, and the episodes got worse. It wasn't until recently that I realized how bad they had become.

In the deepest parts of my memory, before she sang, she laughed. But laughed with a slow, warm clarity at my childish questions like where clouds came from or why some deer had sticks on their heads. Back then, she was the one who held and rocked me, the one who cared for and comforted me. We shared with each other our wildest dreams. We skipped through the snow in the winter and shouted into the night sky how much we missed my father. Somewhere between then and now everything fell apart, like the threads of an old blanket unraveling until there is nothing but a heap of string.

Now, I'm the one holding the threads of what she once was between my useless hands with no knowledge of how to knit her back together. All I can do is hold her and yearn for the mother she once was.

After several moments, I lay her on her bed and pull the sheets up to her chin. Removing the bloodied handkerchief, I survey the gash on her forehead and breathe a sigh of relief that the wound is crusted over. Inching out of her room, I close the door and sink down to my heels with my head leaning back against the door.

I have nothing left.

Nothing left to eat.

Nothing left to trade for more medication.

That vial was the last I had.

TWO

FISHING

Sunlight chases away the sounds of crickets and toads, replacing them with songs of birds. I skulk through the forest, the glow of the early morning light bathing the Northern Forest in hues of oranges and yellows. Pine trees stretch over my head, casting dappled sunshine across the forest floor.

My chest tightens with anxiety as a glimmer of water shines through the trees ahead. *Perhaps, if the dragon from yesterday had killed us, we would have had a quick and merciful death instead of this agonizingly slow descent. We wouldn't be left with this impending threat of running out of medication—or starving to death.*

My anxiety eases as I near the rippling stream. Few dare into these forests, mostly because of the close proximity to the northern Dragon Lands border. Many have gone missing or been found dead here.

But I have no choice.

If my father or brother were here, I wouldn't need to fish for our survival. Maybe I would be somewhere halfway across the kingdom writing poetry, painting, or courting a man who's wickedly good at dancing. But instead I'm here, and they are there, buried beneath what little we could honor them with: two small rickety crosses near the river. The years and weather have stripped the woods of their rich browns, fading them to shades of gray. I don't let my gaze linger for long. Because each sidelong glance at the crosses is a reminder.

A reminder of how incapable I am.

A reminder of how helpless I am.

Yet it strikes like an insult to their memories to not stop and think of them.

I chew at my lip, biting back a surge of remorse. This is my twenty-second year. I'm twelve years older than my brother was when he died. Yet I'm still trapped in the moment. It's nearly comical that I'm the one caring for our mother now. Because out of the two of us, he would have been able to dig us out of this shitty fucking hole we're stuck in—despite him being older by only four years. That's simply who he was: confident, capable, and strong. If he inherited those attributes from my father, I'll never know for certain. My father died before I was born, and after my brother passed, my mother rapidly declined past the point of coherency.

I avert my gaze from my brother's cross to the river. The water glistens in the light of dawn, its glassy surface rumbling with a hidden danger. I scan the water, but the fish trap isn't where I set it yesterday. Instead, I find it about twenty yards farther downstream.

I hold my breath as I tread toward the bend of the river where an edge of the wooden contraption peeks out from a cluster of rocks. With each step I mentally beg for a fish to be caught in the trap. Because if not...I don't know what we will do. We have no medicine, and I have nothing left to trade for more. There's no telling what will become of my mother without her medication, even if only for a day. But I can't give that possibility space. It scares me too much.

My heart sinks as I reach the trap. No fish, and the fucking trap is broken. The body of the contraption is ripped in half, with the second piece missing.

Some asshole bear must have come by, seen the easy meal, ripped out the fish, and went on its merry fucking way. The realization I won't have any fish to trade today crushes me, and I tremble with the weight of my reality. Tears sting the corners of my eyes as my desperation bubbles to the surface.

We are fucked.

So very, very fucked.

Either we will starve or my mother will become so deranged without her medication she'll burn our house down. I pull the trap out of the water with shaking hands. A thick haze of hopelessness clouds over me, and I grip onto the wood as if it might calm the emotions threatening to overwhelm me. The wood creaks and snaps in my grasp. With a guttural scream, I fling the trap behind me, hoping to release the feelings of dread with it. Instead, the trap slips from my sweat-slickened hands and rockets into my father's cross, pulling it part way out of the ground.

My shoulders sag. What have I done to deserve such a damnation? Maybe this is a terrible dream I can't seem to shake. But that's the thing: no one is here to save me. No one is here to tell me it's going to be okay.

This is not a dream.

The weight of our fate looms, threatening to pull me under its vicious tide. I scramble for any semblance of sanity. My instincts drive me to memories of Cole and how he'd remind me to ground myself in the world around me.

I look up. Blinking back any tears threatening to creep up on me.

Five things I see.
Four things I feel.
Three things I hear.
Two things I smell.
One thing I taste.

The process distracts me from my own hopelessness—distracts me from myself. My racing thoughts slow as I shift into another perspective. An electric blue butterfly floats on a breeze across the water and disappears into the throng of trees. My pounding heart quiets, and my panicked breath levels.

After a few moments, I trudge over to the unearthed cross, kneeling as I reach a hand toward its wooden surface.

"I'm so sorry, Father," I croak, shaking my head against the next well of sadness. I push the cross back into the packed earth, but my efforts are met with resistance. My gaze shifts to the ground as I clear away splintered trap remnants and crumbs of dirt.

My fingers brush against something cold, and a zap of energy zings its way up through my fingertips. I recoil with a gasp.

Is my lack of food over the last few weeks leading me to the point of hallucinations?

I creep closer for a better look. Buried under the cross, a smooth black surface gleams in the sunlight. I tug the cross out of the ground and place it next to me, revealing an oval-shaped black stone underneath.

If it's not the most flawless river rock I've ever seen—

My fingers brush over its surface, and the stone hums against my skin as if it bottled the electricity of a storm. I pause, my intuition urging me to leave it there. Or report it to the Padmoor council. But something else calls me to it, as if something whispers on a breeze.

I rub my eyes with the heels of my hands. Perhaps the buzz in my skin is a figment of my imagination. Would the council laugh at me if I took a riverstone to them and reported it as something else? Or perhaps they would pity me?

I'm probably overthinking it—wouldn't be the first time.

I pull the stone free from the earth and cradle it's cold, heavy weight in my hands. I brush a thumb across its glassy smooth curves, the black surface lustrous in the sunlight.

If it is a riverstone, it would make a nice matching set of earrings, ring, and bracelet. It might catch enough of a penny to keep us afloat with food and medicine for a considerable amount of time.

And if it's not a riverstone?

I suppose it's a risk I must take. Because if it is a dragon egg, I'll spend my last seconds gasping for air with a noose around my neck. And my mother will be damned.

THREE

WILLARD

By the time I make it to the outskirts of Padmoor it's after noon. Clouds skitter and dissipate, and harsh sunlight streaks across the angled rooftops of the town. I pull the hood of my cloak over my face, shading my eyes. Buyers bustle back and forth between the merchant carts lining the main road. Charred gouges shred the cobblestone street, edges of buildings blackened by yesterday's attack.

Dragonfire is unlike regular fire. Fire burns everything flammable. But dragonfire scores its target, marring everything in its path.

As I walk further down the street, the frenzy of the crowd thickens. Each Arterian's stare flicks over me with the same expression.

Wide-eyed.

Distressed.

Terrified.

It's the first dragon attack here in years. And while it was only a matter of time, the event is enough to send people into a panic. Civilians stock up on what they can, in case another dragon comes. In case they aren't as lucky next time around, and not even the King can save them.

Because dragons are ruthless.

Vicious and savage creatures determined to destroy anything and everything in their paths. They are loyal to none.

The King declared war on dragons long ago to save us from the wicked beasts. And we might have eradicated the dwindling species if sympathizers hadn't split off for the Dragon Lands to our north.

Rebels: the more precise word for what most Arterians call sympathizers. They revel in bloodshed and worship the winged beasts of the sky. We're encouraged to report any suspicious activity or persons to our town council. Turning in a rebel garners respect, and reporting someone you know? Honorable. It signifies you value your kingdom more than any loyalty to the people you love.

Besides, refraining to report a known sympathizer means a guaranteed execution. Especially since rumors began circulating in recent years that those same rebels were attacking the northern cities of Arterias. We are lucky we haven't been targeted.

Yet.

Perhaps it was only a matter of time.

But it's not something I can consider right now. I don't

have the luxury of time—we will probably die of starvation first. Unless some gods-assigned miracle saves us from this slow death.

I used to daydream a man would rescue us. On some fateful day, I'd be wandering the main street and bump into a handsome foreigner, his luxurious clothes pressed and lacking the stains and tears of my own. In my dream, I was always puzzled at why he was so captivated by me. It certainly wouldn't be my clothes, draping loose on my frame where I'd lost weight from malnutrition. Nor would it be the brown freckles dusting the red tinted blush of my cheeks, signifying my days in the sun. No, it would be my hair.

Definitely the hair.

I imagined the way his gaze followed the cascade of my silvery blonde hair down to my ribcage. He'd profusely apologize while helping me gather whatever I had dropped, and our eyes would lock. It would be then, in that moment, he'd fall head over heels in love with me, and I'd be whisked away to whatever castle he dwelled in. And I would never again have to gut, nor eat, another damn fish for the rest of my life.

A shoulder shoves against mine, and I'm clipped out of my thoughts.

"Watch where you're going," a familiar voice snaps.

As I turn toward the voice, I catch her wicked, angry stare. Cole's younger sister: Vivian. Like her five younger sisters, her long raven hair shadows her pale skin. Cole was a stark comparison with his tousle of flame-red hair and soft hazel eyes. The girls look like their father. And I wish I could have met the woman Cole resembled.

His mother died during childbirth with their youngest sister, Rosetta. And since then, their father spent most of his time working to provide financially for his children. Cole naturally assumed the role of guardian and protector of all his younger sisters.

"Viv—" I blurt. Somewhat relieved to see her, and anxious to ask how Cole is.

"He went to see you before he left, you know. And you couldn't even bother to answer the door." Her voice is laced with an extra layer of venom.

She had never been a fan of me. Cole always assured me she was naturally standoffish. But I always suspected it was because she thought I would take Cole away from them. And then they would have no one.

The realization dawns on me, my mouth falling open. The only day she could be referring to was the one where I fell asleep by the river for nearly half the day. I wouldn't have ignored a knock at the door, especially if I knew it was Cole. Not when part of me still yearned for any opportunity to see him again.

I reach out to her with a hand. "I...I had no idea, Vivian—"

"You're a bitch, Kat. He loved you," she snaps, recoiling from my grasp. "And one day, he'll find some pretty girl in Blackfell and forget all about you." She swivels away from me to storm back into the crowd.

My shoulders sag as I watch her fade into the crowd. Part of me is tempted to follow her, and to explain it was all a mistake. But the other part of me knows it's no use.

Someone else bumps into me, and I reflexively clutch my satchel. The movement reminds me of my objective.

Walking down the main street, I pass by the battered awning where I met Cole ten years ago. The merchant there had been the go-to for selling honey. That fateful day was my mother's birthday, and she had been sick with a nasty cough. While she told me very little of medicines growing up, I remembered her mentioning honey coated sore throats. But the merchant declined my offer of a freshly caught fish for a bottle of honey. It wasn't until Cole offered to trade me a fire poker for my fish that the merchant changed his mind.

"What the hell am I supposed to do with this?" I had asked, feeling awfully skeptical of Cole's intentions.

To think Cole would try to lead someone astray was now laughable.

He had smiled. Slowly, until it was wide, warm, and welcoming. "Well, some of the nobles use it to stoke their fireplaces. But I say it doubles as a weapon. Or if you needed a toothpick for your horse, I guess that'd work too."

I didn't need any of those three options. Surprisingly, though, the merchant did. That day I walked home with honey, Cole left with my fish, and the merchant got a brand new fire poker.

It wasn't until years later Cole admitted the fire poker was valued well over the fish and honey combined. Could have fooled me.

I cut away from the main street and down an alley. The

same locked door I pounded on yesterday opens with ease. Ducking my head, I slink through Willard's arched doorway.

I've been coming to Willard for years after Cole introduced us. While some pin him as a little crazy with radical practices and beliefs—I find him endearing. He's become as familiar to me as if I knew him my entire life. Willard is kind and fair, even when others aren't. Maybe it's because I'm one of a few who actually listens when he goes off on his rambles.

"Willard?" I call as I lower my hood.

Candles of different shapes and sizes scattered across the room illuminate the cozy shop. An old withered chair seats half-haphazardly stacked books, and on the ground next to it is a bucket collecting drips of water from the ceiling. A collection of odd-shaped bottles line multiple shelves layered on the stone walls. Some glasses are half-full, and others have only drops left. I avert my eyes from the jars with animal parts floating in them. A mixed scent of must and smoke hangs in the air.

"Willard?" I call out once more. I pause after taking a few steps into the room, not wanting to venture further if he isn't here.

"Comin', comin'!" a call comes from the corner of the room. Willard backs out of the curtained room he calls his study. When he twists to face me, he greets me with a lopsided grin. His eyes soft within the deep wrinkles etching his face. His shoulders curve more than his usual posture, arms full of books. Before I can scold him, his knees buckle from the weight.

I jolt forward, catching him before he can fall face first. A few books clatter to the ground.

I gather the books, piling them onto a table with a frown. "Willard, didn't I tell you not to carry this many on your own?"

Willard turns a grateful smile toward me. "Ahh, Katerina! I haven't seen you in a week. I was startin' to worry about you."

"I dropped by yesterday, but your door was locked. Did you not hear the Carnyx?"

"Ahh, ahh. Yes." He uses a pinky finger to swipe the innards of his ear. "Sorry, I mustn't have heard you knockin'."

If it were anyone else I might have been frustrated. I could have died. But I believe him—the years haven't been kind to his hearing. And if he did hear me, he wouldn't have hesitated to let me in.

I pat his shoulder forgivingly. "Look, I came by yesterday because the fish have either been getting smarter or something else has been catching them. I wanted to ask if there was any way I could get some medication now, even if it's only a few days' worth."

"Katerina, I can't—"

"I'll pay you double."

"Katerina." He sighs. "You know I would for you. But I can't. I have to get the supplies from the council, first. And I don't have much to give, myself."

My heart sinks. It leaves me no other choice.

"I have something else," I whisper as I pull out the stone and present it to him.

Willard sucks in a breath and takes a step back, his hand covering his open mouth.

I flinch at his response and glance back down at the stone, confirming I didn't pull out a decapitated head instead.

"Where did you get that?" His voice is tight.

I inch forward and offer it to him.

He hesitates. Cautiously, he takes the stone from me and inspects the surface with a gentle stroke.

"I found it—"

He shoves the stone back into my chest, and my breath wooshes out.

"Never mind! Don't answer that." His hand shaking, he points at the door. "Return it at once. Don't tell anyone. Don't show anyone."

"Willard—"

He vigorously shakes his head, his lips tight and eyes wild. If I didn't think Willard was pale before, he's definitely pale now.

"Go!" His voice trembles as much as his hands do.

My heart hammers in my ears, and I'm frozen where I stand. What am I supposed to do?

"I said go, Katerina," he grits out.

Stunned at his uncharacteristically severe voice, I step back and out of the shop. In the few seconds before the door closes between us, his voice drops to a whisper.

"You shouldn't have shown me that."

FOUR

TRAPPED

My mind reels with each step taking me closer to home. The clamor of the busy main street falls away to silence as I leave Padmoor. The quiet secludes me within my own thoughts. I find myself ruminating over the intensity of Willard's tone. Perhaps he was drunk. Maybe he was mistaken.

Or maybe I'm the one mistaken, and this is a bad idea.

But Willard instructed me to return the stone where I found it, and I'm too far from Padmoor now to report it to the council. Besides, if it isn't a stone, what would a dragon egg be doing out here?

Maybe it's a fancy riverstone and Willard thought I stole it out of desperation, and he wants me to return it before someone realizes it's gone. In the solitude of the rolling grass-dusted hills around me, I peek in my satchel's opening. The stunning black stone shines, my fingers edging toward it as if bewitched to touch it…

I rip back my hand and snap the bag shut, before tossing a glance over my shoulder at the distant outline of Padmoor.

I'll report it to the council tomorrow.

In the meantime, I'll prepare a new fishing trap. As soon as I get home, I slink into our outdoor shed for materials. My gaze lingers on my mother's dusty bow-and-arrow hanging on the wall.

If only archery skills were genetic.

If they were, I'd be gifted enough to be an archer for the military. Like my mother was. Maybe even skilled enough to be an archer for the King. The pay alone would cover our medication and food costs. I brush my fingertip down the bow's string, a line of dust coats my skin. All I need is time to practice.

But time isn't a luxury I have.

I gather materials and work the rest of the day bending and weaving inside our home. The sun sets by the time I stop. Blisters nick my fingers, and my stomach roars with hunger. I'm partly relieved my mother hasn't stirred since I've been home.

The trap isn't complete enough to warrant it a successful one. Slumping in the chair I've been sitting in, I chew my lip, pushing the trap onto the table in defeat. The candlelight scatters dancing shadows across the opposing wall. I watch in silence, hoping for some hidden sign or answer. But nothing comes to me. Instead, I flick my gaze over to where my mother carved into the wall last week.

Secrets never die, they're just buried in a grave.

Secrets never die, they're just buried in a grave.

Secrets never die, they're just buried in a grave.

Secrets never die, they're jus

Over, and over, and over. Until the fourth row down it pauses halfway through the sentence, where I stopped her. I started hiding any sharp objects, for fear she might someday turn it on herself.

Or…me.

Leaning back into my chair, I rest my heels on the seat across from me. The seat she used to sit in. How I would do anything to have her back in that chair. Or anything, at all, just to have her back.

Perhaps I'll feign ignorance if it truly is a dragon egg. Insanity from malnutrition…maybe my mother's mental illness is genetic?

With a sigh, I push to my feet. There's no use in ruminating on it. Not when I can do that tomorrow.

I blow out the candles and shut all of the windows. By the time I've tip-toed back to my room and collapsed into bed, exhaustion drags at my eyelids. I stare at the ceiling and the wooden pillars slanted above me.

They tie me back to the forest. To my father and brother. The forest makes me feel so small, and my problems so minute in comparison. That it really, truly doesn't matter. Whether tomorrow is the day I die. Or the day after. At least I wouldn't suffer anymore.

Because I'm not cut out for this. I wish I could switch places with my brother or father. I know they'd figure a way out of this. They'd take better care of my mother than I've been able to. I wonder if they'd be as ashamed of me as I am of myself. Because at the end of the day, I'm incapable. Useless. Helpless.

My eyes fall closed, and I drift into sleep.

A sharp creak and crash rips me out of my slumber. My eyes flash open to orange-bathed beams above me. I'm not sure if it's morning, or how I've managed to sleep in so late.

"Katerina!" my mother screams.

I whip out of bed, blinking away the sleep as my gaze focuses. A wave of unsettling heat washes over me. Flames lick up the side of the wall and the dresser near my door, crackling from the intense heat.

"Mother!" I run toward the door. Another loud crash sounds outside my room, and the ground shivers under my feet. I hastily grab the doorknob, the heated metal sears my hand. I jerk back. Snatching my cloak I left draped over the edge of my bed, I wrap the fabric around my hand before twisting the knob and pushing the door open. It stops after a few inches. On the third attempt, I ram my shoulder into the wood, an ache flashing in my arm. Still, the door doesn't budge. My breath comes out in pants from the exertion and smoke filling my nose.

A familiar set of blue eyes flashes in the small gap between the door and frame. My mother frantically stuffs a bag through the opening, her nimble fingers working the satchel inch by inch. "Take it!"

I grab the bag, tugging it until the pressure releases and it slips free. Rivers of perspiration glide down my neck and back. My gaze flickers to the fire, now only a few feet away and climbing toward the ceiling. Thick smoke weaves its way into my lungs, tickling my throat. I slam against the door once more, desperate to get to my mother, but the heavy wood barely budges. My breath quickens with growing realization—I'm trapped.

"Listen to me!" my mother shouts over the roaring flames. "Find Cole, and take her back to the Dragon Lands. You aren't safe here. Don't come back. Trust no one!"

"Her? What are you talking about?" A cough steals my breath, the mix of heat and smoke burning in my chest. "Meet me at the front. Can you get to the front door?"

She shakes her head with soft, misty eyes. Despite her tears, the glassy look I've come to know is missing. In fact, her entire demeanor is different—lucid in a way she hasn't been since before my brother died. "I love you so much, Kit."

My heart plummets. She hasn't used that nickname since I was a kid. Since before she got sick. With a grunt, I drive my shoulder into the door again, but another cough racks my body. My eyes burn from the smoke clouding the room.

"Stop!" Mother reaches through the gap of the door and touches my cheek. "If you don't go now, you'll be dead."

The tenderness of the gesture and clarity in her gaze paralyzes me.

Something crashes in another room, and she whips her head over her shoulder before turning back to me. "Go. Now!"

The dresser to my left collapses, swinging toward me. I jump out of the way, dodging it just in time. When I peer into the gap where my mother was only moments before, she's gone.

I fumble backwards, shoving my boots on without tying the laces and throwing her bag over my shoulder. My own satchel sits on the ground near the bed, the flap open, and the stone missing. Panicked, I scan the room, searching as flames creep closer. From the corner of my eye, an orange light reflects off a dark, shiny surface peeking from beneath the edge of my bed. I reach for the stone, but the surface singes my fingertips. Crying out, I jerk my hand back.

The stone, I realize, is no longer whole but fragmented into pieces. As though it's been broken open like a chicken egg.

I drop to my knees and squint through darkness and smoke for a better look. A pair of reflective orbs shine back at me in the light of the dancing flames. Before I can register what's before me, the orbs blink and race toward me. A small dark creature scampers up my arm and onto my back as I writhe. Every doubt it was a "riverstone" is wiped away.

Before I can remove the creature from my back, another loud shriek rips my attention to the ceiling. Above me, the wooden beams scream as flames engulf it. One buckles under the attack, swinging down and rocketing into the side of the wall near the window, shattering the pane.

The window.

I dive through its gaping mouth and land on my face. The creature on my back jumps off and disappears into the shadows of the night. I push back onto my feet, struggling to stay upright as another cough chokes my breath. I circle to the front of the house and my skin crawls at the raging inferno decimating our small home. The only home I've ever known. Walls slump inwards, parts of the roof cave in, and a near-blinding flare pulses in the night. I race for the front door and find it stuck.

"Mother!" I punch the wood, desperate for it to open. Pledging everything I am to get to her. I have to get her.

I have to save her.

Balancing on one leg, I rear back and drive my heel into the door.

Once.

Twice.

Panic sinks me, like a heavy rock in the pit of my stomach—this isn't working.

I dash to the window leading to her room, but the walls groan, and the glass explodes. Embers spout from the fire, whipping across my face. I duck my head into the crook of my arm as an earth-shattering tremor reverberates over the ground. Before I can react, the walls of our home ripple like liquid and collapse.

A tidal wave of smoke races toward me. With no further hope of saving my mother or our home, I finally turn and run for the forest. The wind rips past me, chilling my sweat-coated skin and breaking it out into goosebumps.

I don't slow until I've reached the forest.

My chest heaves and breath sputters. I fold to my knees and release a ragged cough. I don't stop until I'm choking. My heart pounds, and my body trembles with each labored breath I suck into my lungs.

I dare a glance back toward the cottage, mentally begging my mother's silhouette to walk out the front door and escape the flames stretching into the night sky.

A loud crack splits the night and sparks burst into the air. The last of my hope dies in my chest as what's left of our home caves in.

A quiet numbness washes over me, broken only by the echo of my mother's voice in my head. I crack. And sob.

My chest is heavy and empty all at once. A raw pain, unlike anything I've ever experienced, tears through every inch of my soul.

The world spins around me before I fall to the forest floor. A distant pain roars in my skull as I connect with the ground. Stars twinkle in my vision before they turn black, and my mother's voice echoes inside my head.

Trust no one.

FIVE

DAEJA

An aching pain pulses in my skull, and my lungs strain with each rasping inhale. A rattling cough holds my breath hostage, and my eyes fly open as I suck in air. The rest of my senses spring to life one by one. Smoke taints my nostrils. My hand rests in front of me, blades of grass tickling my palm. I test my fingers by curling them inward, digging them into the cold hard earth. I'm laying stomach down on the ground, the dark silhouettes of trees stretching up into the night sky. An obscure hum rumbles far off in the distance.

The shadows shift, and small shadowed limbs and claws emerge from the black. I scramble to my feet. A black lizard-like creature stares at me with wide, white eyes. Unblinking. Unmoving. The animal chirps at me…*chirps?*

I fumble for something nearby and find an embarrassingly small stick, pointing it at the creature. "Get back!" I hiss.

The creature blinks, taking another step forward as I wave the stick wildly. Its gaze locks onto the wood in my hands. As I swing the stick, part of it splits from the main branch and flies off a few yards away. The creature darts after it, trotting back toward me with the stick in its mouth.

The moonlight highlights the animal's small, daggered teeth clenched around the stick. I freeze as the creature drops the stick at my feet and backs up a few paces. When we sit in silence for a few moments, I test it. I wave the stick again, and the creature watches my every move. Chucking the stick as far as I can, I bolt in the opposite direction toward the river.

The trees and river flash by me, and I finally slow as I approach my father's and brother's crosses. Surely, I would have lost the creature by now. I drop to sit by a tree, trying to even my breathing through hacking coughs.

Glowing eyes bounce toward me, the light of dawn reflecting in its pupils. I fish into the satchel my mother gave me, hopeful for something to defend myself, and whip out a dagger.

"I will use this!" I declare.

The creature slows and drops the branch a few yards from me, locking eyes once more and waiting. I stare it down through narrowed eyes, hoping it'll scurry off if I'm intimidating enough.

Instead, the creature carries the stick over to me, clearly unbothered by my dagger, and drops the branch inches from my toes. It backs up with a wiggle of its snake-like tail, eyes wide with what I assume is anticipation. The creature's proximity affords me a chance to study it. Dazzling black scales armor its body, and nubbed horns line its small head. It's about the size of a large lizard except…lizards don't have wings.

A dragon.

My mind races…*what if Willard turned me in? He couldn't possibly, could he? We're friends. Is that why my mother warned me not to trust anyone?*

My mother…

Tears creep up on me as my new reality settles in. My life's mission was to keep her alive—to take care of her—and I failed. It all swims back: the roof melting, the exploding window spraying glass shards, the smoke blotting out the stars.

A tremor snakes up my hand holding the dagger pointed at the dragon hatchling. Could this creature have been the one to start the fire? Maybe it was the reason my mother died. A sob consumes me at the thought of her, and the reminder of her absence. I'm nearly drowning in desperation for all the things I wanted to hear from her. From our very last moments together.

I love you.

I cling to the words. Replaying them over and over in my mind as if they were something I could audibly hear. Last night was the first time I heard them in so long. Perhaps the first time I heard them since my brother died.

Died. And now they were all dead. My eyes narrow at the little beast, and my fingers clench into the hilt as I hold the dagger steady. Aiming it straight between the two wide, white eyes. Since I was still sitting against a tree, the creature had a much better angle to attack me. Yet, if I tried to inch up to my feet it might become threatened. Dragons were unpredictable.

I should kill it first. Before it attacks.

The hatchling blinks slowly at me. Something about the soft movement freezes me. The fish I caught I could never look in the eyes as I gutted them. The idea of killing something while looking it in the eyes…it was too much. In a way, it felt barbaric.

The dagger falls from my hand and clatters to the ground. I sink my head into my hands. I can't. I can't do it. Despair's daggered claws sink into me and pull me down. Down far enough where I don't care what happens to me anymore. I should have died with my mother. I should have died a long time ago. It should have been me instead of my brother. A cry shakes my body, my palms growing wet with each shed tear.

Something nudges my boot, and I look up.

The creature sits, its eyes round as it chirps. It nuzzles against my leg, and I quickly shift away. My mother's words an echoed whisper in my mind.

Take her to the Dragon Lands.

My mouth parts, and I wipe away rivers of tears. *Her…who else would she have been referring to?* The rest of what my mother said echoes in my mind.

Find Cole, and take her to the Dragon Lands. You aren't safe here. Don't come back. Trust no one.

The urgency in her voice, the clarity in her eyes. It was as clear as I have seen her in so long. But what I couldn't wrap my head around was how she could have possibly been lucid.

"You're a her? How did she know about you?" I croak, almost immediately bemused I'm speaking out loud. And to an animal, at that.

The hatchling scurries toward me again as I hold out an open hand to pause her, but the tip of her nose brushes my palm. A shock of energy sings in my hand and trembles up my arm, my body writhing in response. A burst of air flares out from around us, rustling the leaves of the trees and blades of grass.

Daeja.

I don't know how or why. There's no one around me to whisper it, nor is it spelled out in the sky. But somehow I know that's her name. I pull my hand back and look at my open palm. A faint white ring wraps around the middle finger of my left hand.

The dragon hatchling—Daeja—takes my flat open hand as an invitation and climbs up to sit in my palm. Cautiously, I bring her closer to my face to look at her. Part of me is nervous this may be when she decides to strike me. But where I expect malice, danger, and ferality—there's a softness, trust, and…something else I can't quite put my finger on.

Before I can think better of it, I hold out a finger to inspect her wings. She takes the moment to lean into my hand and rubs her cheek alongside my finger.

Admittedly, for being a dragon, she's actually kind of… cute.

"You're an odd little thing," I mutter. How would my mother know about dragons or the Dragon Lands? Why would she possibly spend her last breaths telling me such a thing? And could I trust she was telling me these things in a sane state of mind, after her years of manic episodes and hysteria?

…I can't do this.

If I couldn't keep my own mother alive, how am I supposed to keep a dragon hatchling alive? If I'm caught, I'm dead. Not to mention that's if I don't die from a rebel attack, starvation, or the cold.

I set the dragon hatchling down on the ground.

"Just keep going north and you'll eventually get back to your lands." I point toward the jagged mountain tops of Dragon's Back Ridge stretching above the forest.

I gather my satchel, but the hatchling snags my dagger off the ground before I can grab it. I jolt forward, and she dodges me. Her eyes sparkle and tail quivers. She bounds off, and I stumble after her.

"Hey, get back here!" I hiss and follow her darting shadow. "Put that down! You'll hurt yourself!"

She squeals at our game of chase and stops at the river's edge. Dropping the dagger, she leans forward to sniff the water. Her body teetering far too close to the river's depths.

My pulse races as I manage to catch her by the tail before she falls in. It's the first time I've ever been fast enough. My attention momentarily flickers over to the two crosses before Daeja wriggles in my grasp and I let her go. Collecting my dagger off the ground, I place it back into my satchel.

The morning light catches the shine of…*coins? Where did she get this?* I pull out a brown journal, loaf of bread, and a flask of water. Every item I sift through, the seriousness of my mother's commands sinks in. She had planned this. She had thought this through. But it still didn't explain all the questions and doubts I had swirling around me.

King Aaric closed the northern border long before I was born. It's a nearly impossible quest to get to the border alive and alone. And that doesn't factor in with an illegal dragon. *Maybe that's why she told me to find Cole first…he could help me.*

My mother met Cole multiple times. Although, it was difficult to get any sort of indication on whether or not she approved of him. Not when most days she was either sleeping or having a mental break.

I have to admit, a part of me wants to see him again. Craves to see him again. Perhaps make amends.

My gaze floats back over to the two crosses. *What would they do?* I wait for an answer—a prod in a specific direction—anything. But I feel nothing. Despite how much it hurts, I think of my mother. Daeja watches me curiously, her head tilting far to the side.

If it was my mother's last request, I'll honor her memory by doing it. *I have to find Cole.*

Recounting my interaction with Vivian, Cole has to be in Blackfell. Blackfell is a few week's trek from here. Maybe a bit more at my pace and if I stick to the cover of the forest for as long as I can.

Before we leave, I linger at my father's and brother's crosses. My fingers trace the rugged grains of the wood as Daeja sniffs from afar. I shove a branch into the ground next to the other two. Sadness wells in me because I can't honor her memory with something more. I kiss my fingers before pressing them to the wood. I turn away quickly before I can cry again.

Leaving all I've ever known behind.

SIX

THE JOURNAL

We are moving slow. Too slow. I toss a look over my shoulder to see how far behind Daeja is. Her strides are far too short. And as more time goes on, her movements drag in exhaustion.

After deliberating, I turn around and place her in my satchel, but as I attempt to shut the flap, she hisses and climbs out. In liquid fast movement, she snakes up my arm and perches on my shoulder. My skin burns in the wake of her sharp talons.

The next attempt to place her back in my bag is just as unsuccessful. This time, she wraps herself around my neck. Despite the vulnerable position it puts me in if she decides to attack, it's... oddly comforting. Like a warm, dragon scarf. This may be the closest I ever get to being wealthy, since only the rich wear scarves. And fur ones at that.

Guess I have them beat with my scaled one.

I give in to her preferred spot wrapped around my neck—at least this way we can travel faster. She nuzzles into my neck with a chuff, and I flinch at her touch. It would be easy for her to sink her fangs into my throat from this angle.

But she doesn't.

And part of me lacks the depth of fear I should feel if she did.

The sun dips low behind the tree line stretching out before us. Soft hues of greens and golden light bathe the forest around us. My entire body groans against the effort to walk. Daeja is fairly quiet, aside from her head shifting against my neck as her gaze darts around at every little noise. We eventually stop at a rocky overhang for the night. As we settle in, I reach for the journal tucked into my satchel and set it on my lap.

A leather strap ties the two front folds closed. I trace my forefinger over the insignia etched into the weathered brown cover, leaving a thin layer of dust coating my finger. The silhouette of a dragon perches on top of a capital A. The dragon's long whip of a tail finishes out the crossbar of the letter. I edge open the cover, and my breath catches at the first page.

A Comprehensive Study of Dragons

By Leland Blackwind

Fire incarnate.

Flame in flesh.

Blood of power.

I slam the cover closed with both hands, my heart thumping wildly in my chest. I press my hands down on the journal's cover, as if it might fight against me and spring open at any given moment. Sweat coats my palms, and as I glance to my left I catch Daeja's bewildered gaze.

Leland Blackwind—*my father.*

My father's journal.

And at that, a *rebel's* journal.

A snort escapes me at the absurdity of it all.

If the King himself were here, the last thing I'd worry about would be a rebel's journal. The dragon hatchling herself climbing into my lap would be damning enough. Daeja nuzzles into my ribs as my breath slows. I stare at the back of my hands keeping the journal closed. The ring of white encircling my middle finger is so faint, I almost wonder if it was a trick of the waning sunlight.

Everything I thought I knew...I didn't.

With shaky hands and a burning curiosity, I pry open the journal again and read.

There is much we have discovered about dragons over the years, and yet, so very little we do know.

The origin of dragons is one of the biggest conundrums and is widely speculated. Most believe that the gods who created this world once resided here and created man and woman in their image. But they created dragons to embody the elemental forces. And to maintain peace and order amongst humans and creatures.

Man and woman were commanded to live in peace with dragons, trusting the dragons to provide a cosmic balance. And the dragons were to trust the humans' laws. A system of checks and balances.

This collection of my dragon research has been accounted for by elders and first-hand experiences.

The names of these elders have been redacted for the safety of their persons and loved ones.

Shall this journal exist outside of the libraries of Agonsreach and I deceased, I beg the reader to burn this journal and all of its contents. Abstaining to do so could mean the death of many innocents, both human and dragons alike.

I stare at the page. Unsure whether I should read on or toss it into the river gurgling nearby. But there it says: to burn this journal and all of its contents. Knowing I can't grant my father's request, I turn the page to continue reading.

Dragons of different forms are sketched across the pages. Some of which I've never seen before: ones with no wings, ones without front legs, and others that resemble a snake.

Various measurements of wingspans and detailed illustrations of eyes and skulls litter the page alongside sections of scrawled notes.

Fire dragons: All dragons of this breed breathe fire. They typically live near volcanoes and cannot tolerate colder climates. These dragons avoid water and cannot swim. Other atypical abilities observed in fire dragons: telekinesis of earthly matter such as rocks, triggering earthquakes, and manipulation of fire.

Earth dragons: Dragons of this breed are quite stationary and sedentary within forested areas. These dragons are normally ingrained in their environments, so much so that it's often hard to locate them. It's unknown if they consume other sources of energy outside of solar. Myth has it these dragons can accelerate healing and control plants. Similar to their preferred environments, earth dragons are incredibly sensitive to fire and ice.

Water dragons: *Water dragons are hard to observe, considering many of them live in the depths of the ocean for a majority of their lives. They are mostly seen when they travel to shallower waters in the bays, lakes, and rivers for mating season and to lay eggs. It's a mystery as to how long they can survive outside of water. These dragons have a myriad of abilities: echolocation, spouting jets of boiling water, camouflaging their scales, and producing electric shock waves.*

Air dragons: *The most elusive of the breeds, these dragons are rumored to dwell within the northern hemisphere of the Dragon Lands. These dragons were executed by King Aaric when he came into rule. The last air dragon spotted by humans was at the castle of Vitalis shortly after the Great War.*

Dragon hatchlings haven't been observed often, due to the danger of getting close enough to collect any data.

We do know dragons are considered hatchlings for the first few months. It can take months to years for their scales to completely harden. Due to the lack of hardened scales, the vulnerable hatchlings typically stay with their kin until they're able to defend themselves.

Hatchlings are not born with the ability to fly but learn over time. Should they have any magical capabilities, they usually don't surface until well into their adolescence.

Females are notorious for being the biggest, strongest, and most territorial of the species. Additionally, they seem to have a deeper connection to their magical abilities. Females with hatchlings or eggs are especially dangerous and should be avoided at all costs.

As far as we can tell from books rescued after the Great War in Vitalis, dragons have roamed the earth for thousands of years. But the first time a human bonded a dragon was centuries ago.

The very first dragon rider.

It's rumored the first dragon rider had blood of magic and that was why the dragon bonded them.

Dragons are especially sensitive to magic, and bonding a human was undoubtedly a massive risk. Bonds between dragon and human far exceed any other emotion. A bond that surpasses love itself. It is of sacrifice, justice, and the essence of what makes this world good.

But with such a bond, comes a price.

Once bonded, a pair cannot be separated. They become intrinsically one. Shall one die, the other shall too.

The generations before us whispered only elites and those in their blood lines could bond dragons. After Queen Elara and her dragon died, her brother King Aaric took the throne. Under the new King's order, all dragon riders were captured and executed. The bonds between humans and dragons were severed.

Causing a war between man and dragon.

I turn and steal a glance at Daeja as she frolics through the tall grasses nearby. A blue butterfly floats past her, then circles back and lands on the tip of her nose. Daeja's eyes widen, and her gaze flicks to me, her stance cautiously rigid.

I give her a reassuring smile, and she looks back at the butterfly, its wings twitching in the breeze. In the blink of an eye, the butterfly lifts off her nose and flutters back through the clearing. Daeja chases after it, her immature wings flaring and disturbing her balance. She topples over then quickly rises again and stumbles as she continues her chase.

I can't imagine Daeja growing into the gruesome, vicious beast I've grown up believing her kind to be.

My thoughts wander to that morning in Padmoor and the man racing down the street. The fire. If dragons weren't dangerous, why else would the King outlaw them? Especially when his own sister was a dragon rider.

I set down the journal and rub my hands together, breathing warmth into them to melt the sharp sting of cold.

"Stay here," I tell Daeja as I turn on my heels to find some branches.

She bounces after me—*so much for that.*

She sniffs around as I collect potential kindling in the darkening forest. A creak and snap from behind me catches my attention. I swivel to find Daeja seesawing toward me, stumbling every few steps with a branch double her length protruding from her jaws. She drops it at my feet.

"Great find, thank you," I chuckle. Stacking her branch

on the pile I have clutched in my hands, we return back to our makeshift camp.

Cole showed me how to start a fire long ago when he lit our fireplace one cold winter. Thereafter, I couldn't help but request he help almost every winter night. Admittedly, it was an excuse to see him.

The first time we touched was when I tried to replicate him striking a flame. I was miserably bad at doing so. He gathered my hands in his and delicately showed me the motions to create a spark. He flinched at our initial touch. At how cold my hands were in his. He brought my hands up to his lips and breathed on them. My hands warmed, almost as much as my cheeks. When he realized the intimacy of it, he apologized and quickly shifted to explaining that if my hands were too cold it would be hard to grip the stone the right way. At the time, I told myself it made sense.

He couldn't possibly be interested in me.

As I recall the memory, my heart tumbles down a flight of stairs. Each drop more painful than the last. I miss him. I miss the glowing amber of his eyes that reminds me of a cozy fire on a frigid winter night. His smile like when the sun emerges after a rainstorm. How his heartbeat hums like the rhythm of my own. I've always craved every existence of him, whether he was here standing in front of me or tucked into the memories of my mind. But I can only have the latter. It terrifies me that more time will pass and I might forget the shade of red his hair is. Or the pattern of freckles staining his cheeks. Maybe misremembering how he felt pressed against me, when it was just me and him. Here I am, without him. Living in a reality where we said we would never be.

I start breathing into my own hands, warming them before I pick up the rocks. The only thing sparking with each unsuccessful strike is my frustration. Daeja watches me with a tilted head, her head flopping from one side to the other with every scrape.

A small spark flares and bounces over onto the piled branches. My hope rises, before it sinks again as the ember fades.

Daeja creeps forward and nudges the collection of branches, one of them falls to the ground.

"Hey, stop!" I try to pull her back.

She noses my hands away with a chirp, turning back to the branches and opening her mouth. A soft glow burns in her throat, traveling up and out of her mouth in a small spurt. A ball of flame, no bigger than the size of my palm, barrels forward and past the branches. A bush nearby catches fire, and I scramble to throw the water I have in my flask on it. By the time I've expelled the fire by smothering the flames with my cloak, I glance over at Daeja who sits near our collection of kindling. Now glowing with fire.

"You did it." I breathe in relief. Even if she almost caught the rest of the forest on fire. I push away the whispered thought it might have been her that set my home on fire. That she was the reason why my mother died.

Daeja curls into a ball in my lap, and I stretch my hands out across to the fire.

I should destroy the journal. My father specifically wrote to burn it. But my longing for him makes me pause. The journal is all

I'll ever know of him. The last thing I'll ever have of my heritage. *Will it really matter if I keep it when I have a dragon hatchling? Perhaps I can burn it once I'm done reading. Why else would my mother want me to have it?*

A loud pop of burning wood splits the air. My heart jumps at the sound. I attempt to level my breathing, struggling to avoid the memory of the raging fire in our home just days ago. Closing my eyes, I shut out the creeping anxiety and delight in the warmth of the fire kissing my skin. My body relaxes with a sigh.

We will live to see another night.

A raging fire disrupts my dreams, the red flames transforming into blue and then white. My mother's voice haunts me, echoing around me as if I were stuck in an infinite cave.

Find Cole.

You aren't safe here.

Trust no one.

Kit!

A scream splits through the repetitive warnings, but I can't tell if it's hers or mine.

My eyes flash open, and I fling forward. The sudden motion dislodges Daeja from the crook of my chest, and she flops to the ground with a squeak. Sweat cakes my hair to my face, and I'm struggling to catch my quickened breath. The looming dread of premonition fogs over me.

Ground yourself…five things…five things.

I scan the darkness for five things I see, when Daeja shakes her body like a dog beside me, her wings slapping against her sides as she wiggles. The movement momentarily distracts me from my panic. She rubs her cheek alongside my sleeve, nudging her snout underneath my elbow to lift my arm and wriggling her way between my arm and side. Her wide eyes stare up at me, her head cocked to the side. I scratch under her chin. The stroke melts her into a light purr, and her eyes flutter closed.

I scan the pile of soot where the fire was earlier tonight, but any semblance of flame is long gone. Part of me anticipates it coming back to life as soon as I look away. For the flames to creep up and consume me. I lie back down and watch the heap of ash until I can't keep my eyes open any longer.

It's been days of traveling near the river. I think. I'm starting to lose track of the time.

Every chance I get, I read another page of my father's

journal. And when I'm not reading, I theorize what his face looked like. My blue eyes and silvery blonde hair are from my mother.

Since my brother had brown hair, I could only guess my father had the same shade. I trace my features with my fingertips as I read, clinging to every word he's written.

The Elders decided my time as a researcher in the realm has concluded.

We have sent several requests over the years to King Aaric to discuss peace between our lands. All of our correspondence has gone unanswered. But last month, the King finally acknowledged us.

With the severed head of one of our messengers.

Shortly thereafter, the King's guard attacked our southern post near the border. Our outpost gained the victory and managed to capture a King's guard.

This morning, my mentor sent me to the outpost. It wasn't until I met with the elders that I was briefed on the recent attacks. They explained the dire need of why I was to stop my research on dragons. That I was needed for a new mission.

I am to return to the kingdom disguised as a King's guard. To do research, even more critical than the study of dragons. This study is to ensure the survival of the Dragon Lands.

Of our realm.

To find out why our requests for peace are ignored.

We gathered what important information we could from the guard. Enough for me to practice the knowledge so I can blend in seamlessly. Next week I set out on my new quest.

Only one rule has been made urgent to me.

One that can mean life or death.

Avoid direct interactions with the King himself at all costs.

He is unstable.

He is unpredictable.

He must not be trusted.

And if that's not enough to scare me: he killed his own sister to rule.

I shut the journal. *My father was sent as a spy?*

My mind reels trying to piece together how he could have met my mother. All I knew growing up was my mother was a fantastic archer. So much so, she was drafted into the military at a young age and stationed at the northern outposts. Archers were well paid positions, considering they were our best defenses against dragons. One pierce of an arrow in the correct spot could bring a skyward dragon to the ground.

My father, a rebel.

My mother, a loyalist to the King and kingdom.

Why did my mother never tell me how he died?

SEVEN

HORNWOOD

I'm out of food. I should be used to the feeling of hunger, but it scrapes at my insides, blurring what little mental coherency I might have left after the long days of walking.

The gods must be smiling down on me because a faint outline of a town breaks the horizon in the distance. A few hours later, I paused on the outskirts. Judging by the tattered and worn roofs and the position of the town from Dragon's Back Ridge, it's Hornwood. I watch the townspeople shuffle back and forth between the streets, my hands sweating at the thought of having to dare into town.

If I get caught—Daeja and I are both dead. But if I don't go, I'll starve.

Dead again.

I swallow against the knot building in my throat and flick

a glance toward Daeja perched on my shoulder. Her wide, white eyes meet mine. She dips her head low, and I pull my cloak's hood over me. Daeja falls into silence as I tuck her back behind the fall of my hair. As if she somehow understands what's at stake.

I'm hoping the cover of my hair is enough to conceal her. Praying she has the sense not to wiggle or chirp as we pass through the crowds.

I try to quiet my nerves as we near the huddled buildings. Large gaping holes filled with murky water litter the roads. The townspeople zip by, muddy footprints scattered across the cobblestone road. Every lingering stare of passersby spikes my heart rate. I push by fast, tucking my head down as I go.

I watch where each of my steps land, trying to avoid any lifted cobblestones, pits in the ground, or water that might make me slip. Any stumble could dislodge Daeja, and then we'd both be doomed.

I find a merchant with baskets of bread loaves, their line wrapping into the busy street. I debate whether it's worth the risk. The longer I wait, the greater the chance of getting caught. A mother with her young daughter stands in front of me. The little girl bounces back and forth, a doll hanging from her grasp.

Shouts erupt from deeper into town, and the crowd parts for a man racing through with multiple bottles held tight to his chest.

Another man appears hot on his heels, shouting and pointing. "After him! He's stealing my whiskey!"

People split to either side of the road as the thief sprints down the cobblestone. I jump back as the mother in front of me snags her daughter, ripping her out of the way just in time to dodge the thief. But the quickness of the movement knocks the doll out of the young girl's grasp, landing on the ground a short distance away.

Daeja growls as the thief rockets past us, and the mother's eyes find mine. I smile nervously, grabbing the doll off the ground after the thief disappears.

"Must have been my stomach…" I mutter, handing the doll back to the little girl.

The mother mouths her thank you, and they turn back into the line. When I make it to the front of the line, I fish out a coin and place it on the table. The baker frowns with a shake of his head. This would at least buy me one loaf back home. I slide him another to be met with the same response.

"Are there any other bakers in town that might have something I could purchase? Even if it's spoiled…I'm traveling, and I can't afford anything more than this."

His eyes soften. "Unfortunately, our taxes have nearly tripled to pay the King for repairs to the town. Everything is expensive here, but if you go south to Groveden, you might have better luck. It's a four day trek from here."

"What about Blackfell?" I ask.

"That's maybe another four or five days east."

My heart sinks. I'm not sure we can last another four days, especially at our pace. I nod my thanks and turn back to the road, my heart and hope sinking with each step taking me out of the town.

A tap pats my shoulder, just under where Daeja lies. I turn, in part to avoid any further touching that may expose Daeja but also to see who it is.

The little girl with the doll presents me half a loaf of bread, then she scurries off back to her watchful mother. The woman smiles at me before dipping her head. The two of them disappear into the crowd.

I swallow against the tightness in my throat from such a kind gesture.

I tear off a piece of bread as I lean back against a boulder, offering a piece to Daeja who wrinkles her nose at the smell. With a shrug, I pop the piece into my mouth as I watch the distant outline of Hornwood from the shelter of the forest.

Four to five days until Blackfell. If I push myself, maybe I can get there faster. Maybe three, if I can start tonight.

Daeja must have slipped off. Because a few moments later, she bounds toward me with wide eyes and a dead mouse hanging from her mouth. She drops her kill on my lap as I squirm and shuffle backwards, its limp body flopping to the floor.

She waits. Watching me expectantly with a tilted head. Her gaze shifts back and forth between me and the mouse.

I shake my head with a muffled laugh as I realize what she's asking. "No...thank you. I umm...you have it."

She slurps up the mouse, taking two quick chomps before she swallows it whole and slides herself into my lap. I absent-mindedly run a few fingertips between the horns crowning her head down to where her shoulders meet her spine. In the amount of time we've been together, she is already nearly the size of a kitten. I trace interlocking circles over her back, lulling her into a slumber as I flip open my father's journal.

The first few weeks at the castle have been quiet. I was reassigned from my post at the library to deliveries, due to the previous guard breaking his ankle. I was thankful for the slow pace of the early weeks—it gave me enough time to settle my nerves. To get into the routine. I learned the only way to write in private is if I excuse myself for the bathroom. Any other moment is full of watching eyes or fading footsteps in the hallways.

During my first shift on deliveries, a batch of crates arrived with 'FRAGILE' written in large letters across the wood. As I took the deliveries into the castle, a liquid sloshed inside the crates with each footstep.

My lead directed me to a new hallway and down a spiraling staircase. Halfway down the staircase the temperature dropped, and the humidity rose.

The castle sits atop a mountain, built into a towering cliff side. And with how many steps it took to get to the bottom of the stairs, I guessed I was in the basement, if there was such a thing.

No windows lined the walls. No doors. The only light to chase away the shadows came from the torch my lead held. We walked in darkness and silence until he came to a stop.

The hair on the back of my neck stood up, and a thick, electric tension hung in the air. Something I couldn't quite put my finger on. He opened a large door, having me place the crates inside the dark room behind it. Collections of empty bottles and vials lined the walls and shelves.

It dawned on me, slowly. Wine. They were storing imported wine and beer. It all made sense—the King liked to throw extravagant balls and parties. Or so I had been told. But a party of this size would only indicate a large event...like a victory.

Like if you had won a war.

Today I asked another guard if it was only the King we guarded here. Or if anyone was assigned to guarding the royal family. He shushed me, his eyes wild as he looked around to make sure no one else was listening.

He gripped my elbow, his fingers sinking into my flesh as he pulled me into him. "You must never speak of them around the King."

The guard admitted the King fathered many bastards and hadn't married since his first wife. Apparently, our voices were hushed to protect the shame of the King's children out of wedlock. Nobody knew of the King's first wife, who she was, or what happened to her.

I learned the King had been alive for a long time when I was apprenticing in the Dragon Lands. He had ruled for almost one hundred and fifty years. The King's lifespan was unheard of across the entire realm, and those in the kingdom had been spoon-fed a story that he was appointed by the gods to rule them. But few of us knew the truth of it.

I squint to read in the fading daylight, until I finally give up and close the journal. Fighting a yawn, I gather my belongings, place Daeja on my shoulders, and walk east. As I near Hornwood for the second time, the lights of homes flicker off for the night as people turn in for bed. I keep to the outskirts, slinking slowly between the trees as I watch the town's perimeter.

As I pass the northern side of town, a shuffle breaks the silence of the night. I squint through the dim starlit forest, making out a group of men gathered near the town's border.

I drop into a crouch behind a bush, and Daeja stirs against my neck with the sudden movement. Holding out a finger to silence her protest, I strain to listen.

From this distance, I should at least be able to pick up indistinct chatter. Slowly, I peek up over the top of the bush. Men slink through the shadows without a word among them, exchanging cryptic hand gestures and nods.

They're speaking to each other in...sign language?

Their torches cast wicked shadows across their dark leathers. They break into smaller groups and spread out around the surrounding homes. Using rope, they tie double knots around the door handles, securing the other end to a wagon stacked heavy with boulders in the center of the road.

Horror grips me as several of the men drag their torches around the perimeters of the homes. When they finish, they throw their torches onto the roofs and disappear into the night.

Rebels. They're trapping them!

I scramble for a plan and begin to weigh my options. When

the last of the men disappear into the night, my moment of opportunity presents itself. I have to help them. Smoke snakes in the sky, and distant shouts pierce through the quiet. I run for the nearest house, my satchel slamming against my hip, and Daeja's talons sinking into my shoulders. I pause once I reach the front door. I'm instantly brought back to that night at my home. To how helpless I felt.

I push through the overwhelming emotions.

Using my dagger, I try to shear the rope, pushing the blade hard and fast against the thick cord. But it doesn't budge.

Fuck! This isn't working.

Sweat begins to coat my hands, my neck, everything. The blade is far too slippery in my hands, and I'm not strong enough to cut the cord.

The door shudders and stills. Shudders and stills. I spot a small window to the top right of the door and push onto my toes to look in.

My eyes widen when I see her: the little girl from the market. That same doll gripped tightly in her small hand. Her mother holds her and speaks to a man. He pulls and pushes feverishly against the door, as if testing the lock. I slam a fist against the window and the hot glass nearly splits the skin on my knuckles. The three of them whip their attention toward me.

"The door is tied off!" I scream over the sound of roaring flames.

They stare at me, trying to decipher what I'm saying. I shift my focus to my surroundings for something to break the glass but only find small rocks the size of a coin.

The door thuds again, and as I peek back into the window, the father is ramming into it with his shoulder.

"It won't work! We have to get you out through the window!" I point repeatedly at the window.

They shift their gazes to each other. The father disappears into the thick smoke of another room, returning with a chair. I back up in time for him to smash it against the window. The second attempt splinters glass everywhere. The heat of the fire swells, and I wipe away the sweat that trickles down into my eyes from my forehead.

I stretch my arms into the window. "Here! Climb through, and I'll help pull you out!"

They lift their daughter first. Her arms outstretched with the doll clasped in one hand. As she gets close, the father's grip falters with a wicked cough. I slingshot forward, broken glass scraping the undersides of my arms as I try to grab for what I can. My fingers close on the soft fabric of the doll, and the girl falls just out of my grasp. Her body hits the ground with a thud that makes my stomach sick.

I shove the doll down into my bag to free my hands once more. "Again! Again!"

But the mother and daughter's movements are sluggish, and the father is unresponsive on the floor. A thick fog of smoke clouds the room, burning my eyes.

"Hey! What are you doing?" A man charges me with a sword from the left, stealing my attention for a moment.

By the time I look back into the window, all three of them are on the ground.

Motionless.

I'm not sure if they're unconscious from the smoke. Or worse. *I can't think of worse right now—*

"Wake up, wake up, wake *up*!" My throat burns at how hard I scream. But they don't move. Black smoke spills throughout the rest of the room, clouding my vision of them.

The man's silhouette in my periphery grows larger and larger. My gaze is pulled away from the window, and I back pedal as the space between the man and I closes quickly. Hesitantly, I turn and run for the trees. Daeja hisses in one ear as my heart pounds in the other. A cough sputters my breath, and I slow because of it. The racing footsteps close in. A hand grabs the back of my hood, and I spin to try and dodge him.

"Daeja!" I cry.

I turn to face him head on as he narrowly avoids grabbing where Daeja lays. Before I can act, her weight leaves my shoulders as she lunges off me and onto him. He screeches in surprise, his sword clattering to the ground, and his grip on me falters.

The man falls backwards, his body thumping heavily on the ground. Daeja's mouth is latched onto his nose as she wriggles her body back and forth vigorously.

Swiping the man's sword from the ground, I charge as he recovers and grabs Daeja with both hands. He rips her from his face, rolls, and pins her tight under his hands. She wriggles with a stolen cry as his hands clench around her small throat.

I don't give it a second thought.

I sink the sword into the middle of his back. The blade slices through his flesh with a squelch I wish I could block out.

He freezes. A wheezed breath squeaks out of his mouth.

I pull the sword free and kick him off Daeja. He crumples to the ground effortlessly, stilling as he stares up at the night sky blankly.

My blood rushes in my ears, and my hands tremble as I toss the sword to the side. I blink through blurry eyes when I drop to my knees to gather Daeja in my hands.

"Are you okay?" I whisper through a tight breath.

When she opens her bright white eyes, it unlocks a torrent of relief in me. I pull her into my chest, cradling her weak body.

She saved me.

A rough, cracked purr rumbles from somewhere deep within her chest. I dig in my satchel for my water flask, and my hand briefly brushes against unfamiliar fabric. My brow furrows as I remove it from my bag. Starlight illuminates the object, and I release a choked gasp.

The little girl's doll.

EIGHT

IS IT YOUR FIRST TIME?

I direct my attention back to the city of Hornwood and my heart withers. Dark smoke shrouds the night sky. In the distance the home of the family collapses followed by the town buildings. One by one, they fall away to heaps of ash.

I couldn't save them.

A swarm of rage and despair drowns me. I can't ground myself, not when everything around me is fire.

I grab the rebel's sword and stand at the edge of the flames. Ice spreads through my chest, like some disease waiting to consume me.

I'll fucking kill them.

My body shakes with fury. I turn away from the flames, blocking out every thought. I can't let myself think about it. If I let it in—if I allow myself to feel—the anguish will consume me.

I put one foot in front of the other, walking until I'm not sure how long it's been and I collapse near a river. As I lie on the cold hard earth, screams echoing inside my skull, I retreat to memories of Cole to stay afloat.

Three summers ago.

The sun starts to creep above the canopy of trees. My gaze floats over to my father's cross, and I wonder if he would approve of Cole. The river behind my father's and brother's crosses rushes with the runoff of melted snow from Dragon's Back Ridge. A thick layer of heat settles over the forest, and I pull at my collar sticking to my skin. I fan myself with a hand, unable to distinguish whether it's as hot as I think it is or if my nerves are getting the best of me.

A familiar thud of approaching footsteps catches my attention. As I turn to look over my shoulder toward the sound, the dappled sunlight catches the burnished flame of Cole's hair. His broad shoulders sway with a silent confidence. I can't help but admire the way his clothes cling to the curves and angles of his concealed brawn and power. I flick my attention to something else before he catches me staring.

Two birds fly by between us, somersaulting in the air as they dance and disappear off into the trees. As Cole approaches, I cock my head to the side, wondering what he holds in his hands.

He flashes me a smile, presenting me with a bow. "Surprise."

I gape in utter shock and realization. The string, which was once snapped in half, is whole once more. Even the wood gleams from a fresh polish, free from the gouges that had once scarred the wood.

It's my mother's bow.

Gratitude swells within me, and my voice comes out strained through the knot tightening my throat. "I...don't know what to say. How did you—"

"Don't worry about how." His smile warms his eyes.

Repairing it must have cost a significant amount of coin. Guilt surfaces, and as I open my mouth to refuse such a generous gift, he interrupts me.

"We can start practicing today."

"Today?"

"Today," he confirms.

I look down at the bow in my hands, suddenly doubting every ambition I've had. I always wanted to be an archer like my mother. If I could be half the archer she was, I could give us a better life. But the snapped bow—broken long before I was born—was always a problem. Now freed from that limitation...what if I'm not good enough?

"Do you...not like it?" Cole asks gently, noting my hesitation.

"No, no. It's not that. I just…" My voice drops to a whisper, "I don't really know where to start."

"Is it your first time?"

I nod, and he opens his hands, silently asking for the bow. He demonstrates for me, patiently narrating each step before handing the bow back to me to replicate.

I squeeze my hands around the bow, praying I can keep my grip steady between my sweaty fingers. As I pull the string back and narrow my eyes at a spot across the river, the bow wobbles in my trembling hands.

Cole glides in behind me and corrects my elbow with a soft touch. His arms surround me, his face dangerously close to mine and his body brushing against me. Wrapping his hand over the top of mine, he aims the bow higher. A blush creeps to my cheeks. He clears his throat and steps away. I try not to let my shoulders sag at the sudden departure.

"That looks great! Now all you need is an arrow. Here, let's have you aim at"— Cole points to a tree stump across the river and hands me an arrow—"that trunk over there."

Hope bubbles inside me at the size of the target he's selected. Maybe I can impress him as well as myself. Ignoring my hammering heart and quaking hands, I notch the arrow and pull back the string. After slowing my breath, I narrow my eyes on the trunk and release the string on an exhale.

The first shot goes rogue and sinks several yards in front of the trunk. With Cole's encouragement, I shoot three more arrows.

The first two fire off into the forest behind the stump, but the third lands in the river between two rocks.

Cole pats my shoulder. "Hey, that was a great first try! Most people wouldn't even be able to clear the river."

I'm not sure if he's trying to be nice or if he's genuinely impressed. Taking his boots off, he rolls up his pant legs, revealing corded calves and a hint of muscular thighs. I clear my throat, diverting my attention and rolling up my own pants.

With my stubborn insistence, we cross the river to fetch the arrows. I block out thoughts of being swept away, thankful for Cole's steady hand holding mine as he leads us across the river. Rolling up my pants deemed a useless measure, as the water reaches up to my hips.

My foot glides off an underwater rock and I slip backwards. Cole catches me, pulling me into his arms before I can dip completely underwater.

His round eyes meet mine. "Are you okay?"

I nod, biting down my fear at the memory of my brother's fate in this same river.

"I got you," Cole whispers, to me and my fears.

We reach the other side, and Cole collects the arrows from the forest while I retrieve the one lodged between the rocks. I tug the arrow several times, but it won't budge.

"Is it stuck, or broken?" Cole crouches down beside me.

I yank at the arrow once more, and it comes loose. The motion of my effort throws me sideways into Cole, and we tumble backwards onto the riverbank. My elbow jabs straight into Cole's abs, and his breath saws out. The arrow escapes my grasp, flying off a few feet away from us, and my face lands on Cole's muscled chest. I lift my head off his chest, my eyes meeting his, and my skin heats with embarrassment.

"Are you okay?" we say simultaneously and laugh awkwardly in unison.

I'm close. Far too close. Full lashes frame his glowing amber eyes, and a dark ring encircles his irises. The pulse in his throat flickers. The brown freckles staining his cheeks remind me of the patterned stars in a night sky, and my attention settles on the soft curve of his lips. Before I'm lost to the temptation, I twist away. But I'm stuck. His arms are wrapped around me, trapping me for a long second before he remembers to let me go. A faint blush blooms on his cheeks as I return to my feet.

I wipe my sweaty palms on my pants then extend a hand to help him up. He takes my hand, lifting to his feet, then retrieves the arrow I left on the ground. Our eyes lock again, and he pauses a step away from me. We're so close, if I lean into him my head would tuck right under his angled chin, and I would fit perfectly in his strong arms. It's not the first time I've yearned to be there.

He hands me the arrow, and I take it without breaking our eye contact, flinging it behind me. Before I can stop myself, I crash my lips onto his. I underestimate my power, and he stumbles backwards until we find ourselves on the ground again. But this time, we don't allow any space between us. He kisses me soft and slow, wrapping his arms around me and pulling me into him. My heart flutters at his delicate touch. He wants this too—it's not all in my head.

Sliding one hand to my neck, he cradles my head. We melt into each other until I finally pull away.

"What was that," he whispers, his gaze flickering between my eyes and lips.

"Is it your first time?" I echo his comment from earlier.

He laughs. "I've been wanting to do that for a while. But I didn't think you felt the same."

"I didn't think you felt the same," I murmur.

He twirls a lock of my hair around his finger before tucking it behind my ear. In that same movement, he slides his finger around my ear and down my jaw toward my chin, guiding me into another kiss.

I wish we could stay like this forever.

NINE

I'VE GOT MY MONEY ON THE BIG GUY

Present day.

I dug a shallow grave with the rebel's sword and buried the little girl's doll near the river. Daeja helped me find two branches, and I cut the strap from my father's journal to tie it into a cross. I must have gotten lost because the river is northwest of Hornwood, which means I turned back. I should be more upset, but a dark cloud of numbness dulls every hint of emotion.

I trace the grip of the rebel's sword, my fingers brushing the swirls engraved into the hilt.

I'll kill every last one of them. The thought is a whisper in the dark recesses of my mind, the severity of it startling me. It's the only thing that makes me feel anything—aside from the relief Daeja sustained no major injuries.

My thoughts linger on my father. *Had he been alive, would*

he have made the same decision? Could he have trapped and slaughtered hundreds of innocent lives?

The questions and fear of discovering more than I'm prepared for keeps me from opening the journal again.

As the days drag on, my disorientation grows. I'm not sure how much time has passed or even what day it is. I avoid sleeping at night. If I'm honest, I'm scared other terrors lie in the shadows, waiting for me to falter before they strike.

The sky melts from midnight black to sunrise. My eyelids drag closed, and I fall forward, catching myself on my hands and knees. I sink my fingers into the grass, lifting my brows to keep my eyes open. My arms tremble from pure exhaustion as I stare at the ground.

Daeja slides off my shoulders, and pokes her head into my vision, staring up at me with her unblinking white eyes.

"I'm okay," I croak.

Gods...is that my voice?

She chitters, bumping her scaly cool nose to mine.

I nod and flop to my back. "I suppose I can rest...just for a bit though." My muscles twitch at the sudden inactivity. I close a hand over the hilt of my sword and turn my head to call Daeja to rest with me. But she's missing from the spot she was moments earlier.

"Daeja?" I push up to my elbows to scan the forest around me. My gaze bounces from tree to tree, bush to bush. But she's nowhere. I hold a breath, waiting for a flicker of movement. "Daeja!"

I must be out of my godsdamned mind—the same spot where she sat earlier, and the spot that was empty milliseconds before, is where she sits once again. She tilts her small head to the side as though confused.

I rub the heel of my hand over one eye and watch her figure blink out of existence before me. *What the fuck, am I hallucinating?*

I scramble forward, patting the area where she had sat.

My fingertips jab something scaly. Double tapping the invisible mass with two fingers, and Daeja's body flashes into view again.

"Did you just...did you just do that on your own?"

She stretches her neck and flares her nostrils. Then, squeezing her eyes shut, she disappears again. Seconds later, she reappears.

I race for my father's journal, flipping back to the pages detailing his dragon research. I scan the passages, but nothing mentions disappearing dragons. Daeja's round black muzzle rests on the spine between the pages, her big eyes staring up at me.

"What are you?" I ask.

Dark clouds clog the sky through the ridges of the leaves above me. A deep thunder rumbles. In the distance between the gaps of trees, an orange light glows against the dreary blue mist. My hope flickers. It has to be Blackfell.

It *has* to be.

A drop of rain splatters against the ground. Daeja flinches against me. Another falls, hitting her in the head, and she hisses. Her eyes scan our surroundings, waiting for the next attack. As more drops fall, she snaps at them. It drags a chuckle out of me.

By the time we near the town, the rain picks up to a drizzle. I turn to look at Daeja on my shoulder as I pull my hood up and double tap two fingers against her scaly side. She disappears, as if she were swept away by the wind. We've come to discover she can only disappear for short spurts at a time. And even that is a monumental effort for her. But it's one I hope we can use to our advantage.

The black roofs of the town confirm it's Blackfell. I follow a crowd through the puddled streets and into a building full of laughter and roaring conversation. Overhead chandeliers and torches lining the walls illuminate the great room. People flock toward the center of the building, where clangs of metal ring out. Between the gaps of the massive audience, two men swirl and strike.

I slide through the crowd to make my way to the bar, thinking and hoping I might be able to find out information about Cole. Drunk people are always good at talking.

"I've got my money on the big guy. He's second best in the kingdom to Darian Raventhorn," a man I try to skirt around tells his companion.

His companion scoffs. "Darian isn't as good as everyone makes him out to be."

"You're saying that because you've never seen him fight. He was trained by Jurrock himself," the first one counters.

"Do you want to bet money on that? He got passed up to captain a squad. Can't be all that good."

The first one's voice drops low, "Really? Who beat him?"

"Some fiery red-head from Padmoor. The man is brutal. He single-handedly took down a group of rebels and killed the lead with his bare hands—"

I freeze. *It can't be…can it? Cole wouldn't be able to kill someone—let alone with his bare hands.* The clamor of the fight melts away as I stop. I stare at the two people fighting in the ring, but I strain to listen to the men's conversation.

"—and left the bloody redhead on a spike near the border to scare off the rest of the rebels."

The first man shakes his head. "I'll believe it when I see it."

"You callin' me a liar? Go look at it yourself. Up north about thirty miles from here."

"I'm not daring north of Blackfell."

"Well, then, maybe you can go ask him yourself. Their squad is over there." The second man jabs a finger over his shoulder.

My heart tumbles and races as I follow his direction toward the back left of the building. I push up onto my toes, trying to peer over the shifting bodies of the crowd.

Red hair gleams against the grey-washed stone walls. Cole's hair sweeps down toward a soft beard brushing his jawline. He's different from the man I remember. He's no longer the clean-shaven man with a shorter haircut who left home.

His jaw is set in a hard line, and his forehead creases in concentration as he stares down at paper strewn on the table. Someone from his group points at a spot on the page. He nods thoughtfully and tips back his mug to swallow its contents. Standing and gathering the pages, he sets down the mug before turning to talk to the men around him. A waitress struts over to him and motions toward his mug. Cole shakes his head with his signature glowing smile. It softens the rest of his rugged, dangerous features. Popping her hip, the waitress tilts her head back and bats her lashes.

I'm not the only one who thinks he's gorgeous.

Cole hands the woman a small pouch before he and his group slip out of a back door and disappear. When the door shuts, I snake my way through the crowd.

A loud clash of swords splits the air, and the crowd erupts into a frenzy. The jostle falters my step, and Daeja's claws sink into me for grip. I grit my teeth to avoid shouting. By the time I reach where Cole sat, it's been a few minutes.

I burst out of the back door, the cold air whipping me in the face. Each direction the road splits into is void of any hint of Cole.

He's gone.

Rain blurs my vision as I break into a sprint down the main road. Daeja bounces with each fall of my step. My hopes sink at every empty alley and vacant road.

Each passerby I ask if they've seen a military group walk

through. The fourth person I ask mentions a military outpost northwest of Blackfell near a lake. By the time I leave Blackfell and reenter the forest, the rain ceases, and the cloud cover lightens. The sounds of the forest are broken by the unmistakable clashing of metal against metal.

My hand wraps tighter around the sword at my side. I slow my pace and stick to the cover of shrubs and trees, slinking closer to the sound until the trees break into a clearing. I crouch behind a shrub and peer over the ragged top. Sparse bits of green grass sprinkle the ground, surrounded by trampled earth and...*drag marks?*

My observation is interrupted by two men fighting with swords, one of whom is far outmatched by the other. Taller than me by an inch or two, his sandy blonde hair whips through the air each time he dodges his opponent's sword.

His towering, brown-haired opponent ruthlessly hacks cut after cut, handling his sword with such ease his long chestnut hair dances around his face.

Men and women circle them, shouting encouragements.

The dark-haired male advances, flicks his wrist, and effortlessly disarms his opponent.

The onlookers fall silent as the sword flies several feet away.

Looming toward the unarmed, golden-haired man, the victor swings his sword once more. His opponent falls onto his back, narrowly dodging a slice to his chest, and the crowd breaks out into shouts of disgust.

A voice cuts above the rest and everyone falls silent. "Darian, that's enough."

The golden-haired one shuffles backward and fumbles for his sword on the ground, grabbing it just in time to block the next swing.

The brown-haired male, Darian, snorts. "The rules in war are that the weakest links die.

This mop will either be killed or get us killed. No use in giving the kid any hope." He takes another step forward, his sword raised in preparation to swing again.

The other male rolls out of the way.

From the sidelines, a man in a white shirt and dark pants jumps to his feet, his red hair vibrant against the light of the moon. Cole.

"Darian, you ruthless fuck. That's an order." Cole plucks a fistful of Darian's shirt, ripping him back before he can strike again.

Darian spins, but Cole twists the sword out of his grasp and glares at him. Darian swings his fist, the punch connecting with Cole's cheek and spinning his face in my direction.

I flinch at the hit.

The muscles of Cole's back and arms ripple under his tight shirt. He whips back around and cuffs Darian on the jaw. They quickly turn into a mash of fists and fury: spinning, dodging, and whaling until Cole sweeps a leg to the back of Darian's knees and he drops to the ground.

Pinning him, Cole grips Darian's shirt in one hand, the fist of the other clenched and ready to deliver the next blow.

"Are you done?" Cole roars.

Darian mutters something under his breath then spits in Cole's face.

Cole raises his fist but pauses. Hovering over Darian, he bares his teeth and glares.

Waiting.

Tense moments pass, and nobody dares breathe.

Leaning away, Cole finally shoves up to his feet. His chest rises with each heavy breath, his eyes narrowed and watching Darian. The clear victor, he extends a hand to help Darian up.

Darian scoffs and ignores Cole's offer, standing on his own and cupping a hand to his nose gushing with blood.

With an exasperated sigh, Cole removes his shirt and throws it at Darian. "Go see Marge. Or go get a drink. I don't care what you do, just get the fuck out of my sight."

Without his shirt, the sunlight glints off the sweat-slickened crevices of Cole's chiseled torso. His muscles dance under his skin with each stride, a newly discovered authority and confidence exuded by the way he walks toward the golden-haired male. I would have never imagined the boy I met ten years ago having such raw power and ferocity. But I can't mistake his red hair, nor the deep gruffness of his voice.

"Are you okay, Archie?" Cole pulls the blond man to his feet.

"Oh, yeah, I'm good. I almost had him. I was taking it easy on him." Archie brushes off his chest.

Cole's lips quirk up into a slight smile before he clasps him on the shoulder. "You did good. With your tenacity, we are a force to be reckoned with."

Daeja's breath huffs into my ear, pulling me back to the spot where I crouch. I'll have to wait until tonight, and grab Cole without attracting anyone else's attention.

A flutter of nervousness tickles my stomach as thoughts pour into me. Is he still angry with me? Will he even help me? And if he doesn't help me, what will I do?

Because he's the only one who can help me free Daeja.

And he's the only one I can trust.

TEN

TEA PARTIES AND DRUNKS

9 months ago.

Trees unfurl with bursts of green, the whisper of spring amongst the leaves. The morning sun melts away the chill of winter, and rich purple alliums flower the gnarled roots of trees.

Heavy footsteps pull me out of my admiration, and Cole's figure glides through the distant tree line. I slink behind a tree trunk and lie in wait.

The footsteps stop, and I peek around the tree. Cole crouches over the alliums and picks several of the flowers from a thick cluster. He scans the forest, his amber eyes sweeping closer toward me, and I dart back behind the trunk. Silence falls, and after a few heartbeats, I dare one more peek.

Fingers wrap around my shoulder and spin me. My back hits the tree, now behind me.

Cole's face dips into my vision, his fingers threading into mine and pinning my hand above my head. He trails kisses up my neck to my jaw as I giggle.

I push my fingertips into his chest. "You're late."

He hands me the flowers. "I know, I know. I'm sorry. Arabella really wanted to play tea party."

I look down at his clothes in disappointment. "I would have rather you'd worn the dress."

He laughs and pulls me into a hug. We sway back and forth in each other's arms, his chin resting on the top of my head. He pulls back from me, a soft smile on his lips.

"I've missed you." He twirls a piece of my hair around his finger, and tucks it behind my ear.

A signature Cole move I dream of, even when we are apart.

"I've missed you." I mirror. "And I've been thinking…"

He stops swaying. "Yes?"

I fidget with the chained ring around my neck. His mother's ring. His proposal from a week ago fresh on my mind.

"What if we go somewhere else?" I whisper.

Cole tilts his head to the side. "What do you mean?"

"What if we went to Stoneshire? We could move there, start a new life. I could learn a new trade. Maybe practice archery. I could get good enough to hunt, or try to get into the military. It could be a good life. A better life."

He brushes my cheek with a thumb. "I'd go anywhere with you."

"Then let's go. Tomorrow."

He drops his hand from my face. "I…I can't leave my family. And what about your mother? You can't leave her."

"She would come with us."

"But my sisters couldn't?"

Words spill out of my mouth in desperation. "Well…they have your father. And Vivian will be eighteen? Willard spoke to me of a possible cure for my mother. There's been accounts of people cured of lameness and disease in Stoneshire by a blue flame. He said sometimes there's seasonal shifts in—"

"Willard isn't the most dependable source of information. You know that," he murmurs.

"It's a risk I have to take. And if it's seasonal I can't wait, I have to go."

"Kat, listen to yourself. You're going to travel across the entire kingdom, with your sick mother, for a rumor that Willard shared with you. The same one who kept his pet goat's teeth to try and bring it back to life? He's a drunk. A nice person…but a drunk."

The soft way his gaze settles on me is enough to crumble every wall of defense I have.

But I can't give in. Not now.

"I have to do this, I have to try. We could always come back." I offer.

"I'm all they have, it'll crush them—"

"—they have your father." I counter.

"He isn't around, Kat." An anger creeps into his voice.

My own frustration and desperation bubbles to the surface.

"How are we to be together then, Cole? What happens if I get there, and I can't come back?"

"Then don't go—stay. Stay with me." He squeezes my hands in his. "I need more time. I'll figure out a way we can be together, and we can go to whatever town you want. Wherever."

This conversation isn't going how I planned, or hoped. My stomach twists into knots at the thought of traveling with my mother on my own to the eastern part of the kingdom. Not to mention how much I will miss Cole. How much I don't want to leave him.

But I can't sacrifice finding a cure for my mother. Not when it may be my only chance to help her. And not when the last time I didn't act, someone I loved died.

I search his golden eyes. "I don't have time. Willard said it's a fickle thing, and nobody knows how long it will last."

"Then how do you know it will still be there by the time you get to Stoneshire?"

"I don't. But I can't sit here, waiting and wondering. I have to try—just come with me, please."

A muscle in Cole's jaw flickers before he shakes his head. "Arabella and Rosetta won't understand, they're too young."

"I was only a little older than Arabella when my brother died. And Rosetta is much older than I was. They'll understand."

"Kat, you can't even talk about him. You can't even say his name. I'm not going to do that to them."

"I turned out fine."

"Fine? I know you're desperate to fix this. You were forced

into a situation that should've never happened. I can't do the same to them."

I slip my hands from his grasp. My heart sinks, part of me wanting to give in and stay here with him. But I can't let that part of me win.

Cole's voice drops into a plea. "Don't do this, please. This isn't fair, Kat. You're trapping me."

"Trapping?"

If anything, I was trapped. If I stay here with him, I lose the only opportunity to save my mother. I may live the rest of my life in regret for not taking the chance. Even if it means going by myself. If my brother were still alive, he wouldn't hesitate.

I stare at the ground as I unhook my necklace with shaky hands. "Then if you feel so trapped, I'll make it easy for you."

I place the necklace in his palm and turn away from him. Doubt creeps in, stalking me like a predator ready to pounce. Before Cole changes my mind, and before I stop myself…I run.

Through the forest and farther away from Cole, trees are a blur of color in my peripheral vision.

He calls my name, and when I don't slow, his footsteps race after me. I approach the tree line, trees giving way to rolling hills stretched off into the distance. Cole catches my forearm and spins me toward him. His anguished expression floods me in guilt.

But it's better this way. I must get my mother to Stoneshire, with or without him.

"Kat, please, I love you. Can we please talk about this? I didn't mean it like that—"

I pull my arm out of his grasp. The unspoken meaning behind it pains me as much as it does him. I block out my emotions—this is the only way. If anyone has the power to convince me not to go, it's him. And if I stay here a second longer, he'll do it.

I avoid his eye contact. "Don't touch me. Don't talk to me again. Leave me alone."

Without another word, I race back home. Footsteps don't follow me, and my name isn't called out on the wind. He respects my request.

Part of me wishes he didn't.

ELEVEN

NEVER BETTER

Present day.

The sun set an hour ago, the daylight faded to shadows. I've mapped out the military outpost from the outskirts. A crumbling stone wall encircles the outpost and beyond it are rows of tents, several fortified buildings, and collections of tables and barrels. An outlook tower faces north toward Dragon's Back Ridge, stretching high above the rest of the settlement.

I creep closer to the outpost, my footsteps undetected in the clamor pulsing from the center of camp. Melting my body against the stone wall, I peer through a gaping hole. A group of men and women gather around a large crackling fire leaping into the night sky. My skin crawls, the flames triggering a wave of nausea inside my stomach.

A man clears his throat, and the group falls silent. "While he's fairly new to the squad, I want to toast to our captain, Cole. With hard work and determination, anything is possible."

The rest of the squad erupts in cheers. Cole grins, his head humbly lowered as people near him swing their mugs into his.

"To Cole!"

"Hurrah!"

The shadows accentuate each sharpened cut of his jaw. The glowing flames highlight the strong chords in his throat.

Gods, I'm mesmerized by the sight of him. Admiring his muscled features distracts me from the wicked flames.

Darian rises to his feet from across the group and strolls toward Cole. The group stills in anticipation. Cole watches warily, but his posture doesn't falter or shift into one of defense.

Darian pours his flask into Cole's mug, eyes trained on him in a silent challenge. "I like the way you try, Red."

Cole narrows his eyes, raises the mug, and downs the entire thing in a few gulps. A satisfied exhale slips off his lips. "Thanks."

Darian stares for a long moment with a venomous grin, before turning and slipping away from the group, disappearing farther into the camp. The rest of the squad eases, many of them smiling, laughing, and resuming their conversations.

Archie, who's sitting next to Cole, wraps an arm around Cole's neck. "Our fearless leader! Someday, I wanna be you when I grow up."

Cole shakes his head with an embarrassed smile, murmuring as he playfully pushes Archie. The two of them drop into a hushed conversation when Daeja peers out through my hair, chirping.

Cole flashes a glance my way, and I duck behind the wall. Glancing sideways at Daeja, I hold a finger to my lips, and she slips back into my cloak. They couldn't have possibly heard her, could they? I dare another peek and meet Cole's gaze.

I freeze.

He flinches, the color in his face drains, his mouth parting open.

Shit, maybe this is a bad idea.

Archie jabs his elbow into Cole's side, prompting him. Cole shakes his head, scattering his red hair. Unable to tear his eyes away from me, Cole pats Archie's shoulder with a few mumbled words, and then walks in my direction.

My pulse spikes, and my plan for what I'll say or do escapes me. Panicking, I dart back toward the forest.

I slip behind a tree and turn my focus to Daeja sitting on my shoulder. "I need you to understand me. You have to stay quiet. You stay hidden until I bring you out. Or we're both dead."

Her white eyes blink, and she bumps her forehead against mine.

Shuffling leaves whisper nearby, and I hurriedly tuck Daeja back behind my hair, securing my hood over my head. Edging around the tree, I catch a glimpse of Cole blundering through the forest, scanning the darkness through squinted eyes.

"Psst!" I hiss.

He stumbles, whipping toward my direction and eyes rounding as his gaze settles on me. "…Kat?"

I drift closer, stopping at an arm's-length from him.

Hesitantly, I reach out to touch his cheek. Surging relief and longing constricts my throat. My mind races with all the things I want to say: I'm sorry. I love you. All the 'I shouldn't haves'.

But I start with one word. "Hey."

He leans his cheek into my hand, and I brush my thumb over his soft beard. His strong, calloused hand wraps around mine, his lips blooming into a sad smile. Taking my hand from his face, he kisses the back of my hand.

He breathes. "I miss you."

Sadness, longing, and heartbreak fill those three words.

I take a half-step closer to him, and a sweet, metallic scent wafts over me. Daeja's claws sink into my shoulder, reminding me I'm pushing my limits. This close to him, and I'm fighting against my desperation to touch him. To kiss him. Gods, and those incredibly warm eyes…

He sways too far to the left, and I catch him before he can fall.

"Are you…okay? Are you drunk?" I correct his stance back to a straight position. "Where are you staying?"

He points erratically in one direction, his intoxication now obvious. Looping my arm around his lower back, we return to the outpost. His focus shifts over to me with a lazy grin every few steps, his balance slipping and he nearly tumbles forward. I palm his chest, steadying him and praying he doesn't fall.

"It's been one hundred and forty-two days since I've told you how beautiful you are," he slurs out.

I side-glance at him. Clearly, he's too drunk for counting.

"There I am." He nods toward a stone building near the western wall of the outpost.

"Is it safe?" I whisper.

He wraps his fingers around mine, both of our hands resting on his chest. "You're with me. I'll never let anything happen to you."

After I've checked the coast is clear, we slip into his quarters. We shut his door, ceasing the lull of chatter from those still gathered around the fire. I blink through the darkness of his room, my vision adjusting slowly. A bed layered with sheets folded into a neat press is tucked against the opposite wall. To the right, a wooden desk houses stacks of organized letters, a quill, and a half-empty glass bottle. To the left, an old, withered trunk is set on the ground, its lock gleaming in the darkness.

I help Cole to the bed, and he plops down on the mattress, his gaze clouded. Crouching, I unlace and pull his boots off as his eyes drag closed. I've never seen him in such a state-he's always so perfectly composed.

"Cole?" I murmur.

He tips over, his thick brawny frame landing on the mattress with a thud. Eyes still closed, he mumbles back an incoherent response. His breathing slows as he drifts off into sleep.

Backing up slowly, I remove my cloak and pile it on top of the chair by the desk. Removing Daeja from my shoulders, I place her on my piled cloak and scratch her under the chin for a job well done. She kneads the material a few times, her claws ripping out strands of my cloak before curling her body into the fabric and settling into sleep. I rid my boots and slip into the sheets beside Cole. A smile pulls at my lips as I study him in the darkness.

I brush the red hair sweeping into his forehead back, tracing my fingertips over his cheekbone and jaw, skimming the edge of his beard. It makes him look so much…older. Dark lashes press against his freckled skin, and the strong bridge of his nose points down to his soft full lips. I kiss him, ever so gently I question if I've even touched him.

His lips quirk up into a grin, mumbling in drunken satisfaction. Shifting closer, he nuzzles into me. I rest my hand on the side of his face.

The sight of him chases away my fear and hesitations.

The feeling of his pulse beneath my hand is a sanctuary.

The sound of his steady, even breath, a lullaby.

The smell of him is home.

This is where I belong.

I fall asleep, and for the first time in a long time, I dream of home. But it isn't engulfed in flames.

It's me and Cole, rolling down the grassy hills near Padmoor as if we were kids again.

TWELVE

NOT DEAD

Cole stretches himself awake next to me. When he opens his eyes, the color drains from his face. He scrambles away from me, whipping his gaze around the room and rubbing an eye with the heel of his hand.

"Kat! What the—" he pauses. His eyebrows knit together, his voice dropping to a whisper, "I—is this real? Are you really here?"

I nod, a smile spreading from my lips.

Hesitantly, he reaches out a hand to twirl a strand of my hair around his finger and tucks it behind my ear. His breath catches, realizing I'm not a figment of his imagination as his skin touches mine.

"I—I thought you were dead? I was told your house caught fire." His voice is hoarse.

I grab his hand and rest it on my chest. My heartbeat dances underneath his touch. "Not dead," I whisper.

Cole pulls me tight into his arms, crushing me into his broad chest. "I can't believe it…I thought last night was a dream or a hallucination. I've missed you so much." He looks around the room. "Where's your mother? How did you get here?"

My throat tightens enough for my voice to come out strained. "She's…dead. She was trapped in the fire. I tried to get her out but it all happened so fast…"

He brushes comforting strokes down my arm, rocking me gently until my emotions settle to a controllable level. "I'm so sorry, Kat. I'm so, so sorry."

I nod, chewing my lip and trying to divert my attention to something else before the wave of despair takes over. Daeja pops her head up from the chair, and Cole freezes. He snatches a sword by the bed.

I throw an arm out in front of him. "Stop. She won't hurt you."

"She?"

"Yes, Daeja. She's been with me since our house burned down."

He stares at me like I've lost my mind.

"You've *named* it? Kat!" His voice drops to a whisper, "It's a dragon. If we were even rumored to be in the same area as her and not report it, we would both get the noose. Not to mention she could turn on us at any moment. She could torch this whole place to ash in seconds."

I wrap my hand around his holding the sword. "She's not like that, she's just a baby."

Daeja jumps down from the chair, her nails scraping against the ground as she stretches her front legs. A stretch rolls through her spine and shakes the tip of her tail. She leaps into my lap with a weary glance pointed at Cole.

Cole flicks his attention back and forth between the two of us. "And how do you know that? How in the world did you end up with a dragon?"

"I found her egg by the river."

"So she hatched with you? As she gets older she will become more and more dangerous—"

Daeja hisses.

I pat Daeja's head to quiet her and toss a look toward Cole. "She's not like the others. The last thing my mother said was to find you and take her back to the Dragon Lands."

His grip on the sword relaxes. "Your mother said that? Kat...your mother..."

"I know, I know. But Cole, you should have seen her. She spoke to me with such clarity and conviction. It was like she was herself again. If it weren't for her, I would have died in that fire, too."

"I know you loved her." He tries to grab my hand, but his gaze flicks down to a glaring Daeja and drops his hand. "You did everything you could for her."

"Not everything. I need to do this one last thing. Please...I need your help. I have no idea how to get there from here. You could come with me? We could set her free at the border, and then we could run away together. We could go anywhere and live the life we've always wanted to."

His eyes soften. A sad smile spreads at the thought. "I can't leave this squad. I'm their captain. At this rank, leaving it would have deadly repercussions."

"Even if we left for just a few days?"

"I'm not sure it would only take a few days."

My face falls, my words as soft as a breath. "I can't do this without you..."

The words land gently as if they were snowflakes on water.

Cole chews at his lip, a muscle in his jaw feathering as he considers. Breath by breath, the tension slowly melts away. His heavy sigh finally breaks the silence. "I'll need time to think of something. But she can't stay here. There's too many people that could see her. We need to keep her out of camp."

"Well then, where can we stay where we won't be seen by your squad?"

He shakes his head, daring to reach across to grab my hand, his grip on me firm. "Not we, Kat. *Her.* I need you to stay. I've lost you once...I can't bear to lose you again."

"She's a baby, and she can't protect herself," I argue and look down at her curled in my lap. A purr rumbles in Daeja's chest as I caress her under her chin. "If we kept her here in your room couldn't we hide her in that trunk?" I point over to where it sits by the wall.

"No, we store a lot of our correspondence in there. If we

were to be audited or invaded, my room would be the first they checked. Keeping her here would be even more dangerous than out in the forest."

"Well, I can't leave her. Where she goes, I go."

He searches my eyes for a few moments in silence. Begging me. When I don't relent he sighs in defeat. "Then we need to go now. Before too many people are up and asking where I am. You can stay near the lake, and I'll reassign patrols to focus on the forest north of the outpost."

We both stand. I wrap my cloak around me and raise Daeja to slip behind my neck, pulling my hair forward over her. Cole moves for the door as I gather my things. He brushes the opening apart an inch and looks around before we exit and turn left to the forest behind his building. We slip between the gaps of the crumbling wall.

"Hey!" Quick steps approach us from behind.

Cole's hand tightens around mine before he drops it.

We've been caught.

THIRTEEN

THIS WAS A MISTAKE

"Cap! Wait—"

I turn to face the approaching voice. Archie bounds toward us, the modest brown military clothing a size too large for his lean frame.

"We needed you to...oh. Who is this?" Archie's eyes widen as they connect with mine. The daylight catches the dirty blonde wisps of his hair and meld it into a golden halo behind him.

Cole interjects before I can respond, "This is Kat..."

A bearded man approaches us. The man's weathered face pulls into a suspicious expression, his long light hair swept neatly to the side as he strolls toward us. "Captain," the man nods in greeting and flicks a hard look at me, "I wasn't aware we were having visitors."

Shit. The military doesn't allow visitors.

Daeja's weight is awfully heavy on my shoulders, and I fight the temptation to shift my posture. I'm praying to the gods she continues to stay quiet. I only know how panicked Cole is through the years I've known him—a very slight twitch sparks between his thumb and forefinger.

But his voice is as smooth as water. "Good morning, Carlisle. Meet my sister, Katerina. She's not a visitor. Her mentor passed away recently, and I thought we might be able to use the extra help."

His sister, of all things? But perhaps I don't have to play the part for long.

"And you got approvals from the General?" Carlisle challenges.

I steal a glance at Cole and the muscle flickering in his jaw.

"No. Not yet. I planned on including the request in this month's report. Marge desperately needs the help, and I imagine the General would approve the urgent request."

Carlisle watches me with narrowed eyes. I'm unsure if he buys it or not. My heart hammers in my ears as I ponder what it will mean for Daeja and I if they turn us away. If we end up having to venture to the Dragon Lands alone, without Cole's help.

Carlisle clears his throat and flicks his attention back to Cole. "I suppose we could use extra healers."

I swallow, darting my gaze over to Cole. A *healer?* I have no experience or knowledge. I can try to fake being his sister, but how can I fake being a healer?

Cole dips his head. "Thank you, Carlisle. Could you assist

us in finding Katerina her own room? Preferably close to mine and the outer west wing if possible."

Carlisle blinks at the request. "We can relocate some of the supplies in one of the northern storage tents."

"If that's all we have, then that will work. Thank you."

"I'll assign it right away. In the meantime, this is for you. It's urgent." Carlisle hands a letter to Cole and disappears off into the camp.

The corners of Archie's mouth stretch into a wide grin, the gesture wrinkling his brown eyes as he holds out an open hand to me. "Hi, Kat! What an honor to meet you, I'm Archie Stormbane."

My heart races as I eye his open hand, my own slick with sweat. In one motion I wipe my palm on my side before I meet Archie's hand and shake it. "Nice to meet you too, Archie."

An awkward, tense silence falls between the three of us. I'm starting to wonder if Archie can hear the pounding of my heart or see the fidget of Cole's anxious hands.

"Is there…there's something in my teeth, isn't there?" Archie asks and closes his mouth as he works his tongue over his teeth.

Cole tucks the letter Carlisle gave him into the chest pocket of his jacket. "Arch, do you mind securing an extra seat at breakfast for Kat?"

"Of course! Right away, Cap!" Archie bows and turns on his heels to stride back to camp.

Cole chuckles as he watches Archie go. "I keep telling him not to bow. That's reserved for the King, but he's adamant."

"You have an admirer? That's sweet." I breathe a sigh of relief. Turning my head to the side, Daeja's hot breath whispers against my ear.

Cole surveys around us, his voice dropping low. "That was far too close."

I gently smack his arm, hissing under my breath. "Yes, but what the hell, Cole? Apprenticing a *healer*?"

"It'll be an excuse if we get any questions. You know visitors aren't allowed in military outposts. So if your guise is as an apprentice, it could cover us."

Daeja pokes her head out between a layer of my hair and tilts her head at Cole.

I quickly usher her back into the cover of my hood. "What happened to staying near the lake and reassigning patrols?"

Cole grimaces. "I might have...panicked. Look. Let's get you something to eat, first, and we can figure out a plan. Can you leave her in the forest for an hour or two?"

"Absolutely not." I slip a hand back into my hood to scratch Daeja. "I can keep her quiet."

Cole's copper hair rustles as he shakes his head. "Too risky."

"Well, either I stay with her out in the forest and you tell the rest of your squad there's a change of plans—"

"I can't do that, it'll raise suspicion—"

"What do you propose then, Cole?"

"She can't stay with you. She'll get the both of you killed."

"Well, then I leave with her on my own to the Dragon

Lands," I bluff. I'm not a fan of manipulation, but I'm hoping it's enough of a threat to convince him.

His body goes rigid, confirming it worked. At least partially.

"Trust me. I can keep her…" I hook a finger under Daeja's chin and lead her out from the cover of my hair, then double tap two fingers against the side of her neck, "Hidden."

Daeja evaporates from view.

A collective murmur hums around us as we pass rows of crowded tents and reach the heart of the camp. Staring eyes weigh on me as we pass other soldiers. Cole guides me with a light touch on my lower back.

We approach a cluster of long tables accompanied by groups of soldiers bent over their breakfast plates. Cole briefly announces and introduces me to the squad, before pulling out a chair for me to sit.

Archie slides a plate in front of me. The smell alone would make me groan if I weren't surrounded by strangers. My mouth salivates as the steam off the fresh pancakes snakes up into the morning air. I grab a fork and steady myself to take small bites. Choking may be an embarrassing first impression here. The first bite melts into my mouth, and I sag at the taste.

Daeja growls in my ear, and Archie flicks a questioning look at me as he sits across from me.

I lean my head to the side to nudge her quiet. "Sorry." I laugh sheepishly. "I haven't eaten in awhile."

Cole sits next to me, subtly throwing me a side glance. As Archie directs his attention to Cole, I stealthily nab a piece of the pancake and bring it up to my neck. Daeja's hot breath warms my fingers as she sucks the food out of my grasp.

Now please, stay quiet.

Archie's words are muffled around his mouthful of pancakes as he asks Cole, "Do you think Kat and I could be sparring partners?"

"Kat's here as Marge's apprentice, so she won't be sparring," Cole answers.

"Ohh…got it. Well that's too bad, Kat, because you could spar with the best."

"I don't doubt that," I say with a smile.

Archie mirrors my smile, his cheeks stuffed full of pancakes. He absent-mindedly flicks a knife round and round his fingers, nearly slicing himself in the process. The metal knife gleams with an expensive sheen compared to the dullness of mine and Cole's.

"Where did you get that?" I ask, digging out any excuse for conversation to mask Daeja's sounds.

"Oh, this?" Archie twirls the knife in his hand again. "I brought it. It's from my home back in Helmbrook."

Cole chuckles. "You mean to tell me, out of all the items you could bring, you brought your own silverware?"

Archie studies the hilt with a smile. "It reminds me of home." He stabs the knife into a pancake and brings the next bite to his mouth.

My thoughts drift to Daeja. I hadn't realized how attached I am. Until now. The weight of her hangs on my shoulders. Somewhere along the line, it became as familiar to me as the breath in my lungs. Her presence is something intimate. Something that feels like home.

As I survey the soldiers gathered around us, it becomes clear to me. She is now something I am willing to risk my life for. My duty for fulfilling my mother's last request is spiraling into something more. Something I can't quite explain.

Cole fidgets and shifts more noticeably with each passing breath. His fingers tap against the table. As I finish my last bite, he excuses us and whisks me away.

His voice is low as he leads me away from the tables. "You can stay in my room until yours is ready."

Part of me is relieved. It'll mean less watchful eyes.

As we enter Cole's room, the both of us sag with a sigh. I lower my hood as Cole pulls the letter Carlisle gave him out from his jacket and tosses it onto his desk. The *urgent* letter.

"Aren't you going to read that?" I ask as Daeja slithers out from my hair.

"Not right now. There's nothing more urgent than you."

I blush at the implication.

"Okay so…" Cole runs a hand through his hair. "I can't

have you stay with me because it would be odd to have my sister sharing a room. But I can't protect you if I'm not near you—"

A knock sounds at the door.

Fuck.

I pull my hood back over my head as Cole opens the door.

Carlisle doesn't even try to mask his pointed stare at me. "Marge is requesting to meet Katerina."

"Now?" Cole asks.

"Unless you'd rather wait. But I wouldn't recommend testing that woman's patience. Are you otherwise occupied?"

Cole blows out a weary breath. "Very well, then. I'll make an introduction."

"Most of the supplies in the storage tent have also been relocated," Carlisle reports.

Cole voices his appreciation and dismisses Carlisle. To not press our luck, I reluctantly agree to keeping Daeja hidden in the trunk in Cole's room for the brief time we will be gone. Each step further away from Daeja prickles an uneasiness in my chest as Cole leads me toward the southern part of the outpost. He opens the door to one of the largest stone buildings I've seen here yet. The scent of honey and mint hits me as we sweep into the building. Cabinets full of glasses, bottles, and vials line the walls.

"Good morning, Marge," Cole greets.

An old woman fixing the beds against the opposite wall turns to us. Her wiry gray and white hair sweeps up into a bun, stray hairs strewn about her weathered skin.

She grabs a wooden staff with black gloved hands, her

cold gray eyes settling on Cole. "Cole. What's this I hear of an apprentice?"

Cole's fingers flutter anxiously. "My sister Katerina has decided to pay me a visit. She had been apprenticing for our town healer back home, but unfortunately, he died. I was wondering if during her time with our outpost she could follow you? That way she can continue her studies until she's able to return home and find a new mentor."

"I don't recall agreeing to such a thing," irritation laces Marge's response.

But Cole meets her heavy gaze, his voice utterly calm. "Last I remember, as a captain, I don't need your approval."

Marge shifts her squinted gaze to me. Her staff taps against the hard stone ground as she hobbles toward us. I try not to swallow under the intensity of her stare picking through my clothes, my hair, my face. Everything in me is ushering me to shrink back behind the cabinets. In case she somehow knows Cole's lying.

An uneasy silence falls between the three of us, until Marge looks back at Cole. "If it's only for the interim, and if she won't be in the way."

Cole clasps his fidgety hands together. "Great, thank you, Marge—"

"Have her here tomorrow. Immediately after breakfast."

"Tomorrow. Of course." Cole uses an open palm to lead me out.

"Nice to meet you!" I call with a half wave as we shuffle out the door. As soon as the door shuts behind us, I twist to Cole with a hiss. "There's no way I'm going to be able to fake it!"

Cole throws out a hand to silence me as two men pass us. After they disappear from view, Cole ushers me back toward his room. As soon as we open his door, my heart drops.

The trunk where we placed Daeja is tipped over. The lid is wide open, and a disarray of contents spill out onto the floor. But no Daeja.

This was a mistake.

I jet to trunk, tipping it back over and scanning the floor, picking through piles of letters and correspondence and—

Cole clears his throat. He holds the sheets on his bed up, revealing Daeja curled into a ball, her nose tucked under her tail. Sleeping.

At the commotion, she lifts her head, her eyes blinking heavily as she yawns.

My breath blows out of my lungs.

"Let's get you to your room. I have to attend sparring soon, and it should be a bit more private than my quarters." Cole rests a hand on my shoulder, his thumb stroking me reassuringly. "I can bring you food and new clothes afterwards."

"What's wrong with what I'm wearing?"

His gaze softens as he places both hands on my shoulders. "Nothing is wrong with them. But you've been wearing these for years. Not to mention if this is all you've traveled with."

I follow his gaze down to where he's touching me. Dark stains mottle the material.

Cole's voice drops to a wistful tone, "I can't imagine living in the same clothes for months on end has been very comfortable."

My eyes round with shock. "What? Did you say *months?*"

"Yes. The fire happened almost three months ago."

My mouth goes dry, and my mind fumbles for proof of it. I attempt to recount my days and memories and…nothing. I can remember events but not the days. Or the weeks.

Or the months.

I thought the cold weather could be attributed to how far north we traveled. Not because we were at the tail end of fall. The way Daeja's weight leaves my shoulders sore…how much bigger she is. It all makes sense. The fear of how completely out of my mind I am creeps in.

But Cole's tender touch anchors me. "What's wrong?"

"Nothing, I'm fine." I swallow.

"I know you're not fine when you say you're fine." He squeezes my hand. "If you don't want to talk about it yet, that's okay. I'm here when you're ready. In the meantime, let's get you settled and with some clean clothes. We can get your current things washed if you prefer it over what we have. Deal?"

"Deal," I squeak out.

Daeja, Cole, and I head to the western storage tent, now adjusted to accommodate our stay.

As we step inside, a damp scent of must and earth wafts over me. Small holes sprinkling the ceiling cast beams of golden light onto the floor, swirls of dust dancing within it.

"You deserve so much more than this," Cole breathes after he closes the door.

Daeja pokes her head out from my hood, and I scratch under her chin for a job well done in staying quiet and still. I make my way around the room. The tent has to be nearly three times the size of the other tents inhabited by soldiers. I suppose it made sense, considering this was where they stored their supplies. Remnants of those supplies were still stacked in rows of wooden crates against one of the walls. Thick wooden posts support the angled roof, and Cole leans back against a thick wooden door with his arms crossed.

I toss a look over my shoulder at him. "Is it safe?"

He shrugs. "Probably the safest place for you right now."

Hesitantly, I pull Daeja out from my hood and set her on the ground. She sniffs around the room, inspecting every corner. She finally jumps up onto the bed, wiggles her way underneath the sheets, and stills as she slips off into sleep again.

I turn back to Cole. "We can't afford to stay here long-term. What do you propose?"

He nearly flinches at the word propose. Perhaps our history had a much heavier effect on him than I could possibly imagine.

The glowing amber of his eyes swirl with pain and regret before it fades, and he responds mechanically, "I don't have an immediate answer. I'd need a couple of days to figure out a plan. Maybe even get a map—"

I saunter over to him. His cream-colored sleeves are pushed up to reveal chords of muscle lacing his forearms. As I get closer and closer, his fingers flicker to life.

I pause a step away from him. But the fidgeting doesn't stop. Hesitantly, I reach for his hand and wrap mine around his, stilling his quaking fingers.

"Cole…" I whisper. "I'm so sorry for that day in the forest."

He shakes his head, biting his lip as he looks down at our intertwined fingers. "You have nothing to be sorry for. You were trying to save your mother. I'm sorry I didn't go with you. I should have—"

"You were doing what was best for your family." I smile sadly.

"But you were my family, too. I wanted a life with you," his voice dips low, and his eyes catch mine.

Were. Wanted. All the things of the past. My face falls, and he slips his hand out from mine. Digging between the layers of his shirt, he fishes out something metal. It gleams as the light fragments off it.

The necklace with his mother's ring.

He unclasps it from his neck and holds it in his palm. "I wore it every day after you left."

An offering. A question. Perhaps he doesn't hate me as much as I thought he might.

He swallows hard. "Kat, I—"

I crush myself into him, pressing my lips to his.

I love you, too. He doesn't have to say it for me to know it or feel it.

He sighs into my mouth, easing into my embrace.

I cling to him. As desperate as someone would be for air

as they drowned. Grasping, melting, holding. His hands find the sides of my face as he kisses me back. I press into him, shifting him back a few steps. His back thuds against the door, and something falls to the ground with a 'clink.' He pulls away from our kiss and drops to a crouch to pick up the ring he dropped.

He kneels in front of me, eyes flicking up at me. His mother's ring in his hand.

This is the moment—this is it.

Something shuffles outside, and he frantically pushes back up to his feet, shoving the ring into a pocket. His chest rises with exaggerated breaths, and his eyes round.

His throat bobs as he swallows. "We have to be careful. Really careful, Kat. They can't know you're not my sister. There's so much at stake. There's so much we have to figure out—it…it doesn't mean I don't want to—" He's fumbling for words, bracing himself against a wooden post as he shuffles backwards away from me.

I can't tell if he's spooked or if he's fighting himself to keep from ripping my clothes off.

"Okay," I breathe, ghosting a touch on his hand with a smile. As if I were calming a wild animal. "It's okay."

The tension in him lessens.

With a sad smile, he gazes down at our hands, now laced together. "The past few months I've been worried for other people: my family, my squad, the towns. But since this morning I've only been able to think of one person. You. I'm worried about you.

Because if something happens to you…I won't be able to survive it." He flicks a look up at me. "Not again."

I rest my other hand on his cheek. "Nothing's going to happen to me, Cole."

It's all I can think of to answer him.

Even if I can't promise it.

FOURTEEN

A BLUE FIRE

Cole brings dinner and several sets of new clothes later in the day. I can't help but snicker as he turns away while I change. As if he had never seen me naked before. Such a chivalrous act, for someone I know has a feral drive whenever he lets go of his impossibly tight reins.

He must be taking this 'being careful' thing seriously, if he can't bother even a glance.

Perhaps he knows deep down, like me, he doesn't have as much self-discipline as he'd like to have. That a simple look would be enough to tear down every boundary he's trying to set. I suppose it only makes me respect him even more.

Cole isn't able to stay long. He leaves shortly after, commenting that he's going to try and convince Marge to give me a few days to 'settle in' before apprenticing with her.

His tone hints he's not too confident.

Half the dinner Cole brought—chicken—went to Daeja.

Every piece I tossed her she swallowed nearly whole. I don't think I've ever seen her eyes so dilated.

With the dwindling daylight and Daeja curled into the corner of my arm and chest, I open my father's journal.

It's been about a month since I've been here. The military general, Jurrock, appeared for a meeting with the King today. They whispered behind closed doors while a group of us were there to guard the windows. We stood at each arched window encircling the meeting room, staring out to ensure no stray arrows came through the glass. I had never seen, nor heard of an arrow piercing glass and striking someone behind it before. But I didn't question it. I did as I was told.

We were ordered to not take our eyes off, or shift away from, the window frame. I strained to listen to the King and Jurrock's conversation. I could only catch words here and there, with dragons and rebels grabbing my attention. It took everything in me to not turn and try to read their lips.

Their conversation paused with the sound of footsteps.

Out of my periphery, I saw the King move toward a guard near the door. Both of the King's hands cradled a round crimson object. Light reflected off the object in a brilliant sheen. Ever so slowly, I turned my chin toward their direction for a better look.

It looked like...a dragon egg.

The King demanded the guard take the egg to the 'lock.'

I straightened my view back to the window before the King turned, and we were all ordered out.

What was the King doing with a dragon egg?

A few nights have passed since the King ordered the dragon egg to be stored in the 'lock.' I've been itching to find out where the lock was and who had access to it. The first step was to find who the guard was. But the information I gathered with only a second long side-glance wasn't enough to determine who it was. He had short brown hair. That's all I knew.

And it didn't narrow it down much. Most of the men here had short brown hair. I examined each guard's profile as I passed them in the halls or as we ate. Hoping to think, "Ahh! That was his nose!" or "That was his ear!" But there was nothing. No indication or pull of who it might have been.

But tonight at dinner, the lot of us sat and discussed the incoming shift changes. With the sun setting sooner, and the nights growing longer, we had to transition our stations and hours. One man looked at my lead and asked about the candidates to replace him in the lock. He was taking leave to spend some time with his terminally ill wife.

Many who overheard the conversation watched in confusion. I realized only the handful of us guards who were in the room that day would have ever heard of the 'lock.' My lead shook his head silently in warning and shifted the subject.

Got him.

This morning I strained to listen to the two guards whispering next to me at breakfast.

"The King was shouting last night," one said.

"Okay? So? The King shouts all the time."

"Yes, but he wasn't shouting at anything. Anyone. I was stationed outside his door all night. And unless someone scaled the walls to the top without being caught, he was alone."

A thoughtful silence settled after the word 'alone.'

"I...even opened the door and peeked at him. His back was to me, but he was in a full blown conversation. There was no one else there."

I knew the King killed his sister to rule. That in itself took a certain level of insanity. But to be talking to himself?

"Did he see you?"

"Of course not! I didn't take more than a few seconds. I wouldn't still be here if he had—"

"Gentleman." Our lead came up behind us and clasped me and the guard beside me on the shoulders. I tried not to choke on the food in my mouth.

Our lead called an urgent meeting, and we all gathered in the training room.

Once everyone was settled, he called two names forward. I watched in surprise as the two broke from the group. The two who had sat next to me whispering.

Our lead ordered them to kneel—a custom standard for promotional ceremonies. Excitement danced on their faces. It was the last thing we saw before their faces twisted in anguish as they were decapitated.

My hand flies to my throat, my pulse skittering under my skin. I slap the journal shut, and Daeja's head jolts up from where it was tucked into my side.

"Sorry, girl," I whisper and stroke a thumb over her head.

She wiggles herself back into my ribs, and I slide the journal under my pillow.

That wasn't something I wanted to end on, but the light in my room starts to dim as the last light of the day fades. I stare up at the ceiling until sleep eventually pulls me under.

Something wet grazes my cheek. I use a hand to swipe it off and turn to my opposite side. A sniff pulses in my ears, and another wet flick tickles my face. Except this time, it doesn't let up.

My eyes flash open, and I shrink away from the sensation.

Daeja's wide eyes twinkle in the starlight. Staring directly at me.

"What? What is it, girl?" I grumble.

She whines, nudging her nose under my hand. I pat her, and she grabs a mouthful of my sleeve and pulls.

"What are you doing?" I whisper.

She tugs until I sit up, before she pounces off the bed and

scurries over to the door. Dragging her front claws down the wood, the grating sound shoots me to my feet.

As I dart over to her, she scratches more insistently. Frantically.

I grab her, pulling her into my arms and placing an ear against the door. Did she hear something I couldn't?

But it's quiet.

I flick a look down at her. Cautiously, I open the door a few inches to peer out. An orange glow of a fire pulses from the center of camp, blocked by shadowy silhouettes of soldiers gathered around it.

Daeja moves fast. Too fast for me to stop her. She jumps from my arms and slips out the door. Her body flickers, as if testing her newly acquired disappearing skill.

Cursing, I sprint after her. She skirts left, away from the center of camp and around the backside of the storage tent facing the forest beyond. The farther away we get from the glow of the fire, the harder it is to track her in the night.

As we reach the outpost's crumbling stone wall, I jet a glance over my shoulder toward camp. No one follows us.

Daeja disappears into the shadowy forest beyond.

Once I'm in the thick of the trees, I call her, "Daeja?"

I tip-toe around shadows stretching across the forest floor. Scanning every lifted tree root or pile of leaves.

"Daeja," I whisper again, hoping she will reveal herself.

My breath is stuck in my lungs as I scan the stillness of the trees. My eyes search the shadows, my heart sinking with every passing second. I reach a break in the tree line giving way to a glittering lake. Off in the distance, a soft glowing moon hovers above Dragon's Back Ridge. As I cup my hands to call for her again, the shadow of a large fallen tree shifts. White ghostly eyes blink at me, and my breath loosens.

I close the distance between us, scooping Daeja into my arms. "What has gotten into you?"

I draw her face to face with me. Her hot breath billows against my nose. Setting her down on the ground, I watch as her attention jets over her shoulder, and she stills. She swings and launches at her own twitching tail, spinning circles, and grappling with outstretched claws. She eventually ends up on the ground.

A smile lifts my lips at the innocence of it. I can't place why she might have slipped out until the scent of the forest lingers over me: sap, earth, and cedar. Flooding me with memories of home. I didn't realize how much it reminds me of my father, my brother, and my mother.

How much I miss them.

What if keeping her at the camp is a mistake?

Perhaps she was safest out here. In theory, she should be able to take care of herself, given the fact she's a dragon: a flying, fire-breathing—

Wait—flying. If she could fly, she could at least get away if she were in trouble. If something kept me from being able to return her to the Dragon Lands myself, she could go on her own, at least.

Daeja jumps back up to her feet, her tail clutched between her teeth as I crouch down near her. I take a fingertip and start at the bridge of her nose and slowly drag it up between her eyes, over her head and down her neck between her shoulder blades. I stop at the joints of her wings and recall my father's journal entry about hatchlings. Gently hooking a finger under her wing, I lift. Her wings flare to life. The newfound weight makes her topple over, and I catch her before she falls. Once I steady her, I stand.

"Ok, now fly!" I call out and point to the sky.

She tilts her head with a blink but doesn't move. I raise both of my arms above my head and flap them. The muscles above her eyes raise in question. I jump into the air as I flap, and I'm sure if anyone else saw, they'd think I've lost my damn mind.

"You can do it! Just like this!" I pause to see if she's catching on.

She jerks her chin up repeatedly, like a series of small nods, and pauses. Watching me.

I gesture again with a flap of my arms and jump.

She lifts her chin again.

Oh...*she's encouraging me.*

I chuckle. "No, no. Not me. *You.* I don't have wings." I reach forward, delicately grabbing her wings and flapping them.

She looks at her wings and wiggles them slightly. Her eyes round in amazement and realization that these things are attached to her.

"Now flap them, and fly!" I hint at the motion again.

She grits her teeth at her first attempt. But she isn't able to lift off the ground. She just slowly falls to the side. We try again and again, until I realize she might need a running start. My gaze travels over to the lake, my heart pounding in my ears.

It makes the most sense.

If she crashes, it'll be into the water.

But what if she can't swim? What if she drowns?

My thoughts spiral. Down and down. And now I'm stuck at the bottom, clawing my way back up as emotions swarm me.

I miss him.

I miss my brother.

Had I only listened to him when he told me to stop playing near the river, he might still be here today. I might not have accidentally knocked him into the current rushing with Dragon's Back Ridge's snow melt. I should have been strong enough to pull him out. I should have been able to save him. But I couldn't.

And I didn't.

I bite my tongue at the surge of sadness and guilt. The fact that I couldn't save him or my mother.

What makes me think this will be any different—

Daeja touches my hand.

The warmth of her breath blows against my sweaty palm. I drag my gaze away from the water and toward her glowing white eyes, sparkling in the moonlight. I scratch underneath her chin, and she melts into a purr. A smile cracks at my lips.

Daeja stills for a few moments. Her eyes focused on the lake ahead. She dips her head and charges for the water. Flapping as she goes.

"Daeja!" I bolt after her.

As her feet graze the sandy shore, she lifts into the air, flapping against the wind and soaring over the water.

The icy cold water sloshes against my shins as I race after her, my voice tight as I whisper, "I don't know if you know how to swim..."

She dips and swerves, and she struggles to maintain a leveled glide. Her dark shadow grows smaller and smaller as she approaches the opposite side of the lake and toward the black silhouette of trees outlined against the night sky.

Turn, turn, turn!

My feet catch fire, and I run for the other side of the lake. I don't know if she knows how to stop or turn. My panic rises as I realize I don't see her anymore. My lungs scream with each stride, my heart hammering in my ears. By the time I finally reach the other side, my cold, wet legs threaten to buckle underneath me.

Daeja's dark shadow is slumped against a tree. I run faster. Closing the distance between us, I fall to my knees beside her.

"Are you okay?" I pant as I try to assess her.

She stands, wriggling and shaking her body, as if she were drenched with embarrassment. I pull her into me, my arms trembling around the warmth of her scales.

"You...did...it!" I say between breaths, pride welling in me as I scratch her cheek. She melts into my touch, as she always does.

Her relaxed expression melts away, her gaze locking in on a spot in the woods.

Something flickers in my periphery. I turn toward it, pressing a hand to her side as I follow her stare. In the darkness, the distant trees pulse a soft glow. Not with the warmth of a fire of orange and red and light. But a cool, icy blue flame floats up from the ground and fades into the shadows like fog.

What is…that?

Daeja bristles, the spikes on her neck and head fanning out. My fear melts to curiosity—it doesn't dance like fire. It lacks the crackles and spits a flame would produce. Completely entranced by the beauty of its color, I move toward it. Daeja follows me and touches her muzzle to my leg. I pause mid-step and meet her round eyes. In the stillness of the moment, a distant hum buzzes beneath my feet.

As Daeja and I draw closer to the light, the hair on my neck stands. I'm oddly aware of how the blood in my veins sing, and the sweat rivers down my back. Close enough now to notice the lack of warmth a normal fire would create from this distance. Mesmerized, I watch how the flames flare and dance.

Is this the same blue flame Willard had mentioned all those months ago? That could have been the cure to my mother's insanity?

If it is the rumored flame, I'm not sure what it could offer me now.

But it still calls to me the same, beckoning me forward with invisible fingers as if I were in a trance.

Daeja and I are a few steps from the edge of its blue fire as my hair lifts and floats up toward the sky. The air tightens around us with a hidden electricity. A jagged glowing crack in the earth sways and whips sporadically, the blue and white flame ebbing and flowing from it. Daeja stiffens beside me as we stand there, staring for a few moments.

She walks to the edge of the cracked earth to sniff it before I can stop her. The wicked flames flare in the same moment, brushing her nose, and she staggers back wildly.

"Daeja!" I hiss in surprise and reach for her.

Daeja's pupils blow wide, the blue reflection of the fire bursting in her irises. Her mouth parts as she crumples to the ground.

I dart forward with a cry, folding to my knees to pick her up. As I brace my hands under her cold body, something shifts. A distant thunder rumbles beneath me, and Daeja rises. I fall back onto the heels of my hands as she grows and grows. Her dark shadow casts over me, drowning me in darkness. Where she had been the size of a kitten before, she now towers above me as high as any steed would.

Like a dark horse with wings.

My mouth drops open. "By the gods..."

But there's no mistaking her round white eyes, nearly opalescent in the soft blue light around us. The wideness of her stare matches my own.

"Why do you look so much smaller?" a voice as slippery as oil and raspy fills my ears.

I scan the forest for anyone else around us, my hand fumbling for a blade I didn't sheathe before we slipped out of the outpost.

"No one else is here," the voice echoes again. Except I realize it's not in my ears. It's in my *mind.*

I whip toward Daeja. Stretching out an open hand toward her as if to halt any sudden movements. *"You…you can hear me?"*

"Yes."

My right hand tremors as Daeja leans forward and presses her muzzle into my palm. The part of my palm that used to cover her entire head now only covers the front of her nose. My fingers…

My…*fingers.*

The light hint of a band that appeared around my middle finger all those months ago when I learned her name has darkened several shades. The ring is now darker than my skin tone.

Daeja breaks our contact, her gaze darting to the illuminated blue river beside us snaking away. The glowing blue mist thins and fades back into the ground until we are left in the dark.

"And…I can…hear you?"

"Also, yes."

The two of us sit in silence at a loss for words. The moon peaks above the tree line, the light scattering across the forest floor and illuminating the bushes and trees around us.

I rise to my feet and circle her, carefully assessing her transformation as I claw for every memory of my father's journal entries. But every attempt comes up empty handed.

I can't recall a blue flame, nor explosive growth spurt. Perhaps I need to consider reading through the rest of the journal a bit faster.

The light casts a silver sheen on Daeja's back, and she

folds her expansive wings into her body. She wiggles, sniffing and inspecting her broad shoulders, whip-long tail, and deathly long talons. A dozen more jagged black horns spike the crown of her head and the nape of her neck.

As I circle around her, I dare a gliding touch against her cool, rugged scales. The rise and fall of her beneath my fingertips is as similar to my own breath.

As I come back face to face with her, I gently tug her upper lip up to reveal rows of serrated fangs. I flick up a look to meet her gaze. Where part of me expected to be fearful, I find myself... sorrowful, in a way.

Stepping back from her, I size up how tall she is, calculating if she'll even be able to fit through the door at camp. My face falls as I struggle to find any solution.

The small hatchling I once had was gone.

"Well, I guess you won't be able to fit on my shoulders anymore."

"Why not?"

I chuckle at the simplicity of her question. It's so at odds with how ancient and smooth her voice sounds now.

She tilts her head to the side, sparking an ember of joy in my chest at the memory of her doing it so often as a hatchling.

Rubbing my hand against the ridge of her nose, she bumps her muzzle enthusiastically into my hand.

"Do you feel any different? I don't understand what happened."

"No, not really. Last I remember, I reached down to sniff the light. My body felt cold and like it was on fire all at once.

Everything was white. I couldn't see anything. And then when I finally opened my eyes, I saw you."

"I wonder where it went..." My attention floats over to where the blue fire was moments ago. I stare. As if I might look away for a moment and it'll be there taunting me, like a ghost in the night.

I thought it could have been a delusion, as I had never heard of it before. But perhaps the magical blue flame Willard spoke of all along was real.

It makes me wonder what else he knew.

It's hard leaving Daeja out in the forest. But no matter how hard I try to come up with an alternative, there's no way I can sneak her back in and keep her at the camp. Not with how large she is. And definitely not with how clumsy she is. She nearly sweeps my legs out from under me with her tail as she spins around to itch a spot on her hindquarters.

We find her a secluded cave near the southern part of the lake. As I leave, my skin prickles with each step I take back to camp. I can't help but glance over my shoulder every few yards to check on her.

"I'm still here," she calls. **"I'll wait for you."**

"I'll come back." I promise with tears lining my eyes.

I push through each wave of fear and guilt crashing over me until I finally slip into Cole's room and update him on Daeja's growth spurt.

Despite his promise to draw the patrol's perimeter away from the southern half of the lake, I can't shake the feeling of unease. Perhaps it's because Cole says he still needs a few days to figure out a plan. And the plan in the meantime is for me to fake being his sister to stay nearby. And to fake being an apprentice.

Apparently, Marge is a hard woman to negotiate with.

Reluctantly, I return to my room. The overwhelming sense of loneliness nearly chokes the breath from my chest. The ring encircling my finger throbs almost painfully.

"I'm still here," her voice floats over to me.

For the rest of the night, every time the next wave of loneliness and uneasiness lurches over me, her voice caresses my mind.

"I'm still here."

"I'll come back." I promise.

FIFTEEN

KATEENA

"Don't touch anything without my permission or instruction," Marge barks.

I retract my outstretched hand. The bottle I started to inspect has a thick green liquid inside, swirling with flecks of fizzled light.

Marge rips the bottle from the shelf in front of me and tucks it back into a corner of a high up cabinet. She locks the cabinet door and shoots me a glare.

"Sorry," I whisper. Turning away, I awkwardly search for something else to do.

She returns the key to a pocket hidden in the side of her dress. "Do you know what ginger looks like?"

"Ummm, it's red, right?"

The exasperated sigh slipping from Marge tells me it's not

the answer she was looking for. *Shit. She's already going to know I'm faking my medical background and it's not even noon on day one.*

"I'm going to go gather some from the forest." She points a black gloved finger at a basket across the room.

When I don't move, she snaps her fingers impatiently for me to fetch it for her.

Marge grumbles, "I can't quite send you out yet since you don't know what to look for." She scoops the basket from my hand. "If someone comes, tell them I'll be back within the hour. If they're bleeding, hold those rags to the wound and apply firm pressure. If they're dying…well…"

She grabs her staff, and I catch the last half of her sentence before the door shuts. "May the gods be with them."

I wait a few moments after the door is shut before slumping back into a chair, unsure of what to do with myself. Temptation urges me to see what other odd potions and oils are stashed in the cabinets. A stab of homesickness hits me as I think of Willard and how willing he would have been to show me everything. More than willing—perhaps ecstatic.

The longer I sit, the heavier my blinks become, and I stifle a yawn. What little sleep I did get last night after seeing Daeja was interrupted by dreams of fire. And of my mother, my brother, the little girl and her family. Their screams were as audible as if they stood in the room with me.

"Daeja?" I test. *"Can you hear me from here?"*

"Yes!"

A smile pulls at my lips hearing her voice. I glance down

at the band around my finger, wondering what it means. If it is somehow connected to the blue flame, and what might have happened if I were the one to touch the flame instead.

"What was it called that you gave me last night?"

"Chicken?"

"Yes. What do chickens look like?"

I can't contain my snicker. Luckily, I don't have to with Marge gone. *"Well, they come in all sorts of colors. They're birds, so they have wings and—"*

"Like me?"

"No, they have feathered wings—"

The door swings wide open, and a man stumbles in. I jolt at the violent entrance. He's tall. Maybe a few inches shorter than Cole. His mass of walnut brown hair is swept every which way, and his cold and calculating green eyes rake across the room. We lock gazes for a brief moment, and his eyes flare with what almost resembles shock. He looks away quickly, gaze darting to the cabinets.

Darian.

"Marge," he hisses out between gritted teeth and takes a few staggered steps toward me, his hand bracing his left thigh.

A large, dark stain blots his black pants, a glint of metal lodged into his leg. I hurry to him and offer my forearm to brace himself against me. He refuses me with a scoff. Droplets of blood splatter against the ground in his wake as he sweeps the room.

"She's out gathering ingredients in the forest," I mutter quickly.

Darian nearly falls into a chair with a grimace.

I scurry over to snatch a rag on the table near the window. "I can go get her—"

"No," he barks. "Just get me the bottle in the back left of that cabinet over there. It's a green bottle with no label."

"I'm not allowed to administer medication without Marge."

"I don't give a shit. Do as I say," he growls. His menacing green eyes dart over to me through lowered dark brows.

My hand clenches around the rag, tilting up my chin in defiance. "I don't know who you think you are, but I don't take orders from—"

"Sorry? And *who* are you?" he sneers. His attention focused back on his thigh as he tries to apply pressure with his hand around the dagger.

I hold out the rag to him. "I'm Katerina—"

"Listen, Kateena," he hisses. He still doesn't bother to look me in the eyes as he wipes a bloody hand on his pants.

I've met men like him before. Snide, rude, and arrogant. It's a wonder how he got through the door with that big of an ego-filled head.

"Kat-*ER*-ee-na," I correct with an eye roll.

"Yeah, yeah, sure. Anyway, make yourself useful, be a good girl, and go grab that bottle before I bleed to death." He flicks his fingers off to the corner.

I bite my tongue to keep the ticking anger at bay, temptation luring me to throw the damn rag at him. But before I can, a movement at the door catches my attention.

Marge walks in with a basket stuffed with snipped greenery and foliage. "Don't you think you've had enough, Darian?"

I motion to his leg. "He's been stabbed."

Marge waddles over, craning her neck before she sucks her teeth. "Katerina, I'm going to need you to help me by pulling the dagger out slowly. Once we have it removed, I'll have to stitch it quick and wrap it. Do you think you can do that?"

"Yes," my voice is small.

Marge works at her cabinet, pulling materials from the drawers and doors. My pulse skitters at the thought that this is the first chance to prove myself. My gaze flickers to the metal lodged into his flesh, and I gulp.

Marge returns and places items on the table next to us. Darian shakes his head at the sight of the needles, and I drop to crouch in front of him. I circle my hand around the handle of the dagger but don't touch it yet.

"Ready?" Marge asks.

I nod.

"Go."

In the moments I close my fingers around the hilt, Darian shifts his gaze back to me.

His lips twitch into a ridiculously sinful smirk. "I love the look of you between my legs. Maybe while you're down there—"

I glare up at him and twist my grip on the dagger ever so slightly.

He throws his head back with a yell and slams a fist into the arm of the chair.

Asshole. That was for Cole, and for Archie. And...maybe for myself, too. Perhaps it'll teach him to mind his tongue.

After I retract the dagger, Marge presses a rag into the gaping wound, and I back away. Marge blots and sews, blots and sews. Her skillful gloved hands work nearly mechanically. Darian occasionally grimaces or clenches his fists, staring off at a wall as he sips from a flask he's pulled from his black vest.

Once he's stitched, Marge applies an ointment and instructs me to grab the bandage she's set aside. As soon as she completes his wrap, Marge wipes her hands clean and returns back to her collection from her outing.

"Probably should tell you to stay off your leg for a few days to let it heal. But there's no point since you won't listen to me anyway, right?" she asks.

Darian rises with a grunt and a sickly sweet smile. "You know me better than anyone, Margie."

He limps past me, not a word or another look toward me. When the door closes, Marge huffs.

"Wicked thing. For your first patient, that was impressive. Had it been me, I might have relocated that dagger into his neck if he talked to me like that." She pulls out contents from her basket and begins to line the countertop with it all.

I shrug. "Well, I guess there's always next time."

A hint of a grin twitches on her lips before it's gone. "Alright, I'll need your help to reorganize what we have since you've managed to take over our supply room. Come over here and start putting these up into the top right cabinet."

We pace back and forth to organize supplies. She shows me various things she collected, and where it all belongs in the healer's quadrant. At one point, my hands start sweating from the nerves of needing to remember it all. A bottle slips out of my grip, shattering onto the floor.

Marge isn't afraid to let me know she's not pleased about that before sending me off for the rest of the day.

Guess I'll try again tomorrow.

I have some free time before dinner, so I return to my room to read another journal entry. Hope flickers within me at the thought of finding something that could tell me about Daeja or the blue flame.

It's been a week since the King met with Jurrock and obtained a fire dragon egg. Jurrock must have left shortly thereafter because I haven't seen nor heard a word of him since. I've been waiting for the right moment to ask questions I'm hoping will lead me to wherever the 'lock' is.

I can't seem to wrap my head around why the King would want a dragon egg, and what he'd be doing with one. Not to mention, an egg away from other dragons could mean the embryo dying from magical inactivity. That time frame had such a wide range—but it's a risk I imagined the King knew.

With his royal bloodline, one theory I had was that he was trying to resuscitate dragon riders. But why fight so abhorrently against us "dragon sympathizers" if you meant to revive dragon riders?

Something told me it was a larger puzzle I couldn't quite piece together...yet. I had to figure out where the lock was with the dragon egg.

So the best plan I could come up with was to lie.

"The King sent me to retrieve the egg. It must be relocated. We need to secure it by guard in the King's quarters until further notice," I had said to the guard that was given the egg the week prior.

He searched my eyes, waiting for me to flinch or falter. But I held him there. After a few moments of tense silence, he nodded and led me to the lock.

Rather than down the spiraling staircases where I expected it would be, we headed upwards. Up several sets of stairs and through a maze of hallways. We stopped at a hidden door blending into one of the stone walls. The guard pressed against one of the many gray stones until they shifted, clicked, and creaked as part of the wall opened. We walked down another long narrow hallway with no lights lining the corridor. The only light came from the small torch clutched in the guard's hand.

Wicked shadows danced along a heavy metal door at the end of the corridor. It was one of few doors in this castle I had seen that wasn't made of wood.

We both walked inside, and my insides instantly curled into a knot.

Inside the small room, several eggs were in wooden crates. By the flickering torchlight, various colors peeked out from the gaps of the wooden cages. One egg was large and red with veins of black. One was a shiny blue, another a dull white, and a fourth egg green with dark speckles. Each dragon species was accounted for: fire, water, earth, and air.

But what caught my eye was the egg in the middle of them all. It wasn't nearly as large as the others, but the light sheened off its smooth surface.

In all of my days, I had never heard of, nor seen, a black dragon egg.

"Well, what are you waiting for?" the guard challenged.

I quickly grabbed the black one. A magical energy hummed beneath my hands at the mere closeness of the egg, and I held down a shiver. I glanced at the others. Guilt swarmed me that I didn't have enough arms to carry them all.

It dawned on me as we exited, and the guard locked the door behind us.

I had told the guard I needed to retrieve the egg.

One.

And there were multiple.

How did he not question me which one?

It confirmed the black dragon egg must have had some significance.

As I broke away from the guard on the main floor and toward the King's quarters, I fumbled through a plan. If I got caught, there was no way I'd get out alive.

They'd find my journal, and what information they didn't already know would be confiscated.

I contemplated destroying this journal before they had the chance to read it. I considered the fireplaces in almost every room in the castle. A special unit was assigned to keep them all going—day and night—no matter the weather.

It would only take minutes before the journal was ash.

My thoughts swim as I recount the fateful day I found Daeja by the river. A black dragon egg buried underneath my father's cross.

It must have been Daeja.

SIXTEEN

DINNER TALKS

At dinner, I convince Archie I'm capable of getting my own plate, much to his dismay. He mentions using my elbows to get through the line. Something about him makes me laugh nearly every time he speaks. Not the obligated laugh, but the kind that starts off as a genuine smile and cracks into something greater.

As Archie and I settle into our seats, Darian slides in next to Archie. Archie looks at me with an excited waggle of his eyebrows.

Cole clears his throat from beside me. "Darian, this is my sister, Kat—

"We've already exchanged *pleasantries.*" Darian unscrews the lid to his flask, not bothering to look at any of us.

"How's your leg?" I ask not so innocently.

"Just fine, Kateena." He takes a swig from his flask.

"Do you think we'll get to fight rebels any time soon?" Archie asks as he slurps into his soup.

Cole's jaw tightens. "I'd say it's inevitable. I've received word from the General to move our east wing squad south to cover Spillburg who was attacked three nights ago. Which means we may need to spread ourselves thin here."

Archie sits up straighter, his eyes sparkling. "I would love to be a lead. You could even pair me with Darian, if you're worried about him?" Archie elbows Darian.

The sudden movement jerks Darian's grip, and the flask spills its contents onto the table. Darian whips a daggered glare toward Archie.

"Right?" Archie asks him again, the smile on his face fading.

Darian clenches his teeth. "I stopped listening once you started talking."

"Can you say *anything* remotely nice?" I blurt.

Darian drags his heated stare toward me and tilts his head to the side, his brown hair sweeping down into his eyes. "Excuse me?"

Cole knocks his knee into mine. A silent warning.

But I know these types of men. No one owes them a lick of sympathy, nor respect, or fear. And in fact, I bet if I show him a hint of any of those, he'll use it as a weapon against me.

Despite my nerves flinching under Darian's wicked pointed glare, I hold his gaze. "You. Heard. Me."

Darian scoffs. Rolling his neck, he turns to Archie with an exasperated sigh. "Someday, you'll go far, kid." He downs whatever is left in his flask and pushes up to his feet. "...And I really hope you stay there."

"You're a fucking asshole," I sneer.

Archie's spoon drops, clattering into his bowl. Cole tenses, reflexively holding out an arm across my chest.

Everyone around us stops mid-conversation to stare, the chatter in camp dying instantly.

Darian's expression isn't one I've seen before. It's a mix of dangerous calm hinting he doesn't need to oversell his anger. People just...fear him.

He leans onto the table, towering and lurching above me. I tilt my chin up to look him in the eyes.

His whisper sends chills down my spine.

"I *know*."

He spits at the ground before pushing off the table and stalking away. Once he disappears, everyone resumes their conversations. Except this time, a nervous murmuring replaces the normal jabbering.

"What is his problem?" I flick my gaze to Cole. "How is he still with the squad acting like that?"

Cole lightly shakes his head and diverts his attention back to his own bowl. "He's the best swordsman in the kingdom. We need his skills."

"Shouldn't matter. People like that aren't useful to anyone. That sort of attitude is dangerous—"

Archie laughs. "I'm not scared of him. If anything, he

should be scared of me!" He flashes a toothy grin through the gap of his flexed arm.

I stifle a chuckle. "You're right. Now will you put that thing away before I have to run for the hills?"

Archie waggles an eyebrow but lowers his flexed bicep.

"Archie, how are your parents?" Cole redirects the conversation.

Archie's grin flickers. "They're good, they're good. Yeah. I haven't received any letters this month yet. But I know this time of year they're busy getting settled for winter."

Sadness fogs over me. Winter. A few months ago I was doing the same thing—hyper focused on stocking enough food and medicine to last until spring. Now, rather than that, I'm here. An orphan. My biggest concern with winter at this point is how many layers I need to wear in the mornings. I don't have to second guess where my next meal will come from. I look down at the soup.

"Are you hungry?"

"Aren't I ever! More chicken?"

I bite my lip to keep from smiling. *"No chicken, unfortunately. We're having soup. But let me see if I can bring you something else."*

"How are your parents?" Archie asks Cole and I.

Cole taps his fingers against the wooden table. "They're good. Well. Actually, our mother died. But, our father is good. Sisters are all good."

Archie frowns at the news. "I'm so sorry. I didn't know."

Part of what Cole said was true. Both of our mothers are

dead. But where Cole has a father and sisters, I have no one. Just Daeja. And Cole.

"How old are your sisters?" Archie asks.

I panic as I struggle recalling all the ages of Cole's sisters.

Thankfully, Cole responds. "Seventeen, fourteen, eleven, nine, six, and four."

Archie's eyes round as he looks at me. "How old are you, Kat?"

An easy enough reply for me. "Twenty-two."

"And you're...how old, Cole?"

"Twenty-six."

"Wow…" Archie nods slowly with arched eyebrows. "I bet birthday parties are fun."

"Do you have any siblings, Archie?" I ask.

"Yep, I'm the youngest of four. All boys. Two of my brothers are actually stationed in Arterias."

"Wow. The capital, huh? That's impressive!"

"Yeah. All three of my brothers were originally appointed to the King's castle. But my oldest brother was injured and honorably discharged. He's back home with my ma and pa."

"I'm sorry to hear that," I murmur.

Archie shrugs and diverts his gaze down to his hands.

"Do chickens live in the forest?"

Daeja's sudden intrusion catches me off guard, and I clear my throat to keep myself from laughing.

Cole looks over to me, and Archie lifts his head. The both

of them watching me expectantly, as if I announced I needed to say something.

A nervous chuckle rumbles off my lips. "Delicious." I sip a spoonful of soup.

"No. Why are you asking?"

"I wanted to see if I could hunt one myself."

I bite my lip—hard—trying not to laugh. *"You can't, they live on farms. We raise them for food."*

"What are farms?"

Archie's eyes meet mine, his eyebrow quirking up in question.

Shit, I must have been staring directly at him for far too long. Juggling two conversations is proving to be much more difficult than I could have ever imagined.

"Daeja, I have to go. I'll come see you tonight."

I mentally scramble for something to ask Archie. "Have you ever been to Arterias?"

"No. I've always wanted to! I was hoping to be stationed there with my brothers by the time I turned twenty-one."

"When do you turn twenty-one?" I question.

"I'm nearly twenty-two. I uh…didn't quite make the cut. Those stationed in Arterias are the best of the best. They have to be to protect the King."

Cole pipes in, offering an encouraging smile, "And we will get you there, Arch. You're close! I don't think I've ever seen another soldier with your courage. We just have to work on some more technical sword training. I'll even write a recommendation to the King for you myself."

But despite the confidence from Cole, Archie's smile doesn't touch his eyes. He steals a quick glance off in the direction where Darian disappeared.

Realization dawns over me…*he wants Darian to train him.*

The cogs in my mind spin as I piece it together. The way Archie gravitates toward him, desperate for an ounce of recognition or respect, even though Darian does nothing but push him away. The one rumored to be the best swordsman in the kingdom. And that asshole won't even give Archie the time of day.

I chew at my lip, my irritation toward Darian blistering.

Archie's gaze darts behind me, his expression shifting. I turn, following his stare to two men flanking a woman strolling by. All three of them are dressed in dark shades of fighting leathers, the woman a few strides ahead of the two men.

Hair as black as a shadow falls in luscious waves down the woman's back. Her shoulders sway with each step with a cat-like confidence. Dark lashes frame her brown eyes, her skin a rich chocolate and glowing in the dwindling sunlight. She nods to Cole in greeting before her and the two men walk a few tables down and settle into their seats.

"Who is that?" I ask Archie.

Archie's back to eating his food with a feverish pace as he shrugs his shoulders.

Cole answers, "Melaina Silverstone. The other two are Gavin Lonecreek and Nolan Clearbrook. They're from Mistwood."

"Mistwood?"

"Yes, it's the farthest eastern city aside from Stoneshire." Cole pauses. "Well…I guess the farthest city now."

"What is that supposed to mean?"

"A few months ago, Stoneshire was abandoned. The entire town is missing—it's like they up and left. I've been told there was still a fire burning in a bakery's oven. And tea left in a kettle, still piping hot."

"How is that possible? Nobody saw anything?"

Cole shrugs, thoughts knitting his eyebrows together. His expression of contemplation became one I grew to love long ago. So lost within himself.

Cole's voice drops to a murmur, "Nobody knows. Even neighboring towns didn't have answers."

"Has the King been searching for them?" I ask.

"I think he's doing what he can. With the increased rebel attacks, we've been losing a lot of people between civilians and military, so we might be spread a bit thin. That's why we just merged with some of the squad from Mistwood."

My stomach churns at the thought of rebels and the surfacing memory of Hornwood. Archie stills, the seriousness of the situation finally settling in. It's eerie to see him so solemn.

"Do you think…they'll split us up?" I whisper.

Cole sighs with a frown. "I wish I could say no. But I'm not sure. Sometimes we get orders to carry out within the hour." He glances from Archie to me with a small grin. "But I'll do everything in my power to keep us all together."

But how much power does Cole really have?

When I return to my room after dinner, I race to read my father's journal in what little daylight is left before I slip off to see Daeja.

I don't think I'd ever been so scared.

The vision of the decapitated guards replayed in my mind with every step away from the King's quarters, the wooden crate with the dragon egg clutched in my hands. And those guards had only been whispering about the King, as far as I had known.

I had to get out of there.

I couldn't give myself another second to ponder what could become of me. So I focused one step in front of the other. Chest out.

Feigned confidence.

Schooled my panic because if someone saw me, they'd know I was up to something.

It seemed ages before I reached the lower levels of the castle. I didn't have time to make it to the front doors. Plus, my exit would have been far too obvious.

The kitchen had a trash chute, and if I could make it there, I could make it out of the castle unseen. When I reached the kitchen, it was eerily silent. The lights were out, and it was oddly still.

I almost anticipated the King himself melting away from the shadows and snatching me.

But he didn't come.

I slid down the trash chute, out of the castle, and ran south. I knew if I made it past the gate, I had a better chance at making it back to the Dragon Lands.

I never dared looking behind me to see if anyone was following me as I ran through the shadowed streets of Arterias. There wasn't a spare moment I could afford.

The gods had been smiling on me because I managed to make it through the rest of Arterias without much attention.

Arterias faded behind me, and the outskirts of Brookvale appeared out of a fog. I collapsed in the thickest part of the woods. I wasn't sure my legs could carry me another step and if my lungs would ever catch a solid breath. But when I finally willed myself with my last bit of strength, I pulled myself up a tree. I spent the night on my back, draped over a branch high up. The last thing I saw was the starry night sky through the gaps of leaves above me.

It reminded me of home.

I close the journal and gaze up at my tattered ceiling. Clouds skitter across the last streaks of a dark orange and purple sky. The light in my room fades to darkness.

Oddly enough, the vision of a star studded sky comforts me in a way I can't comprehend. Perhaps part of it was because it's the same sky I've slept under for the last few months. The same sky my father slept under.

I slip out later in the night to visit Daeja. Each step further into the forest pulls an invisible string rooted deep within my chest, guiding me to the thicket of trees I last saw her near. A smile warms my face as I make out her glowing white eyes in the depths of the cave.

She bounces toward me in excitement, leaving the shadows of the cave behind and stepping into the moonlight. Rolling her shoulders back, her nose flares in pride. ***I caught a chicken.***

I pause mid-step, tilting my head in confusion. *"What? How could you possibly catch a—"*

Something limp dangles from her mouth. Gingerly, I lift her prey's head to confirm.

A *duck.*

I erupt into a giggle, imagining a dragon her size chasing after a duck. I pat Daeja's thick neck. *"That's umm…not a chicken."*

She blinks. ***"Not a chicken?"***

"Not a chicken."

Perhaps I should have been more direct about what a chicken looks like, as a simple descriptor of feathered wings wasn't quite specific enough.

Daeja's wings lower slightly in disappointment, but she still sucks the limp duck into her mouth and swallows it in one gulp. Her grimace hints it wasn't quite what she had been expecting.

I glance toward the lake glittering off in the distance between gaps of trees. *"I'm not sure how long we will stay here yet. But you have to be careful, it's dangerous out here."*

"Why?"

"Well…because humans can be dangerous for dragons."

"What's a human?"

"People like me that walk on two legs."

She tilts her head to the side. **"But you aren't dangerous?"**

Her innocence lifts my lips into a sad smile. I rub a hand on her cheek and down her neck. *"If you see someone on two legs, other than me, promise me you'll hide and stay quiet?"*

I double tap two fingers against the column of her neck, expecting her to vanish from view. But nothing happens. I try again with no success and drag my gaze up to her face. *"Are you not able to disappear anymore?"*

She squeezes her eyes shut, nostrils flaring, and body tense. She peeks open an eye, staring directly at me.

I snort. *"I can still see you."*

A defeated exhale relaxes her body.

Damn. There goes that idea.

"That's okay, keep practicing. I have to get back to camp, but I'll come see you tomorrow. Make sure you're sticking to the shadows and keeping a low profile—"

"I know, I know."

But how do I tell her if she's caught, it will mean life or death? Not only for her, but even for the one who might stumble upon her.

SEVENTEEN

WE. TOGETHER.

Marge doesn't take long to greet me the next morning. In fact, as soon as I walk into the healer's quadrant, she shoves a glass vial into my hand and barks at me to deliver it to Darian. Apparently, his quarters are near mine. Our rooms are separated by one building, the second and now only, storage tent. My skin crawls at the realization of our proximity.

I bite down on my tongue to keep myself from refusing Marge's order.

When I hesitate, Marge's expression darkens "Today, Katerina. *Now.*"

Clearing my throat, I dip my head and leave the healer's quadrant. My heartbeat thunders in my ears as I pass my quarters and slow at the stone structure two buildings down from mine.

Staring at the thick wooden door, I contemplate leaving the vial at the doorstep.

Pfft, he doesn't scare me. I try to convince myself.

"Who?" Daeja's voice ghosts over me.

"Nobody. A wannabe dangerous two legger." I narrow my eyes and pound on the door.

The door creaks open, revealing a disheveled Darian. His green eyes narrow, and he slowly closes the door in my face.

I blink. Completely caught off guard by the response. But the risk of Marge's discontent if I don't do as she's asked pushes me forward. I beat on the door again.

Darian opens the door a few inches to confirm it's still me, but as he shuts it again, I slam a hand out against the door, propping it open.

His eyes flare, a crooked grin splitting his lips.

Holding down an efforted grunt, I shove my weight into the wood. But as I push into the door, he backs off it, and it swings wide open. I stumble forward, nearly falling to my face before he catches me by my elbow.

As he steadies me back up to my feet, I turn toward him, glaring. He closes the door, shutting out the daylight. The thick stone walls seclude us from the camp chatter outside.

His eyes travel from my face down the length of my body. "What are you doing here?"

I flinch, shifting uncomfortably under his unbearably heavy stare. "Marge sent me."

"Hmmm…" He leans against his door frame, crossing his

arms over his chest. A black sleeveless tunic exposes his tanned, muscular arms. His stupidly tousled brown hair falls into his brow, obscuring his eyes. "And what does Marge want?"

Gods, he looks like an absolute mess.

I freeze. Forgetting what exactly I came for. I fumble for the vial I tucked earlier into my waistband. "Marge wanted me to—"

I catch him eyeing me. The intensity of his stare enough to light fire. A terror lurks beneath my skin of what he might do to me after I twisted that dagger in his thigh. Especially now that we are alone. Away from any witnesses. Away from anyone who could possibly save me from him.

Damnit.

So much for convincing myself he didn't scare me.

I scan every inch of his body, searching for a hint of a sword, dagger, or—

"If you're going to undress me with your eyes, please also use your hands," he rumbles.

I sneer. "I'm assessing your injuries, it's part of my job."

"Ahh, is that what we are calling it nowadays? Might I assess your injuries next? Preferably, without clothes." He pushes off the wall, his gaze floating down toward my lower half. "I find it more...*accurate.*"

Clenching my hand around the vial, I narrow my eyes. "Is that *all* you think about?"

"Oh, no." He snorts as he stalks across the room. No limp stalls his gait from the dagger lodged into his leg just days before. He stops at his bed, sheets rumpled in a tangled mess. He turns his back to me as he adjusts his belt. "I'm being courteous in refraining from telling you what I'm really thinking."

I don't doubt it. And the fact that he thinks he can talk to me as such is infuriating. The sheer boldness of his comments drive me into a frenzied irritation.

The words slip off my tongue before I can stop them. "You're an ass."

He lifts his head, glancing over his shoulder at me with a glimmer of amusement sparking his eyes. "I know."

Glaring hard enough it might sear his skin, I hold out the vial in his direction. "Are you going to take this or not?"

His laugh shakes his shoulders. But the humor doesn't soften his features.

"What's so funny?" I hiss.

"It's just that..." He turns to face me, tying the closure of his tunic.

I'd guess he might have just woken up.

His voice dips to a menacingly slick whisper, "I can't tell if you want to fight me or fuck me."

Pompous fucking asshole. I can't contain myself. I fling the fucking vial straight at him. Adamant it'll clear whatever delusion he has on what my intentions and fantasies are.

He catches the vial before it can smash into his nose. Those forest green eyes darken as he lowers his head, clenching his fist closed. A sickening crunch splits the silence between us, and he opens his hand, releasing splinters of glass and drops of liquid to the floor.

"Tell Marge I said thank you," he growls.

Backpedaling, I immediately regret my rash decision to throw the vial at him. My back bumps up against the wall, my eyes trained on him as he sweeps toward me. I pat my hand behind me for the door handle, finding it quickly and unlatching the door.

"What's wrong?" His head tilts to the side. Regarding me like a predator might its prey before it makes the killing blow. "Do I scare you?"

"No," I lie.

Another laugh rumbles in his chest. He closes the distance between us and pounds his fist above my head against the door, shutting it. A muscle in his jaw twinges as his green eyes lazily trace circles around my face. His calm violence instills a cold terror inside of me. It scares me more than it would have if he exploded. His body inches closer to mine, his breath stirring the hair near my forehead.

"Gods, I love to watch you squirm," he admits on a breath. His eyes are a combination of fathomless green and a soulful blue. Stubble shadows his sharp jawline.

My skin breaks out in tingles. "You don't scare me," I say again, hoping my voice doesn't tremble.

His gaze skims down my neck and arms, his lips perking up in a half-sided smile.

He sees my goosebumps.

"Are you sure you aren't scared of me?" he whispers, his hand lifting to nearly brush my cheek.

I slap his hand down.

A smug grin pulls at his lips. He snickers as he turns away. "You will be, when I'm done with you."

I slip back out of his room, slamming the door closed between us. My heart drums in my chest until I return to the healer's quadrant.

Earlier at the dinner table, I stared at Archie as he rambled on, but my thoughts were entirely focused on Cole. Cole sat next to me, his body turned toward mine, and his lingering gaze challenged every sense of my self-composure. Before I blushed, I nudged Cole's boot with mine in warning. Finally, he shook himself out of his daze.

Maybe I wasn't going to be the one to give us away.

Carlisle swept Cole off shortly after. Archie and I bonded over discussions of food and our upbringing in poor towns. Water dragons destroyed his family's ships out in Helmbrook. When his brothers came of age, they were all sent off to the military. Yet, the way he spoke about the military, his eyes sparkling in wonder…

In that moment, my face fell. His sheer enthusiasm and confidence closely resembled that of my brother, hitting me with a bittersweet pang.

We both agreed we didn't like fish and were relieved

tonight's dinner was chicken. If it were true that you are what you eat, I surely would have sprouted fins ten years ago.

When Archie was distracted, I slipped a piece of chicken into my pocket. Another piece moments later.

After dinner, I make a pit-stop at Cole's room before meeting with Daeja. I rap my knuckles against his door, remembering how his eyes grazed my skin at dinner.

I knock a second time, and the door opens. Cole's buttery smile lifts his face, and he opens the door wider for me to enter. When he shuts it and turns to me, I edge closer.

Cole holds out a hand to stop me.

"What?" I glance at his hand, as if he's trying to show me something.

"Don't…come any closer," he whispers.

When my mouth falls open he continues.

"Listen…it's so hard for me to be around you. I can't get you out of my head."

I smile at the confession and close the gap between us, lacing my fingers into his. "Then don't. But we should probably work on your stare outside of these four walls. You know, trying to keep a low profile and all."

His body tenses as our skin touches.

My head falls back to gaze up at him, my gaze settling on the soft curve of his mouth. I reminisce about all the beautiful things he can do with those lips. Years of declarations, soft kisses, and fiery moments when we're alone.

His breath stirs a heat in my skin, his voice sultry and soft. "Do you know how hard I'm trying not to kiss you right now?"

"Perhaps it's better if you stop trying," I murmur, skimming my fingertips up his muscled chest and to the nape of his neck.

"Katerina..." he growls in warning.

The lethal sound—and use of my full name—sends a shiver down my spine. A warning, and yet a dare.

Fuck it.

I close the gap between our bodies and press my lips to his. He groans into my mouth and hesitantly melts into me. Flicking my tongue across his lip, I push harder into him. His body stiffens, and he pulls away from me. I bite down a whimper of disappointment, my lips growing cold from his absence.

"I can't." He breathes heavily.

"Why not?"

"I'm...I'm trying to do the right thing. We're supposed to keep a low profile—" His voice breaks into a rasp. "Gods...because if I kiss you, I can't stop. And I won't...stop." His hand slides from my face, down my side, and over my hip.

He flinches. "What do you have?"

I blush, opening my pocket for him to see for himself. "For Daeja..."

"A chicken wing?"

I snort. "It's all I could take without drawing suspicion."

A grin cracks his tense features, his head falling into his hand as he rubs his eyes. When he looks back up at me, he's smiling. "You always find ways to amuse me, woman."

"How else do you propose I get her food? I worry if she hunts, she may catch someone's attention."

He sighs and trains his eyes on my pocket. "I've been trying to come up with a plan. I've been able to reassign the patrols away from the southern part of the lake. But I haven't gotten far in terms of next steps."

I blow out a disappointed breath.

"But..." He motions toward the desk and pulls the chair out for me.

I sit as he shuffles through stacks of papers fluttered across the desk. His gaze jumps, looking and searching. He finally snatches a letter and sets it in front of me, resting his finger on the page.

"There has been an uptick in rebel attacks, and they've changed their strategy." He grabs another letter from the other side of the desk, the broken wax seal stamped with an 'A' and points at a new sentence. "They're burning civilians alive. Trapping them in their homes in the late hours of the night and slaughtering entire villages. In the past, we've had dragon attacks to contend with. These rebel attacks...they're precise and planned. But we have no motive, no estimated time of the next attack, no intended targets... nothing."

"Like Hornwood..." I mutter blankly.

He drops to crouch beside me, tilting his head to make eye contact. "How do you know about Hornwood?"

"I was there..." I recount the events. My lips tremble when I speak of the little girl and her family. How I failed. Yet again.

He shakes his head furiously and swipes a tear off my cheek

with a thumb. "You can't beat yourself up about that. I know you. And I know you did everything you could to save them."

"But even my mother—" My voice cracks, and I try again. "Even with my mother I couldn't—"

But I can't. I can't get the words out.

He pulls me off the chair into an embrace, rubbing gentle strokes down my hair. "Shhh. I know, I know. I'm so sorry, Kat."

I pull a strained breath into my lungs, trying to shove all my heavy emotions back into a box to process at a later, more convenient, time.

Cole's raspy whisper brushes against my ear, "When I was told your house burned down with you in it, you died once. But in my mind, I experienced your death every day. I suffered every waking breath, knowing I lived in a world without you..."

I pull away to look at him, and his eyes glisten in torment. He understood me.

He bites his lip, shaking his head to keep tears at bay. "I...I couldn't even escape my longing for you in my dreams."

I lean my forehead to his, cradling his cheek with my palm. His sadness cracks into a shaky grin.

Perhaps death was crueler to those it left behind. To miss, and wonder, and long for. To hold all of those memories in the palm of your hand, desperate to not let them go, but painful to keep them all the same.

He grabs my hands, raining soft kisses onto them. "I wish I could take your pain away. If it were possible, it would be done.

It kills me to see you hurting. But know that I'm here for you. Always. And I'm never leaving."

The pain in my heart dulls ever so slightly with the way he gazes at me and the delicacy of his lips pressing a tender kiss to my cheek.

"Thank you," I whisper.

His hand brushes the chicken in my pocket, his gaze diverted down. "We will find a way to get her to the Dragon Lands. I will help you, even if it's the last thing I do."

We. *Together.*

I smile, hope flickering in my heart. "Then what are we going to—"

"Captain!" a shout comes from outside the room, followed by a pounding on the door.

We both freeze.

Cole scrambles up to his feet, and I follow. He opens the door, and outside, Carlisle's narrowed eyes dig into us.

Blood drains from my face from the one word Carlisle hisses.

"Traitors."

EIGHTEEN

TRAITORS

Cole snatches my hand and shifts his body in front of me. His muscles lock in preparation, his stance rigid and shoulders pinned back. Cole towers at least five inches over Carlisle, and if it came down to fighting, Cole definitely had the advantage. Outside of his naturally skilled hands, Cole's exceptional stature would intimidate just about anyone.

But we are outnumbered here.

Several other men are lined up behind Carlisle, eyes trained on us.

Sweat coats my palms, and Cole gives my hand a quick reassuring squeeze. A subtle, nearly subconscious gesture he'd been doing for years.

"Darian has them gathered near the outlook tower," Carlisle reports. "We are pulling the patrols and assembling the full squad."

Cole turns toward me, releasing my hand ever so subtly. "Go back to your room," he says with a hard swallow.

"Captain, you know the rules," Carlisle calls from behind him.

Cole tosses a glare at Carlisle. "She doesn't need to see this. She's a temporary guest—"

"She is a subject of this outpost. Which means all rules apply."

Cole stands, his body rigid and unmoving.

Carlisle's eyes narrow. "Captain, are you saying you're granting your sister a pass for the mandatory attendance of all the King's military personnel?"

Cole flexes his hand into a fist, his knuckles turning white. He finally dips his head in defeat.

We gather with the rest of the squad assembled near the northern outlook tower. Shoulders brush mine as more people join the crowd. An eerie hush settles over the throng, broken up only by shuffling feet. Every face I stare at is lowered, the night shadowing their faces and grim expressions.

At the top of the stone, moss-dusted tower stands Darian, alongside several other soldiers with torches. Between the soldiers are two figures with black bags pulled over their heads. Their metal shackles gleam in the flickering torchlight.

Cole steals a glance at me, a thick well of anguish darkening his amber eyes, before his face settles into an emotionless, stone-cold mask.

He gives my hand a quick squeeze, his voice softly threaded within his breath. "Look away."

Carlisle motions to Cole, and the two of them disappear into the throng.

Archie slides in next to me and meets my gaze. As I'm about to ask him what's going on, Darian clears his throat from the outlook tower and the shuffling crowd falls still. Cole and Carlisle join Darian at the top platform.

Carlisle calls out across the crowd, "Today, we condemn two dragon sympathizers. Let us be reminded that our King is just, and the law is the law. To protect us from the rebels and dragons, we must uphold our laws, regardless of who they are."

A woman farther into the crowd sinks her head into her hands with a body-shuddering sob, and the man next to her hushes her.

A soldier on the platform rips the bag off one of the prisoners. I don't recognize the offender, but his eyes round with fear. He writhes against the soldiers as they struggle to keep him still and loop a noose around his neck.

My jaw falls open, my chest constricting. Fear locks me in place, each second ticking by painfully slow as it all unravels before me.

The prisoner cries out, "Wait! Wait, please, let me explain—"

One of the soldiers shoves something into the prisoner's mouth to muffle his screams. They unbag the second offender, wrap the noose around his neck, and nudge the both of them toward the edge of the platform.

No.

No, no, no.

How can they not hear them out? Shouldn't there be a trial and questioning?

I scan the crowd around me, waiting for someone to stop this. Anyone to stop this. But nobody moves, their eyes locked on the tower.

I jerk forward, tempted to stop them, before Archie catches my forearm. Glancing sideways at him, he bites his lip and shakes his head.

"On behalf of the King, you are hereby condemned to death by the noose. May the gods grant you mercy," Darian calls.

My gaze swings back up to the tower and connects with Cole's. Sweat drips down the back of my neck, slithering down my spine as my breath catches in my throat.

Look. Away.

A guard shoves one of the prisoners off the platform, and I rip my stare away and down to my heaving chest.

A collective gasp rolls through the crowd. But nothing can block out the wicked crack of the man's necks snapping. Squeezing my eyes shut, I clench my hands around my ears, barely muffling the snap of the second prisoner's neck.

A hand touches my back, and I flinch. My eyes flash open as I turn, finding Archie staring at me, his eyes soft. His lips mouth, *"Kat."*

I slip past him and push through the crowd. Squeezing through the last row of onlookers, I burst into a sprint. I race past the outpost's crumbling wall and into the forest, the dark shadowed trees a flash of black around me. My breath saws in and out of my chest.

It could have been me.

Or Cole.

Moonlight glitters on scattered waves as I race to the lake. Crickets sing rickety songs, and my skin prickles in the chilled night. I sink to the ground, hugging my knees to my chest as I fight to slow my breath.

Daeja's shadowy figure slides through the trees in my direction. As she approaches, she bumps her snout into my ribs. ***"What's wrong?"***

How could I possibly tell her what happened, when she's out here all alone? When the consequences of her mere existence are so great? It would likely scare her. My mind reels with the possibilities and the endless amount of risks. The margin for errors is slim and daunting.

I fake a smile and scratch under her chin. *"Nothing."*

She nudges my side again and pauses. Pulling a deep inhale through her nose, her eyes dilate.

The chicken.

"Have you been eating?" I fish it out of my pocket.

Her eyes glow like the glinted surface of the moon against the night black scales, her head tilting to the side. ***"If I say no, does that mean you'll give me the chicken you brought?"***

A giggle cracks through my fear, and I toss her the pieces of meat. Figures she would have smelled it.

She snatches the pieces mid-air, gulping it down and running her tongue over her maw. *"How big do chickens get?"*

"Not much bigger than this." I motion an estimate with my hands.

She slumps in disappointment.

Chuckling, I rub long strokes across the side of her face. *"One day, you'll eat other things. Like horses, deer, and sheep. They get much bigger than chickens do. You'll be able to hunt them in the Dragon Lands with other dragons. You'll be able to fly freely, and you'll never have to worry about where you can or can't go."*

Her head perks up with an idea. *"I want to show you something. I've been practicing flying, and I can make it to the other side of the lake."*

She circles behind me, stretching her wings out to the side.

I watch her over my shoulder. *"Show me, but Daeja, you should not be flying by yourself—"*

Lowering her head, she charges right for me, shoving her snout between my legs and knocking me backwards. My breath blows out of me, and she snakes her body to roll me back down into the crook of her neck and shoulders. I fumble for something to balance myself, snatching one of her horns, and pulling myself up. Daeja bullets toward the lake, my body jostling with each of her strides.

I cling to her neck, my eyes rounding as we near the water. *"Daeja!"*

The thunder of her steps ceases, replaced by her flapping wings. We lift off the ground just before we hit the water's edge. My heart stops for a few beats as we lift higher into the air, soaring over the lake. The wind grazes my face and whips my hair behind me. I squint through my watering eyes, before squeezing them shut and constricting my legs and arms around her. *"That was not what I meant by show me!"*

She hisses. **"Easy!"**

"I'm going to slip, I'm going to slip, I'm going to slip."

"Don't you trust me?"

My eyes flash open, and I dare a peek below us at the white-crested waves of the lake racing by us. My heart thunders in my ears, my hands slick with sweat. *"It's not you I don't trust!"*

"Stop looking down!"

I shift my gaze up from the water and straight ahead. The trees grow larger as we approach the other side of the lake.

"Hold on."

"As if I'm not already holding on!"

Daeja banks left—hard—and I'm thrown to the right, sliding off her back and dangling from her neck.

She falters and dips lower to the water, shrieking in surprise at the sudden shift of weight.

My legs pedal pathetically below me, my arms trembling in effort to keep clasped around her neck. My sweat-slickened grip slides off her scales, and I fall backwards with a scream.

I don't know if it's seconds or minutes into the free fall, but as I twist to face the water quickly promising to meet me, my body is snatched in the fall. Something yanks my shirt from above me, the wind whispering against my naked back. Daeja's breath warms my skin, the steel of her teeth pressed against the nape of my neck. I grab hold of my collar to keep myself from choking. She lifts higher into the air, the water shrinking below my feet at an alarming pace.

My chest tightens painfully, my heart hammering like a war drum beneath my skin. *"Put me down!"*

"I can't."

"Daeja. Put. Me. Down!"

She snorts. **"Fine. As you wish."**

Her grip on me disappears. A scream rips through me as I free fall once again. I crash into the lake, swallowed by the frigid water. I fight for air, my skin stinging as I race toward the surface. When I break through and suck in a breath of fresh air, I blink water out of my eyes and scan the dark night for her.

"That was not what I meant!"

A numbness creeps into my limbs, each kick and stroke slowing with every passing second. My legs lock up, and my face dips back below the surface. A panic heats my lungs as I struggle to keep my head above the water. But I sink, lower and lower with each delayed kick, until I'm completely underwater. The slowing pulse of my heartbeat echoes around me, my eyes dragging closed.

Daeja plunges into the water beside me. She stretches forward, grabbing a mouthful of my shirt and pulling me up. We break through the surface, a strangled gasp slips from my lips. Her powerful legs swish through the water as she carries me to the shore.

Dragging me out of the lake, she leaves me on the shore, my body convulsing in shivers as I pull my knees up to my chest to conserve body heat. She gathers driftwood and sets them down near me. One of the branches snaps in her jaws, and I flinch.

My mind immediately swims back to the two men who were executed.

A warm glow seeps from the back of Daeja's throat as she unhinges her jaw.

"N—*no. Please, dddon't,*" I say through chattering teeth. I can't fathom seeing a fire right now. My throat constricts at the thought alone. That, and the light could attract unwanted attention.

My gaze sweeps over to the opposite side of the lake toward the outpost. The tree line blocks my view of camp, but a soft glow emits from its direction.

What is happening at the camp now…and who is responsible for cutting down the prisoners? Do they even get a proper burial, and their families a chance to honor their memories? What had they even been caught for, and why couldn't Cole stop it?

My stomach churns. The prisoners likely didn't have anything as damning as an actual dragon. If I was caught, that would be one thing. But if Cole was caught? If I were responsible for his violent death? The thought alone makes me nauseous.

Daeja curls herself around me, angling her wings to cut out the wind. The hot breath from her nose warms my skin, chasing away the shivers and cold.

When I first met her, she had been curling into me for

warmth. And now I was tucked into her side for her body heat, her long neck and tail wrapping around me.

"Why did you do that?" I whisper.

"You told me to put you down."

"Not what I meant."

She snorts, the steam billowing in my face and warming my cheeks.

"Why did you want me to ride you?"

She shifts her body, somehow managing to edge even closer to me. **"I thought we could get to the Dragon Lands faster if we could fly there."**

I gaze up at her. *"We can't go without Cole."*

"And why not?"

"Because—" I pause, wracking my brain for my own reasoning. Because my mother said so. It sounded pathetic. When in truth…it's because I don't think I can do it on my own.

Because I'm scared.

"Because we need him."

"What do we need him for?"

"What do we need anyone for?" I challenge. Perhaps it isn't only my self-doubt. I don't want to be separated from Cole—not again. My heart belongs to him, whether or not I still had his mother's ring wrapped around my finger. The terrifying thought of choosing between him or Daeja lingers in the back of my mind.

"All I've ever known is you…" she whispers into my mind, nuzzling into my side.

I stroke her head with a shaky hand, my hand stinging from the thawed nerves. *"I know. And all I've ever known is him, too."*

"So we have to go with him? How do we know he isn't a dangerous two legger?"

"Because I know him. I know Cole. And I—"

"Love him. I know. I can feel what you feel."

"You can?" I smile at the revelation and lean into her, closing my eyes and scratching underneath her chin.

A purr thunders to life in her chest, shuddering the blood in my veins.

We lay in a silent curl of scales and skin, cold and warmth. Soaking in each other's presence. Listening to the rise and fall of each other's breath.

A thought whispers in the back of my mind. I try, unsuccessfully, to damper it as it rises. I drag my attention out toward the edge of Dragon's Back Ridge etched into the night sky. It stares back: jagged, menacing, and dark.

I should take her. I should go. Before I fail and someone else dies.

But the longer I stare at the distant mountain range, the firmer my decision becomes. There's no way I can make it on my own. Not without a map and not without Cole.

With a hard swallow, I break the peace of our quiet moment. *"I have to go back. I have to figure out a plan."*

If anyone has ever said they can sneak around in wet clothes, they're lying. Every footstep back to camp is a squelch of water between my toes, the drip of my hair snaking streams of water down my spine. My clothes scrape and cling against each other in every stride. My skin rubbed raw and irritated by the time I pass the tree line and near the camp border.

A patrol loops around the west side I'm approaching, and I pause, sliding behind a tree. They pass by me, unnoticing, and I slip past the crumbling wall and toward the faint silhouette of my quarters. My heart skips when someone emerges from the shadows nearby.

I debate ducking and running. But it's too late.

I've been noticed.

"You're um....wet." Darian's rough voice cuts through the silence. His gaze outlines my clothes clinging to my frame.

I hug my arms around myself, suddenly more self-conscious than I am cold.

"Great observational skills you have," I whisper and turn toward my room.

He slides in front of me, tilting his gaze up at the sky with a thoughtful *'hmmm.'*

I follow his line of sight. The stars glitter brilliantly above us in a cloudless night. We both look down and back at each other. A question hanging between us.

After a few moments of silence he says, "And it's not like it's raining."

"I like bathing at night," I blurt.

"And...in your clothes?"

He's got me there. I wrack my brain for a reason as to why I'd be walking through the night dripping wet. Especially so soon after a public execution.

The moonlight glints off his disastrous smile. "Not that I mind seeing you wet. I'd just prefer...different circumstances."

I want to pummel him for being so nonchalant after sentencing two men to their deaths earlier tonight. This fucking asshole doesn't have a lick of remorse.

"And what are *you* doing out here?" I growl.

Suddenly disinterested, he turns his attention to brush something off his chest. "You know, I actually don't really care," he mumbles. Turning away from me, he stalks off toward the direction of his quarters.

Once I'm in my room, I peel the clothes off my skin, draping them over the back of my chair near the desk. When I change into my nightgown, I shift into bed, thankful for the warmth and dryness of the sheets.

"Tomorrow we will figure out a plan," I murmur to Daeja as I drift into sleep.

NINETEEN

TOMORROW I'M ON MY OWN

Darian swings at me in slow motion. I duck, his blade narrowly missing the top of my head by an inch. I swing my satchel at him, as pathetic as it is. His green eyes burn, flickering flames within his irises. With a wicked smile, his irises burst into red, then orange, until his eyes are but an expanse of white, drowning out his pupils. Heat kisses my skin, and the oxygen is sucked from the air.

I clutch at my throat, willing myself to breathe. Flames rupture from the ground and dance around me, flickering between red and blue. Every direction I turn they spring. The cries of the little girl, her parents, my mother, and my brother echo around me. The crackling fire mimics the snapping of a man's neck.

Tears spring to my eyes, and I drop to my knees, covering my ears as they ring louder.

Circling me, taunting me, torturing me. I squeeze my eyes

shut in an attempt to block it all out. I tear my ears off, and when I open my hands, blood bathes my skin. The screams still ring in my head, even louder than before.

Blood of power.

Blood of power.

Blood of power.

I wake with a jolt, panting and laying in a pool of my own sweat.

Five things I see...

I look around, taking notes of my room. Of the desk, the chair, my bed, the tattered ceiling, my satchel. I run through my other senses until my breath slows.

Four things I feel.

Three things I hear.

Two things I smell.

One thing I taste.

I blow out a breath. *It was just a dream.*

Daeja must sense my panic because her watery voice trickles into my mind. ***"I'm still here."***

I brush my hair back from my forehead, settling my panic and fear.

Beams of soft, dawn light trickle through the holes in my ceiling, stretching out across the room and falling onto my satchel. Exhaustion weighs heavily on me, but I rule out going back to sleep. The memory of the echoing screams still haunting me.

I retrieve my father's journal, hopeful I can find some sort of answer to what I need to do.

A few weeks have passed since I left the castle. I've been careful to travel by night. It's the most certain way to not get caught. I'm ashamed to say I've had to steal food under the cover of darkness where I can, but I remind myself it's for the good of the realm.

I have to make it back to the Dragon Lands. I have to take this egg to the elders. The black dragon egg must have some sort of significance. It could even be the key to Arterian peace and freedom.

I smashed the wooden crate to free the egg from its trap and placed it in a bag I stole for easy travel and hiding.

I finally made it to Groveden with nothing but the clothes on my back, the dragon egg in my satchel, this journal, and my sword.

The farther north I got, the poorer the cities became. It hit me that the riches of the King were kept close to his castle. I witnessed thin children playing in the muddied streets of weathered towns, and the sullen faces of the townspeople.

I was so tempted to stop them. To beg them to live a better life in the Dragon Lands. But I knew in doing so I risked everything.

I trudged on and found refuge by the river near Padmoor.

It started to feel more like home, with the thick cover of trees and the bubble of rivers. Even the air seemed clearer here. The smell wet and earthy, and birds singing in the treetops.

I spent a few days tucked into the Northern Forest, mapping out how to make the last stretch to the Dragon Lands. I was so close.

And then I'd be free.

Reunited with the place and people I called home.

I pause, lingering on the last sentence. How could such a corrupt group of people be considered home? What changed, from then to now, that they were responsible for unspeakable acts against the northern towns?

Against innocent people?

I chew my lip over and over again as I think of Hornwood.

Why were they doing this?

When I flip to the next page, my heart sinks to the pits of my stomach. I flip again. And again.

Blank, blank, blank.

Tears well into my eyes. There's nothing left. I would never know how he and my mother met or how they fell in love. While I'm not sure what I expected, the abrupt ending sinks me. As I take my hand off the journal, the back cover inches closed on its own. The remaining pages flutter closed, and I glimpse something scrawled onto the end pages. I flatten the book, turning through the pages again and stop.

The blood drains from my face, my mouth dropping open at what is written toward the back of the journal.

Secrets never die, they're just buried in a grave.

Secrets never die, they're just buried in a grave.

Secrets never die, they're just buried in a grave.

Secrets never die, they're just buried in a grave.

Secrets never die, they're just buried in a grave.

Secrets never die, they're just buried in a grave.

Secrets never die, they're just buried in a grave.

Secrets never die, they're just buried in a grave.

Secrets never die, they're just buried in a grave.

Secrets never die, they're just buried in a grave.

Secrets never die, they're just buried in a grave.

Secrets never die, they're just buried in a grave.

Secrets never die, they're just buried in a grave.

Secrets never die, they're just buried in a grave.

Secrets never die, they're just buried in a grave.

Secrets never die, they're just buried in a grave.

Secrets never die, they're just buried in a grave.

Secrets never die, they're just buried in a grave.

Secrets never die, they're just buried in a grave.

Secrets never die, they're just buried in a grave.

Secrets never die, they're just buried in a grave.

Secrets never die, they're just buried in a grave.

Secrets never die, they're just buried in a grave.

Secrets never die, they're just buried in a grave.

Secrets never die, they're just buried in a grave.

Secrets never die, they're just buried in a grave.

Secrets never die, they're just buried in a grave.
Secrets never die, they're just buried in a grave.
Secrets never die, they're just buried in a grave.
Secrets never die, they're just buried in a grave.
Secrets never die, they're just buried in a grave.
Secrets never die, they're just buried in a grave.
Secrets never die, they're just buried in a grave.
Secrets never die, they're just buried in a grave.
Secrets never die, they're just buried in a grave.
Secrets never die, they're just buried in a grave.
Secrets never die, they're just buried in a grave.
Secrets never die, they're just buried in a grave.
Secrets never die, they're just buried in a grave.
Secrets never die, they're just buried in a grave.
Secrets never die, they're just buried in a grave.
Secrets never die, they're just buried in a grave.
Secrets never die, they're just buried in a grave.
Secrets never die, they're just buried in a grave.
Secrets never die, they're just buried in a grave.
Secrets never die, they're just buried in a grave.
Secrets never die, they're just buried in a grave.
Secrets never die, they're just buried in a grave.
Secrets never die, they're just buried in a grave.
Secrets never die, they're just buried in a grave.

I shut the journal with an audible force and hastily toss it away from me. My mother's words ring in my ears, frightening me. Aside from her rambling about the sun, it was another line she constantly repeated. The vision bursts in my mind, the words carved repeatedly into the wall of what had once been our living room.

I focus on my breathing, counting to ten to level myself. I don't know what it means, and maybe it means nothing, but I have to show Cole. It could have been another manic episode… but then I remember her instructions.

To find Cole, take Daeja to the Dragon Lands, and not come back.

At the time, I thought she meant to not come back to Padmoor. But as I recall the execution last night, my nightmares of Darian, and the flames, I start to wonder…what if she had a different meaning?

What if she meant we weren't safe here in Arterias?

Could I even trust what she said?

I look back at the journal. Could I trust what he said?

I change into day clothes, braid my hair, and throw the journal into my satchel before I head out of my room.

The sun warms my skin as I step outside, and I blink into the morning light.

Shit, it's later than I thought. Marge is going to be pissed. I stride through camp, hoping to catch Cole. Groups gather around the tables for breakfast. I don't know how they have the stomach for it, given two of them were just executed last night.

When I don't find Cole, I head to the healer's quadrant,

afraid I might not make it to tomorrow if I get on Marge's bad side. I'll grab Cole after Marge dismisses me for the day.

"You're late," Marge grumbles when I finally push through the door.

"Sorry, I…" I fumble for an excuse as I set my satchel down on the counter, but can't find one.

She wordlessly hands me a basket. Grabbing her staff, she declares she'll be showing me where to find various plants, but tomorrow I'm on my own. We exit the healer's quadrant, then the outpost in silence.

"So…do you always go this far into the forest?" I ask, my gaze wandering to the shadows and thoughts wandering to Daeja.

"No. But this time of year, we might find swamp milkweeds down near the lake."

"And those are good for…?"

"Reducing vomiting, if you get the right ones."

We approach the tree line giving way to the expansive lake shimmering in the daylight.

I scan the forest around us. *"Daeja? Where are you?"*

Daeja yawns. ***"In the cave."***

Perhaps she was becoming more of a nocturnal creature. *"Good, stay there. I'm out here with company."*

"That's odd," Marge says, slightly bent over and staring at a spot on the shore.

I saunter over to her to see what she's looking at, the sand shifting underneath my boots. My mouth goes dry. Deep paw prints score the sand, long talon marks gouging the ground.

"What…is it?" I feign curiosity and ignorance.

She scans the water and trees around us, before shifting her attention to the sky. "Dragons."

"D—dragons?" I mirror, a genuine fear spiking my voice. But not exactly the reason fear *should* be coating my voice.

Marge inches closer to the lake's edge and slams her staff down into the water. Ripples explode from around her staff and dissipate into the depths of the lake.

Perplexed, I watch her with arched eyebrows. "What…are you doing?"

"Checking."

"Checking what?"

"Shh." She squints, her gaze flicking back and forth around the water's perimeter.

But nothing breaks the surface, and nothing stirs. She finally drags her attention to me, her gaze lingering on me, possibly noticing the sweat gathering on my brow.

She taps her staff on my shoulder to herd me away. "We need to leave now."

"What! Why?"

"Because these…" she motions toward the prints with her staff, "are dragon prints. And they look fresh."

"What would a dragon be doing out here? Wouldn't it have been seen by now?"

"Water dragons typically come from the depths of the ocean to rivers and lakes to nest. It's possible there may be eggs, hatchlings, or a mother nearby. Which means we will need to report it to Cole and have this area heavily monitored."

At the way my eyes round, she sighs. "Come on, let's get back. No need to be scared. I'm sure Cole will have a good plan to keep everyone safe."

Panic surges in me at the thought of patrols monitoring the area. At the thought of them discovering Daeja.

Marge takes the basket as we near the outpost wall. "Go report to Cole. When you're done, you can help me trim these back in the healer's quadrant."

I scurry off to find Cole gathered with Carlisle and Darian near the outlook tower. All of their stares settle on me as I approach.

Overcome by my nerves, I bow my head awkwardly, avoiding eye contact with any of them. "Cole, I need to speak with you."

Cole excuses himself, and I lead him out of the outpost.

Once we pass the wall, Cole begins, "Look, I know last night was scary—"

"Marge found dragon prints near the lake."

He pauses mid-step. "What?"

"But I don't think they're hers. They look too big, and Marge said they might be a water dragon—"

"Show me."

We rush toward the lake, and he drops into a crouch near the prints. His fingertips trail above the imprint.

"This is definitely not a bear or wolf. There's no way we can pass it off as one." He brushes his hand over the print, covering the track.

Simultaneously, we both look up, noticing the rest of the prints. Hundreds of them trailing to and from the water.

Shit.

A branch snaps behind us, and we whirl. Daeja slinks out from the shadows.

Cole's throat bobs as he stares at her. "She's…bigger. *Significantly* bigger."

The daylight accentuates just how much bigger she is, free from darkness and shadow. I start second guessing these prints aren't hers. Because he's right—she is *much* bigger.

Would he actually believe me if I told him of the blue flame? How could I explain such a thing, anyway? Perhaps Willard wasn't as crazy as Cole had thought.

But before I can attempt at an explanation, Cole interrupts my thoughts.

"How are we supposed to keep her hidden? She can't be any smaller than a horse."

"You weren't supposed to come out," I scold.

Daeja stalks toward Cole, watching him thoughtfully and stretching her neck forward to sniff him from a distance. **"I thought I smelled you, I didn't smell any other two leggers."**

Cole swallows, the necklace with his mother's metal ring flickering in the sunlight. He's frozen in place, still crouched over her prints. Motionless, he watches Daeja out of his periphery.

She continues circling around him, sniffing. Inching closer and closer.

"She won't hurt you," I murmur as I stand. I walk over to Daeja, petting her cheek. *"Stop, you're going to make him nervous."*

"Maybe he should be nervous."

I snort, perceiving the slight jealousy in her voice. *"He's our friend. He's on our side."*

Cole clears his throat and inch by inch, stands, his eyes glued to Daeja.

"Are you able to focus the patrols on the northern end? They can concentrate there," I offer.

"I can try. But she needs to stay out of sight. She can't be coming out during the day."

I turn to her. *"He said–"*

Daeja snorts, blinking slowly at Cole. **"I can hear him."**

"You can?"

Cole tilts his head. "What...are you doing?"

I must have been staring in silence at Daeja. "She understands you. And we can...talk."

"Talk?" He looks back and forth between us two.

I nod. "I can hear her in my mind."

"How is that even possible?"

"Remember the blue fire Willard spoke of? We saw it here in the forest the other night. She touched it and grew triple her size. Since then, we've been able to communicate."

The curve of his lips part open in amazement. "Perhaps... Willard was right all along..."

Snapping his mouth shut, he takes a few steps forward and locks eyes with Daeja. "The guards at our tower will spot you if you fly above the treetops. Especially during the day. Keep off the shoreline, otherwise you'll leave new prints." He shifts his gaze back to me. "And you. Keep a low profile. Do as Marge asks, until we figure out a plan."

Daeja sweeps her tail across the sand, clearing the shore of her paw prints. I scratch her under the chin before Cole and I head back to camp.

Cole pauses at the trees right before we get to camp and turns to me, his voice a whisper. "I'm so sorry you had to see that last night…I didn't want you to. I came to look for you after, and you were gone. I was scared you left…"

I flick my gaze up to his warm amber eyes. "You didn't stop it."

"I couldn't." He swallows hard. "I…I don't know what to do, Kat. I feel trapped. I'm terrified to lose you again. But each day you stay here is another risk…"

"Then come with me," I breathe out, edging closer to him.

He searches my face, a frown pulling at his lips before he looks down and away from me. "I can't."

I grab his hand. "Yes, you can. My mother told me to find you and not to come back. I don't think she meant Padmoor. I think she meant Arterias. Maybe she wanted both of us to go to the Dragon Lands. Together."

"We can't stay in the Dragon Lands. Do you know how savage the rebels are? They would kill us on the spot."

I shake my head. "No, I don't think they would."

"And what makes you say that?"

"Because my father was a rebel."

"What? How would you know that?"

I fill him in on my father's journal and all the entries.

Cole's eyes widen and he instinctively grips my arm. "Do you have it with you?"

"No."

"Where is it?"

My face falls as I recall where I left it last. "It's...it's in my bag. In the healer's quadrant."

The thick muscle of his throat pulses with his heartbeat, and he snags my wrist, pulling me toward the outpost. "We have to retrieve it before someone else finds it."

We race back. As soon as we pass the wall, Carlisle appears and marches straight for us. He motions at Cole, tight and urgent, demanding his presence.

Cole's voice drops to a whisper, "If someone finds it, you tell them it was—"

Carlisle closes the gap between us. "You are needed, Captain."

Cole leaves with Carlisle, glancing over his shoulder at me. "*Mine,*" he mouths.

Standing at the healer's quadrant door, I pull in a shaky breath, terror threatening to lock my limbs into place. I've been gone far too long.

Pushing past my fear, I swing open the door. My gaze shoots over to where I last left my satchel on the counter. But my bag isn't where it was earlier—it's slumped on the ground.

I race over to it, crouch and pick it up, only to discover the flap isn't secured. *Fuck—did I not snap it closed before I left?*

A *tap, tap, tap* pulls my attention over my shoulder, and I swivel. Marge hobbles over to me and drops something onto the counter beside me. It lands with a soft slap, and a curl of dust plumes around it.

My father's journal.

TWENTY

THE RIGHT QUESTIONS

I swallow back the knot collecting in my throat and narrow my eyes. "You went through my stuff?"

Marge stares me up and down. "Hardly, child. It fell off the counter. It's a good thing I found it."

I snatch the journal, press it to my chest, and twist my shoulders away from her view. "What is that supposed to mean?"

She's already turned away from me, pouring a concoction on the counter into a glass bottle. Either she's about to request a handsome bribe for her silence, or the King's guard is already on their way, and she's counting down the seconds until they burst in here and free her of me forever.

"Fire incarnate. Flame in flesh. Blood of power," she whispers, her attention still fixed on transferring the liquid into the container.

I clench my hand tighter around the journal. "You…you liar. You did read it."

She stops pouring, setting the bottle down and turning to lock eyes with me. "Keep slewing accusations, and I'll turn you loose to the King himself, Katerina."

"If you've already turned me in, it doesn't matter."

"I haven't."

"And why not? What do you want?"

She grins, pouring the rest of the liquid in the bottle before corking it shut. "I want to go to the Dragon Lands."

The journal almost slips from my hand. Is this what blackmail feels like? "Excuse me?"

"You heard me. I would know that insignia anywhere."

My eyes widen, and I absent-mindedly trace the symbol on the front. "You…you're a rebel?"

She rolls her eyes. "You're not asking the right questions."

"Well, what should I be asking, then?"

"Don't you want to know what it was like? The world we live in today was not what it was. In fact, there was peace and freedom. There weren't these attacks or high taxes. People didn't starve to death. Diseases were treated with care, no matter your income or status. There was community, family, and love. For decades people have been trying to sneak out across the border, to go to the Dragon Lands—free from the King's laws."

She might as well have sprouted her own pair of wings and horns. I watch her with a gaped mouth. Maybe this is some sort of test. I not-so-subtly survey the room around us, looking for anyone hidden behind the cabinets or beneath the beds. I'm suspicious someone is lying in wait for me to agree before springing out to arrest me.

"Our King is…honorable and…kind. He rules for the benefit of his kingdom…" I stare at her. "You can be executed for speaking of the rebels and lands before."

"And you can be executed for having a rebel journal. What are you doing with a rebel's journal, Katerina?"

Can she hear my heartbeat from there? My deafening pulse nearly drowns out the rest of my thoughts and her words. I open my mouth to reply, and the door swings open. Slipping the journal behind my back and into the band of my pants, I tug my tunic over it.

In walks Cole, his focus bouncing back and forth between Marge and me. "Marge, my apologies for the intrusion. But may I borrow my sister for a few minutes?"

Marge nods, turns, and adjusts the jars on a top shelf to make space for the fresh bottle she poured earlier. I swipe my satchel off the ground, sneak the journal into my bag, and nearly run for the door.

Once we are in Cole's room, the door shut, he asks, "Did you get it?"

"Yes…but she found it first."

Stress flashes a twinge in his jaw, his eyes wild as he grabs my shoulders. "Fuck, we don't have a lot of time then. I need you to go, I need you to—"

"It's okay, I don't think she's going to turn us in."

His eyebrows bunch. "Why wouldn't she?"

Retrieving my journal, I present the cover to him and trace the emblem on the front with my fingers. "See this symbol? She knew it. She knew details about dragons and repeated what my father wrote—"

"So, she read it, then?"

"No. She *knew* it. And she asked to go to the Dragon Lands."

He's slow to respond as he processes. "She's…testing you. She's trying to see what you know."

"I don't think she was. And if she was, it's too late to worry about it now." I place the journal back into my bag.

Cole grabs my hands and rests them on his chest, leaning his forehead against mine. His heart hammers underneath my palms.

"I need you to listen to me, Kat. You need to go. You're not safe here."

"I'm not leaving you." I enunciate each word and pull back to look him in the eyes.

His eyes soften. "I'd rather die a thousand times over than live in a world without you again. This may be the worst place for you to be right now—"

"I'm not leaving. We stay together, remember? She's not going to turn us in. The way she spoke, Cole, I know it."

He sighs, shaking his head in conclusion as he unlaces his fingers from mine.

My throat tightens, and I see no other way around it, blurting the words aloud, "We'll burn it."

My heart sinks at the thought of destroying the only piece of my father I have. The last tangible thing tying me back to my family, my heritage. But I would rather lose it, than lose Cole.

His expression softens, hinting he knows the significance of what this means to me. "I…I can't let you do that."

"Yes, you can," I beg. "We'll burn it tonight, and even if she turns us in, there will be no proof of it."

He stares blankly at my bag for a long moment, before flicking his gaze up to me. "Are you sure?"

I nod, biting my lip.

He sighs. "Very well then. We keep it here until then. And if Marge reports it—it's mine. And you get out of here as fast as you can."

My heart swells, knowing damn well I can't let him make such a sacrifice but not bothering to argue with him. Not right now.

We shove the journal deep inside the trunk in his room and leave. When we get back to the healer's quadrant, Marge is gone. My stomach turns sour as my thoughts gallop to all the scenarios of her turning us in and being wrong about her.

"Fuck," I hiss.

Cole squeezes my hand to slow my thoughts. "If she's not here, she might be at the sparring ring. Maybe someone was injured."

We race to the sparring ring out in the forest, and sure enough, she's crouched over and assessing a downed man's leg.

I join her on the ground. "What happened?"

The man's sandy blonde head is leaned back, his thick brown eyebrows scrunched, and eyes squeezed shut in pain. He was one of the three Mistwood transplants, making him either Gavin or Nolan.

"Leg injury. Do you think you can help carry him back to the healer's quadrant?" Marge answers.

I whip my gaze from the man's leg to Marge, doubt creeping in about being able to lift him on my own.

Cole takes a step closer. "I can help—"

"Darian!" Marge barks. "Get over here and help us get Nolan to the healer's quadrant."

Darian's eyes meet mine, and he pushes off the tree he was leaning against, casually strolling over to us.

"I don't need his help," I scoff, desperate to have anyone but him help. I grab Nolan's hand, helping him sit up and looping his arm around my neck. Circling my arms around his torso, I push up through my legs, my knees wobbling and threatening to buckle from lifting his weight. But I only get him a few inches off the ground before setting him back down to catch my breath.

Cole shifts in to help but is brushed aside by Darian.

Instead, Cole strides to the center of the sparring circle, addressing the rest of the squad who watches us with wide eyes, "Let's resume sparring."

A hint of mischief darkens Darian's eyes as he slides in next to me. He flicks his fingers for me to move down and monitor Nolan's leg while he does the heavy lifting.

I stare him up and down. "Pfft."

Darian shoves his arm into me, knocking me out of his way, his voice sultry soft. "Gods, you are *so* hot—"

The admission makes my mouth part in shock.

"—*headed*." He sighs, clearly using the pause to his advantage, and I fall for it.

"Are you always an ass?" I bite.

Nolan chuckles, his gaze flicking back and forth between the two of us.

Darian mutters, "No, sometimes I sleep."

Marge snaps her fingers impatiently at the two of us.

Glad I'm not the only one irritated by his antics.

Darian hauls Nolan up to stand, and I slide to Nolan's other side, wrapping my arm around his lower back to brace him. Darian and I help Nolan back to the healer's quadrant. Admittedly, I'm relieved for Darian's help as I couldn't have lifted or carried Nolan on my own.

"Next…time," Nolan pants. "I'll break your arm…Darian."

Darian chuckles. "It's cute you think I'm afraid of you. I'll get your other leg before you can even touch me."

Nolan snarls. "You spoiled ass—"

"Stop it, the both of you!" Marge warns and pulls the door open for the three of us.

We shuffle into the healer's quadrant awkwardly. As soon as Darian helps lower Nolan onto a bed, he heads for the door. Marge stretches her staff out, blocking Darian's path.

Intensity crackles between the two of them as they stare

each other down in silence, like two wolves circling each other, waiting for the other to strike first.

If I didn't know them, I would have been scared for Marge. But she challenges his glare with a lifted chin, her shoulders back, and posture confident despite her need for a staff to walk.

Maybe I should be scared for *him.*

Darian moves first, swatting her staff out the way and taking another step to the door. Marge swings the wood down on the top of his head, smacking him with a loud *'thud,'* and Darian spins on her with an incinerating scowl.

Nolan mirrors my own gaping mouth and wide eyes at the movement.

"Your life is your own to ruin. But you're not going to make things harder for me by bringing more in here to tend to," Marge warns. "Do you understand me?"

"I don't remember asking, nor caring, for your opinion," Darian quips.

"Speak to me like that one more time, and I'll cut you off."

Darian falls silent, computing whatever it is she means by it. After a few still moments, he ducks his head and leaves. Nolan and I exchange a glance, awkwardly pretending we didn't just witness it all.

I help Marge gather vials and materials while she assesses Nolan's injury. Luckily for Nolan, it doesn't seem to be broken, but Marge instructs him to rest for a few days.

Melaina enters the room and sweeps over to Nolan. "Are you okay? It looked like an awful hit."

Nolan nods. "I'm fine."

Marge commands Melaina and me to take Nolan back to his room, and that I'm dismissed afterwards. The three of us slip out of the healer's quadrant to Nolan's room and slide him into his bed.

Melaina turns to me, tucking a black strand of hair behind her ear. "Thank you for your help…"

"Katerina," I finish for her with a smile.

She mirrors my grin. "Katerina. Nice to meet you, I'm Melaina."

"Nolan," Nolan introduces himself through gritted teeth.

I nod my head to both of them and leave, finding Cole outside waiting.

"How's Nolan?" he asks.

"Marge doesn't think it's broken, but he's on bed rest for a few days."

Cole sighs, running a hand through his hair.

I glance around us to ensure no one else is in earshot. "Why don't you discharge Darian? He's nothing but a menace to everyone here."

"It's not that easy. He's the best swordsman in the King-dom. Chosen by the King himself—"

"Then why doesn't the King have him? Did he piss him off, too?" I hiss.

"The King wanted him to train all of our northern posts. With the uptick in rebel attacks, he's our best bet at teaching our squads some serious combat moves. But he's been refusing."

"Why?"

"Well…" Cole blows out a breath. "I think he's a little pissed. He expected he would lead his own squad. When he arrived, I don't think he realized I would be the captain."

"So, he's thinking his power move is to be a dick to everyone? Can't you negotiate some sort of terms?"

If Cole leaves with me and Daeja, perhaps Darian could take the coveted captain role. Although, considering how it would affect Archie, Marge, and everyone else in the squad, maybe it's a bad idea.

Cole frowns. "Drunks, terrorists, and toddlers aren't worth negotiating with. And he's essentially all three."

I snort, scanning around us in case he's lingering about. "So he's mad at you?"

"Yep."

"Still doesn't explain why he's a complete ass to *everyone* else."

Cole shrugs. "I think in part it's to test me. He doesn't think I deserve the title."

I whip my gaze back to him. "If anyone deserves it, Cole, it's you."

Cole shakes his head, his eyes falling to the ground as his cheeks redden.

I jab his arm to get his attention. "Have you seen the way Archie looks at you? He quite literally bows before you every time he's in your presence."

Cole laughs. "Well, it's misplaced."

"Stop it."

"What?"

"Stop doubting yourself," I command him.

Our eyes lock, and the desire to kiss him heats my chest. I want to kiss away that stubborn modesty of his. The way his eyes smolder before his gaze lowers to my mouth, tells me he's thinking the same thing. As if lured by an invisible force, I take a half step toward him. But he turns away, no doubt to hide the longing he masks from the others around us.

"I can't," I mutter, averting my gaze from the flaming torch Cole holds, to the pile of wood on his stone floor.

I can't incinerate the last tether to my family and my father. Guilt, sadness, and anger swarm me all at once. Guilt washes over me—I can't be the one to burn it. Sad that, after tonight, I'll have nothing left of my father. And angry I can't do anything to change it.

But it's the only way to eliminate any proof if Marge decides to report me. The required proximity to a flame petrifies me as much as destroying the journal. Staring at the kindling Cole collected for us to burn the journal in, my mouth goes dry as I picture the wood engulfed in flames. The crackling branches mimicking a snapping neck. Screams a whispered echo in my ears, and nightmarish words I can't decipher coming to life.

With a shaky hand and eyes still lowered, I hold out my father's journal to Cole. "I can't be the one to do it."

"Are you sure?" he asks for the third time. His fingers close around the journal, but he doesn't take it from me.

I stare at the leather cover. I've lost so much—and perhaps I shouldn't be so sentimental about a silly journal.

In the grand scheme of things, it is only paper and ink.

Struggling, I convince myself that between the journal, and Cole and Daeja, I'm making the right choice.

With a nod, I let my hand slip from the journal. Before Cole notices my glossy eyes, I turn away and head for his door.

"Wait—where are you going?" he asks.

"Just…burn it. I can't stay to watch," I whisper over my shoulder before exiting Cole's room. When I get to my own, I sink into my bed and cry.

At least I fulfilled my father's written wish of burning the journal.

TWENTY ONE

TWENTY-TWO SECONDS

I dream of fire and smoke, haunted by the constant flux of flames from red to blue. Horror grips me in its merciless talons as the faces of the little girl and her family swim in and out of my vision. The shudder of a tied door. Flames licking up the sides of a house.

Beating my fists against a glass window until I bleed, I scream at the girl and her family stuck inside their house. Yet, they still can't hear me, their round eyes staring.

In one blink, they're gone, and I'm pounding on the window of my room back in Padmoor instead. I watch as fire roars around the room, inching closer to the bed where my body lies. My eyes are squeezed shut, a soft smile on my lips. The doorknob jiggles, and my mother's distant cry is muffled by the inferno.

But I don't stir.

I punch the windowpane, again and again. "Wake *up!*"

My scream echoes and morphs into other voices, tones, and pitches.

I jerk awake, my heart racing and sweat drenching my back. The screams from my nightmare still ring fresh around me.

Hugging my knees to my chest, I rock back and forth. Whispering to myself, I attempt to quiet the cries, cupping my hands over my ears. But the screams don't fade.

I blink through the blurriness of sleep.

By now, the screams should have waned.

A bell rings out, and I shoot out of bed. The screams are real. Shoving boots onto my naked legs, I snatch my satchel and sword. I slip out of my room and shiver, my nightgown not providing much warmth against the frigid night air.

Several groups of shadows scatter throughout the camp: screaming, shouting, and crashing. I press myself back against the wall of my room, holding my breath, and tightening my grip around my sword. Another alarm cries out from the outlook tower, ringing out across the chaos.

I have to get to Daeja.

Slipping behind my building, I race for the western wall and the forest beyond.

"Daeja, we're being attacked. I'm coming to you."

"Two leggers?" Panic draws the bond between us tight. **"I'm coming."**

"No! Stay where you are. I'll be there—"

"We have to find out where their vials are stocked," a voice calls from the other side of a tent.

Marge should be in her own room this late at night. But the possibility of her still being in the healer's quadrant, defenseless and vulnerable, pulls me to a screeching halt. If she's killed, it would alleviate any risk of her turning us in. It would essentially solve our problems.

But I can't.

I can't do it.

I have to warn her.

"Hold on, Daeja. I have to make a quick detour, and then I'll be there."

She grumbles her protest but quiets.

I cut a shorter path to the healer's quadrant and slip inside. Burning candles cast a soft amber glow in the room, and Marge hunches over the counter, pouring liquid into a glass vial.

She spins toward me, eyes squinting. "What are you doing here this late—"

"Shhh!" I hiss and blow out the candles in a single breath. Covering her mouth, I rip her into my chest, and the vial in her hands falls to the ground and shatters. Pulling her back from the counter, I shift us both into the farthest corner of the room. She tears my hand off her mouth, and the door swings wide open. Three men enter, weapons held ready as they scan the room, their gazes snagging on the soft smoke rising from the extinguished candles before finally reaching us.

"Daeja, I need you to fly as fast and as far north as you can. Once you pass the mountain range, you'll be free."

"What? I'm not leaving without you!"

"Grab her," one of the men says.

The other two thunder toward us, their eyes trained and weapons angled in our direction.

I step forward and shove Marge behind me, unsheathing my sword.

She stumbles. "My staff, Katerina."

Her staff is across the room, beyond the two men advancing, and leaning against the counter. Clearly, she should retire. She must have lost her godsdamn mind to imply such a thing. Does this woman really believe in me enough that she thinks we'll be walking out of this alive? That she'll actually need her staff once I'm done with these three?

If I make it twenty-two seconds before I die, I'll consider it a massive success on my part.

The men sweep toward us, too close for comfort, and I do everything my body and mind screams at me not to do. I lift my sword, readying my arm with all of the strength I could ever possess.

I fucking *charge* them.

I swing sideways into one man's sword. As soon as our blades collide, the strength of his blow rips my sword out of my grasp, sending it flying back a few feet. An unsettling vibration rings throughout my hand, all the way up my arm. The second one swings for my head, and I duck, the metal grazing the very tips of my hair. His sword catches into the cabinet beside me, the wood groaning at the impact. The man heaves to pull it free.

My gaze darts to my sword on the ground, a few feet away and blocked by the first man who swipes his blade toward me again.

Falling backward, I roll onto my side but not fast enough to dodge the tip of his blade. A wicked sting rips across my arm.

Fuck. There goes my twenty-two seconds.

Daeja's roar echoes in my head, nearly incapacitating me from my next move.

"*Daeja—*"

A vicious slam of splintering wood tears all of our attention to the door. A man, as dark and cruel as a nightmare, surges into the room.

Darian.

He flies in with a boiling rage, decapitating the commanding man in one fell swoop. The man's head thuds to the ground and rolls, his body collapsing a split second after. The other two freeze, before scattering like roaches in the room.

Darian hunts them down, swinging and striking like the graceful lethality of a snake. Cold, calculating, and painfully beautiful. Despite the violent moment, I'm mesmerized by how simple he makes it all seem. Crawling to my sword, I swipe it off the ground and jump to my feet. All three of the intruders are on the floor, soaked in pools of their own blood. Darian rakes his gaze across the room.

Our eyes connect.

A brutality smolders in his eyes, like an unbridled wildfire that could set the entire world ablaze. His chest heaves, lips pulled back in a silent snarl, and sweat drips down his face. "Where is Marge?"

Marge limps past me and pats my shoulder, her touch

stirring the memory I was struck. I clamp down on my upper arm to slow the river of blood trickling down to my hand.

The tension in Darian's face lessens slightly. "Glad you live to see another day, Margie."

He snakes over to a cabinet as he reaches for the flask tucked into his side. Grabbing a bottle from the shelf, he pours its contents into the flask and takes a few hard gulps from the bottle himself.

"Darian," Marge hisses. "What have I told you about proper etiquette?"

"Considering I just saved your ass, Marge, don't give me shit about manners." He wipes the liquid from his mouth with the back of his hand, a satisfied breath escaping his lips. He puts the bottle back onto the shelf and lifts his flask to us before he leaves.

The sound of the alarm bell in the distance dies out before the door shuts again.

"Wretched boy. Couldn't even be bothered to clean up after himself." Marge sneers as she walks over to the bloodied bodies sprawled across the floor. As if he had left broken glass on the ground, rather than three mutilated men.

She turns her attention back to me. "Come here. Let me get a look at your arm."

I don't allow my gaze to linger for too long on the bodies, my stomach roiling with every glimpse. I fix my stare at the ceiling as her nimble hands assess me.

Marge watches my face, potentially noticing my unease. "Nothing but a superficial cut. I can clean you up in a bit…why don't you find Cole first, and see if he can send someone to help clear this out?" She motions toward the bloodied ground.

I don't argue.

Holding my breath and fixing my gaze on anywhere but down, I inch around the pools of blood and out of the healer's quadrant.

A cold silence replaces the screams and chaos bursting in the outpost earlier. I'm assuming we've won, but an eerie tension settles around the camp like an invisible fog. Every direction I scan is empty, no hint of our squad or our attackers.

"I'm okay, Daeja. I'm safe."

"You had me worried something bad was going to happen—"

A hand claps over my mouth, tearing me backward. My shoulders hit a firm chest, and a cold, metal sword presses to my throat. "Don't scream. Don't fight. Or I'll kill you." The words are whispered into my neck, the voice rough and unfamiliar.

My instinct to scream and thrash dies.

"Drop your sword," the man hisses.

My hand flexes on the hilt of my sword, the metal slippery in my hands. I won't be able to maneuver fast enough to avoid my throat being sliced open if I try to run. And my inexperience with sword fighting would also mean a quick death.

I drop my sword.

My captor leads me away from camp, his sword sliding down from my throat around to my back, its tip pricking my spine, prompting me forward. Terror drains my blood from my face as we slip silently away from the rugged stone walls of the outpost, his hand still wrapped around my mouth.

I'm tempted to reach out to Daeja, but even if she could save me from this man, her death would be imminent if she were discovered by Cole's squad.

The man leads me into the cover of the trees, and I scan the forest floor, my gaze settling on a rock. Without giving myself the chance to second guess it, I fling forward, feigning tripping over something, and catching myself on my hands. I roll to my right, anticipating his blade to come crashing into my skull.

He hisses and snatches my braid, ripping me to my feet as shouts thunder from behind us. Pinning me back into the position I was in before, the man claps his hand over my mouth before I can scream, the tip of his sword settling at the base of my throat.

He turns us to face the approaching beat of footsteps and tears me back, step by step, farther into the forest. But the surging group of shadows from the outpost is much faster, and recognizable figures emerge from the mass of darkness. Cole and Archie appear at the front of the group.

My captor growls. "Get back, or I'll sever her!"

Cole goes rigid, his eyes calculating as he raises his open palms to us. He shifts one hand behind him to stop the approaching squad, never breaking eye contact with my captor.

The blade digs harder into my throat, and my skin burns, a hot trickle of blood races down into my nightgown.

*"**Where are you?**"* Daeja's growl is laced with intense panic.

"Stay where you are, I'll be okay!" I lie in fear of risking her

life. The reality hits me over the head as hard as if it were a rock—my mother told me the same thing before she died.

"What do you want?" Cole demands through gritted teeth. "Whatever you want, you'll have it."

My captor snickers. "There's nothing you have that I want."

Cole's eyes darken to an unrecognizable level, his voice dipping into an otherworldly wrath. "If you so much as nick another inch of her flesh, I will rip every breath from your lungs with my bare hands. I will beat the life out of you into another lifetime."

My captor drags the sword down, slicing more of my skin in a taunt.

A shiver snakes down my spine as I witness in slow-motion Cole transform into the pure embodiment of wrath, rage, and fury. He roars—animalistic—lunging as multiple people spring forward to stop him. But it's no use, Cole swings them off of him, managing to shake the grip of them all.

A whirl of silver flashes toward my captor and me.

Cold metal grazes my cheek as the silver passes and sinks into my captor behind me. His grip on my mouth slides off, and the cold sting of his sword against my throat disappears entirely. I whirl, and the man who held me hostage slumps to the ground, a dagger sunk hilt-deep into his gurgling mouth. Blood bubbles out of lips, his eyes wide and hands clawing at his face.

Stepping back, I gasp in horror.

Cole brushes me behind him. "Look. Away."

I stare off into the forest, but I'm unable to block out the sound of squelching flesh. Turning back slowly to Cole, I watch him sheathe his bloody sword, rage still fuming in his pinched features. Lying on the ground in a pool of blood, blank eyes staring up at the stars, is my captor. My stomach churns, and I cup my hand over my mouth.

Cole pulls me into him, his strong arms wrapping around me as if he'll never let go. His heartbeat is rabid inside his chest, and his dilated pupils shrink as he locks eyes with me.

"Are you okay?" he whispers, holding my face between his hands and searching every inch of my skin. His thumb brushes underneath the slice against my cheek, his finger coming away smeared with blood.

"Yes…I–I think so?"

Cole whirls. "Archie, what the hell was that!"

Archie dips his head with a sheepish grin. "I…uhh. I used to throw daggers?"

Cole's voice dips into a growl. "If you missed you could have *killed. Her.*"

"I-I knew I wouldn't," Archie murmurs, blinking at Cole's uncharacteristically furious tone.

I rub up and down Cole's arm to get his attention, then tug his collar when he doesn't budge. "Hey. Hey! Look at me." I pull his chin to face me, resting my hand on his cheek as I whisper, "I'm okay."

Cole locks into my gaze, his anger fading like the darkness after the sun rises. His breathing slows. Finally, he looks at Archie, his voice gravelly, "Thank you, Archie."

The rest of the squad erupts into a cheer. Carlisle breaks

off from the group, pridefully slaps Archie on the shoulder with some sentimental words, and ruffles his hair.

A flicker of movement beyond the distant trees catches my attention. Daeja's nearness is as apparent to me as if it were a sixth sense.

"I'm safe, this time. I promise," I confirm.

Her half snort, half relieved sigh whispers in my mind. The shadows in the forest stills.

I hug Archie, my voice weak. "Thank you, I knew it was you I needed to be scared of."

Cole shifts into his captain role seamlessly. "You're a hero, Arch. Grab your dagger, I'm going to take Kat to Marge. Carlisle, could you please delegate someone to dispose of the bodies?"

Cole ushers the rest of the squad back to camp and whisks me away. We're alone, hidden by trees and bushes, when trembles erupt from my body, and my hands drip sweat. The cold air whispers against my cuts, burning my skin.

Cole stops to take my face into his hands, his voice trembling. "I was…I was so scared to lose you again…are you sure you're alright?"

In the comfort of just him and I, my stomach retches. Holding up a finger, I take a step away from him and hurl into the bushes.

He's quick to pull my hair back from my face with one hand and softly rub circles on my back with the other. My body shudders as I hack again and again until I have nothing left.

Cole's voice is gentle. "I'm so sorry. This should have never happened, and I'm sure you were so scared. Adrenaline can make you nauseous."

I wipe my mouth with the back of my hand and turn back to him to reply. My vision swings into a dizzying blur, and my knees buckle.

Cole slingshots forward, catching me in his arms, and concern furrows his dark brows. "We've got to get you to Marge."

He sweeps me up off of my feet, my head flopping back into the crook of his muscled arm. The stars swim circles above me.

"I'm fine," I murmur, though not convincingly enough.

Marge answers Cole's knock at the healer's quadrant with an exasperated sigh, until she sees my state and ushers us in. Cole lays me down onto a bed, and my gaze wanders beyond him to the dark stains mottling the floor where the three men were mutilated.

"What happened?" Marge demands.

"We must have missed a rebel. He took her hostage." Cole's voice is still thick with worry.

Marge works quickly, assessing the cuts on my neck, cheek, and arm. She cleans the wounds and flicks her gaze up at Cole. "These should heal just fine, she's just in shock."

"She'll be okay?" Cole's wide eyes watch Marge's every movement.

"Yes. Now go. Leave her to rest."

"I'm not leaving her."

"Fine. Who am I to tell you what to do, captain? Stay here, then." Marge rubs an ointment on the cuts, and presses a vial to my lips, demanding me to drink it. "Get some rest. I'll check on you in the morning."

I swallow down the liquid, and each second it settles deeper into me numbs my consciousness.

Cole sinks to his knees beside the bed as Marge leaves the healer's quadrant. He strokes my hair, his touch soft. My vision starts to fade to black. The last thing I feel is Cole's hand wrapped around mine and a whispered, *"I love you."*

Nightmares consume me, and I struggle to breathe through the blazing fire ravaging around me. I'm pulled under, drowning in flames and blood. Screams surround me, until one erupts from my own mouth, and I can't stop myself.

"Shhh, shhh, shh. You're safe. You're with me. I've got you, I'm right here with you." Cole's soft voice brushes against the shell of my ear. His strong, muscled arms wrap around me like a blanket.

I peek open my eyes and turn to look up at him. His tender eyes chase away the haze of my fear. My head falls back against his chest. The steady beat of his heart slows my own. He holds me, rocking me back and forth until I slip back into sleep. The thunder of his heart pulses around me.

But rather than the fire and flames and screams, I hear a chanting of words.

Fire incarnate.

Flame in flesh.

Blood of power.

TWENTY TWO

FINE

When I wake, Cole is slumped over the bed near my legs, his hand still clutching mine. His eyes flutter open and closed, his lashes kissing his cheek with each dragging blink.

As I shift under the sheets, his eyes fly open.

He pulls up closer to me, cupping my face with a hand. "How are you feeling?"

My head is a little fuzzy as I swim back to my memory. "I'm okay, I think?"

"Daeja?"

"I'm here. I was so worried something happened to you, are you okay?"

"I'm okay. I'll try to come see you tonight."

Cole's staring at me. "You didn't hear a word I just said… did you?"

He knows me too well and takes my hesitation as confirmation. "Look, this is getting far too risky, Kat. And the rebels aren't going to let up. They're going to keep attacking us. We are too close to their borders, and I can't keep risking your life. Not to mention if someone catches wind we have a full-grown dragon. You should let Daeja go on her own before you get too attached. You could go back to Padmoor where you will be safe."

"That's not your call, Cole."

"I'm the captain. Of course it is."

I glare. "Don't you pull that captain card on me. I have to get Daeja to the Dragon Lands. You said you would help me—"

"You almost *died* at the hands of a rebel last night. If it weren't for Archie, I would be mourning you all over again—" He pauses, his chest rising and falling. Finally, he grits out, "I can't do this, it's too dangerous, Kat. I can't lose you again."

"Then if it's so dangerous, why don't you train me to defend myself?"

He snorts and shakes his head.

I try again, "If you are so worried about me, then train me."

"I was supposed to protect you, and I—" He swallows.

He doesn't have to continue for me to know what word comes next. *Failed*…I relate to it too much.

He continues, "I'm supposed to protect you. *Me.* I should have been the one to save you. I would have done anything, given anything just to make sure you were safe…" he looks down at our clasped hands as he blinks back tears.

I rub the back of his hand. "Cole, you can't be the one to save me all the time."

His watery eyes meet mine. "Gods, but I want to."

I smile softly. "I know you do."

A heavy, defeated sigh escapes his lips as he diverts his attention back down to our hands. He shakes his head again, as if he already knows he's in trouble for asking. "You think that's what we should do? That's what you really want? To be trained?"

"Is that so awful of me to ask?"

"No…but…I guess now I'll have to be scared you'll kick my ass when you're pissed at me." He flashes me a subtle, handsome smile.

We both laugh.

I knock my fist into his arm, a smile creeping onto my face as I say, "How about tomorrow?"

He levels a disapproving look at me.

"You were the one who said there's been an influx of rebels. Who knows when they will attack next. If we're going to travel north, I'm going to need to know how to defend myself. And next time I might not be so lucky," I murmur.

He chews at his lip but nods his head. "Fine. If you're feeling up for it after training with Marge. But I don't want you pushing yourself."

He leans in to kiss my forehead, and the door swings open. He pulls back quickly enough that when Marge walks back in, he's sitting on the bed, his hands piled in his lap.

Marge shuffles over to us, flicking a wrist at Cole to excuse him off the bed. She presses a hand to my cheek, my forehead, and assesses my cuts. "She looks fine to me. How do you feel?"

"Good," I answer.

"Great. I'd like you to start cleaning those vials over there." She points to a basket on the counter.

"Now? But I—"

"Plenty of things that need to get done around here. But if you're feeling that bad—"

"No, I'm fine." I push up to my feet as Cole offers me his hand to help me up.

Away from the cover of my sheets, I realize I'm still wearing the nightgown from the night before. The hem is shredded, and old blood stains the material in blotches. Cole is already a step ahead, having had someone bring me a change of clothes for when I woke. After I encourage Cole several times to leave and get some rest, he throws me a hesitant look and leaves. I quickly change into a fresh set of pants and a tunic.

I scrub vials until Marge walks over to me. She pauses, watching my hands work while I wash the last one.

"Why did you come here last night?" she asks finally.

I turn toward her. "I umm…"

When our eyes lock I stop scrubbing. "I…I don't know," I admit.

She takes the last vial from me, tucks it into a drawer, and returns with two knives and a clump of mushrooms. We both slice in silence.

Her attention flickers over to me, and she stops cutting, dropping her blade to the counter.

"What?" I ask.

"You're...cutting those wrong," she mutters.

I don't bother to mask my heavy sigh. I can't do anything right in her eyes, and it's starting to wear on me. "You're telling me there's a right way to cut mushrooms?"

"Well, if you keep chopping like that, you might cut your finger off," she quips, shuffling over to me.

She wraps her hands around mine, puppeteering each motion. "Here."

For the first time, she isn't wearing her black gloves. Angry scars wrap around the backs of her hands. The rugged skin is raised and jagged, and the color blends in with the rest of her hands. I always assumed she wore gloves for sanitary reasons. With how often she must come into contact with body fluids and illnesses, I never questioned it.

She notices my stare and lifts a hand closer to my face to observe. I flinch back, embarrassed to be caught staring.

"Dragons," she says and goes back to slicing her own mushrooms.

I check over my shoulder to make sure it's only us in the room. "You were attacked?"

"No." She grins, as if her brilliant mind hid all the secrets of the world, and she's just waiting for someone to ask her the right questions. "Dragonblood."

I stop chopping. "Dragonblood?"

"Shh! Keep your voice down," she scolds.

I stare at her hands again. The scars mimic the wicked lick of flames.

"What were you doing with dragonblood?" I whisper.

"When I was a little girl, I became sick. Within a day I likely would have succumbed to my illness. It was incredibly painful, and I withered away to almost nothing. But my grandmother used the last of her dragonblood. And it saved me."

"What do you mean it saved you?"

"Dragonblood is incredibly rare, and at that, very dangerous. Some that consume it can go insane. They can be granted special powers. They could go blind, or die—and it's a horrible, painful death. The blood will burn you inside like a live fire. Or… it can heal you."

She looks down at her hands and brushes the scars with her fingertips. "These scars are from dragonblood. And ever since then, I wanted to be a healer."

"So…how come you never went to the Dragon Lands yourself?"

"Because the rebels despise Spoileds almost as much as they do the King."

"Spoileds?"

"Yes, when you consume dragonblood it essentially spoils your blood. Some say you will burn in hell for interfering with such sacred, magical blood—" She laughs absent-mindedly. "Maybe that's actually why I wanted to be a healer. To balance out whatever cosmic sin I had committed to…"

She shakes her head to clear the thought from her mind and ushers me out. "You are dismissed for the day. Go get some rest."

As I walk toward my room, I pass by other soldiers, their steps sure and expressions hard. *Out of last night's attack...how was I the only one injured? Unless I woke after the other injured soldiers left the healer's quadrant?* It's another confirmation how critical it is for me to be trained.

Nearing my tent, I smile as I notice Archie standing at my door. A plate of pastries balances on his fingertips. I invite him into my room, and he sweeps inside with me.

"I wanted to come check on you before sparring," he murmurs with a nervous grin.

I smile. "I'm doing fine, thanks to you."

He plucks a pastry off the plate and offers it to me.

"I'm okay for now, but thank you."

He nods and sets the plate down on my desk.

I step forward, tilting my head to the side. "Archie, I never knew you were so skilled in knife throwing."

He blushes. "It was my favorite weapon growing up... but...you can't really use throwing knives in a war."

"Maybe not. But you would be a *killer* assassin." I wink.

He laughs and points at me. "Ahh! I see what you did there!"

And there he is—void of guilt. His regular optimistic self.

I dip my head. "But honestly, you saved my life, Arch."

He mirrors my smile, and his chest inflates. Pride bubbles

through the warmth in his brown eyes and blushing cheeks. He tries to wave me off nonchalantly. "I just did what I had to do."

I squeeze his arm. "Thank you."

His gaze floats over to my sword leaning against the desk for a long moment. "Where did you get that sword, by the way?"

"I uhh…a friend gave it to me."

Archie's eyes flare. "Wow, some friend you have! You have a friend in the close circle?"

"What do you mean close circle?"

"May I?" He motions toward my sword.

I nod, and he retrieves it, stopping a step away from me.

"After the rebels attacked, I found your sword on the ground near the healer's quadrant. Cole recognized it was yours, and that's how we knew something was wrong. We spotted you before the rebel took you into the forest. When I originally picked it up, I noticed this…" He traces a fingertip over the textures on the handle, outlining a ring of circles overlapping each other in the middle. "The mark of the King's most inner assembly. Some say they know the kingdom better than the King—"

He pauses, realizing the insult he implied to the King. "I-I mean, some say they know the King better than the kingdom—" He laughs awkwardly as he runs a hand through his hair. "Okay, maybe I don't know what I'm trying to say. But it's a nice sword."

He hands it back to me. I stare down at the hilt decorated in intricate patterns with hidden intersecting circles.

What was a rebel doing with a sword from the King's close circle?

"Stay away from the shoreline. We have to cover your tracks," I call out after Daeja as she approaches the lake. As soon as the camp fell silent in the late night, I slipped out to see her.

Daeja turns to me, her eyes catching a reflection of moonlight. **"Why?"**

"Because if someone catches you, they'll kill you. Remember?"

"Why would they want to kill me?"

I think of the people who lost their lives in Padmoor. How the dragonfire left scorch marks along the cobblestones. The man who tried to run in the street from the dragon, torched to a heap of ash, and now a distant memory.

But my thoughts fade to the memory of her as a hatchling. Diving around with my dagger in her mouth. Chasing after a butterfly and trying to catch her own tail. The corner of my lips lift into a smile. Maybe if they knew Daeja like I did, they would see she isn't a threat.

"I don't know."

Doubt tightens the invisible bond between us. **"I've been thinking…what if we get to the Dragon Lands and the other dragons don't like me?"**

"Why do you say that? Why wouldn't they like you?"

"What if I'm different? What if I don't know how to be like the other dragons?"

I chuckle as I pat her neck. *"It doesn't matter if you know how—it's what you are."*

"Is that supposed to make me feel better?" She snorts and bumps me with her hindquarters. I stumble forward, thrown off by how powerful she is. She nabs the back of my shirt in her teeth, catching me before I land on my face.

Steadying back onto my feet, guilt swarms me with how out of place she must feel. Stuck in a land that doesn't want her and without her kind. Limited from her natural tendencies and capabilities.

Perhaps I know what can make her feel better, even if it's only for a fleeting moment.

I mount her, climbing onto her back as she turns her head to grin. If dragons can grin. I cling to the horns lining her neck, my hands already anxiously sweating.

"Fly."

She ducks her head and charges for the lake. Her wings flap and thunder, and we lift above the water, her talons grazing the surface. The wind sings around me, stealing my breath as we soar. I don't let my gaze fall lower than her head, for fear of losing my grip and slipping into the water below. The roaring wind dies down, and she slows to a graceful glide.

Slowly, I dare a peek down. The reflection of the moon and stars glitter across the lake's glassy surface. I drag my gaze up to the sky. Remembering the times my mother, brother, and I used to shout how much we missed my father up to the sky, as if he could hear us. Absent-mindedly, I reach one hand up, as if I could touch the stars. Wondering if they were looking back down at me now.

A shooting star streaks across the sky, so fast I almost second guess I actually saw one.

For the rest of the night, we fly in circles under the stars. And for the first time, in a long time, it makes me feel as close as I ever have to all of my family.

TWENTY THREE

KITTEN

"Given the most recent rebel attacks, we are upping our training. We will have mandatory training for all outpost positions," Cole calls out in the center of the sparring ring. Although, Marge is the exception in the entire squad. She mentioned she had more than enough experience and didn't need extra training.

My theory is she didn't want to admit she's too old. And Cole knew better than to argue with her.

Cole is the first to spar and fights against Carlisle in hand-to-hand combat. Cole's moves are short and jerky, holding back his full power. Carlisle is drenched in sweat as he defends, blocks, and dodges again and again. Unlike the duels with Darian I've witnessed, this fight is much more forgiving. Cole swings Carlisle to the ground and pins him until he taps out.

Cole scans the crowd. "Who's next?"

I step forward. "Me."

"I'll take her!" Archie interjects enthusiastically before anyone else can respond.

Archie and I stand in the center of the clearing and face each other, the sun glaring against the edge of my sword as I raise it. Archie unsheathes his own sword, the metal ringing as it's pulled free from its scabbard. Nervousness bubbles inside of me, mixed with relief that out of everyone I'm sparring with, it's him.

Archie waits for me to make the first move. I jab forward, swiping my blade up and to the right. He twists his sword down to mine. Blocked. The metal rings out around us, and a vibration buzzes in my arm. I swing again—blocked. Stepping back from him, I wait for his attack, but it never comes. He steps forward like he's going to but doesn't strike.

"Archie, what are you doing?" I whisper as I swipe my blade sideways at him. "Fight. Me."

He continues to deflect. I leave long pauses between, waiting for him to advance. While I secretly hoped he would take it easy on me, I wasn't wanting this easy.

"Rebels won't give a shit if she's untrained," Darian calls out from the sidelines.

And for once, I *actually* agree with him. Cole shoots a glare in Darian's direction to silence him and then is back to watching us.

"Come on Archie…I promise. It's okay," I mutter as I lunge and cut again.

He's still not attacking me, his focus entirely on defending. His boot catches an invisible lift in the ground. Falling to his knees, his sword falls far away from his grasp. A little too far.

Did he just fake tripping and throw his sword?

Archie holds his arms above his head. "I surrender!"

I roll my eyes, an exasperated sigh slipping from my lips as I offer to help him up. He graciously takes my outstretched hand and leaps to his feet.

I shift my gaze to Cole, hoping he might entertain me. "Cole, will you—"

"I challenge." Darian steps forward into the center, mischief dancing in his eyes.

Cole snaps his head into his direction. "Absolutely not."

"C'mon, it won't hurt," Darian taunts.

Cole glares at the defiance in Darian's voice and bites back, "It might for you."

Darian sneers. "She has the prowess of a *kitten*. But thank you for your concern."

"You know it wasn't her I was referring to," Cole growls.

"It's fine," I assure Cole with a small nod. Part of me is adamant not to lure that simmering wrath of a man I witnessed the night I was captured. Besides, this may be my opportunity to prove myself. I step closer to face Darian, locking my stance to keep my legs from wobbling.

I can't back down. Not on the first day.

"You've got this," Daeja whispers in my head.

The memory of Darian ruthlessly hacking against Archie replays in my mind. The way Darian so effortlessly beheaded three men. How he's rumored to be the best swordsman in the kingdom and trained by Jurrock himself.

Kitten my *ass*.

A kitten wouldn't dare fight a damn wolf.

Darian lowers his chin with a devilish grin and stretches out an open hand, bending his fingers toward him in an unspoken challenge.

I charge immediately, hoping my lack of hesitancy catches him off-guard. Swinging my sword in a hard left, he catches my strike so easily with his own blade, his eyes dance. Sweeping his sword locked with mine up and around, he thrusts me backward. I take a few steps back, narrowing my eyes, and spring forward. I swipe and swing, thrust and cut, each move deflected effortlessly by him. He hasn't even taken a single swing at me, a stupid snide grin settles on his lips. My blood boils in my veins as he begins to laugh at each of my strikes.

He's fucking toying with me.

At least Archie had the decency of not mocking my inexperience.

Channeling my irritation into my attacks, I throw extra force behind each swing.

He dodges again, as if he could do it in his sleep. "You're going to have to do much better than that, *kitten*."

The name unlocks a deep rooted anger within me. How fucking dare he think he can call me such a thing. Impulsively, I lash out with my full strength, sweat gathering on my brow.

With a simple twist of his wrist, he disarms me and grabs my other forearm in one move. He whips me around, twirling me away from him, and pinning my back into his hard chest. The cold metal of his sword kisses the delicate skin on my neck, near the cut from the last time I was held hostage.

Cole shifts from the edge of the ring, fists clenched and ready to pounce. "Darian, if you don't let her go in five seconds…"

"Control your emotions, or they'll control you. We have no room for deadly mistakes," Darian hisses in my ear.

I writhe as his breath caresses the sensitive part between my neck and ear. Every attempt to free myself is unsuccessful, and the memory of him adamant on killing Archie in their last sparring practice resurfaces in my mind. But he doesn't deal the final, killing blow.

"What? You aren't going to kill the weakest link now? How very *anticlimactic* of you," I hiss at Darian, struggling in his grasp.

Darian chuckles behind me, his laugh radiating in my chest. He leans closer, his lips brushing the shell of my ear. It takes everything in me to hold down a shiver. We are far, *far* too close for comfort now.

His voice dips to something only the two of us can discern. "If you're looking for a climax, kitten, all you have to do is ask."

I drop my elbow into his crotch. His sword drops from my throat and clatters to the ground, his startled gasp whispers against my ear. Pushing out of Darian's grasp, I turn to face him. He folds over, his face lowered as he braces his palms on his knees.

Cole springs to my side and muffles a laugh behind tight lips. I don't think anyone else heard Darian—just me. Because if Cole heard the innuendo, he might kill Darian himself.

"I'll take that as a win," I declare, strutting off the center of the sparring ring with Cole.

Archie loops an arm around my neck, chuckling and raises a hand to high-five me. "Remind me to never call you kitten! That's two wins for you today. Maybe you should start training me?"

I roll my eyes and playfully slap his arm. Darian sucks in a loud inhale from where he is still hunched over in the sparring circle and stands. His fuming green eyes raze me before he slips off back to camp.

Good riddance.

After lunch with Archie, I head to Cole's room and knock on his door before inching it open. Cole sits at his desk, his angled chin perched on his fist as he stares down at the papers in front of him. He furiously scans the pages with lowered eyebrows.

I slip into his room, closing the door behind me, and he finally looks over to me.

A smile twitches up at the corner of Cole's mouth. "Hey. Sorry, I didn't hear you."

"Hey." I float across the room to him, circling my arms around his neck and looking down over his shoulder at his desk, wondering what has him so focused.

"That was pretty impressive, you fighting Darian," he praises.

"Oh, but not Archie?"

He laughs, smiling up at me. "Of course Archie, too. Admittedly, he took it a little too easy on you."

"I think we all knew that."

"What did Darian say to you?" he asks.

I bite my tongue, trying to think of what to say. I'd rather not upset Cole about the things Darian said. Cole has enough on his plate already. That, and I'm perfectly capable of handling Darian on my own. "Just that…you're a protective big brother."

He watches me carefully. "If he keeps harassing you, let me know. I'll deal with him. But keep your distance from him—he's dangerous."

I shift my focus from Cole down to the papers scattered on his desk. "What are you up to?"

He sighs and lifts a page up for me to see. "Inventory counts. I have to sign them and send them back to the General. They've been really adamant on ensuring nothing goes unaccounted for. If the counts are off, they'll have my head."

"They'd execute you just because you might have misplaced some bandages?"

"No…I would likely have a warning or two before any disciplinary action. But it's just one of those nuances of being in my position. They're really serious about keeping track." He sets down the paper and grabs a new one. "I also have to send a report of events from the last month. I've been hesitant to mention my sister joined the squad. Let alone I didn't ask for permission before I granted you a position. I'm worried they might audit me under such circumstances."

We both stare at his letter for a few still moments.

"Then tell them," I murmur.

He turns in his chair to regard me. Our faces dangerously close. So much so, his breath tickles my cheek. It's a bad move since we aren't supposed to be kissing. My gaze instinctively darts down to his lips, and I'm oddly aware of his hitched breath.

His gaze flicks back and forth between my eyes and mouth. "It makes me….nervous."

I'm not quite sure if we are still talking about the same thing. But I play the game. "It won't matter, if we're already in the Dragon Lands, right?"

Cole blows out a breath, averting his attention to the letters. "I don't know. I've been thinking, and the best chance at getting through undetected is to wait for a moonless night. No moon, no light. Daeja's scales are so dark, it would be easier to hide her in the shadows. But the next moonless night isn't for a few more weeks."

He taps against the letter he's scrawled several sentences onto. "I'm hoping the General will approve my request for a map of the northern outposts and borders. Perhaps even detailing Dragon's Back Ridge. It'll likely take a few weeks for us to receive it."

"You don't think we could make it without the map, just take a straight shot north?" I ask.

"No because I'm not familiar with where the rebel camps are. I've heard rumors of them sprinkled throughout Dragon's Back

Ridge to protect their borders, but I'm not certain. Running into a rebel's outpost could be catastrophic. Especially given you'd be outnumbered. Do you think you'd be able to wait here a few weeks until we have the map?"

My stomach churns. I'm uncertain if it's the thought of staying here that long or the dangerous path to get to the Dragon Lands. But I nod my head anyway. "I...I think so."

"The start of Dragon's Back Ridge is about a few days' trek from here. Maybe more if we have to move slowly. I'll have a better idea once I have the map."

I lean in and press my lips to his cheek. "Thank you."

His jaws tightens into a smile, and I pull back to look him in the eyes. Our noses brush, and his eyes heat. This close up, my heartbeat must sound like a war drum to him. I find myself completely entranced by the smoldering amber of his eyes. The way I gravitate toward the curve of his soft lips–

"Three weeks," he interrupts my observations, ripping his gaze away from mine.

It takes me a few seconds to shake myself out of my stupor. "What...about Marge?"

"What about her?"

"She said she wouldn't turn us in. She wants to go to the Dragon Lands..."

He raises an eyebrow. "And you want her to come with us?"

"I..." *Don't know.*

My mother's words ring in my head. *Trust no one but Cole.* Did that also apply to Marge?

But the more I think of my mother and all the things she's ever told me, the more my mind whirls. At the end of the day, could I even trust her and her sanity? I wasn't even sure if I could trust the words of my own father, someone I had never met before. Someone who had been a rebel, for that matter. But something lingered within my gut, just a touch out of my grasp for me to fully understand it.

My voice drops to a whisper. "I've been thinking about the journal, and...what if we're on the wrong side?"

"Of course we aren't on the wrong side. The rebels have been slaughtering towns of innocent people—"

"But what if it wasn't the rebels? What if it was someone else?" I shift uncomfortably at the possibility.

He levels a look at me. "And who else would it possibly be?"

"I...don't know." I avert my eyes down to my fidgety hands. "But my father's journal mentioned the King executed all of the dragons when he came into rule."

"Well, dragons can be dangerous. He was only doing it to protect his people."

I throw a narrowed glare at him in warning. Part of me instinctively defensive of Daeja and her kind. "But that's not just it. There was a mention of dragonriders. And the execution of them, too."

"Rebels," Cole answers.

I shake my head in frustration. "What do you know of Queen Elara?"

"Who?"

"Exactly. The journal spoke of a Queen Elara who ruled before King Aaric did."

"I know the King had a wife, but she died—"

"She wasn't his wife. Queen Elara was his *sister*. And King Aaric killed her."

Cole freezes, his face blanching.

I meet his wide-eyed gaze, begging for him to consider what I thought could be the truth. "My father said he was spying on the King and saw multiple dragon eggs. That's how I found Daeja's egg—buried in his grave."

Cole blinks rapidly as he digests the information, his words slow. "Perhaps…he had…to kill…"

But even he can't seem to find a reason why. He wouldn't ever be able to kill one of his own sisters, and the longer he sits with the information, the more his expression knits in conflict.

His final question lingers in my mind for the rest of the day. "But can you really trust your father's journal?"

After we ate dinner, most of the squad split off from the tables to sit around a campfire and drink. A common occurrence—I've come to notice—in the squad's routine. But the thought of having to get close to the flames is enough for me to refuse the invitations.

"You don't drink?" Archie asks innocently and covers quickly with, "It's okay if you don't! I don't really, either."

"I do. I just…would prefer not to drink—" I pause, trying to find the right excuse, my attention settling on where the soldiers pile branches to burn. "There."

He looks over his shoulder, following my gaze. "There?"

Darian takes a seat at the edge of the campfire, watching the rest of the soldiers setting up, his eyes picking at me from across the distance. I turn away and back to Archie with a nod.

"We could go somewhere else if you wanted?" Archie offers.

"That would be weird, don't you think? If we showed up for the liquor and left?"

He shrugs. "I think that's what most of them do, anyway."

An idea sparks me. "I know where we can get our own bottle."

Grabbing Archie's elbow, I pull him to the healer's quadrant as the last bits of sunlight fades, darkness settling around the camp. Archie covers his mouth with a hand, unsuccessfully masking his snickering until I pinch him quiet.

"You'll get us caught." I giggle.

Marge isn't present when we slip into the healer's quadrant and inch over to the storage. I peer through the cabinets, searching. Plucking a glass bottle tucked back onto a shelf, we tip-toe back out into camp and to my room. I close my door, and a bubble of laughter erupts from both of us.

Archie plops down into the chair near my desk, and I sit on the edge of my bed. I throw him the bottle, and he catches it with ease. Uncorking the bottle, he sniffs the liquid, and pauses with a grimace. After my encouraging nod, he tilts it back and takes a drink.

"People actually like the taste of this?" he scowls.

I laugh. "No, I don't think so. But people don't drink it for the taste."

"Will I start to hallucinate? Because if I start to see my Great Aunt Becky, I'm never listening to you again."

I tilt my head to the side. "What's wrong with Great Aunt Becky?"

"She used to pinch my cheeks and pull my ears. I used to think it's why my cheeks are always so red and why my ears stick out."

"Your ears don't stick out, Arch. Besides, your natural blush is kind of cute."

He grins at me, takes another drink, and hands the bottle to me. He coughs and sputters, pounding a fist against his chest.

"But no, you won't hallucinate. You'll just feel a little… lighter?" I take a few swigs and swallow down the burn. "Out of everything, that's what scares you the most? Your Great Aunt Becky?"

"No…there are other things. Like owls," he whispers.

"Owls?"

"Yeah, they're creepy. Have you ever seen one twist its head?" He shivers at the thought. "And whistling at night."

"Why's that?"

"I know it seems so silly…but it's a bad omen."

"If you think that's silly, fire scares me."

"Fire?" he repeats.

"Yeah…" I mutter, glancing back down at the bottle in my hands, taking another gulp.

He shrugs the longer he sits with my answer. "That's pretty logical, though. Fire can be scary."

"And myself." My voice drops to a whisper, so low I'm wondering if he heard me.

He blinks, raising his eyebrows. "You know…don't take this personally. But…you're really not all that intimidating."

I chuckle. "Ahh, so now you tell me the truth? I must have forgotten to mention they say alcohol unleashes what you've always wanted to say."

Maybe I should slow down. Before I say too much.

But the words fall out of my mouth before I can stop them. "No. I'm scared I'll make the wrong decisions. That I'm not capable. That no matter what I do, even if I'm trying to make the right choice, it'll still destroy the people I love. And that scares me."

"Trying to do the right thing is scary," Archie agrees softly.

Our eyes connect, solemn and somber. It's unsettling to witness him with such a mellow expression, as if he's containing a silent, hidden storm waiting to break a sunny day. And it's the first time I've noticed how much his smile softens his face. Without it, and his dimpled cheeks when he grins, his angles are sharp. If he didn't have his infectious cheery optimism I'd come to know, I would never think he's a soldier.

A sad tension lingers between us, hanging like an invisible fog.

"More?" I lift the bottle to him, trying to break through the silence and heaviness of the moment.

He shakes me off. "If I have any more, I might throw up."

I laugh and stand as I cork the bottle shut. My feet move sluggishly beneath me as I walk over to the desk to set the bottle down.

Archie's face pales. He jolts to his feet and covers his mouth with his hand. "I feel like I'm going to be sick."

He wobbles, and I slingshot forward, steadying him before he falls. We both giggle as we lock eyes and sway as if there's a hidden wind in the room pushing into us.

I try to settle him. "You'll be okay. Let's get some fresh air. That always seems to help."

We slip out of my room and off into the night, a stumbling mess of heavy feet and hushed giggles until we get to the outer wall of the outpost. My arm linked into his, and both of us taking turns to brace the other. I don't pull my foot quite high enough to clear a rock and trip.

Archie is pulled down with me, and we hit the ground with a thud. Another laugh bursts from our lungs. I push myself up to my hands and knees as my gaze scans the forest ahead.

"Dae...ja?"

"Yessss?" her voices hisses, as if deep underwater. ***"Why do you ssssound ssso...different?"***

"Think there's any dragons out here?" Archie asks from beside me.

I glance sideways at him, rising up to my feet and dusting my pants off. "We probably scared them off by now."

"Stay where you are," I warn Daeja.

"Look," Archie says, still lying on the ground. He shifted to laying on his back, his hand outstretched and pointing to the sky.

I follow the direction of his finger toward the star-studded sky stretching out above us. "Have you...never seen the stars before?"

"No, it's just...this far north. At this elevation. They're so clear here."

I lie down next to him, shifting close to him for body warmth. Leaning my head against his shoulder, we stare at the stars in silence.

"That looks like a soup ladle," he says, pointing at a collection of stars. His arm sways as he struggles to keep still. "A... *spinning*...soup ladle."

"Maybe that's just the hunger talking," I whisper.

He laughs. "You're probably right."

I shift my attention back in the direction of the forest. "We should get back. Before something hungry this way comes and thinks we look like a soup ladle."

"Is that supposed to be scary? Because it's not." He flashes me a toothy smile. The kind of smile that warms his whole face, the crinkles near his eyes deepening.

I giggle. "I might be a little drunk. So I'm not sure how much sense I'm making."

We both help each other up. Stumbling back to the camp, we say good night with a hug, and part our separate ways. I watch him go with a drunken smile.

He might be my first friend here.

TWENTY FOUR

THE EXISTENCE IN BETWEEN

A dull ache pounds in my skull, a remnant of last night's shenanigans with Archie. I rub circles on my temples as sunlight leaks into my room. With a groan, I push up to my feet.

"Daeja?"

"Mmphmm?" Her voice gravelly.

"How has practicing the disappearing thing been coming along? Any luck?"

"No...no luck."

I frown. That'll make things a bit harder, considering we're to stay in camp until Cole gets the map. *"That's okay, keep practicing. Cole says he's working on getting a map for us and we'll wait for a moonless night and be on our way to the Dragon Lands. In the meantime, I'll be practicing sparring. If you feel any sort of pain...don't worry about me. I'll let you know if I'm seriously hurt. Don't come barging in to save me, okay?"*

She snorts in annoyance, the sound loud enough I flinch.

"No promises."

"Daeja," I scold. *"I don't need you to save me, I won't be in danger. And if someone sees you, you'll blow our cover. At least for the next few weeks, I need you to keep a low profile."*

Her growl rumbles in my blood. **"Fine. But I refuse to stand by if your life is at risk."**

Little does she know, our relationship alone is grounds for that.

"Thank you."

She falls silent as she slips back into sleep, further proving my theory she's something nocturnal. Tucking the bottle Archie and I drank last night into my side underneath my tunic, I head to the healer's quadrant. Hopefully, I'm early enough to beat Marge so I can return the bottle unnoticed. Cole's mention of inventory counts rings in my mind, and I wonder if they also tracked the supplies in the healer's quadrant. Though, I recall Darian hadn't appeared to be concerned. Even Marge's biggest worry seemed to be drinking etiquette. As long as we weren't drinking directly from the bottle like Darian was…*oops. Guess what she doesn't know won't hurt her.*

Opening the cabinet, I tuck the bottle back onto its shelf as the door opens.

"What are you doing?" Marge's gaze narrows in on me.

"I…" Shit. I can't even lie at this point. "I'm returning this."

She hobbles over, raking me with a glare, and rips the bottle from my hands. "That's not where that goes."

I stiffen, waiting for her to insult or berate me. But she doesn't. She slides the bottle back onto a different shelf.

She looks me up and down, her eyebrow raised. "You look a little disheveled this morning."

I snort at her honesty. "Good morning to you too, Marge."

"Ginger."

"Excuse me?"

She sighs. "Ginger. It's good for the morning fog."

Even after I've finished the concoction she makes me, my head still pounds. My fingertips are uncomfortably swollen as I steady the broom in my hands and sweep the floors. I'm halfway through the healer's quadrant when Marge turns to me.

"You're dismissed for the day."

"What? Why?" I glance down at the pile of dirt I've swept and all around me, expecting I'm making a bigger mess than I'm cleaning, and that's why she wanted me out.

"Because you're a bit lousy when you've had too much to drink the night before." She shoos me along with a flicker of her wrist.

I open my mouth to reply, my cheeks heating.

She shakes her head. "You come back tomorrow. Fresh."

"Okay," I agree, hesitantly. "I'm sorry, Marge."

She dips her head, and I leave the healer's quadrant for my room.

Walking through the outpost, I pick out my angled roof

stretching into the sky ahead, when a shadow sweeps straight toward me. Darian eyes me, his gaze picking me apart from head to toe.

I jut left to walk around him, and he mirrors my move. Pivoting, I move right instead, and he follows. What was supposed to be an easy, quick return to my room has become an awkward dance of steps and with someone I wouldn't be particularly fond of dancing with. The first two instances I would have pinned as an accident. But with Darian, I know he's toying with me.

Admittedly, I'm a bit too hungover to tolerate it, my self-discipline wearing thin. "Can you get the fuck out of my way?"

There's that stupid, delirious tilt to his lips. "And what is the reason you're in *such* a pleasant mood this morning?"

I growl through gritted teeth to keep myself from shoving him out of my way. "You're aggravating—"

"—ly handsome?" He tilts his chin up, watching me.

"No. There was no continuation of that sentence." I slide to the left, trying to inch around him.

But he slithers along with me, each step closer and closer. "Well, I can think of a way to fix both of our attitudes…"

"If it's not fighting you, then I have no interest." My shoulder clips his arm as I shove past him.

"How disappointing. I would have proposed a different 'F' verb," he tosses over his shoulder.

I don't even bother to look back. Instead, I raise my middle finger at him as I walk back to my room.

I managed to rest for a few hours until everyone gathered for sparring practice. My raging headache slowed to a more tolerable level. At sparring practice, Cole calls for volunteers, and Melaina rises first. I jump to my feet, eager to prove myself. Archie's face sags in disappointment. But I know Melaina won't take it easy on me. She also won't fuck with me like Darian did.

Cole and Melaina exchange a hesitant look, but Melaina reluctantly agrees with a silent nod. The two of us ready our stances in the center of the clearing, eyes trained on the other, swords held in preparation.

Twenty-two seconds…if I can make it that long, I'll be proud of myself.

"You can do all of that and more," Daeja coos in the distance, reading my mind.

A smile tugs at my lips, my spirits instantly lifting.

Melaina and I explode into a frenzy—swinging, cutting, and thrusting. I have to say, I'm jealous of how graceful she is in the way she spins and swings. And here I am, sweating and breathing heavily, my hair stuck to the nape of my neck.

Only a minute passes until she disarms me, but at least I made it longer than I anticipated.

If I can't hold my own against someone in the same squad, how am I to ever fight against an actual opponent? Self-doubt creeps in as stealthy as a lion. The only potentially dangerous thing about me is I have a dragon.

Melaina plucks my sword from the ground and hands it to me, and we both walk out of the center together.

"Has anyone ever told you, you're a little obvious?" Melaina murmurs as we join the group of onlookers.

"A little obvious?" I repeat, unsure of where this conversation is about to go.

"When you're about to swing left, you kind of take a half-step forward. It makes it predictable what your next move is going to be."

"Oh…I didn't realize."

She pulls me back by my elbow, further away from the crowd. "That's okay, I used to do the same thing, until my father pointed it out. Here. Stand straight, balance your weight between your legs, and bend your knees. No. Not that far—like this," she instructs and demonstrates the steps.

"So when I swing at you…" She pulls her blade down, slow across mine. "It's easier to block. Or maneuver for a strike."

I nod and twist my wrist to flick her sword away from me.

She nods her head. "Good! Just keep practicing like that."

"Thanks, Melaina." I grin. "Did you learn sword fighting from your father?"

"Yes. He was Jurrock's second in command. So whenever he was home, he would teach me how to defend myself. My mother was never a fan of it, so we often did it in secret." She chuckles at the memory.

A twinge of envy twists my heart that she had the opportunity to have such a memory with her father.

Her full lips fall as she gazes down at her sword. "I learned the rest from Nolan and Gavin when he died."

I frown. "I'm so sorry for your loss."

She nods, eyes still fixed on her sword. The weapon's silver sheen is mottled with patina, the hilt shining in comparison to the condition of its blade.

One of her dark fingers caresses the length of the metal. "Thank you. He died an honorable death years ago. Rebels attacked a town and tried setting it on fire. He was trapped, and this was all that was left of him."

I stiffen as I think of Hornwood, hoping the color doesn't drain from my face. My memory rolls over me like a fog. I swallow hard, trying to push through the tension collecting in my throat. The memory of my mother dying in the fire all those months ago flashes in my mind.

A heavy sigh escapes her lips. "Then I joined the military, to save anyone else from having to lose their loved ones. My mother wasn't too fond of the idea. I think the only reason she allowed me to is because of Nolan and Gavin."

"Why do you say that?"

Melaina huffs and rolls her eyes. "Apparently, Gavin swore an oath to my father when he was his apprentice. He feels like he's obligated out of honor to keep me safe. And Nolan, I'm not sure...I think my mother paid him. I keep thinking if I rise the ranks I can pay him to leave me alone."

I glance over to where Nolan sits. His leg seems to have healed, although he's been a bit hesitant to participate in sparring. Gavin sits next to him, quiet and still, thoughtfully watching a pair of soldiers sparring in the clearing. His raven black hair is swept back from his taut face.

"If it's any reassurance, I think you'd do just fine without them," I reply.

She smiles as she sheaths her sword. "Thanks, Katerina."

"You can call me Kat."

After dinner I slip into my room, closing my door behind me, and I freeze. Someone has been in my room. Laying atop my desk is a bundle of rich purple flowers, strikingly colorful in the muddy palette of my room. Their heavy floral scent wafts over me, and I absent-mindedly brush my thumb over a petal.

Alliums.

Only one person knows they're my favorite flowers.

I blush at the thought of Cole stealing some moments away from his busy captain schedule to pick them for me. A giddy smile tightens my cheeks, and I bite into my lip.

A folded piece of paper is tucked into the flower's stems. I pull it out, reading the note:

What you are to me, I may never be able to justify in the significance of words. But you are, always have been and always will be, my beginning and my end. And every breath of my existence in between.

My chest swells and bursts, each careful curve of Cole's handwriting carving his name into the depths of my heart.

Once it's dark enough, and the chatter of the squad around the campfire dies down outside, I slip off to Cole's room, eager to thank him for such a thoughtful gesture before I head out to see Daeja.

Something has me hesitating at his door, but I push past it and tap against the wood. The door swings open, Cole's face softening as he sees me. His ruffled red hair is swept in a handsome disaster across his brow, his shirt uncharacteristically wrinkled. The top few buttons of his tunic are undone, exposing part of his deeply muscled chest. I avert my eyes before I blush. He opens the door wider to let me in and shuts it softly behind me after I enter.

The soft glow of a candle warms his room, scattering exaggerated shadows across the floor. I tear my focus away from the flame, unease bubbling under my skin. Cole leans back against his door, watching me.

He isn't wearing shoes. In fact, he isn't wearing much at all. His belt is missing, along with the many layers of attire he normally wears. The lack of formality slams into my heart, reminding me of the humble, shy boy I met all those years ago.

"Sorry, were you sleeping?" I murmur.

He shakes his head. "No, just got back from patrol. Are you okay?"

He knows me all too well if he's already picking up on how nervous I am. From the fire. I think. I swallow as he ghosts toward me and stops a step away from me. Clenching and unclenching my fists, I try to calm my frenzied anxiety at the thought of a live fire dancing freely behind me.

He tries once more, concern furrowing his eyebrow. "What's wrong?"

When I hesitate to answer, he reaches forward and grabs my hand. My palms are slick when he squeezes his hand around mine.

"I haven't uhh…." My gaze darts over to the candle, and while it's a split second movement, he follows it.

I swallow hard. It sounds so silly saying it out loud. A fucking candle makes me nervous, of all things. Preposterous and pathetic, and yet, he crumbles every wall of defense I have with the soft caress of his calloused fingers.

"Since Hornwood, fire makes me nervous," I finally whisper.

"I can fix that," he says softly. Dropping my hand, he strides over to the candle and blows it out in a single breath.

Within a few blinks, my vision adjusts to the scattered light seeping through the door frame.

He returns to me, stopping a breath's distance away. "When I was young I used to be scared of fire, too. It didn't serve my father well, considering he expected me to assist him in the forge. He taught me fire can destroy, but it can also do other things. It can light our darkness in the night. It can meld things together, making them stronger than ever."

My gaze skips to his mother's metal ring nestled in the crevice of his chest. "Why did you leave me those flowers, Cole?"

His throat bobs. He's still not close enough, his body rigid with tension. "Because I wanted to remind you how much you mean to me."

A stupid smile rips across my face, despite my every effort to hide it.

A spark of heated electricity fills the air between us, and it's only a matter of time before I'm struck. I make the first move, gliding toward him, and weave my fingers into his.

He shakes his head, flinching. "Kat, we shouldn't…"

"We shouldn't…what?" I ask innocently, pulling our intertwined hands to rest on my chest so he can feel how much my heart races for him. How much it calls for him. Desperation overrides my pride for the familiar intimacy we once had. I'm aching for his delicate touch and melting into a puddle of buzzing and burning desire. I long for his hands on me, tangled in my hair, his lips whispering against mine. Gods, the way he'd say my name.

"You don't know what you do to me," he says, nearly breathless.

Grabbing the backs of his arms, I push up onto my toes and kiss him lightly, and his hands rest on my hips. He gasps silently as I pull back from him, our noses brushing, and his eyes still closed. Resting his head forward on mine, he shakes his head wordlessly. I snag his collar, pull him down closer, and kiss him again. Our lips brush gently at first, until we transform into melding and molding. I flick my tongue across his lips, and he opens his mouth to me. We slow into a tantalizing tease and stroke of flesh and heat. Moving closer and closer until we are sharing shaky breaths. Each movement is more jerky, more frantic, more desperate.

Until, that is, he withdraws breathily. "We shouldn't be doing this. We can't, Kat. I—"

"I love you, too," I whisper against his mouth and roll my body into his, sealing his lips closed with mine. If he thinks this is just sex, he's sorely mistaken. And if he thinks I'll desert him again, he's wrong. It's just him and him alone. And I need him. The intimacy, the closeness, and the fire of what we once were.

He staggers backwards, slamming back into his desk, the wood creaking at the sudden force. Withdrawing from my mouth, he flicks his attention to the door, his hands clenched tight around the lip of the desk, and the veins in his arms bulging with tension. He drags his gaze back to me, his breathing ragged. "I can't. I can't keep touching you. Because I won't be able to stop myself."

Sliding my hand up his chest to his face, I brush my thumb over his bottom lip before leaning in and kissing him. I cup the front of his trousers with my other hand, rubbing against his length as I murmur against his mouth, "I don't want you to stop. I need you."

He seizes my wrist, removing my hand from his crotch.

I look up at him through my lashes, my breath still heavy on my lips. "If you don't want this, then just say it."

He grunts. "It's not that I don't..."

"Then what? What is holding you back? I don't need chivalry, Cole, I just need you. Tell me no if you don't want this."

"I...can't," he nearly whines, his grip around my hand trembling. His breath saws in and out of his chest, his hair even more of a mess than when I first came into his room. But there it is—raw desire roaring in the intensity of his eyes, locking me in and begging me to release him. The bands of muscle in his throat are pulled tight, his jaw clenched.

All of it releases in a single breath as he shakes his head. "Gods, I always want you. Every beat of my heart is a profession of what life you instill in me. The day I no longer want you will be the day I'm buried in the ground, far from feelings or thoughts. Because it's you. Always you."

"Then shut up, Cole." I lean forward, pulling my wrist out from his weak grip. "Save the chivalry for some other time, and kiss me."

He snakes his fingers through my hair and curls them into the strands at the base of my skull, leading me into him. His other hand rests on my lower back, pressing my hips into him. For the first time since I've been here, he kisses me. *Actually* kisses me. Slow and deliberate, strong and sure, his mouth claiming mine.

Finally.

As if brick by brick, the walls he's fought so hard to keep fortified come crumbling down. Each movement more assertive.

I can't help it. We've always been electric. But there's a new edge to him—a new him I'm hungry to unravel. My mouth parts, and I tease his bottom lip with my tongue. He groans before opening his own mouth, and our tongues clash in a furious dance, a blistering heat sparking between us. Our movements catch fire, and there's nothing left to do but burn.

His lips slide from my mouth down to my jawline, trailing his kisses lower toward my neck.

Brushing my hand down his shirt, I follow the muscles etched into his abdomen and dip my fingertips into his waistband. I slip my hand underneath his clothes and wrap my fingers around his hard length. He moans into the side of my neck, the sound rumbling against my skin. I smile triumphantly.

He grits out choppily as I stroke him. "You…make it… so…hard—"

"So I can tell."

"—to have any self-control," he finishes with a husky breath.

I lean forward, whispering against his ear, "Then let it go."

The ferality he's been hiding unleashes. A growl rumbles in his chest as he rips me off the ground into his arms, his hands gripping the back of my thighs as my legs wrap around his waist, my hands around his biceps to steady myself. He spins us, placing me on his desk.

We work together to tear my clothes off, and I fling them across the room. Now naked, I become painfully aware of how the months of traveling and lack of food pulls my skin taut over my bones. I shift, self-conscious of how different I must look compared to the last time he saw me.

A soft smile breaks his hardened features as he brushes a thumb over my cheek. "Gods, you're infinitely beautiful."

He dips his head low, taking his time as he delicately presses one kiss at a time along an invisible line drawn down the center of my body. My forehead, nose, lips, chin, the hollow of my throat, and between my breasts. Each touch melting every bit of my self-consciousness until it's gone.

Knotting my hands in his hair, I tug him to my breast.

He grazes his teeth across the tip of my nipple before sucking it into his mouth. My head sinks back, hitting the desk with a moan. He presses a few fingers to my mouth to quiet me.

Switching his mouth to the other breast, his fingers knead the first one. I roll my hips up closer to him, and he unlatches his lips from my breast, his wolf-like eyes meeting mine through dark lowered brows. The most devious smile splits his lips, and he withdraws from me, kneeling down on the ground before me.

Grabbing my legs, he pulls me to the edge of the desk in one swift tug. He snatches my ankles and sweeps my legs up to rest on his shoulders. His glowing, yellow eyes stare up at me from between my naked legs.

"Is this what you want?" he rasps.

"Please...need," is the best I can answer, my chest and core unbearably tight.

His fingers sink into my thighs, pulling them apart. A hot, wet flick skims my slit, and a shot of lightning rockets into my core. My hopelessly hungry body squirms in response for more. He obliges in a series of careful and slow flicks, licks, and sucks. I clap a hand over my mouth to keep myself quiet, squeezing my eyes shut to fight each whimper and moan squeaking out of my mouth. He quickens, chasing after my pleasure. Each movement quicker and firmer, until I'm teetering toward an edge I'm sure to fall off of.

I lunge forward, snatching his hair in my hands as if it'll secure me. "Cole," I whisper.

He digs his tongue deeper inside of me, his nose rubbing circles against my clit. My toes curl, and my thighs instinctively squeeze together, but he keeps them parted with sure hands.

"Cole!" I hiss again, my eyes flashing open.

He doesn't stop, devouring me lick by lick. His eyes lazily flick up to meet mine, that all-knowing glint in his eyes. Gods, his eye contact alone makes me crumble.

My back arches off the desk, a cry slipping from my lips as I shatter. I slap a hand back over my mouth, silencing myself. His fingers dig harder into my inner thighs, pinning me open as he finishes me off.

When I stop trembling from the aftershocks, he plants a kiss on my slit and kisses up my body to my mouth. The ache and need rushes in again on a new tide.

We tear his clothes off and fling them to the floor like an afterthought. The dim light etches every crevice and angle of him in tantalizing shadows. My gaze crawls over every inch of him, down to the deep V cutting between his hips and dipping down to his eager cock.

Fuck, he is incredible. Every month here has chiseled the marble of him into a statuesque build that's meant to be worshiped—meant to be cherished and ravaged all at once.

I stretch onto my back, lifting my hips to him impatiently.

He teases my soaked entrance with the head of his meaty cock, and his heated gaze finds mine. But he pauses, waiting for permission. I grab his throbbing cock with a nod and rub the tip against me, my wetness teasing his jaw slack before I guide him into me.

As he slides into me, filling and stretching me with a slow burn, I moan.

His eyes flutter closed, his head sagging forward and mouth parting in pure ecstasy. "Fuck…oh, fuck."

My breath sticks in my lungs as I wait to adjust to his size, and I open my legs wider for him. Slowly, inch by inch, he moves closer, burying his thick cock inside of me until he's completely filled me.

He leans down and nibbles on the sensitive skin between my ear and neck, his hand resting around my throat as he begins to rock his hips into me. I melt under his touch, a liquid fire flaring inside of me as his heavy, tight breath whispers near my ear. I curl my legs around his waist, inviting him closer.

Gods, I would surrender every part of me to him. Anything to keep us here in this moment. Connected as one.

His rhythm catches fire, thrusting harder into me. My body clenches around his width, plummeting us both into a heap of staggered, heavy breaths. I grapple for him, my eyes rolling to the back of my head as I sink my fingertips into his shoulders. He slams his hips into me hungrily, and the desk creaks underneath us. He freezes and sweeps me up into his arms, carrying me over to his bed.

As soon as we fall into the comfort of his sheets, he's back to rolling his hips into me. His strokes become deeper, his hand still wrapped around my throat, and his forehead leaned into mine. Both of our gazes are focused on where he plunges into me, his cock glistening with my arousal every time he withdraws. My body writhes in response to each plunge, each achingly, deliberate pump is ecstasy. My legs shake, and I'm begging him to move faster to fill that void. As my mouth falls open to moan, he kisses me, capturing each groan and whimper from me. I thread my fingers into his hair, my racing heart threatening to drown out the smacking sound of our sweaty bodies sliding against each other. A heavy, tight tension coils in my core, roaring to an inferno begging for release. I'm lost in the abyss of him. Lost to his scent, his touch, his sounds—his everything.

"Cole..." I warn.

He locks eyes with me, beads of sweat glistening on his forehead. With a nod of his head, he covers my mouth with his hand to silence my whimpers and kisses my forehead.

I dig my fingers into his back, clinging to him with such an effort that he flinches. My body sings in euphoria as I spiral into an earth shattering high, my skin blazing as I shudder and quake underneath him.

My eyes roll into the back of my head as I cry out, and he keeps that pace and depth until my legs stop shaking, and I'm able to catch my breath. His hand slips off my mouth to cradle the side of my face. He kisses me, claiming my mouth as his. Drilling his hips into me over and over, his breathing becomes more strained, movements more choppy, until he curls himself into me and succumbs to his own pleasure. Sinking his face into the crook of my neck, he bites into the pillow behind me to strangle his groan as he fills me with his release. His body weight pins me down with a heavy comfort as he fights to catch his breath.

We lay there: naked, sweating, and panting as he kisses my neck and jaw.

"Gods, I've missed that." I breathe as my heartbeat slows from a gallop.

He smiles in agreement and showers me in tender kisses around my face until he reaches my mouth, and kisses me—long and slow. Intentionally, and deliberately.

"I love you, Katerina Blackwind," he vows between my kisses.

He shifts off me and onto his back, pulling me over to lay on his chest. One of his arms wraps around my shoulders, and the other traces light circles on my side. He presses another kiss to my temple.

As our breath slows, we flutter into sleep.

Connected once more, as we were.

As we always will be.

I stir awake, Cole's warm body cradling me from behind.

His thick arms wrap around me, securing my body to his, each rise and fall of his chest echoed in my own breath.

Inching myself out of his grasp in hesitant movements, I slowly drag the sheets off of me.

"No…not yet. Just a bit longer." Cole's sleep roughened voice brushes my ear. He pulls me in tighter against him, nuzzling his face into the crook of my neck.

I turn my head toward him and whisper, "I have to go. People might ask questions if they notice your sister is sleeping in your room."

He grunts, his eyes still closed. "I'm so close to saying fuck it all."

Still fastened in his grip, I twist toward him, brushing a lock of hair out of his face. "Soon. We'll leave and go to the Dragon Lands where we don't have to pretend anymore."

His eyes flash open at my touch, his pupils dilating in the dim light. Sadness erodes his features into something sullen. "This is all I've ever wanted. You. Here. With me. Every moment away from you is torturous. Promise you'll stay with me. Promise you won't leave without me."

A part of my heart crumbles. Perhaps I hadn't realized the extent of how much our day in the forest all those months ago affected him. How afflicted he was after having gone months thinking I was dead. The way he watched me so intensely, as if I might be gone in the next blink. The pure rage exploding from him the night I was held hostage, when my life was at risk. I could only imagine how dark, traumatizing, and lonely it had been for him.

An abyss of sadness and turmoil rages within his pained eyes as he waits for me to respond.

I lean my forehead into his. "I promise."

He twirls a piece of my hair around his finger a few times before tucking it behind my ear. In that same line of movement, he drags his fingers along my jaw to rest under my chin and tilts my face up to him. It's so intimately him that I melt. His lips brush mine, softly. As if any harder and I may shatter underneath his touch. I melt into a puddle of smiles and kiss him.

"I love you," I whisper.

Those three words light a fire within him.

A smile cracks through his torment, his eyes crinkling at the corners. "Gods, I am pathetically in love with you. Addicted and consumed. Sometimes I feel like I can't think straight." He presses a kiss to the tip of my nose. "There could never be enough of you that I love. Until the sun rises in the south and sets in the north, I will always be yours."

Our fingers intertwine, and he pulls our hands toward his mouth. He pauses, his gaze fixed on my hand.

His thumb caresses my middle finger. "What…is this? You didn't have this before."

Even in the dimness, the dark circle around my finger is stark. The fact that Cole has every inch of my skin memorized has me grinning like a buffoon.

"I've had it since I found Daeja," I answer.

"Weird…" He flicks his gaze back up to me.

Fighting against the urge to stay, now exacerbated by the

way he watches me with a lingering sadness that's hard to miss, I slide out of his bed.

After I leave Cole's room, I slip into the healer's quadrant. The little I do know of herbs and medicine is the power of pennyroyal. A green leafy plant with bursts of pale purple flowers. It's been used for generations as a contraceptive and at heavy dosages, can be lethal.

I pick out a few petals from the stash in the healer's quadrant and pop them into my mouth before I manage to get back to my room without spotting anyone. I change into a nightgown and shuffle into the cold linens of my bed.

As I lay staring at the ceiling, I can't keep my mind off Cole. How the slowness and ease of his fingertips against my skin could calm any storm. The way he never shies away from telling me how he feels. How he is the perfect balance of gentle and unyielding. I've always been addicted to his presence. Every time I'm near him, I feel such a cosmic pull to him. It's easy for me to lose control when I'm around him, as if all my common sense goes out the window. He makes me reckless—not in the sense that I'm careless in a world outside of him. But reckless when it comes to my heart for him. I find myself wanting to bow before him and surrender every bit of myself on a silver platter. I'm only lucky that he feels the same.

Gods, I love him.

TWENTY FIVE

HURT THINGS BITE

Daeja stalks toward me, shadows swarming around her as she approaches. In the dim starlight, it's a menacing view. One that would have caused anyone else to turn tail and run. She stops a few feet away, tilting her head to the side as she sniffs. ***"You… smell…"***

I snort. *"Well if that isn't the most pleasant way I've been greeted—"*

"Different," she finishes.

Maybe because…I blush as I consider how to explain it to her. All day today we shared scattered gazes across the distances separating Cole and I. A flirty grin here. A lingering stare there. A brush of a shoulder and skittering fingertips across my lower back as he passed by. It was tantalizing. And unbearable.

If I struggled pretending to be his sister before…gods, was I struggling now. Every active effort to not stare at him and reminisce of our previous night was a strain.

Daeja's eyes narrow in comprehension. ***"The Red One."***

She closes the gap between us, and I pull her down toward me, leaning my forehead against hers. My eyes fall closed, and my breath deepens. I rub her favorite spot under her chin, and a purr roars to life in her throat. It's so much deeper and rougher…my skin quakes at the thunder of her rumbling. I pull my head back, and her glassy white eyes meet mine. Her breathy exhale blasts my hair back from my face.

"Will the Red One come with us to the Dragon Lands?"

"Yes, he'll come with us. Cole thinks it's about a three to four days' trek from here to the border. Once we have a map, we'll have a better idea of what our path will be."

She staggers back from me with dragged blinks and sneezes. Dragon snot splatters my face, and I wipe it off with my hand.

She ducks her head. ***"Sorry."***

I fling the fluids off my hand onto the ground. If I fall into the lake tonight, it'd save me from a bath. Although, with our recent flight exercises, I have yet to fall into the lake again.

Yet.

My days have mostly consisted of training. Well, more like cleaning and errands with Marge. And practicing sparring in the afternoons. A few days ago, we worked on shield work. Unsurprising to me, I struggled to keep a shield up with one forearm and swing a sword with the other.

A separate day we worked on archery. As I drew the string back, the familiar wobble of my arm clutching the bow resurfaced. Immediately, I remembered the last time I attempted it: with Cole wrapped around me, his breath whispered against my neck after he restored and gifted me my mother's bow. After I released the arrow, I couldn't help but glance over my shoulder at Cole. He was already watching with a grin, as if he was remembering it, too. And just like all my previous attempts, I pathetically missed the target.

Every.

Single.

Time.

Since injuring Nolan's leg, Darian had been moderately tame. Whatever hold Marge had over him was clearly convincing. Then again, if Marge had so much as threatened me, I would have done cartwheels naked through the center of camp if she demanded me to.

Today is the first time we spar with nothing but our fists and feet. I still struggle to convince Archie to use more force against me. I've reminded him time and time again holding back doesn't do me any favors—I have to learn somehow. While every day seems a little bit better, he's still taking it easy on me.

"I challenge." Darian's voice rings out across the clearing as he nears the center where Archie and I concluded sparring. Darian sure loves to make a scene and do whatever he can to piss Cole off.

Cole glares. "No."

Darian laughs. "Quite the protective big brother, aren't you Red?"

"I mean it," Cole growls. A muscle jumps in his jaw, and everyone in the crowd falls silent at the uncharacteristic threat in Cole's voice.

"It's fine, Cole. I can handle it myself," I attempt to diffuse the situation. "Besides, last time we were in this circle I got the win, remember?"

Feigning confidence, I stare Darian down with clenched fists and hope it's enough to convince everyone else I'm not scared. Maybe even myself.

"I love the confidence in this one," Darian goads.

I jut my chin at Cole, irritated he still hasn't moved from his spot. Reluctantly, he drops back to the edge of the audience. Rather than taking a seat like many of the onlookers, he stands next to Archie, the both of them at the ready. Like at any moment they'll spring to my aid.

I center my breath and power my stance, clenching my hands into fists. Darian lazily walks around me, his hands open and relaxed. But the way he stalks circles around me—determination lining his steps—it's as if he's hunting me. A hidden hunger burns in his eyes, like he hasn't eaten in weeks and here I am—an easy catch.

I search for a way to get myself out of this situation. With wolves, you raise your arms above your head to make yourself larger and intimidating. And with bears, you remain calm and slink away, as running will trigger their instincts. I take the latter approach and stare back, stillness rooting my feet to the ground despite every nerve screaming at me to run. My skin crawls every time he slips out of my periphery and slinks behind me, but I refuse to play his game by following his every move.

He wants me to be scared.

He wants me riled up.

As soon as I give into his intimidation is when he'll strike. I just know it.

Hushed questions rise in the crowd, and confused looks are exchanged as Darian circles me again and again.

His pacing stops behind me, out of sight. He hums thoughtfully.

I give in, glaring at him over my shoulder. "Spare me the theatrics and get to the point."

"You have lovely legs…" he whispers under his breath. "But I can think of better places they could be."

I roll my eyes. "Have I given you any reason to think you can be as suggestive as you are with me? Because I assure you, I'm not interested."

He snickers, edging dangerously closer to me. I turn forward to face away from him, picking out nervous stares from the rest of the squad positioned in front of us. Part of me is glad I can't see Cole from this angle—he might beat Darian into the ground if I shoot him even one nervous glance.

Darian's whisper brushes the hair on the back of my head, "Just trying to help. Your stance isn't—"

"I don't *need* your help, asshole—"

One second, I'm standing with my back turned to Darian. The next I'm knocked to the ground. He swept my legs out from under me in a lightning quick move. The muscles in my side groan in pain at the sudden collision with the earth, and I scramble to my hands and knees, shooting a daggered glare at him.

I scramble to my feet and swing a punch toward his face.

He catches my fist in his hand, his fingers wrapping around my knuckles far too easily, trapping me. "You missed, kitten."

I snatch his throat with my other free hand, a frustrated growl escaping me. My fingers are ridiculously thin around his thick neck, but I squeeze as hard as I can.

The tip of his tongue flicks across his lower lip before he smiles deviously. "Harder."

"What?" I hiss, flinching in bewilderment.

"I said, *harder.*"

Digging my nails into his skin and gritting my teeth, I sink my fingers into his throat as hard as I can.

He gazes down at me, a sneer pulling at his expression. "Really? That's it? Pathetic. You'll never last more than a minute."

Did I have anger issues? Before this moment, I would have said no. But something about Darian unlocks a side of me I've never experienced. Never knew existed. A wild, unfettered temper I'm finding hard to comprehend. "I hate you," I seethe.

He snorts, clearly unbothered. "Get in line, sweetheart. The line starts behind me."

With wicked speed, he seizes the wrist of my hand wrapped around his neck and twists me into submission. I fold down, pain roaring to life in my wrist, and terror steals my breath that he might break me. But instead, he spins me to face away from him. He rips me into him, pinning my back against his chest, and restraining me with his arms.

I squirm, trying to wriggle free from his hold. When that proves futile, I throw my head back and connect it with his jaw, a new flare of pain rippling in my skull. His grip on me falters, but he hooks a leg in between mine and tears me down to the ground. Before I can roll away, he pins me onto my back. He traps my hands above my head, and my injured wrist screams under his hard grip. His hips straddle my own—it's even more intimate than the last time we fought.

I bite my tongue to keep myself from blushing, raking my heated gaze across his barbarously smug face. Attempting to dislodge him, I buck my hips up, and he laughs.

"Must be over-compensating," I grit out as I wriggle and strain underneath him.

"Is this you asking to test that theory? Because," he leans down, his smooth, shaved cheek gliding against mine as he whispers into my ear, "I would be happy to oblige you."

"Let me go," I demand.

"Only if you beg me."

"*Fuck* you," I spit.

"Mmm, I love that filthy little mouth of yours," he says with a wink.

I exert all my strength and energy into rolling him to the side, but he braces against me. I'm trapped, and each of my attempts to escape is unsuccessful. Everyone stares, their attention as heavy as if it were bricks weighing me down. Embarrassment heats my cheeks, and with that triumphant grin of his, there's no doubt he recognizes it.

Asshole.

"We're done here," I hiss.

He finally releases my wrists and gets off of me. As soon as I'm on my feet, I stalk off, far too mortified to try my hand at sparring again and avoiding eye contact with every person I pass.

"Hey!" Archie calls after me. "Kat! Wait. Where are you going? Are you okay?"

"Yep. Fine. Going to get some water, I left my flask in my room." I can't even look in his direction, I'm fuming and flustered.

"You can have some of mine? I'm happy to share?" he offers, still following me.

I toss an apologetic glance over my shoulder at him. "Thank you, but I'll catch you at dinner."

Once I'm in the privacy of my four walls, I push my sleeve back and dare a peek at my wrist. My hand trembles with the surging ache, and I grip my forearm, hoping the pressure will make the pain stop. Rotating my wrist slightly, I wince.

I slip off to the healer's quadrant, avoiding the main pathways in hopes of not running into anyone. Gods forbid Darian himself. But the camp is quiet—everyone must still be sparring. As I walk into the healer's quadrant, Marge is facing away from me and shifting things around on the counter.

She doesn't even glance in my direction. "One of the first things I learned as an apprentice is hurt things bite."

"I'm not hurt," I retort, trying to ignore the throb in my wrist.

"I wasn't referring to *you*." She finally turns to me and tosses me a folded bandage.

I catch the dressing with a terse, awkward nod and wrap it around my wrist tightly. I'm not quite sure what to say, so I ask the first thing that comes to my mind. "What were you talking about when you told Darian you'd cut him off?"

She stops whatever she's been organizing and stares at the wall for a long, considering moment before turning her attention to me. "I don't think that's any of your business."

I nod, regretting having asked it and turn to walk out.

"You two have more similarities than you think," she says.

I pause a few steps from the door. "What are you talking about?"

"I know you and Cole lost your mother. So did he."

I glance at her over my shoulder. "And how would you know that?"

"I've known Darian since he was a boy. He wasn't always like who he is today. We either outgrow our grief, or our grief outgrows us."

I turn to face her fully. "Doesn't give him the right to be an asshole to everyone."

She shrugs. "You're not wrong. His sister was always my favorite, anyhow."

"Was? How did she die?"

"Well, she didn't really die," Marge murmurs. She grabs a vial in the cabinet and brings it to me.

I swallow its contents without question. The liquid numbs my throat as it slides down, and a tingle sings in my veins. The pain in my wrist dissipates, and she directs me to go clean the empty vial.

"Then why did you say *was?*" I call over my shoulder as I scrub the glass vial.

Her voice dips with sadness. "She's in a coma. Has been for over ten years. I'm not quite sure what she would be like now..."

"Oh..." I respond awkwardly. "I'm sorry to hear that—"

The door bursts open, and we both whip toward the sound.

Gavin pops his head in, his black hair falling into his eyes. "Marge, Katerina. Blackfell has been breached by rebels. We're called for an emergency meeting near the outlook tower."

TWENTY SIX

NIGHT WHISTLING

I fetch Marge's staff and hand it to her. We walk out together and meet the rest of the squad gathered near the outlook tower. The memory of the two men executed pricks an uneasiness in my chest. I stare at the base of the tower, terrified if I gaze up at the top I won't be able to stop replaying the vision of the men dropping to their demise. Whispers shuffle around us until Cole clears his throat at the top platform.

Everyone falls silent.

"Blackfell has been breached, and there seems to be a stalemate between the rebels and the town. We need to get there quickly, before the rebels make a move. I'm assembling two groups in the event this is a trap. Groups will be split from the center of camp: north and south. Carlisle will lead the northern half that'll stay here to guard the camp. Southern half comes with me, and we will head to Blackfell to reclaim the town. Grab your weapons, and prepare yourselves for a fight. We will leave at sundown and surprise them in the cover of darkness."

Which means I'll stay here, as part of the northern group. And Cole will go to Blackfell.

My heart sinks into the pits of my stomach at the thought of being separated from him. Marge pats my shoulder and leaves the throng. The squad's nervous anticipation bubbles around me as people scurry off into opposite directions. Cole walks toward me, the people splitting off and breaking to let him through. As if he's a rock and the crowd is a river forced around his wake.

He rests a hand on my shoulder and whispers, "I don't want to be separated from you, but I have to ask you to stay here."

I shake my head profusely. "No. I'm going with you."

"It's too dangerous."

"It would be just as dangerous here as it would be with you, if it really is a trap."

He grunts. "Yes, but here you have Da—" he catches himself before he says Daeja's name.

"Then she can come with us," I plead. "Please. Don't do this."

"If she's seen, we're all dead."

I grab his arm and tug him toward my room. The door shuts out the noise behind us and silence falls between us.

A muscle flickers in his jaw. "Believe me, this is just as hard on me as it is you. But it's in your best interest."

"Cole." I dare a touch of my fingers on his chest. "We're

supposed to stay together, remember? You asked me to stay. With you."

He sighs, gaze lowered and avoiding.

I try again, pulling his chin to look me in the eye. "I promised."

His voice drops to a whisper, "You did..."

A war rages within his eyes, his eyebrows knit together. He blows out a breath. "Sometimes I wonder if you know how much power you have over me. And it's instances like this where I realize, you do know...bring whatever medicinal supplies you can. Marge can stay here, and you can take her place with us. You're to stay back from the battle in the outskirts of Blackfell. And if there's the slightest threat, I want you to run. You don't look back. You don't stop to think of me. You run. If something happens to me, I want you to take her to the Dragon Lands."

"I—" my voice catches at the thought of going without him. Of leaving him and living in a world without him. No. I start to shake my head.

"Kat, promise me," he urges, gripping my hand in his.

"I'll fly," I reassure.

"Huh?"

"I won't run, I'll fly. Daeja and I have been practicing."

He blinks. "Practicing...flying?"

"Well. We've only done it a few times. But I can do it."

A knock sounds at the door, and Carlisle calls from the other side. "Captain, a word?"

"One moment, Carlisle!" Cole shouts as he unclasps the

necklace around his neck and places it in my palm. The metal of his mother's ring is cold against my hot skin.

My breath hitches as he closes my fingers over the ring. He leans his forehead into mine, his hand still holding my fingers closed over his family heirloom.

"I love you," he promises in a hushed whisper. With his other hand, he draws me into his soft lips. But he pulls away—far too quickly—and ends with a kiss on my forehead.

He slips out of my door and disappears off into the night.

I clasp Cole's necklace around my neck, strap my dagger into my thigh sheath, and sheathe my sword. Sucking in a deep breath, I ignore the buzzing in my veins and head toward the healer's quadrant.

"Daeja? We're going to Blackfell. There's been a breach by rebels. I'll travel there with the rest of the squad and meet you on the outskirts of town near the forest."

"I'll head there now—"

"No. Wait until the sun sets. And stay behind us so you aren't seen."

I swing open the door to the healer's quadrant and find Marge collecting bottles. She turns to me, raising an eyebrow.

"You're staying here, and I'm taking your place at Blackfell," I explain.

"Says who?"

"The captain."

She blinks at me slowly, then tilts her head to a fully stuffed bag. "There's bandages, splints, needles, and thread in there. A few vials for pain. Use them sparingly."

I can't imagine her having to make the trek there and how vulnerable she'd be near a battle. It gives me a sliver of relief that I'm going in her place. But my hands tremble under the heavy responsibility. I've never had to stitch a wound, nor apply a tourniquet on my own. As I turn for the door with the bag on my back, I lock eyes with Marge.

"Thank you for saving me, all those weeks ago," she murmurs.

"No…problem. Are you saying this because you think I'm going to die?"

She pats my shoulder. "You'll be just fine."

It does nothing to quell my uneasiness. But I leave the room before I think about it too much. I head to the center of camp where a group of people thickens as more join. My shoulder brushes Archie's as I come to stand next to him. He flashes a nervous smile, his hand busy twirling a dagger.

"What's taking Darian so damn long? Someone fetch him," Carlisle calls.

Archie raises his hand to volunteer, and I smack it down.

But Carlisle sees the motion. "Archie?"

"No, I'll get him," I interject. I speed toward Darian's room, not leaving a moment for Archie to argue. I slam a fist into Darian's door. When he doesn't answer, I push the door open and enter hesitantly.

Darian's shirtless, pulling his pants up his thighs and tightening them at the waist. When he turns fully toward me, I get an unobstructed view of his chiseled olive-toned chest. A deep V lines his hips and lower abdomen. Where Cole is thick and powerful muscle, Darian is smoothly carved elegance. The muscles in his arms flex and work as he slowly buttons up his pants.

My breath catches, and I shield my eyes with the back of my hand.

He snickers. "Have you never seen a man before?"

I fumble for a shirt draped over the back of a chair, throwing it at him blindly. He cackles at my unmistakable nervousness.

"Can you hurry up? You're the only one missing from the group," I grumble.

"They can wait. They have to wait for me."

"You are such a pompous piece of—"

"I know."

I whip a glare at him, thankful his torso is now covered by the shirt I threw him. He has yet to button up the front of it, though. The dark fabric dips low between his chest and abdomen.

I avert my eyes again, my gaze sweeping around his room. A cluttered mess of sheaths, belts, and clothes lay in a heap on the floor near his bedpost. Tangled sheets and blankets wrestle on his bed. A black coat drapes over the chair pulled out from his desk, waiting for someone to trip over it. Piles of papers are scattered around his desk. One piece of parchment snags my attention.

Drawn on a large curling paper, pinned down by books at the corners, is the unmistakable outline of Dragon's Back Ridge.

A map.

Beyond the northern part of Dragon's Back Ridge is a hint

of the Dragon Lands, covered by other papers. I'm kicking myself for not noticing it the first time I came in here.

"We're going to be…late," I warn, though partly distracted by the map on his desk.

Darian stalks toward me, grabbing two swords leaning against his desk. "We? Aren't you supposed to be staying here? You know, northern part of camp and all."

"In that instance, shouldn't you also be staying?"

He shrugs. "They need me."

"And they also need me," I counter.

He snorts as he sheathes his swords, the slither of metal splitting the air between us. "Big Red really will do anything to keep his eyes on little sister, huh? If he knew better, he would have you stay here."

"It was my decision," I hiss, my fists clenching with his implied insult at Cole.

He points at the door and tucks a flask into his side. "Let's see what you've got then."

The sun set maybe an hour ago, and an eerie stillness hangs around the town of Blackfell. Last time I was here, it was raining.

Luckily, only a few clouds scatter across the night sky. The moonlight ebbs in and out of the thin puffs of black.

Our squad is huddled and crouched near the outskirts of Blackfell as orders are whispered among us. The night chill seeps into my skin as the wind picks up, and I try to clench my hands still. But they tremble as I shiver, and my teeth clatter in response.

A weighted warmth cloaks my shoulders. I glance to my right as Darian retreats from draping his jacket over me.

"Your chattering is annoying as fuck, and I'm trying to focus," he grouses.

"Or are you just trying to piss Cole off?" I counter.

He snickers and turns his attention back to Cole who's commanding plans and orders with the rest of the group. Holy gods, Cole will lose his godsdamned mind if he sees Darian's jacket on me.

I rip the jacket off as I whisper, "You are always on your worst behavior."

"For someone who hates my behavior, you have yet to tell me to stop."

"Maybe it's because I know you won't." I offer the jacket back to him.

He muffles a laugh, his eyes still fixed on Cole. "Well would you look at that. Look who knows now. Maybe I am starting to rub off on you."

"I wouldn't say rubbing off on me. You just push my buttons," I grumble, shaking his jacket to get his attention.

"I'd rather undo them."

I swat the jacket at Darian, and he ducks with a smirk.

Cole pauses announcing the plans to the group, glaring at Darian with a whistle. "Something you need to say?"

Darian shakes his head nonchalantly, a sly grin still on his lips.

Slinking away from Darian, I leave his jacket on the ground and shiver again as the wind whips at my skin. I slide in next to Archie, who is also forcing himself not to tremble.

"Are you okay?" I mutter, leaning my shoulder into his.

His wide eyes meet mine with a gulp. "Whistling at night is bad."

My mind cuts to the time we spent in my room drinking, speaking of our greatest fears. Owls, Aunt Becky, and whistling at night. And Cole just whistled to get Darian's attention.

I steady a hand on Archie's arm. "We're going to be okay."

He nods, even though his wide eyes still stare at Blackfell in the distance. "How do you do it?"

"How do I do what?"

"How are you not scared?"

"I am…I just…pretend I'm not? Feign confidence? Sometimes it'll force you to be brave."

He pulls in a shaky inhale. The rest of his body is rigid for a long while before his gaze narrows in determination.

With Cole's silent command, Archie jumps to his feet, pointing his sword at Blackfell with a hearty shout, "Let's fucking get 'em!"

He charges toward Blackfell, arms pumping and feet

skimming the ground. I catch the bewildered gaze of Melaina for a moment before she launches to her feet and runs toward Blackfell too, Gavin and Nolan right behind her. The rest of the squad roars to life and follows Archie, who isn't quite fast enough to keep the lead on them for long.

Cole's mother's necklace is hot against my skin as I watch his flame-red hair disappear into the distance with the rest of the squad. What little is left of my heart slams fearfully in my chest.

Each second ticking by where Cole isn't in my direct line of vision, challenges his command for me to stay here on the outskirts. What if they needed me? What if I could help them?

Well…if Cole is pissed at me for not following his orders, I'll take it.

Because if he's pissed at me—it means he's still alive.

TWENTY SEVEN

TWO LEGS AND WAR

"Daeja?"

"I'm here."

We move to each other, following our magnetic pull through the shadowed forest. My jaw is unbearably tight with unbound anxiety, and I'm having a hard time taking my eyes off Blackfell, despite being unable to see any of our squad now.

A sliver of my tension vanishes once I graze my fingertips against Daeja's nose. *"I know I said I would wait here with you… but I have to get closer in case they need me."*

She growls, the sound vibrating under my touch. **"Then I'm going with you."**

"You can't. If someone sees you, we're both dead." I tap two fingers against the side of her neck, but nothing happens. *"See?*

If you were able to vanish again, we wouldn't have to worry about someone seeing you. You're far too big to hide now."

"You can't keep telling me to stay back, meanwhile you run head first into these dangers. I have to protect you."

"No, I have to protect you." I jab a finger into the tip of her nose.

She scoffs and whips her tail at me. **"I don't need protecting."**

I duck, barely missing her swing. *"Just because you're bigger now, Daeja, doesn't mean you can take care of yourself."*

"Oh? You're just as defenseless, if not more, than I am."

"I'm not arguing with you. You stay here, and if I'm not back in an hour, you leave for the Dragon Lands on your own."

She roars, and I have to shut her maw with my hands. I scan our surroundings over my shoulder, even though I know the sound of the battle is likely loud enough to drown her out, and I'm the only one out here.

"Dammit, Daeja! Be logical for a second, there's no way I can defend you and me."

"You're right. You can hardly defend yourself. We are in this—together."

This must be what it's like for Cole. My gaze narrows, and she matches my expression.

I sigh, seeing no way out of it. *"Fine. But you stay behind me, and if I tell you to go, you go."*

"Fine."

Though deep down, something tells me she won't.

The distant roar of the battle grows louder as we slink closer to town. We edge around the southern perimeter, weaving in and out of buildings at an achingly slow pace. A thick layer of sweat accumulates between Marge's bag and my back.

I peek from around the corner of a building, through an alley dumping into the center square of Blackfell. In the distance, a throng of people ebb and flow in a dark sea of war. But what catches my attention is the several groups of people sitting eerily still between me and the battle. I swallow hard—one of them writhes on the ground.

I hold out a hand to Daeja. *"Stay."*

Inching closer, I press my side to the alley wall, meshing my silhouette into the shadows. As I get near the end of the alley, I realize the man on the ground wriggling has his mouth gagged, his hands and feet tied. He thrashes to free himself, and someone appears dressed in black, their back to me. The shadowy figure kicks the hostage until he stills, the rest of the hostages watching with wide eyes. Their captor drops into a crouch and wraps the rope tighter around the motionless hostage's arms and legs.

A rebel.

"They're tied up, we have to free them."

But everyone else is preoccupied with keeping the fighting rebels at bay. The lone rebel dressed in black paces by the group of tied and gagged civilians, watching them intently.

I creep closer. *"Daeja, I have a plan."*

"Psstt," I call.

The rebel whips toward me. I wave, trying to snag his

attention to the alleyway. His gaze narrows in on me, and he charges. Turning, I race back down the alley toward Daeja hidden around a corner, the man's heavy footsteps echoing behind me like thunder. I can't pump my arms and legs fast enough. He catches up to me within a few strides and snatches the back of my neck and hair, ripping me toward him.

Daeja slinks out from the hidden corner and bolts forward, reaching behind me, she snaps the man's head into her jaws. His grasp disappears from me as she rips his head free from his body and tosses it far off into the shadowed alley. His body slumps to his knees before collapsing forward. My heart races as I pat my neck and chest. I scan the man's decapitated body, cringing at the mess of fluids and flesh strewn about the ground. Clenched in his hand is the chain of Cole's necklace. I pry his rigid fingers open with trembling hands.

The clasp of the necklace is broken, so I pocket the chain and suck in a shaky breath as I slide the metal ring down my finger. I had always imagined wearing it—but never like this. Never in a reality where Cole could die at any second. A chill and calmness spreads through me as if it were ice singing in my veins. It floods me until my body buzzes with energy.

"He'll be okay," Daeja whispers in my mind.

I glance at her with a hesitant smile, and I am grateful for her grounding and comforting influence. Perhaps I would never be as skillful at daggers like Archie. Strong in hand-to-hand combat like Cole. Or the best swordsman like Darian.

But I have a fucking dragon. And that makes me feel powerful. It makes me feel a little bit...

Unstoppable.

I race back down the alley toward the group of hostages, unsheathing my dagger from my thigh and dropping to my knees near the one that was kicked still by the rebel. I scan the square around us, nervous another rebel may emerge from the shadows. *"Daeja, watch my back. Let me know if someone is coming."*

"Got it."

Sawing my dagger through the rope binding the man's wrists, I fling the cords to the side as the man's eyes blink open.

I pull the gag from his mouth. "Are you alright?"

He nods, eyes still wild with fear. "Yes. Yes, I think so."

"Is anyone else in your group hurt?" I ask.

He shakes his head.

I hand him my sword. "All of you need to go south to the forest. Be quick. Take this and defend yourselves should someone follow you. Wait in the forest for me, I won't be far behind."

I work quickly, freeing one hostage at a time with my dagger. Each one I release slips away from the town square. Freeing the last civilian, I glance over to the alley where Daeja lies in wait, reflections glimmering in her pupils as she surveys the surroundings.

I stand, taking a few steps into her direction when a scream pierces through the chaos, chilling my blood.

I follow the sound and find Archie sinking against the wall of a stone building, his mouth open wide in a cry and hand cradling his arm. A rebel creeps closer to Archie, wielding an axe dripping dark red…

Blood.

The rebel raises his arm to swing again, and I charge. I throw my dagger without a second thought. It flies across the distance but doesn't go as far as I hoped. The blade sinks into the rebel's heel, and he shrieks, swiveling toward me. It's enough of a distraction, though, and Archie catches my gaze.

"Go!" I mouth.

Archie scrambles off, disappearing into the throng of people as the rebel races toward me. I pat my side for my weapon, panic flooding my veins as I recall giving my sword to the hostage. And I just flung my dagger, now far out of my reach.

I'm fucked.

I turn, eyeing the distance between Daeja and I. Her roar splits the air, and she barrels down the alley toward me. But it won't matter—the rebel will get to me first.

The rebel closes the distance between us, and I backpedal, clenching my fists and readying myself for whatever fight I can possibly muster. In slow-motion, he raises his axe, the metal gleaming and swings it down toward me.

Cole slams into the rebel from the side with a mighty roar, ripping him into the ground. In the blink of an eye, Cole rears up, jumping to his feet while the rebel struggles to stand.

I watch in horror as something as quick as a burst of lightning shifts in Cole. A vicious ferality unlocks in him as he thrusts his sword into the man's chest. The rebel falls back down to the ground with a gurgling cry, and Cole rips his blade free. A shaking rage tightens Cole's features, his eyes entirely focused on the rebel as he swings his sword down. Again, and again. The rebel lies motionless as Cole hacks repeatedly into his flesh. A wicked shiver races down my spine.

"Stop," I whisper, the words soft on my lips as the war rages around me. But only I hear it.

The man's blood splatters Cole with each strike, the corpse shuddering with each contact. But Cole doesn't cease—crazed by his own wrath.

"Cole, stop!" I throw my hand out as if to stop him, but he doesn't react. A loud '*whoosh*' and roar flares to life in the background as noise swims back to me. I lunge at Cole as he swings down again, catching his forearm in my hand and stopping him. My hand shakes at the effort of bracing against his strength.

He whips to me, his face stained red with blood. His lips are pulled back into a snarl, his teeth splattered with crimson. And his eyes…they roar with an inferno that makes me shrink back.

It takes a few moments for him to see through the haze of his anger—to see me. I watch it recede, as a fog might fade when the sun comes out. His sword falls to the ground with a clatter, his breath racing as he looks down at his hands coated with blood. They begin to tremble.

A deep, guttural horn blows into the night, cutting above the rest of the uproar. I stiffen, shooting a glance back over to Daeja whose dark figure flashes and flickers toward us. Her silhouette winking in and out of vision, as if she were a shadowed mirage.

Now wasn't the time to be practicing her vanishing skills.

"The Carnyx...Daeja, get back to the forest! Someone's spotted you!"

"Go!" Cole says and pushes me. His blood-soaked hand leaves a red print on my shoulder. "Take her, and get out of here, Kat!"

Before I can ponder it, I race back to the alley. *"Where are you? We need to go!"*

Daeja's silhouette shimmers at the end of the corridor, and I sprint toward her. She nabs the back of my shirt in her mouth, lifts me off the ground, and bursts into a run. I bite down a shout of surprise. My feet dangle below me, and my hands grip at my shirt clenched in her jagged teeth. She leaps onto the city wall and launches into the air, her wings flapping and steering us clear of the pathways to Blackfell.

"You couldn't wait for me to get on your back first!"

"You said we needed to go. I didn't think we had the time."

She flares her wings as we approach the thick of the forest, flying low, down near the tops of the trees. Flapping hard and slow to ease her descent, we land, and she sets me down carefully.

I adjust my shirt, tucking it back into my pants. *"Did anyone see you?"*

"No. The only two legger I saw was the one whose head I removed. The others you freed went a different pathway."

I gaze up at her. *"You...you did it. I saw you vanish a few times."*

"I did?"

Nodding, I scan the skies, but it's blocked out by trees stretching above us. My nerves knot in my stomach at all the reasons why someone might have sounded the Carnyx. The first reason being if Daeja was spotted.

"Stay here. I need to check and see if the hostages made it out okay."

I'm relieved she doesn't argue.

As I run toward the open plains of the pathway to Blackfell, I make out a group of people huddled against large boulders. I recognize the man I handed my sword to, along with all the others I freed.

"You all made it out okay?" I manage through tired breaths.

"Yes, thanks to you." He hands me back my sword. "We are so grateful for the King's support."

I absent-mindedly trace my thumb over the intertwined circles etched into the hilt.

Before I can respond, an elderly woman hisses in the back of the group. "Those rebels brought dragons."

When I turn to Blackfell, my heart drops. A flare of red branches up into the sky, followed by thick, dark smoke choking out the light from the moon.

"Who sounded the horn?" I ask. "How do we know it was dragons?"

"Everyone knows the Carnyx is saved only for dragon sightings. And look at that fire. There's no way that could have come from a few torches. It has to be dragonfire," the woman answers.

"Did you use fire?"

"No?"

No dark figures dip between the clouds. Could someone have seen Daeja in the fleeting moments she might have been visible?

A dark mass of people head toward us from Blackfell. I take a few steps back, my hand gripping my sword. Others behind me gasp and point with shrill cries. As I ready myself to command the people behind me to run, every fear dissipates when I catch a glimmer of flame-red hair.

My hand releases my sword to the ground. "It's okay, that's our side."

I don't try to fight the urge to race to Cole—I fly to him, nearly tackling him to the ground. Burying my head into his chest, I silently thank the stars, gods, and everything sacred he's alive. The scent of smoke, blood, and metal washes over me. Sweat mixed with fire.

He hugs me back.

Relief floods my soul, and I pull back to face him, almost forgetting I can't kiss him. The temptation dies quickly at how close I am to his face. Blood splatters his skin, his red hair matted with it. My stomach flips, and we take a step back from each other.

Cole stiffens as he notices the group of civilians behind me.

"It's okay. They were the hostages," I confirm.

"How did they get here?" Cole asks.

The man I loaned my sword to answers, "She saved us."

After I confirm with a nod, Cole switches his attention to

counting through the remaining squad around us. Darian, Melaina, Nolan, Gavin…he freezes. Terror in his eyes.

"Darian, where's Archie?"

TWENTY EIGHT

FEIGN CONFIDENCE

Darian rolls his eyes, a cut above his brow bleeding into the crease of his eyelid and snaking down his cheekbone and jaw. "How should I know?"

"I asked you to look out for him?" Cole growls, his fists clenching.

"I might have been a little preoccupied trying to save Melaina's ass," Darian spits back and jerks his thumb at Melaina.

She glares back at him with a grumble. "I didn't need your help."

Cole shoves past Darian, hard enough for Darian to take a few steps back to balance himself.

"Where are you going?" I call out, following him as he strides away from the group.

"To get Archie. I'm not leaving him behind."

I lunge after him, and he rips his arm from my grasp.

He spins a stern look on me. "I command you to stay."

He breaks into a sprint toward the roaring flames of Blackfell.

My heart sputters as his figure grows smaller, and he disappears. My feet are stuck to the ground, not because he commanded me to stay but because of my fear of the flames, the sweltering heat, and the crackle of burning wood resembling snapping necks.

Swallowing hard, I try to force myself to go after Cole—to go after Archie. To try and save the one who saved me all those weeks ago. There's no doubt in my mind if our scenarios were switched, Archie wouldn't hesitate for a second. But these fucking legs won't move, and my head won't stop screaming at me to stay.

I shift my focus to Darian. "Go after him."

He scoffs. "What makes you think I owe you anything?"

"If it were your sister, you'd go."

He flinches as if I've slapped him. It unlocks something in him, a mixture of emotion I can't quite place. With a hint of a snarl, he turns and runs after Cole.

"Daeja?" I call out internally.

"I'm still here."

I'm tempted to look over my shoulder at the pines behind us for her, but I don't. *"If they don't come back soon…"* A lump forms in my throat at the thought of losing Cole and Archie.

"I understand," she whispers back.

The squad and freed civilians around me are staring. Multiple conversations break out around behind me.

"We should go after them," Melaina says, unsheathing her sword and readying herself to run back.

"Doing so would be suicide," Nolan argues.

The frenzied chatter erupts, and I lose track of who is saying what.

"Cole went out."

"Cole is crazy."

"Why did Darian go with him?"

"Did Darian actually save you?"

"Yes."

"Let's take half of us and go after them, they'll need back up."

"Or we should wait here. If they don't come back quickly, we should check the outpost in case it's a trap."

"Then if it is a trap, we're already dead."

I run. Away from the chatter to Blackfell. I don't let my hesitations or fears lock me down as I push through each stride. Feigning confidence. Thinking of Archie—of daggers and soup ladles.

"I'll be right behind you."

"No. Stay until I call you."

She grumbles, and a shadow flickers through the trees beside me, following me. *Damn stubborn dragon.*

"I heard that."

The fire grows larger and larger as I get closer to the city. I avert my attention down to my feet, narrowing my focus to putting one foot in front of the other. Sweat collects on my brow, my neck, my back, my palms as I speed toward Blackfell.

I stop at the entrance of the town—a wall of fire engulfs the buildings, the roofs, the sky. I sink onto my knees. There's no way they are getting out of this. The way the flames dance, I can see the little girl's face again. Her small eyes rounded in terror. The rest of her family's faces flash in my memory, along with my mother and brother. All of their screams linger at the edge of my consciousness. I clench my shaking hands around my ears as they grow louder and closer, transforming from screams into a chant.

Fire incarnate. Flame in flesh. Blood of power.
Fire incarnate. Flame in flesh. Blood of power.
Fire incarnate. Flame in flesh. Blood of power.

Fixating on the flames, I wait for them to morph from red to blue, as they always do in my nightmares. I drop my hands from my ears, slowly succumbing to the madness of the chanted words. I'm swept into an out of body experience. Hypnotized, and against my own volition, I reach my hand out toward the fire. Cole's ring on my finger is the only confirmation it's actually my hand. My fingertips brush the edge of the wicked flame when a shadowy silhouette emerges from behind the wall of fire. The figures morph until I recognize the sway of steps, and the angled set of broad shoulders.

I back away, and Cole bursts through the fire, cradling Archie, both of them doused in blood. Darian steps through the flames right behind him, his sword drawn as he surveys the outskirts of Blackfell.

"Is he okay?" I breathe, rising to my feet.

Archie slowly blinks open his eyes and peers up at Cole, his voice raspy. "Y-you….you came back for me?"

Cole smiles sweetly and nods. "Of course, I did. I'd never leave you behind. You're the best soldier we have."

Darian's shoulder clips the edge of mine as he passes the three of us.

Maybe it was a cheap shot to mention his sister…but I breathe a sigh of relief it worked. We return to the squad and rescued civilians, and I dress Archie's injured arm, wrapping it tight and giving him a vial for the pain. I assess the rest of the squad and civilians. We've lost a handful of men and women in battle. Others that have survived require splints and gauze.

After I've tended to who I can, Cole splits us into three groups. Darian's to lead the front of the pack. Archie and I will be in the center group with the civilians and others who are wounded. And Cole will fall to the back group with Melaina, Gavin, and Nolan. I instruct Daeja to wait in the forest until we've gone far enough ahead for her to follow us back to camp.

Archie insists he can hobble back to the outpost on his own but leans against me for support. I loop my arm around his waist to brace him, catching him every time he stumbles.

"Did you injure your leg?" I pause and crouch to search him for any stab wounds or blood I might have missed earlier.

He winces as I brush his thigh. "I was trapped under a column. I feel more dizzy than anything."

"It's probably from the blood loss. Are you sure you'll be okay to walk back the whole way?"

His voice cracks. "Yeah, totally fine."

I narrow my eyes at him but don't push him. "You were trapped under a column?"

"Yeah, the fire grew so fast. I've never seen anything like it. The buildings started to collapse, and as I tried to escape, part of a column fell on me."

I stand. "Did you see any dragons?"

"No. Did you? I saw you were there—saw you throw that dagger...I'm pretty sure you saved my life. Where did you disappear off to? I never saw you again."

"I helped the rest of the civilians get out." It's not a complete lie but still uncomfortable to present to Archie nonetheless.

It's a long walk back to camp at our pace, and by the midway point, we pause to let Archie catch his breath. Cole offers to carry him the rest of the way, but Archie declines—the stubborn thing. Cole directs Darian to switch spots with me, but I refuse to leave Archie alone with Darian. Instead, Archie wraps his arms around both mine and Darian's neck for support. Darian, surprisingly, hadn't said a single thing the entire way back to camp. As soon as we get Archie down into a bed in the healer's quadrant, Darian departs without a word. A twinge of regret surfaces inside of me for what I said to him about his sister. My thoughts flicker over to my brother for a moment, before I block it all out.

Several beds around us have injured patients, blood smearing their skin and clothing, limbs and torsos wrapped in linens. The heavy scent of alcohol stings my nose—reminding me of Marge's explanation as to why we have so many bottles of liquor in the healer's quadrant. Not only does it help with pain relief, but it also disinfects wounds.

Marge finishes wrapping a woman's ankle before shuffling over to Archie and me. "Are there any others?"

I tuck my hair back behind my ear. "I'm not sure. We might be the last. I bandaged and wrapped who I could before we returned."

Together, Marge and I clean the gash on Archie's arm. Marge then begins to stitch up the wound. He throws his head back, wriggling through the pain.

"Boy, if you don't hold still I won't be able to stitch this properly," Marge warns.

"Does that mean it'll leave a cool scar?" Archie asks through gritted teeth.

"Means you might lose your whole arm if you don't sit still," she hisses.

He stiffens, squeezing his eyes shut and quiets. I muffle a laugh, knowing it was a slight over-exaggeration by Marge. The door creaks open, and in walks Melaina cradling an arm.

Her brown eyes flick up to meet mine as she breathes. "Hi…"

I help her settle into the bed next to Archie as Marge finishes stitching his wound closed.

Out of my periphery, Archie shifts to sit up a little straighter. He tosses a nonchalant glance our way. "Melaina, right?"

She nods with a slight smile. "Yes."

"Archie Stormbane." There's a certainty to his voice I've yet to witness—as if he's mustering every ounce of control into those two words. Feigning confidence.

Marge finishes stitching Archie's arm and hobbles over to Melaina. "How can we help you, Melaina?"

Melaina flinches, dumbfounded. "I…umm, seem to have done something to my arm. I was hoping someone could take a look."

With Marge's instruction, I sit next to Archie to dress his newly-stitched wound.

Marge twists and turns Melaina's arm, her eyes narrowing with each flicker of movement. "Are you sure this hurts? I don't see any cuts, bruises, or lacerations. And you don't seem to flinch any which way I move it."

A faint blush creeps onto Melaina's cheeks, and she flinches. "I—I guess it kind of hurts like that."

But her delayed reaction makes me turn away toward Archie to hide a smile. She's faking her injury, for whatever reason. My eyes connect with Archie's, and I have a sneaking suspicion I might know why.

Marge catches on too, as she rakes Melaina with a head-to-toe glare. "Well, you seem fine to me. Come back if it hurts again. We've got enough to do here."

She brushes Melaina out the door and turns back to me and Archie, who's watching Melaina leave. Marge pauses, resting her hands on her hips as she flicks a look back and forth between Archie and me.

"Well?" she challenges.

I blink, realizing I haven't quite finished wrapping Archie's arm and spin the fabric around his arm frantically. Archie drags his gaze down to my working hands, clearly not wanting to make eye contact with Marge.

I pat Archie's shoulder. "There you go, Arch. All done."

He pulls up his arm, flexing the bicep and winces at the motion.

I swat his arm down by the wrist. "Don't do that, you'll aggravate the stitches. Now…let's take a look at your leg."

"Are you asking me to take my pants off?" His cheeks redden. "Because I'm fine. Truly."

"Would you rather Marge look?" I ask.

Too late—Marge closes in.

He stiffens, his wide eyes flicking back to me with a shake of his head. "This is so embarrassing…"

"Nonsense! It's part of our job," I encourage.

With a defeated sigh, he glances away from us as he shimmies his trousers down so we can assess his thigh. Rich purple and black rings mottle his pale skin. Marge lifts his leg and shifts it side to side, round and round, despite his grunts.

Marge hands him a vial of green liquid. "I don't think it's broken. Might be badly bruised. But drink this, and take it easy for the next week. You've suffered a lot of blood loss from that cut on your arm." She darts a look over to me. "Katerina, can you take him back to his room? I want to keep the beds open in case any other patients come in."

By the time Archie and I step out into camp, the rush of adrenaline wears and wanes, leaving a dragging exhaustion weighing down each of my steps. Dawn can't be more than a few hours away. Carlisle leads the Blackfell civilians to the barracks, while Cole gathers several patrols to perimeter the area. Lucky for us, it seems like Blackfell wasn't a trap. Yet still, a nervous buzz lingers in camp.

"Daeja, are you back at the lake? It looks like they are doubling down on patrols. I'm sure Cole will keep the patrols off the southern part of the lake, but just in case, stick to the shadows."

She yawns, the sound splitting my ears. ***"Got it. I planned on sleeping, anyway. I'm quite tired."***

"You helped me save all of those civilians tonight." And yet, they would never know a dragon was the reason I was able to free them. Had it only been me, I likely wouldn't have been able to escape the rebel holding them hostage. *"And you saved me...thank you."*

"Always. You know, you save me every day, too."

I bite my lip to hide my smile. *"I'll come see you tomorrow night, once the initial buzz of the battle wears down."*

I hobble along with Archie into his tent, and I help him into bed, unlacing his boots and ripping them off his feet.

"Are you okay?" I whisper.

"Yes. Definitely. I was a little scared but...feign confidence, remember?"

I glance up at him and stand. "Archie, don't listen to me. I don't know what I'm saying half the time."

"I think you know a lot more than what you're saying."

I arch an eyebrow at him, prompting him to explain.

"I thought I was going to die. I watched as everyone disappeared into the distance. No one could hear me screaming for help, and the flames got closer and closer. And just as I came to accept my fate, Cole came back…for me. I should have died."

I shake my head. "No, you shouldn't have died. And you didn't."

"I didn't…" He breathes, as if trying to accept the reality of it.

I pat his knee with a smile. "And I'm glad you didn't."

He mirrors my grin, but it fails to touch his eyes. "Me too…it made me realize something."

"What's that?"

"I've been lying to you. To everyone."

I stiffen. "About…what?"

His head sinks, like he's been at war with himself for ages and actively avoiding my eye contact. "My name isn't actually Archie…"

I try not to let my thoughts run away, but my pulse skitters. "Oh?"

"Yeah…it's…it's Archibald."

I blink at the anticipation for something so small and… unsurprising. Guilt slams into me at how much I've been lying to him. Here he was, remorseful for something as simple as his legal name, and yet I hide my true identity from him. Hiding an enormous dragon-sized secret from him.

He nods, downcast with guilt as he peers up at me. "I know, I know. I'm so sorry I didn't tell you sooner. It's just that, I always thought Archie sounded so badass. Archibald is so…childish. Tame. It didn't sound like a soldier."

I sit on the bed next to him slowly. "Thank you for sharing that with me."

He's playing with his fingers, knotting them over and over. "Please don't tell anyone."

I rest my hand on his. "I promise, I won't."

"Thank you." He breathes, and his fidgeting hands calm underneath mine. "It's been eating me alive for a long time. I haven't told anyone else."

I smile. "I'm honored to be the only one you've shared it with. I'll take it with me to the grave."

"There's…one other thing."

I can't help but narrow my eyes in suspicion.

He grimaces. "I…I sort of told my ma and pa I was promoted to captain."

"What? Archie—"

"Yeah, I know! I…it's just that they have always been so proud of my brothers. I've always been the one with the least success. I could never make it in war with throwing knives. And my brothers have been rising in the ranks and…it just…happened. I know I shouldn't have." He buries his face in his hands.

"Shh, it's okay, Arch. You just wanted your parents to be

proud." I rub a hand up and down his uninjured arm before squeezing his shoulder.

He unveils his face. Tears glisten at the corners of his eyes, threatening to spill down. "I just feel like I've been living a lie. All I've ever wanted was to make them proud. As soon as I turned eighteen I enlisted. It's been years. I've been trying to train and become better at sword fighting, but my training hasn't been what I thought it would be. I thought I would've been promoted to Arterias by now. I feel like I'm nothing but a let down."

My fists clench. He doesn't have to mention Darian for me to know why his training has been less than ideal.

"You're not a let down, Arch. We'll work on it. I'll do everything in my power to help you." I lock eyes with him, willing him to listen to me. "Look. I'm proud of you. Cole is proud of you."

He snorts, looking away from me. "Cole had to save me. He had to turn back and risk his life and everyone else's to save me."

"Yes, but *you* saved *me* first."

A powerful silence settles between us, but he still won't look my way.

I grab his chin, turning his face toward me. "You saved me, Archie. No one else would've been able to do that. Cole couldn't. The rest of the squad couldn't. But you did. That rebel would have slit my throat in the forest if you hadn't stepped in."

The words land and stick, his panicked breath slowing as he processes my words. The watery glaze of his eyes lessens.

"You saved me," I repeat, wrapping my arms around him

in a hug. He melts into my embrace, leaning his forehead into my shoulder.

"I'm proud of you," I whisper. Pulling back away from him, I wipe a stray tear from his cheek. "Now, get some rest because you're going to need it to recover if we're going to get you promoted to Arterias."

He smiles and dips his head. "Thank you, Kat. You're a true friend."

I return to the healer's quadrant. It's oddly silent, and there's less patients than when I left with Archie.

"No one else came?" I ask Marge.

"A few, but you did such a good job, not much else was needed," she answers.

I swallow, a smile tugging at my lips at her subtle praise.

"Come here," she commands, patting an empty bed.

I obey and take a seat. She brushes a clean rag to my forehead, and I wince as pain sizzles in my skin. The rag comes back bloody as she blots my head. I must have been injured at some point, though I don't recall a moment I had been.

"This is a little deeper than I expected. Let's stitch it up, just in case." Marge retrieves the materials and lowers a needle into the flame of a candle.

I watch her with interest and a slight nervousness, but I'm unable to pinpoint if the root cause is the needle or flame.

She must notice how wide my eyes get because her expression softens as she murmurs, "Not a big fan of needles?"

"No," I confess, though not fully.

"The trick is to look away. If you can't see it…" her fingers rest on my forehead in preparation, "…you can't feel it as much."

"That doesn't make any sense," I whisper. The needle pierces my flesh, the sharp pain pricking my forehead. I focus on the candle resting on the counter instead, absorbed by the flickering flame.

"Fear accentuates pain. So if you don't pay attention to the emotion, you're better off to process the sensation." She stitches me up quickly, then leans back to look me in the eyes. "Are you okay?"

The question catches me off guard. I flinch, pulled out of a haze. "I—I think so."

I try to not think of Cole and the way his eyes burned. The splatter of blood against his face, and the dead man's flesh squelching under his blow, again and again. Nor how close we got to losing Archie. I draw in a deep breath, pushing the racing thoughts back into a box and closing the lid.

Marge rests a hand on my shoulder. "Why don't you head back to your room and get a good night's rest? You're dismissed for tomorrow. I'll take care of any stragglers that come in."

I shake my head, opening my mouth to argue with her.

She pats me. "It's an order, Katerina. Go."

By the time I get to my room, I collapse into my bed, boots on and all.

My emotional, mental, and physical exhaustion pulled me into a dreamless, dark sleep. When I woke in the morning, I was almost more tired than I had been before I slept. I skip breakfast and slip off toward the lake, longing to be near Daeja.

Beams of sunlight cast blinding sparks of light on the lake's surface through the tree line. Birds dip and skim across the scattered waves. Daeja approaches me, her footfalls heavy on the forest floor, and her tail swishing back and forth.

A trilling croak tears our attention to the shore.

Daeja flinches, mere feet away from me as she swivels toward the sound. A toad stares at us with glassy black eyes, leaping a few paces toward us. Daeja's lips curl back to reveal razor-sharp fangs, a threatened hiss escaping from her as she flares her wings. The toad leaps forward again, its throat expanding with another croak. Daeja scurries behind me, fear emanating from her.

I chuckle, turning to her and patting her head. *It's just a toad. It won't hurt you.*

Her eyes narrow at the creature, her nostrils flaring as the toad's throat expands again. The toad takes another leap forward, just a few feet from us now. Daeja's frozen behind me.

"It's likely more afraid of you, than you are of it." I crouch down in an attempt to show her there's no need to be afraid.

Daeja slides out from behind me, her eyes determined. She sucks in a loud breath and attempts to imitate the toad by inflating her throat. The toad blinks but doesn't move.

Daeja lowers her head a few inches above the ground,

glaring at the toad and blows. The toad flips over before scrambling to its webbed feet and bounding back off toward the lake.

I giggle, sitting down and patting Daeja's thick neck. She never ceases to make me laugh.

She turns away from me and backs up to sit on my lap. Except she's far too big now, and I roll away before she can crush me under her weight. Her catlike pupils expand in realization, and instead, she rests beside me and lays her chin on my lap. I stroke the bony ridge of her nose, each black scale cool against my fingertips. Her slanted eyes flutter closed, and a content purr rumbles in her chest. Trailing my fingers up to the crown of her head, I brush her horns, now longer and thicker than my arm.

The sunlight glints off the silver of Cole's ring around my finger. A reminder I haven't seen him since we returned from Black-fell. My stomach flips—I'm unable to decipher whether it's because I'm haunted by the memory of him beating the rebel to death or because of how close I came to losing him.

But one thing is for certain—we have to get out of Arterias. And if I can steal Darian's map, perhaps we don't need to wait until Cole receives one.

Daeja's eyes flash open, her pupils expanding and narrowing back down to slits.

"What is it?"

"Do you hear that?"

I still. An uneven thud of footsteps approaches behind us. My breath catches, and I scramble to my feet as Daeja rises. I tap two fingers to the side of her neck. She vanishes for a brief moment but flickers back into view, the strenuous events from yesterday having drained her energy. Her wide eyes meet mine.

I point toward the trees. *"Go, hide!"*

She dashes off and slinks behind a thick grouping of trees. Except...as she stills behind a trunk, she's too wide. Her tail and the edges of her horns peek out from the cover of the tree. I rush toward her, motioning her to squeeze tighter behind the tree's silhouette, but it's no use.

A squeak comes from behind us. "Shit!"

Shit.

I turn. Archie's mouth is dropped open in a silent gasp, and his hand fumbles at his side for his dagger. His face is ghost white, his eyes wide as he gawks at Daeja. I race toward him before he can run off and alert everyone.

He staggers forward, sweeping me behind him, and raises the dagger. "Kat, run!"

Terror floods my veins. He clenches the dagger in his non-dominant hand, considering his throwing arm was the one injured last night. He might be inaccurate and hit her. Or be accurate enough to hit her. Slingshotting forward, I whip his arm down and tear the dagger from his grip before he can throw it.

He hisses, "What are you—"

Daeja slinks out from behind the trees and growls. The sound reverberates around us, and birds from nearby trees shoot into the air with a cry.

"Stop, you'll scare him."

"That's the point." She bristles as she raises her head and flares her wings, a silent snarl curling her lips.

"We don't want him scared!" I throw her a warning glare. *"He's a friend. He's safe."*

Archie screams and charges toward Daeja with hobbled steps as he pulls another dagger from his side, waving it in the air.

"Archie, stop!" I dash in front of him, blocking his path to Daeja.

He pauses, his hand still raised with the dagger. Those brown eyes flick between me and Daeja. "What are you doing!"

Daeja stalks forward from behind me and lowers her chin onto my shoulder. Watching Archie, I reach a hand up and pet Daeja's cheek.

Archie's eyes grow even wider, and he drops the dagger. "You…you have a *dragon!*"

"Daeja, meet Archie."

Daeja's black tongue licks over her muzzle in anticipation. Her intentions are as apparent to me as if they were my own.

"No, no. Meet—not meat."

"A clear misunderstanding," she grumbles.

"And Archie, this is Daeja. I need you to swear you won't tell anyone—"

"How did you even…why—" He sighs and takes a slow step backwards, betrayal glistening in his brown eyes. "I thought we were friends. How could you not tell me?"

Something inside my chest weakens as I recognize his

misery. I dare a few steps forward and reach out for him. "We are friends, Arch—"

He takes another step back to avoid my touch, shaking his head.

"Please. Don't tell anyone," I plead again, my voice weak. "I-I can't…"

Daeja chuffs from above me. ***I'll eat him. No body—no worries.***

"No eating, Daeja! You're not helping!"

"She's just a baby. I'm taking her to the Dragon Lands to be with her kind. I'm going to set her free," I explain.

"A baby? How is she considered a baby, Kat?" He motions up toward her. "Look at her!"

He has a fair point. She's not as small as she used to be, and I could only guess how much bigger she will get.

My heart pounds in my ears, my fingers fidget around his dagger I confiscated earlier. "Archie, please. I'm begging you."

The memory of the two men hanging from the tower replays in my mind. How they begged to explain their situation. I couldn't imagine it would have been as damning as the one we're in now. The fate of those two men would become my own. Possibly, even Archie's demise, if he was found to have kept Daeja a secret. By his calculated focus and rigid stance, he's weighing it, too.

Shit, I didn't want any of this. Maybe we should go now, save all of us from the impending possibilities. Forget the map.

Archie shakes his head. "Who else knows?"

The question has me dumbfounded. If he finds out Cole

knows, will he be more convinced to keep Daeja a secret, considering Cole saved his life? But I can't risk Cole—I can't pull him into this. If Archie decides to report us to the King, at least Daeja and I can fly to the Dragon Lands. But Cole would be stuck here and executed for treason.

Yet, lying to Archie, my friend, feels traitorous in itself. I can trust him...*can't I?*

"Nobody," I answer.

"Nobody?" he challenges.

Daeja leans forward and snorts, the air blasting Archie's hair out of his face. It's enough to distract him from my inability to answer his question.

I take the opportunity to close the space between Archie and I. Taking a leap of faith, I place his dagger back into his hand and wrap my fingers around his. "Archie, please. If our friendship means anything..." My eyes search his in desperation. "We will be gone by the end of the month. You won't even have to worry about keeping the secret for long. Please, promise me."

He glances down at our hands. "I...I promise I won't say anything."

I sigh and sag in relief. "Thank you."

He nods reluctantly and turns away, pulling his hand out from my grasp.

"Wait, where are you going?" I call after him.

"Back to camp," he responds as he sheathes his dagger.

"You're...upset with me?"

He stops mid-step. "I trusted you. I told you all of my secrets."

"I'm sorry, Arch. It wasn't because I didn't trust you. I didn't tell you because I wanted to keep you safe."

He snorts, glancing at me over his shoulder. "Well, it's too late for that. If they take you down, I'm going with you."

A snowstorm of emotions flurries inside my heart. I'm overwhelmingly honored by his loyalty, despite the risk of keeping such a massive secret. The thought that my decisions may very well lead to his demise is equally as terrifying.

He grabs the second dagger he dropped to the ground before disappearing into the forest toward the outpost.

"I won't let anything happen to you," I whisper, hoping it's a promise I can actually keep.

TWENTY NINE

WHO DO YOU TRUST

Every time I caught Archie's gaze over the last few days, he looked away. It's starting to make me nervous…because maybe I made a mistake in trusting him. I shouldn't have put him in such a conflicting situation—but he hasn't said anything about it. He hasn't spoken of Daeja again. I'm not sure if I should be relieved or concerned. And every time I try to have a conversation with him, he finds a way to excuse himself.

I've been itching to see Cole—anything to confirm he's safe and alive. But something in my stomach tenses at the vision of him hunched over the rebel's dead body. Every time the memory resurfaces, I shove it back down, choking it off from the light of my mind.

I spend a majority of my time in the healer's quadrant, sneaking off to see Daeja when I can. We spend our time at night flying over the lake, edging closer and closer to our impending deadline. We need that map. And as much as I don't want to consider it, my mind snags on one thought. If Cole can't come with us, could we leave on our own?

I deliberate whether or not I should steal the map from Darian's room. But when I recalled our last interaction where I coerced him into rescuing Archie by exploiting his sister's memory, I change my mind. I can only imagine what Darian's unfiltered rage could mean for someone like me—I'm back to square one with him. We need Cole to get a map, and that means I needed to talk to him.

I'm bent over the sink in the healer's quadrant, washing bottles and vials. A knock sounds on the door, and Cole strolls in. A huge weight lifts off my shoulders at the first glimpse of him in days.

"I'm going to go fill this with water," Marge says, a flask in her hand and her staff in the other. She shuffles out, leaving Cole and me alone.

He blows out a breath. "Hey…"

I take a few steps into his direction. "Hey…I've been wondering when I'd see you."

A gash crusted in blood cuts his temple down to the top of his cheekbone. Darkness blooms under his eyes, and his normally warm gaze is dull.

I reach up a hand hesitantly to brush my thumb near the cut. "Does it hurt?"

He looks away, breaking our eye contact. "No."

"Well, we should get it cleaned anyway. Especially since it's been a few days."

"No need, I'm fine. I just wanted to check in on you."

"Well…I'm not fine." The confession trembles on my lips. I want to tell him everything. How Archie knows about Daeja. The map in Darian's room. How terrified I was I almost lost him and Archie. But I can't ignore the sullenness of his features: the sag of his shoulders, his mussed auburn hair, and weary gaze. I grab his chin and pull his face to me, demanding eye contact. "And I can see you aren't either. What's wrong?"

"Nothing," he mutters. But his eyes say otherwise.

"Are you really going to make me dig?"

He turns his face out of my hand and shifts away. "I just came here to check on you, that's all."

"Cole—" I catch his arm in my hand. "I was scared."

He pauses. Slowly turning back to me, he drags his gaze up to meet mine. I flinch as I recall the moment looking into his eyes at the battle. The brutality in them. The way blood stained his cheeks as vividly as his own freckles now. The memory connects to the emotions I've been forcing down, bursting through the lid I keep trying to cram shut.

Scared of losing him.

Scared of *him*.

Maybe it's all the same.

I continue, my voice wavering, "I was scared to lose you—"

"I know, I know," he whispers. Absent-mindedly, he touches

the side of my face, brushing his thumb in slow strokes against my cheek. "But I'm okay. Everything is going to be okay."

But it doesn't feel okay. Something feels off.

"Tell me it won't happen again," I mutter.

"I wish I could, but I can't. This is war. And with me being the captain…it probably won't be the last time."

My heart sinks, despite his statement already being something I understood deep down. "Then let's leave. We don't need to wait until the moonless night. I know where a map is. Let's go now—"

"It's too risky," he deadpans.

"It'll *always* be risky."

"I am not willing to cut corners if it means endangering your life," he warns.

"Risk will follow us everywhere we go, can't you see that? Even if we wait until you get the map and a moonless night, it doesn't solve everything. There are so many dangerous scenarios after that. And then what do you expect will happen once we get to the Dragon Lands?"

A sad smile blooms on his face. "I don't know."

"Have you even heard when we'll get the map—"

Marge bursts back into the room. I casually slink back away from Cole, hoping the sudden movement doesn't trigger Marge's suspicion.

"Are you hungry?" I ask Cole. "Have you eaten anything since Blackfell?"

"No."

"You should still eat something," I murmur.

He's back to avoiding my eye contact. "I'm not hungry."

I glance over at Marge, hoping for her support, but she continues rearranging bottles on a shelf, ignoring every word exchanged between Cole and me.

I try again, "You need to eat something—"

Cole turns away from me entirely. "I've got to go check in with Carlisle on patrols. I'll see you later."

I watch the door close between Cole and me as he leaves, my stare lingering on the spot for some moments after. Someone clears their throat, interrupting my daze.

I turn to Marge, waiting for her to speak. "Yes?"

Her back is to me as she works at mixing together concoctions. "Nothing. I didn't say anything."

"Is there something you *want* to say?"

"Give him some time. He'll come around. War and death is hard," she calls.

I nod, peering down at my hand and where his was moments ago. I'm still wearing his mother's ring. On my other hand, my middle finger is stained with a dark circle. I clench both hands closed and turn toward Marge.

"Marge…you want to go to the Dragon Lands. But there are dragons and rebels. What makes you think you'll be safe there?"

She chuckles. "Getting right to the questions today, aren't we?"

"How did you know about that water dragon at the lake?" I press.

"Because dragons have been around for thousands of years. And our elders were responsible for sharing all of that information. Books can be rewritten and destroyed but memories cannot. Words cannot. My grandmother used to tell me about dragons and their riders when I was a young girl."

"Riders?" I murmur.

"Before the King came into rule, humans and dragons shared this realm equally. Some dragons would bond humans as dragon riders. It's a mystery as to how dragons chose their bonds, but some used to think it had to do with your blood."

Blood of power…perhaps that was why it was written in my father's journal. "Like if you were a Spoiled?"

"Oh, no. I don't think dragons take to Spoileds very well. In fact, I think if they sensed that you were one, they might try to kill you. They must have some sort of scent or sense to know if you've been Spoiled…I'm not exactly sure what the translation is."

"What do you mean by translation?"

"In the olden days, before the King ruled, there was an ancient tongue. When Aaric came to rule, he burned all of the books and libraries. There are few elders that still whisper of the forgotten language."

"And you know the language?"

She chuckles, the motion of it shaking in her shoulders. "You sure ask a lot of questions."

Was I annoying her? Or was she avoiding the question because she was suspicious I might turn her in? By now, I imagine she must trust me, considering how much she's shared. At least a little.

"You're the only one I can talk to," I whisper. It's not a full truth, but I have to protect Cole. And now Archie. "How do you know whom to trust?"

She shrugs, her focus still fixed on preparing a salve. "You don't."

"Then why are you sharing all this information with me?"

She pauses and turns to me. "Because I trust you, Katerina."

Our eyes lock, and my heart skips a beat. I try not to smile too hard.

She snorts. "Don't make me regret that. As I imagine, you must trust me now that you know I haven't turned you in."

I dip my head. "Yes, I do."

"And if you're asking me all these questions," she adds.

"Sorry," I say sheepishly but not seriously.

Since the battle at Blackfell, the camp has buzzed with an extra liveliness from housing the civilians we rescued. Temporarily, anyway, as Cole worked with Carlisle on plans to relocate them. I imagined having extra mouths to feed and people to protect is stressful on Cole. Every time he catches my stare, he disappears or looks away.

I've started to wonder if he's avoiding me.

We are all crowded around the tables for dinner. With this many extra people, we've been designated certain meal times and rations. A little girl spins circles near one of the tables with a long branch in her hand. She screeches as she swings the stick back and forth. Every swipe hits the edge of the table or the side of a tent. My gut drops in horror as she swings it straight into Darian's calf, who sits at the table taking sip after sip from his flask.

He whips around with a glare and tears the branch from the girl's grasp.

I spring forward, ready to rescue her. "Darian—"

He shakes his head at the little girl and scolds her with a finger. From this distance, I can't hear what he's saying. But he gently corrects her posture, shows her how to flick her wrist, and hands the branch back to her, pointing at his thigh. She freezes, and he stabs his finger into his leg again. She rears back and smacks the branch into his leg, his face tensing in pain as he nods in approval. He jabs a thumb over his shoulder toward a group of other kids, and she sprints off, waving the branch with a shriek as the group of kids disperses.

So, he will gladly train a five year old. But he refused to train Archie and the rest of us? Where it could mean life or death? While the sentiment of the first scenario is admittedly sweet, the rest is infuriating.

Why doesn't he want to train us?

Darian perches his feet up on top of the table, leans back, and lifts the front legs of his chair off the ground. He hooks one arm back behind his head and takes another pull from his flask.

My eyes narrow, and I storm toward him. His gaze darts over to me, and his eyes playfully pick me apart from head to toe. The corner of his lips perk up in a crooked grin, but as I close the distance between us, his attention flits away. As if he couldn't be any less interested in me. The way he flips back and forth so easily between two extremes is enough to give me whiplash.

He sighs in exasperation. "I'm busy right now. Can I ignore you another time?"

I glare down at him. "No. I need to talk to you."

He sneers, examining his nails. "Afraid to break it to you, but I've never been a conversationalist. I'm sure your golden-haired boy can be of use, for once. That kid never stops talking."

I cross my arms over my chest. "Don't even start—"

"Run along now." He ushers me away with a flick of his wrist.

I snatch a fistful of his shirt and yank him forward to have his chair rest all four legs on the ground.

"What the hell?" he growls and tears my fist from his shirt.

"I need a moment alone with you. Take me to your room," I hiss. Admittedly, it's the wrong choice of words…but it's too late.

He blinks back surprise, which melts into a sinful lick of his lips as he smiles.

"*Shut up,*" I spit.

He snickers. "I didn't say anything."

"I know, but it's what you're thinking."

He tilts his head dramatically to the side, his brown hair sweeping into his brow. "Oh? And you know what I'm thinking, now?"

I roll my eyes, gritting out each word through clenched teeth, "Just take me to your room."

"You don't have to tell me twice." He swings his feet underneath him, standing in one eager and swift motion.

As we duck into Darian's room, I scan around the cluttered mess. He still hasn't bothered to tidy up since the last time I was here. Though, I suppose it is an accurate depiction of the man dwelling here: messy and chaotic.

My gaze skitters over to the map still pinned under books on his desk. At this angle, I can't study it long enough to decipher it while being discreet.

"So...you have me. Alone, in my room." He grins. "Did you want me to make the first move?"

The only logical way to deal with Darian, I'm beginning to realize, is to ignore his antics completely. "I need you to train Archie."

Darian snorts. "Ha! Such demands from someone who has nothing to offer me."

"Well then, what is it you want?"

"World domination."

I roll my eyes and cross my arms, shifting my weight onto my left leg. "Seriously?"

"Seriously."

We stare at each other, and I wait for him to finally admit what it is he wants. But he confesses nothing.

I sigh in exasperation. "If I ask you nicely, will you do it?"

"No," he responds plainly.

"And why not?"

"Because he's a lost cause."

I growl through gritted teeth, "Don't fucking talk about him like that."

He tilts his head to the side at the irritation sharpening my voice, and a grin pulls at the corner of his mouth. "Why are you so defensive of him?"

"Because he's my friend. And you're being impossible at helping anyone but yourself."

"I know," he taunts as he leans back and crosses his arms with a smile, mirroring my stance.

It enrages me. I can't tell if he's doing it to piss me off or if he really doesn't care.

"What is your problem?" I finally ask.

He opens his hands and arches his thick eyebrows, prompting me for more clarification. As if he has more than one problem.

"What is your problem with Archie?" I snap.

He scoffs and swats at the air. "As I said before, that kid is hopeless. I might as well be with a squad of muskrats."

I glower at him. "He's optimistic."

"No, he's *unreal*istic."

"He looks up to you!"

Darian rolls his eyes. "If you were smart, you wouldn't attach yourself to such an easy target."

"Why are you such a fucking asshole to everyone, huh? Archie is kind. And the rest of the squad are *nothing* but good to you." I jab a finger at his chest.

A muscle in his jaw flickers, his gaze dropping to where I prodded him. When he draws his eyes back up to mine, staring through lowered brows, they simmer with a hidden anger.

"And yet for some reason, out of everyone here, you save me from your piss-poor attitude. Instead, I get your flirty bullshit and unwanted sexual innuendos." I spin on my heel and storm off, opening the door a few inches.

"Because you don't expect anything," he fumes.

I swivel toward him. "What the hell is that even supposed to mean!"

"They think I'm supposed to save them. They think there's some good in me and I owe it to them." He pounds a fist into his chest, his voice getting dangerously louder. "There's not!" He growls, like something hisses in a nightmare. "And *you.*"

Thundering toward me, his anger rips across his features and roars in his green eyes. Too afraid to turn my back to him, I back-step slowly out of his room.

"There's no expectations with you. You know what I am. Void of pressure or responsibility to be good. That's why I don't even have to try to be an asshole to you. Because you know I am. And I don't have to prove that to you." He spits at the ground, stopping at the threshold momentarily as he braces his hand against the door. His voice dips to a depth that sends shocks to my spine.

"And don't you *ever* fucking mention my sister again."

He slams the door in my face. The walls shudder with the shear force and strands of my hair blow back from my face. A sharp ringing pierces my ears. I stare in shock with my mouth open wide before I physically shake it off. Another soldier walks by, staring at me with wide eyes before he averts his gaze.

I slip back into my room, swallowing against the guilt tightening my throat as I think of my brother. How much I would have done in his name. How angry I would have been if someone used him against me.

I deserved that.

I went too far.

THIRTY

A SACRIFICE OF VIRTUE

Cole hasn't made it to dinner. Again. Worry settles in the pit of my stomach like a bag of stones.

"Cole…?" Archie asks at the dinner table. The worry in his eyes mirroring my own.

I shake my head. "He's just tired. Trying to catch up on sleep. A lot of loose ends from the battle."

I'm not sure if I'm trying to convince Archie or myself.

As soon as I eat my fill, I take a tray of food to Cole's room.

A drip of sweat trickles down the back of my neck. I don't know what I'm nervous for, but the prickling unease is undeniable—blooming from every corner of my body. His mother's ring is heavy and cold on my finger.

I strain to listen for any sign of Cole behind his door. Waiting for any scrawl of pen on paper. Any hushed conversations or deep, sleepy breaths. But it's silent, so I knock against his door.

With no answer, I twist the doorknob and slowly push it open. If he's out on patrol, at least I can leave the food for him.

As I walk into the room, Cole is lying on his back in the bed. His eyes drag toward me from where he was deep in thought staring at the ceiling. Dark circles edge his eyes, his hair a tangled red mess. The lines on his forehead are etched deeper than before. At least the blood and dirt has been cleaned from his skin and hair.

A cold dagger sinks deeper into my heart as more time passes, and he looks worse. Something is seriously wrong. As I close his door, he pushes himself onto his forearms and sits up. My eyes wander to the cut grazing his cheek, relieved no sign of infection marks his skin. One less thing to worry about.

I lift the tray as I walk toward him. "Hungry?"

"No," he mumbles.

"Well, you have to eat something. I haven't seen you eat since the battle—"

"I know. But...I can't. I can't eat anything."

Slowly, I sit next to him on the bed, afraid I might spook him if I move too fast. "Why? What's bothering you, Cole? I know something's wrong."

He sighs heavily and looks down at his clasped hands. "I don't really know...how to talk about it..."

I place the food tray at the end of his bed and rest my hand on his thigh, brushing my thumb against him in soothing strokes.

Our touch sparks a slight smile in him before it fades. "I...I've never killed someone before."

My thumb pauses on his leg. "But...before I found you,

someone said you stopped a rebel group. That you beheaded their leader and put it on a spike near the border—"

"No. While I did stop their group from infiltrating the outpost, Darian was the one who put their leader's head on a spike, much against my command not to. I took it down the next day. Their leader wasn't supposed to be executed, he was supposed to be a prisoner. Darian actively defied my orders."

Silence falls between us, like a knife tearing through the space. I realize it's the first time I've ever been so physically close to him and yet, felt so far away. Like he's holding me back at an arm's length and doesn't want to let me in. After all this time, he's trying to protect me—but I don't need his protection.

"You had to do what you had to do," I whisper.

"I've never wanted to kill anyone, though. I know it was inevitable in this role and in the military. I just wish I could have… prepared myself…I guess. When I saw that rebel swing at you, it just happened. The thought of him hurting you. The thought that he might kill you and take you away from me. I just—" His head dips low, red hair covering his face as he clears the tension in his throat. But it's unsuccessful, his voice is still hoarse. "I couldn't stop myself."

I nod, struggling to find the words to comfort him. "Hey, you're a good person. You didn't mean to."

"But I did. I did mean to. And in the moment, I *wanted* to." He avoids my gaze, his attention fixed to his hands. The muscles flex beneath his skin as he clenches and unclenches his fists. "And then when we got back and I realized Archie was missing…I don't know. I swear I could have killed Darian then, too. I imagined wrapping my hands around his throat..." He bites down on his trembling lip. "Gods, I feel fucking *awful.* I can't get it out of my head. That's not who I am, nor who I want to be. But what if... what if I don't know who I am anymore? What if I'm not the same person I thought I once was? It—it scares me."

"Then let me remind you." I breathe, leaning in to kiss him. To remind the both of us.

This is Cole.

The same Cole who taught me how to make better fish traps so I had a better chance at surviving back in Padmoor. The same Cole who traded me a fire poker so I could give my mother honey when she was sick. The same Cole who played tea party with his little sisters and would have taken the blame for my father's journal so I wouldn't be executed. Who stormed Blackfell, aflame and crumbling, to rescue Archie. The same Cole who risks his life again and again for me. Who loves furiously and defends those who need it with every fiber of his being.

He is courageous. Honorable. Loving. And everything I could ever want in a man.

He sighs into my kiss, and I climb closer to him. As I swing my leg over him to straddle his hips, he pushes away from me. I blink in confusion as my eyes meet his.

Something else flickers in his hazel eyes—is that...is that *fear?*

"Wait," he whispers. Tears line his eyes as he twirls a piece of my blonde hair around his finger and tucks it behind my ear, dragging his touch underneath my jaw to tilt my face up toward his. "I just need this last moment of you and I. One last time of us. Tell me you love me…tell me one more time."

"What? Of course I love you. Why would it be one last time? What is it? What's wrong?"

A crack splits the dam he has walled up against the emotions hidden behind his eyes. A single tear slips, rolling down his cheek, as his breath hitches.

"You're scaring me," I mutter, swiping away his tear with a finger.

His voice cracks in pain. "I've royally fucked up, Kat. I thought I was doing the right thing. But I see now I should have told you this a long time ago. I was just so fucking terrified to lose you again. I put my heart above telling you the truth."

My stomach curls into a ball of knots, his voice is laced with something grave and dark. Something strained, desperate, and scared. I hold onto my breath, and I slide off him.

"I-I don't know how to say this." He shakes his head. "Can you promise to listen to me until I'm done?"

"What is it?" I demand.

"I need you to promise me to listen until I explain everything. Please—"

"Just get out with it." My skin prickles in anticipation.

Another tear slips from his eyes. He watches me with pinched brows, blinking slowly as if we're saying goodbye forever. Dipping his head in defeat, he squeezes his eyes shut, as if he can't bear to look at me any longer. "I'm…engaged."

My world stops turning. The air is sucked out of the room, and my vision spins. Every breath is a shard of glass tearing deeper into my heart. Stunned as if he slapped me, I mutter, "You're joking."

Maybe I hadn't heard him right. Maybe this is only another sick, awful dream. I shake my head, as if it'll clear my ears and I'll process what he actually said. Shaking my head as if it may shake me awake, and I'll be in another time and place. Where I'm not here. The motion of my head quickens to a furious speed as his words settle on me like fallen ash. I blink through the disbelief and surging emotions threatening to drown me.

My voice pitches higher through my tight throat. "You're joking." I repeat. Gripping his arm, I shake him, desperate for him to look up at me. "Tell me you're joking, Cole!"

He shakes his head, still unable to look me in the eye.

"Since when?" I croak.

He sinks forward, elbows on his knees as he buries his face into his hands. "Since I thought you were..."

Dead.

He can't even say the words. But it hangs between us nonetheless. And yet...he couldn't bother to tell me the first time he saw me? Or the nights thereafter? Rage flares in me wicked hot, burning me from the inside out. My body trembles from the threat of combustion, and I clench my fists to keep myself from exploding.

He sucks in a breath, finally glancing over to me. "I'm so sorry. I didn't know how to tell you. I tried so many times. I just couldn't find the right time—"

"The right time would have been before you *fucked* me. That would have been the right time." The words are venom on my tongue, each word increasing in hostility and pitching higher.

He tries to reach out to me, and I rip my hand away, finally thawing whatever had frozen me to the spot next to him. I can't race for the door fast enough.

"Kat, please! Kat, wait!" His voice is edged in desperation. "Let me explain. Please, *I love you!*"

I swivel toward him, pointing a finger at him as if it'll still the anger inside me. "No, *fuck* you, Cole. How could you keep that from me? Maybe you were right. I don't know you anymore, either. Because the Cole I knew would have told me. He wouldn't have lied."

The words spill out of my trembling mouth. I'm struggling to maintain any semblance of composure. Rage and betrayal roar inside me, drowning out every other thought and feeling.

I rip his mother's ring from my finger and shove it into his hand. "Here, you'll probably need this for your fiancée."

"No, wait!" He's trying to calm me down, grabbing me by my shoulder. But he can't save me from this hell. It's too late. All that's left to do is burn.

I pull away from his touch. "Don't fucking touch me. Don't touch me ever again. Leave me the fuck alone."

He has the godsdamn audacity to look at me with tears, as if this hurts him more than it does me. I burst out of his room, but he's hot on my heels.

Carlisle strides up to Cole. "Captain, you really need to hear this."

"Hold *on*," Cole grits.

"It's urgent and can't wait. It's from the King."

Cole grunts, and his footsteps behind me cease. I race straight back toward my room, my blood rushing in my ears.

"Daeja? We are leaving."

"What?"

"Yes, tonight. Now. Meet me near camp, and we'll go."

Every doubt creeping into my mind of taking Daeja to the Dragon Lands on my own is snuffed out by the anger raging inside me. I burst into my room, shoving my belongings into my satchel and scrawling a note for Marge and Archie. They're essentially the same—thank you for everything, I'll always consider you a friend. I hope to see you again.

I can already imagine Archie crying, and Marge pissed I didn't take her with me. I hesitate in the heat of the moment but push through it before I can think for too long. Before I change my mind. Maybe I'll come back, and if not, maybe they're better off without me, anyway. I don't have the emotional capacity to consider the outcomes nor the ability to handle anything other than the boiling rage threatening to implode inside of me.

"On my way."

I grab my sword and slip out of my room. As I close my door, I catch a glimpse of the drooping flowers on the desk Cole had given me all those weeks ago before I slam it shut. I glance toward the north when my attention snags on Darian's room. The silvery sheen of the moon peaks above his angled roof.

"The map. I have to get the map."

I slink over to his room, glancing over my shoulder as I go. Once I'm at his door, I knock and wait. Nothing. Checking my surroundings once more, I attempt to open the door.

Locked.

Fuck the map. We'll just have to get there on our own. I round the corner of Darian's room and spot Daeja's silhouette off in the woods beyond.

My toe catches on the side of a crate tucked in the shadows against Darian's room. I stumble to my knees and whip my gaze at the wooden thing. A liquid sloshes inside of it, and in the moonlight, I can make out red letters plastered across the side: *FRAGILE.*

Not sure what a crate of wine is doing out here.

Daeja's silhouette ripples in the shadowed trees up ahead as she begins to approach camp. As I walk toward her, a fist grabs the back of my cloak. I'm ripped back and thrown face first into a wall. An aching pain splits my cheek as I connect with the cold stone.

"What the *fuck* are you doing out here?" someone growls.

My heart races as I dig for an explanation. When I don't answer, I'm spun around and shoved with my back against the wall. My shoulders groan in pain with the violent contact. A hand wraps tightly around my throat. Another hand presses a dagger to my chest. Darian's glare burns into me, his teeth bared in a silent warning. I struggle against his grip, wriggling like a worm under his pin. When I don't answer his question, he tightens his grip around my throat.

I gasp. "You're choking me—"

"I asked you a fucking question."

"Daeja, get out of here, get to the lake before he sees you." My rage melts into fear, and I panic, trying to keep him from looking over his shoulder at her. All he would have to do is turn.

"What do you want?" he hisses again. The tip of his blade burrows into my chest. I'm trying to think of something. Anything. The fear of Darian finding Daeja overrides all of my lingering rage, betrayal, and hurt. Black bleeds into the edges of my vision from the lack of oxygen.

Daeja stalks toward us, her wings flaring. ***"I'll sear every inch of his flesh for putting his hands on you."***

"No—go!" My impulsive gaze flickers over to her shadowy silhouette for a split second.

Darian's eyes narrow before he turns his head to follow my gaze. There's only one thing I know might distract him enough so Daeja can slip away. The only thing I can think of to save us.

"You." I breathe.

He freezes. Something in his gaze falters. His stare bounces back and forth between my eyes. His grip softens around my throat, but there's still a bite to his words. *"What did you say?"*

"I said...I want..." The afforded slack allows me to grab fistfuls of his hair, and I yank him toward me. "You."

I kiss him.

"Go, Daeja, before he sees you."

Darian flinches in shock. But it's only a second before he shoves back into me and kisses me—hard. It's taut and tight. Nothing of the gentleness, the sincerity, and the warmth of Cole. Just as we battled in the sparring center, our tangle is just as tense. We move our mouths over each other, grappling for the upper-hand. Neither of us stopping or ceasing. He presses his hard body into me, pinning me into submission against the wall. Moving away from his mouth, I kiss and suck his sinfully smooth skin on his angled jaw and throat. The tension under him waxes and wanes until he thrusts into me with a ferocity and burning need. Shoving me harder into the wall. As if he needs me closer.

It's working.

I run my hands under his shirt and caress his sides, my fingertips tracing each crevice and mound of muscled abs and pecks.

I hate him, I tell myself. *I just have to make this convincing enough so he doesn't catch on.*

A brief whisper of a thought flickers in the back of my mind...then what are you doing?

I hate him, I hate him, I hate him.

Gods, I can already hear his voice inside my head. *I know.* But something shifts in me. The hate fueling each flicker of my fingers against his muscles, each caress of my lips on his hot skin transforms into something else even more dangerous.

But where do I stop? And how can I stop? What if...what if I can't stop?

The pressure from his dagger against my chest disappears. Something clatters to the ground. His grip on my throat shifts down to seize my hips, and he lifts me off the ground. I wrap my legs around his waist instinctively, and he shifts himself right between my legs. He crushes his groin into me with a gods almighty sinful pressure.

Oh, gods. It's working too well. Even working on *me.*

He shouldn't feel this good. His touch shouldn't be as magnetic as it is. Every stupid graze of his lips on me has me gasping for air, every brush of his fingers makes my heart skip a beat.

Breaking from the kiss, he sucks on my earlobe and drags his tongue across the soft spot behind my ear—that sweet, sensitive spot never failing to betray me. I surprise myself with a moan, and his cheeks tighten into a victorious grin. My core rushes with molten desire, melting the last of my inhibitions. I find myself devastatingly hungry for *him.*

I feel myself falling. Sinking deep into a thick haze of lust, as vividly as if I were slipping off the side of a cliff. I reach out, desperate to anchor myself into anything that'll keep me from plummeting. But each grip vanishes with his hot breath whispered into my ear and the tease of his soft lips against my skin. He lures out and taunts each of my dangerous cravings I didn't even know existed.

His mouth travels down my neck toward the swell of my breasts. My legs squeeze tighter around his waist, my shoulders rolling back. He trails his hot tongue deliciously slow across my skin, leaving me shivering and wanting.

Before I can think better of it, the words slip off my lips. "I want you...take me to your room."

His teeth nip the top of my breasts. "I don't need to hide. I'll take you right here, right now. Everyone can watch me fuck you against this wall."

My fingers curl into his thick brown hair, my voice coming out in a strained whisper, "Please, Darian."

Without another second of hesitation, he carries me into his room, honoring my request. He sucks and nips at the crook between my neck and shoulder as we burst through his door. After he kicks the door closed behind him, he sets me on my feet. I tear the satchel off my shoulder and toss it to the ground, eyes glued to him as he lifts his shirt off. But rather than glancing away, I trail every tempting, sexual edge of his body.

He ghosts over to me as I lift my shirt, his deft fingers unhooking and unclasping every layer on my body. I fling my shirt off, the cool air peaking my nipples. He drops to his knees in front of me, a trail of his hot kisses snaking down my navel as he works to shimmy my trousers down. My pants collect into a puddle at my ankles, leaving me naked, and his gaze sweeps up to my face. His green eyes are hungry through the set of his deviously angled brows.

He drags his sinful tongue against my inner thigh, edging closer and closer to my center. My head falls back, and he stops before his tongue can touch me. I sway, and his strong hands grip my hips to steady me.

His breath warms the space between my legs. "Tell me what you want."

I shake my head, squeezing my eyes shut. I don't want to say it. I can't give the deepest, hungriest desires in me, words. Gripping his hair in my hands, I pull his face closer between my legs instead. I tremble in anticipation of having his mouth on me.

He snorts at my impatience. But then heavily inhales my scent before burying his face between my legs. There is no hesitation, no limitation to how easily he sucks and licks me. Swirling his tongue around my throbbing clit, he devours every inch of my wet, hot skin. His fingers dig into my hips as I jerk with breathy moans.

"Mmmm." He groans at how wet he's made me, pulling back to peer up at me from between my legs. "Gods, you taste as good as I thought you might."

He watches me, that sly smirk on his lips as he feasts on every bit of my pleasure. I can't help but think of how ridiculously seductive he is. Whispering things to me between my legs even I can't understand. He drives his tongue into my hot, wet entrance as he uses the tip of his nose to rub circles against my clit.

Fuck. I'm in way over my head.

I whimper, my legs trembling beneath me as he races me to a climax. My eyes flash open, each breath ragged in my chest. "Please. I can't take it. Just fuck me already."

Mercifully, he gathers me into his arms and lays me on his bed, hovering over me. As if every waiting moment is agonizing, I sink my frantic fingers into the edge of his pants and pull down. His thick cock springs free. I gape at the naked glory of his body, pulled into touching every inch he'll allow me. His body is carved into deep angles and lines from years of vigorous training, all the way from his chest down to his hips. The perfect set of abs sit just above his delicious, thick, straining cock. A molten rush of anticipation tingles in the pits of my stomach.

He pulls back to look at my nakedness with a slow lick of his lips. The sight of him alone makes me want to crumble, my knees weak at the uncontrollable desire to sit on his face. To have him fuck me and fill me. Touching me, teasing me, and doing all the things I desperately need him to do.

Taking two fingers, he teases my entrance as I eagerly buck against him. He works my delicate flesh, swiping his skilled fingertips up and down, agonizingly slow, until his fingers glisten with me. As I lift my hips to him, silently begging, he finally pushes his fingers into me as I whimper and writhe.

He doesn't take his time. It's rough and exhilarating as he pumps hard and fast. I find myself grinding against his hand feverishly. He has me at the pathetic mercy of each stroke, and I'm dipping my head back into the pillows with each delicious slide of his fingers. He adds a third, and I gasp as he eases into me until I'm on fire for something more—for *him*. Starving for him to fill the aching need he's created in me.

I creep closer to an orgasm, my legs shaking. "Darian, please. Slow down, or I'm going to come."

He doesn't slow, his eyes wicked as he flicks his tongue across his lips and smiles. "Good girl. You're going to come for me on my fingers. For the rest of the night, you're not going to stop coming until I say you can stop. Do you understand?"

I'm not sure if I should be afraid or exhilarated. But I don't have long to consider which because I burst at the seams and climax around his skilled fingers with a cry.

He lurches forward, stealing my scream with a kiss. His fingers slow inside me as I spasm again and again. As the trembling in my legs subsides, he pulls back from our kiss.

His nose brushes the tip of mine, and his thumb snags at my bottom lip. "If I could bottle that sound…"

I reach out and wrap my fingers around his hard cock, hoping it's enough that I don't need to admit aloud I need him.

His heavy lidded eyes flick down to my hand wrapped around his length and back up toward me. His voice comes out on choppy breaths. "Tell me. Tell me what you want."

I stroke him, rubbing my thumb over the head of his cock. "I want you to fuck me. Hard. Show me how much of an asshole you really are."

His eyes cloud. A darkness seeps over his features, the light winks out of his expression. Slowing the rhythm of his fingers inside of me to a halt, he removes them. But rather than immediately sinking his cock into me, he flips me over to lay flat on my belly. He rips my hips up, my ass perked up for him. Gripping the width of my hips, he positions himself closer to me. His cock grazes my wetness.

"I'm going to fuck you until you purr, kitten," he rasps, his voice thick with his own desire. The head of his thick cock sinks into me slowly, pushing deeper inside of me. Every inch of him spreads and stretches me in a burning ache, the fullness of him makes my jaw fall open.

"Fuuuck, you feel good," he whispers. "Just a little more. You can take one more inch…yes. That's it. Yes, good girl."

My insides scream in ecstasy when he finally fills me to the brim. He adopts a delicate roll of his hips into me. Each stroke I surrender more and more, clenching my fists into his sheets. I bite down a muffled cry as he digs his fingers into my hips to steady me while he puts more strength into his thrusts, pounding into me. Hard and quick. To the point I'm clinging to every breath like it may be my last. The wet smack of our naked skin against each other fills the room, and gods, it drives me wild. I never knew how much I needed to hear the sound.

The thickness of him fills me in an enigmatic inferno. He drills into me over and over until I find my hips sliding back impatiently to meet him, chasing his rhythm for more. My lips part to let out a moan.

"Yes. Sing for me," he begs, his voice shallow and husky. He fucks me faster until we are both moaning in sync. Threading his fingers through my hair, he pulls me up onto my hands and knees. Slamming his hips into me. Harder. And harder. The pressure in me builds until I teeter at the edge, begging for release.

"Come for me. Again," he whispers against my ear. Reaching his hand down between my legs, he expertly rubs circles against my sensitive clit. With his other hand tangled in my hair, he tears my head back so I'm staring up at the ceiling. He bites into my shoulder as he thrusts in time with his fingers rubbing on my clit.

I unleash a cry as I erupt, shuddering and quaking on his

cock. A swim of stars twinkle in my vision as I climax. Gods, I swear my ears ring with how hard I orgasm.

"That's a good girl," he growls into my ear.

I'm not sure how much more time passes, as I'm lost in a timeless haze of madness and lust. Only able to focus on the now and how inexplicably feral he makes me. But I do know I climax at least three more times. I've fallen into his sheets and pillows, unable to keep myself upright on my trembling arms and legs. I'm lost to his utter control and intoxication while he fucks me into the squeaking mattress.

When I throatily scream into his pillow, spasming around his cock for a sixth time, something changes.

He spreads my legs wider as he drills into me, his voice tight and choppy. "Gods, your scream is going to make me come—"

He roars.

If it isn't the hottest thing I've heard yet, I'm not sure what would top it. He fills me with his release, his pumping slows to a stop until he pulls out of me. He collapses onto the bed beside me with a huff, his breath sawing in and out of his chest. My heart slows from a race to a sink. The fog of my desire fades and melts away. Overwhelming regret looms as I come down from the earth shattering highs.

What have I done?

THIRTY ONE

ME AND YOU

"See you tomorrow," Darian casually rumbles, his eyes closed as he still lies naked on the bed.

I nearly run out the door, fumbling with my shirt to try and tuck it into my pants as I go. I can't get out fast enough, and I can't think straight. Racing to my room, I enter and shut the door, sinking down to my heels. I stare wide eyed across my room at the opposite wall.

Oh, fuck. Oh gods. What is wrong with me? What in the fuck was that...

I bury my head into my hands. My mind reels, searching for answers, but I come up empty handed every time. I'm taken aback by how easily I slipped. Disappointed in my lack of self-composure. I should have at least tried to take the map. I smack my cheek for not considering it sooner. It's far too late to sneak back in to get it.

"Are you okay?"

Daeja's voice makes me nearly jump out of my skin.

"No. I mean...yes. I..." I sigh, running a hand through my hair. *"I don't know, Daeja. I fucked up. I just made a huge mistake."*

"I'm right here," she murmurs.

"Where?" Panic laces my voice. My breathing speeds up as realization settles around me. Last I saw her, she was just outside of camp.

"I went back to the lake as you asked. It's okay. Take a deep breath."

"Okay...okay." I rub my eyes with the heel of my hands as I process the events from the last few hours until I realize...shit. Pennyroyal. I need pennyroyal.

"I need to grab something from the healer's quadrant."

"I won't leave without you."

I scramble to my feet. If I'm still going to try to leave for the Dragon Lands, I should at least take a contraceptive. My heart thunders in my chest as I slip out of my room and out into camp. I can't help but throw a glance over my shoulder at Darian's room before I go. The slim possibility of running into Cole this late at night has me profusely sweating. I manage to make it to the healer's quadrants unseen and begin to pick through what herbs we have on the counter.

Fuck. We are out of pennyroyal.

Before I can panic, I turn to the shelves and begin to sift through bottles and vials. "Where is the godsdamned pennyroyal—"

"What are you doing here this late at night, Katerina?" a voice calls from behind me.

I whirl, not moving fast enough to conceal the vial I'm gripping onto as if it may save my very life. Part of me eases when I make out Marge's hunched silhouette. But the shadows cover her expression, and she stands in the doorway eerily still. My skin prickles as if caressed by her gaze.

Did she happen to catch what I said about the pennyroyal? I swallow, unable to come up with a good reason as to why I might be here so late at night. The thought of explaining my reason to her is both mortifying and terrifying.

Thankfully, she doesn't allow me more than a few seconds to answer.

"If you're looking for pennyroyal, we're out. Soldiers tend to celebrate when they realize how close they've come to dying. We need to restock our supplies tomorrow. You'll be fine to wait until morning."

I nod, clearing my throat as I place the vial back on its shelf. The thought of waiting until tomorrow morning has my stomach working in knots. I dip my head, and she holds the door open for me as I shuffle out. I slip out of camp, beyond the crumbling wall to the forest.

I meet Daeja near the lake, and she nudges my elbow up, lifting my arm into the air so she can slide herself against me and settles her muzzle into the crook of my chest. Her gentle breath slows my own.

After a few quiet moments, I climb onto her back and settle between her neck and shoulders. Without a word, she takes to the skies.

She doesn't ask. She doesn't say anything.

I remember her telling me before she could feel what I felt. Does she feel the shame eating at me, like a vulture feasting on a corpse? Does the guilt I feel rip into her like talons of a predator, leaving nothing left but a carcass of bone and blood? The thought of such a heavy emotion bleeding into her own self-consciousness plummets me into more guilt.

"Don't."

She glides over the lake, and the smallest morsel of peace settles over me. Up in the vastness of the night sky, I'm reminded of how small and insignificant I am. It dulls the overwhelming emotions consuming me like a rabid animal I can't control.

How did I ever get through the loss of my brother or my mother? Or the failure of saving the little girl in Hornwood? The more I think about it, perhaps I never did process the pain. Perhaps it all still lingers in the back of my mind, and it always will. Yet, the things I struggle with now feel so trivial in comparison. So self-inflicted. As I gaze down at Daeja's muscled neck and brush my hands across her scales—it clicks.

She is my gravity. The one constant thing securing me to this earth, despite doing the complete opposite—soaring through the crisp night air. With every heartache and failure, she's been there all along.

My gaze floats up toward the scenery ahead of us. The jagged mountaintops of Dragon's Back Ridge stretch into the star-studded sky like angry claws reaching for the heavens. The border between us and the Dragon Lands. All we have to do is go north.

My racing mind eases to a manageable pace with each inhale. The fog of my guilt and shame lifts. I'm finally able to think more logically. We need the map. And I need pennyroyal. I could steal the map from Darian's room. Get pennyroyal in the morning. And gather as many supplies as I can: food, water, extra clothes. It'll get colder the further north we get with us flying at high altitudes.

But where I get stuck is the people I've met here. Do I leave Marge? And do I leave Archie, without saying goodbye? The thought of leaving Archie—alone—pains me. Even if I know he'll be fine without me.

Yet, something keeps me from guiding us to the Dragon Lands. Something about it is inherently wrong. Maybe it's the fear I've already fucked up so much, and I'm scared the next decision I make will end in even more catastrophic ramifications. I don't trust myself, I realize.

And *that* scares me.

Perhaps there's still a part of me that doesn't want to leave Cole—that doesn't want to lose him completely. Even though I may already have, and even though he lost a piece of me. The thought of him with someone else destroys something intrinsic in me.

Gods, I'm a mess. My heart is shattered, and I clutch the pieces to my chest, desperately fearful I may lose another piece of myself at any given moment.

How can I love someone, and yet hate them all at the same time?

Daeja turns left, and I instinctively lean into her, bracing myself as she lifts and dives. She's holding back, though. It all comes so easy to her—like a second nature close to breathing or blinking. The sound of her wings thunder behind me. The wind cuts into my remorse and frees what tears I have from my eyes until I cry.

I reach a hand down and caress her neck, remembering when she was so small her entire body fit into the palm of my hand. The memory wraps around my heart and squeezes me in a painful way.

I'm jolted with a burst of warmth and joy, the pure emotion chasing away my darkness. My vision of a baby Daeja perched in my hand, staring up at me with her round eyes morphs. The memory shifts to me looking at...*myself*. Through Daeja's eyes.

I gasp and almost slip from her neck. In the vision, my hair is matted, and my dull eyes are sunken with sadness. Cheekbones jut out from my features, threatening to puncture my taut pale skin. Even the natural blush of my cheeks and nose is muted. The freckles dusting my nose and cheeks are stark against my ashen skin.

But I'm flooded with love, warmth, and safety. It shuns out the darkness of my thoughts and feelings.

"Me and you," Daeja whispers along our bond.

A smile splits through the bitter cold entrapping my heart. In the memory, I scratch Daeja under the chin for the first time. My foreign, dull blue eyes stare back at me. Her purr ignites a spark of life to my eyes.

The rest of the night and morning I cling to it. To that sliver of peace and love.

To Daeja.

To my relief, Marge offers me pennyroyal first thing in the morning when I report for duty. Later in the day after sparring, we gather for lunch. I sit across from Archie, wary of where Cole glides through the outpost chatting with several different soldiers. Relief washes over Cole's face when he notices me. I tear my attention away from him. Archie is droning on about Mistwood facts when I pick up the strut of a predator in my periphery.

Darian stalks by, takes a seat next to Archie, and winks when our gazes collide. I bite my lip to keep myself from blushing, staring at Archie in an attempt to look at anyone but Darian.

But Darian's eyes bore into me possessively. I'm pleading to the heavens Archie doesn't notice his newly aimed attention at me.

Archie clears his throat and peers over to Darian. Clearly, Darian and I both missed whatever Archie has said or asked.

"Shut up," Darian says, his eyes not wavering from what I imagine is the curve of my throat down to my chest.

I flick a glare at him, finally meeting his gaze. *Asshole.*

Archie flinches. "But I wanted to know if—"

Darian finally tears his stare away from me and toward Archie. "Do you not understand the concept of 'shut up?'"

I slam a fist into the table, pinning Darian with a leer. "Would you fucking leave him alone for once?"

Archie's eyes round, a nervous chuckle shaking his chest. A shoulder brushes me, and Cole settles into the seat next to mine. Darian shoots to his feet with a snort and walks off.

"Good riddance," I half-whisper as I watch Darian go.

Cole tosses me a sideways glance before taking a sip of water. He still has no food in front of him, just as I have nothing in front of me. I've been avoiding looking at what Archie's eating, for fear of it surfacing whatever may be left in the pits of my own gut.

Cole stretches a hand out cautiously for mine. "Hey...I've been wanting to talk to you. Can I get you alone for a moment—"

I jolt to my feet. "I've got to go. I'll catch you guys later."

Cole's gaze weighs on me as I leave. The space between us tears at me. I nearly run for my room, but before I know it, I'm passing my door and headed toward Darian's. The same door slammed in my face just days ago. The same one we burst through last night in a tangle of heat, lust, and...whatever else it was. I reach a hand forward to knock, hesitating, before forcing myself to rap my knuckles against the wood.

Darian pulls the door open, his face melting into a sinister grin when he realizes it's me. He leans a shoulder into the doorframe and flicks the door open. "Come in."

I slink past him into his room, my breath catching when I stare at the tangled sea of sheets on his bed. The memories of last night flash into my mind— digging my fingers into his sheets, his body pressed into mine, gods how good he felt.

I swallow.

Darian strolls over to his desk, plopping into his chair. He leans back, perching his dirty boots on the desk as he uncorks his flask. He takes a swig, and my eyes travel to the map underneath one of his boots.

I inch forward, motioning toward his flask. "A little early for that, don't you think?"

Now it's his turn to ignore me.

"So, you've come back for more?" he chirps. "Admittedly, I got carried away last night. Next time, you won't be able to walk straight when I'm done with you."

I roll my eyes, ignoring the shiver racing down my spine as I stalk over to him. My voice dips to a whisper, "No. I've come back to tell you that last night didn't happen."

"Oh? Really? Hard to say it didn't happen. I'll forever remember your gods-pleading moan and delicious skin in great detail."

"It didn't happen," I hiss. "And it's *not* going to happen again."

He laughs and kicks his feet off the desk, swinging them beneath him as he stands. His green eyes darken. Walnut brown locks of hair sweep down over his forehead, tickling the dark lashes lining his eyes.

I glare. "I'm serious, you cocky bastard."

His eyebrow quirks at my word choice. "Cocky, huh? Is that meant to be an insult or a compliment?" He takes a thumb and drags it down his tongue and bottom lip, so sensually slow I find myself holding my breath.

"Need I spell it out for you? It was a mistake," I growl.

"I'd love to agree with you, kitten." He reaches out and swipes his wet thumb slowly across my cheek. "But then we'd both be wrong."

I shove him away from me, his muscled chest firm under my palms.

He smirks. "You had a little bit of dirt there."

I don't believe a bit of it. "You're deplorable."

"I know."

"Is that all you ever know how to say?"

"What's the point in arguing with you? I'd rather spend my time and energy doing…something else." He breathes and looks down at my lips.

Turning away from him, I scan the map when I notice several letters scattered across his desk. One thing jumps out at me toward the bottom of every one of them.

'Love, Celeste.'

My eyebrows raise, and my mouth parts in surprise. Great. I've now slept with *two* taken men?

He notices my stare and shifts his body between me and the desk, covering my sight line of the letters. Leaning back against his desk, he crosses his arms over his chest. "Nosy little thing, aren't you?"

I mirror him and cross my own arms, leaning back into one hip. "Those all from your lover?"

He laughs. "No. Why? You jealous?"

I wrinkle my nose and shake my head. "Absolutely not."

"Oh my gods, you're actually…jealous?" He laughs again.

"What would I have to be jealous of?" A muscle ticks in my jaw, and I clamp it down. I turn and walk to his door. "You're so conceited."

"You'll have to try harder to insult me," he calls.

"I'm not insulting you, I'm describing you," I sneer and slam the door shut behind me.

I'll have to figure out another way to get the map. One that doesn't include sleeping with Darian again.

THIRTY TWO

BROTHERS

For once I'm mentally begging for Marge to keep me in the healer's quadrant with her. She dismisses me for the day, but I don't know how to ask to stay without drawing suspicion or questions. She insists I attend sparring to keep up my training.

I head to the sparring ring and settle on the opposite side of where Cole sits. His head snaps up, his attention focused on me. I didn't think it was possible, but the bags under his eyes have worsened. His hair is ruffled as if he's gone weeks without restful sleep. I rip my gaze away from him, pity rising like bile, and divert my attention to the sparring circle.

Darian is in the center with Archie, instructing several other soldiers in combinations. Rather than ruthlessly hacking at Archie, Darian's slow in his movements: redirecting Archie to a new position, teaching him how to block and advance. Archie's eyes sparkle in admiration, while Darian keeps his commands short and gruff.

Archie flashes a smile in my direction. Darian scolds him for losing focus, but follows his line of sight, and his eyes connect with mine. A bead of sweat runs down my neck as he steals a glance down my body and back up.

"Come step in for this pup, since he seems to be too distracted," Darian calls out to me, jerking his head at Archie.

Archie's mouth falls into a frown as he tries to argue.

I shake my head. "I think he's doing just fine."

"Then come stand in for me," Darian orders.

Archie nods enthusiastically. With a sigh, I obey, unsheathing my sword as I stride across the clearing.

"If you lose focus like that in a battle, you'll either die or get an arm cut off," Darian scolds Archie as I draw near.

"What doesn't kill you makes you stronger, right?" Archie offers with an optimistic smile.

"No. What doesn't kill me better fucking run," Darian grumbles.

Archie's lips thin in confusion. "I…I don't think that's how it goes."

Before Darian can say anything else, I step in between them. Archie and I practice slow spins and turns, strikes and blocks. Darian ghosts a touch against my waist to correct my stance in one position and knocks the tip of his boot between my feet to spread my legs wider. My breath hitches, palms sweating as I focus on Archie's face. Archie and I return to sparring, and despite white-knuckling the sword's hilt in my hand, it slips from my grip as I block Archie's attack.

"I think that's enough for today," Darian says neutrally and walks off.

I exchange glances of surprise with the rest of the soldiers in the ring. Apparently, I wasn't the only one caught off guard from Darian's sudden decision to train everyone.

I snag my sword from the ground, muttering under my breath, "I still suck at this."

"Yeah, me too," Archie admits.

I toss a look into his direction. "You're not even going to argue?"

Archie blinks. "Oh...well. You don't suck!"

I laugh at the obvious lie.

He rolls his eyes. "Okay, fine. But you know what? We can suck together. And that's better than sucking alone."

I loop an arm around his shoulder, careful not to put too much pressure on him. "How's your arm?"

"Man, Marge is some sort of magician. It's definitely sore, but I can still swing it. She just told me to take it easy!"

I raise an eyebrow, motioning to the sparring circle as we walk over to join the rest of the onlookers. "And…this is easy?"

He chuckles nervously, patting my shoulder. His smile fades quickly as his voice drops to a whisper, "Please don't tell her. She scares me."

My head tilts back with a hearty laugh.

When we get back to camp, Cole strides straight toward us from across the camp.

"Hey, I'm going to go check on Marge. I'll catch you at dinner?" I smile at Archie.

He nods, and I break off toward the healer's quadrant, quickly slipping into the door before Cole can catch up to me.

"I thought I told you you were dismissed for the day?" Marge narrows her eyes in suspicion.

"I just wanted to make sure there was nothing else I could help you with—"

Cole enters the room. "Hey."

My gaze flickers over to him, my jaw tensing. Damn, wasn't quite fast enough.

"Did you want to get something to eat with me?" Cole asks me.

I shake my head, avoiding his eye contact. "I'm fine, thanks."

He tries again, "You should still—"

"I said I'm *fine*," I level, skewering him with a glare.

He flinches. "Okay," he whispers. His gaze falls to the floor in defeat, before reluctantly turning to leave. The door shuts behind him.

"Brothers can be a little overbearing, can't they?" Marge asks from behind me.

I laugh half-heartedly, not sure how to answer her. When I think of my brother, he was anything but. He was kind, sweet, strong, and independent. "Yeah…how do you know? Do you have a brother?"

"Two of them. I was the youngest of three. We were all healers aside from my eldest brother. He was in the military."

I glance at her over my shoulder. "Are you close to them?"

"I was. My eldest brother died in battle against the King years ago."

"Your brother was a rebel?"

She nods. "He left for the north when we were in our thirties. It nearly broke my other brother's heart. They were twins— critically connected, as if they were one soul split into two bodies. When my eldest brother died in the battle, my other brother went a little…crazy. He started dabbling in blood magic to try to bring him back. But he lost himself and died trying."

"I know how it feels to lose a sibling. I'm so sorry to hear that, Marge."

A sad smile warms her eyes. "Sometimes love is our greatest strength. And sometimes it's our greatest weakness. It all just depends on how you wield it."

We stand there, letting the words soak into the silence of the moment.

She retrieves a glass of water and hands it to me. "Stress, grief, and shock will ruin your appetite. Take a few bites here and there to revive it. I still need your help around here. Make sure you're taking care of yourself. Otherwise, Cole might go a little crazy himself trying to mend you. "

I smile and nod before I take a sip.

She rests her hands on her hips, watching me. "Now…you came back wanting to know if there was anything else you could help me with? We could always use more ginger. See if you can find any in the forest."

As I leave the healer's quadrant and pass the camp's crumbling wall, a movement catches my attention. Out of the corner of my eye, I spot Darian's cat-like stalk from across the camp. His gaze is as intimate as a caress against my skin. I pick up my pace, and he matches it. We reach the trees, and he's hot on my heels, close enough I could throw this basket at him. Or an elbow. I'm starting to consider both.

"Ahh, so we've gotten to the ignoring part?" Darian's voice is as soft as velvet.

"Are you expecting some sort of thanks for finally training the soldiers you were sent here to train?" I call from over my shoulder. "Because you won't get one from me."

He snickers behind me, wraps a hand over my shoulder, and spins me to face him. "One night with you was more than enough of a thanks."

I sneer. "You're infuriating. Is there a reason you can't leave me alone?"

A grin pulls at the corner of his lips, as if he had been waiting all along for the question. "Because I know you—"

"You know *nothing* about me—"

"That's where you're wrong. I know exactly who you are." He tilts my chin up to face him. "Because you're just…like…me."

I swat his hand off my face. "I'll never be like you."

He laughs. "Except, you are. You're angry. You believe you're better than me only because you *think* you can hide it better. But I see it."

I turn and walk away, not interested in carrying the conversation further.

Yet, his voice still rings out as he follows me. "The only difference between you and I, is I don't give a fuck."

I ignore him, crouching down near a bunch of wild chamomile by a tree trunk. Pulling my skirt up to access the sheath on the side of my thigh, his gaze grazes up my leg.

He shields his eyes with the back of his hand with an exaggerated gasp. "Have you no modesty?"

I glare at him. As if he hadn't seen every bare piece of my skin and every vulnerable angle of me days ago. I shear the stalks of the flowers and place them into my basket.

"Daeja, I've got someone following me in the forest. Stay hidden, and don't come out."

"Sorry, I didn't quite hear that. Can you say it again?" Darian chuffs.

I whip to him, flabbergasted. Did he somehow read my mind? "How did you—"

"How did I manage to get so devilishly handsome? I ask myself that every day. Or…were you going to ask about my wicked intellect?" He leans back against the tree trunk and crosses his arms over his chest. "I could also divulge how I've mastered cunnilingus—"

"You are terribly annoying," I blurt.

He cocks his head to the side, his hair sweeping down across his temple. "You think so?"

"I know so."

He laughs. The sound shakes in his arms and chest. If he wasn't so damn annoying it might be an endearing sight, the way it warms his angled and sharp features.

"Now go away—" I start, but I pause as the sunlight catches a patch of grass a few yards away. Sunlight illuminates lavender flowers sprouting from the ground, their long green stalks gently swaying in the breeze.

He follows me over to the flowers, watching me with fascination. Intrigue pulls one of his eyebrows up in an arch at the awe warming my cheeks. I slice into the stalks of the flowers, freeing them from the ground and inhaling their familiar scent. Forcing any thought of Cole out of my mind, I'm brought back to the memories of the river in the northern forest, of my home, and of my family.

"What are those?" Darian interrupts.

I sheathe the dagger on my side. "What's it going to take for you to go back to camp?"

"Tell me what those are. Some rare medicinal flower?"

"No, they're alliums. I used to pick them in the forest near my home..." I trail off as I stare at the splendid raves of purple flowers, brushing a petal with my thumb.

Darian's cunning, if anything. I don't have to explain that the flowers remind me of a home I once knew.

My mother used to tell me smell was the strongest sense

tied to memories. My eyes flutter closed, the scent of the alliums bringing me back to her. To the days where my biggest worry was catching fish—not delivering a forbidden dragon to the Dragon Lands, while avoiding being caught and condemned by the King and his people. And definitely not sleeping with a man I barely knew because I told myself I was protecting Daeja, when in part it was because I was pissed at Cole. And the other parts are confused by how exhilarating my night with Darian was? Maybe even enjoyed it?

No.

I wasn't quite ready to consider that.

I flash my eyes open and turn to look at Darian. But he's gone. I catch a glimpse of him over my shoulder, his silhouette disappearing into the trees beyond back to the outpost.

At least he's a man of his word.

At sparring the next day, Carlisle hands Cole a scroll, prompting him to open it immediately. Cole skim reads the paper, his eyes widening and flicking up to me as he mutters some command to Carlisle.

I turn my focus back on practicing combination moves

against Melaina. I keep faltering in the transitions or forgetting to block in between. Unlike Archie, Melaina doesn't hold back. In a real battle, I would have already died at least five times.

"Good afternoon, squad!" a strong female voice rings out across the clearing.

All of us pause mid-spar and turn to the voice. A woman glides to the edge of the sparring circle, her dark glossy hair shining in long waves down to the bottom of her ribcage. A long, sweeping dress hugs her torso, falling at her waist in a cascade of rich blue fabric. A cluster of white pearls pin back sweeps of her hair, flaunting her high angled cheekbones. She's gorgeous. And it's obvious I'm not the only one who notices—everyone turns toward her with greeting smiles and wide eyes.

Cole breaks from the other side of the crowd and crosses the center of the sparring ring past me to her. My heart sinks at the way she beams at him, batting dark, thick lashes.

"Hello, captain," she murmurs softly—considerably different than she addressed the squad. The two words alone are sensual and intimate.

Cole dips his head low in greeting. "Hello, Celeste. My apologies we hadn't formed a proper welcome for your arrival. It seems we received your letter only moments ago."

She smiles. "Proper welcome not needed. I'm just happy to see you."

Cole breaks eye contact with her and addresses the squad. "Sparring is concluded. Let's all get lunch and refreshments."

Everyone around me scatters and floats over to Celeste's vicinity like moths to a flame.

She must be Cole's fiancée. And if not, we may have even more problems than I'm aware of, based on her unabashed admiration for him. My heart splinters at the thought of him with her, after I spent so many years yearning to be the one with his last name. And now, the closest I can get to that is pretending to be his sister.

I slip away from them, moving against the crowd.

"Kat!" Archie calls, standing with Cole and Celeste, ushering me over with an enthusiastic hand gesture.

Dammit. If only I could melt into the ground right here. I might be able to avoid Cole, but Archie I cannot. I swallow hard, struggling to mask my resentment as I drag myself over to where Archie is.

Archie closes the gap between us, looping an arm around my neck, and pulling me into his side. "Celeste said she wanted to meet you!"

Celeste's eyes sparkle as she gawks at Cole when we approach. My stomach tumbles hard enough I might puke. Celeste finally drags her attention away from Cole to me, her eyes crinkling at the corners as her smile drags her cheeks upwards. The deep blue of her eyes are dazzling.

"Ahh, Katerina! I'm so happy to finally meet you. I'm Celeste, Cole's fiancée."

I can't miss the obnoxiously cheerful emphasis on 'fiancée.' She holds out an open hand to me.

I panic, trying to casually wipe the sweat off my hand onto my sides before I meet her handshake. "Hi, nice to meet you too, Celeste."

We break our handshake, and I notice the subtle wipe of her hand on the side of her dress.

"And a very big congratulations to the two of you. I wish the both of you nothing but happiness." I dare a side glance at Cole.

His hands twitch, but his features are schooled into indifference.

"I've got to report back to the healer's quadrant. It was nice meeting you, Celeste," I excuse myself.

"Oh, of course! So lovely to meet you as well. I would love to talk to you about our plans at dinner," Celeste says.

I bite my tongue not to say anything else. With a nod, I bow my head before I disappear off back into camp.

I don't give a fuck about their plans.

THIRTY THREE

THE ART OF STITCHING

I've tried keeping myself busy in the healer's quadrant with Marge. Desperation had me almost offering to scrub the damn floors with a toothbrush, if it meant not having to leave the comforts and safety of these four walls.

Marge watches me suspiciously. "Is there a reason you are so adamant on staying in here lately? I said you were dismissed over twenty minutes ago."

I scan the room, searching for an excuse. "I know, I know.... it's just—"

My eye catches on a tear in one of the bed sheets. I dash over to it, a bit too eagerly, and grab the material.

"I noticed this was torn." I nearly vomit out the words, hoping to gauge some sort of response or command from her.

She rests her hands on her waist, cocking her hip to the side.

My breath quickens. "A-and I think we should fix it. You know? Make it really…homey in here."

She squints. "Homey?"

"Yes, homey! And…I've never been taught how to sew. Maybe you can help me practice, so someday I can stitch someone on my own?"

She laughs. "You've got a ways to go. But if you're not going to tell me why you're so reluctant to leave, I won't push you. Though, after this, I'm leaving to go bathe. Whether you decide to stay here or not, I'll leave up to you."

She points at the drawer with the needles and threads as she takes a seat on the bed. I retrieve the materials, hand them to her, and sit next to her.

Her focus shifts to the sheets. "Stitching someone and sewing aren't necessarily interchangeable. But if you can get familiar with a needle, it'll better your stitchwork."

She effortlessly winds the needle in and out of the torn sheet gracefully. For some odd reason, it reminds me of the way Daeja glides in the night sky. Like a second nature. Like breathing.

She removes all the threads she stitched, giving me a fresh slate. "Here, you try."

I stare at the sharp delicacy of the needle and the thinness of the thread. Gripping the needle between my fingers as I watched her do, I note the sweat beading on my skin, and I'm already apprehensive under her watchful eyes.

Marge's voice is soft. "It's okay to be nervous, but it won't bite you."

I glance at her sideways, and lie. "I'm not nervous."

She chuckles. "Katerina, don't you lie to me. I know by now when you're lying."

I swallow and try to thread the needle. Jerkily, I follow the same stitches she created. "I'm just not good with my hands."

"And why do you think that?"

"I've always had a hard time. My hands get so sweaty, and it makes it hard to grip things. I almost slipped—" I stop myself from divulging mine and Daeja's flying to her.

I try again. "I…slip all the time with weapons. Swords are so hard for me to hold and swing. My mother used to be an archer, and I can't do that either. Same with daggers, axes, and everything else I've tried."

The needle develops a mind of its own, jerking out of my slippery fingers and pricking my other hand.

I wince. "Shit."

"Watch your mouth, woman," Marge scolds.

"Sorry…" I mumble around my thumb, sucking the blood oozing out of my finger.

"It's okay to not be good at things. I'm not good at those things either." Marge stands and hobbles over to the prep area. She pulls open a drawer and digs out something black.

"Yeah, but you're good at healing. And sewing." I motion to the needle and thread laying on the torn sheet.

"That came with years of practice. The more you practice,

the better you'll get. We all start off terrible. You'll get there—you have the drive, and I have no doubts you'll accomplish whatever you put your mind to."

I smile at the encouraging words she's decided to share with me. But it quickly fades as her sincerity reminds me of my mother. She knew when I needed to be pushed outside of my comfort zone and knew when I needed to be encouraged first.

"What's wrong?" Marge asks, noting the fall of my features as she sits beside me again.

"I just…I thought of my mother. And I miss her."

Marge gently brushes her hand over mine. "She would be proud of you."

Guilt swells inside of me as I remember the many years I dreamed of a different life. A life where I didn't have to fish to provide for my mother and me, where I didn't have to pick between us going hungry or her getting low on medicine. And now that I'm here, living a different life just like I had begged for, all I can do is miss those times. Looking back, it all seemed so simple.

Here I am today, living a life where all of my decisions are blinded by anger or fear. I almost left without saying goodbye to Marge and Archie. I slept with a man I barely know and can hardly stand, even though my heart belongs entirely to Cole. I should have left long ago with Daeja. But the truth is, I'm a coward.

I laugh, trying to mask the feelings threatening to pull me under. "I don't know about that."

"But I know. I've seen the way you defend that Archie boy. Heard how you had saved those Blackfell civilians. You saved me from those rebels, despite me giving you no reason to risk your own life. I could have turned you in, and yet you still defended me. You're patient and kind. Strong willed and ambitious. I've seen how furiously you try to learn, whether it be fighting or medicinal."

I suck my lips in. She doesn't know the reason I asked to learn about sewing in the first place was to try to furiously avoid Cole. And Celeste.

Maybe Darian, too.

"But I keep making these mistakes..." My vision blurs with tears as I glance down at my hands, attempting to sew again and shoving all the emotions back behind a facade.

Her voice is gentle. "It's okay. We all make mistakes. Here," she takes my hand and places whatever she retrieved from the drawer in my palm, "you can have these. It's my extra pair."

I unfurl the ball of black to find a pair of gloves. *Her* gloves.

I shake my head. "I can't take these."

"Yes, you can. Besides, I really only wear this pair anyway." She motions to the ones on her hands.

My thoughts flicker to the last time someone gave me a gift—Cole placing his mother's ring in my palm and closing my fingers over it.

"Go on," Marge encourages.

With her insistence, I pull the gloves onto my fingers. Gratitude surges in me at such a generous gift. I flex my hands in the material and smile at her.

She pats my leg, rises, and hobbles toward the door. "Alright, well you can stay here and keep practicing for as long as you want. But I need to go bathe. I'm quite tired from the last few days."

"Hey, Marge?"

She turns to look at me over her shoulder. "Yes?"

"Thank you."

For the first time since I've known her, she actually smiles at me. Really, truly smiles. The gesture lightens her face, the wrinkled lines in the corners of her eyes deepening. She dips her head, then slips out the door.

After a few breaths, I steady my hands and thread the needle again and again, until I feel I've mastered the shake in my hands. The material of the gloves keeps my hands from slipping and blocks the needle from piercing my skin. The stitches in the material aren't nearly as neat as Marge's, but at least I can say I've done it.

At least I can say I've tried.

I debate staying in the healer's quadrant for the rest of the night. I could sleep in one of the beds to avoid the walk to my room. Placing the needle and thread back in the drawer, I gather what courage I can. With a deep breath, I push the door open. The sun has settled behind the horizon, the last of its rays coloring the sky in yellow, oranges, and reds. Chatter and laughter surge from the center of camp, and as I walk toward my room, I run into Archie.

"Hey, Kat! I've been looking for you!"

"Ahh, sorry. I've been practicing stitching in the healer's quadrant." It's an excuse, but at least it's true.

"I suppose next time you'll sew me up?" He winks.

"Probably not yet. Though, hopefully, there isn't a next time where you need stitches!" I scold.

He loops an arm around my neck and pulls me into a tight side hug. "No promises. You hungry?"

"No."

"Okay, well, you can still sit with us! Cole and Celeste have been waiting for you."

He leads me to where the tables are, lined with almost everyone from the squad. I pick Cole out first. Next to him is Celeste, completely enveloped in the sight of him as she speaks. Her hand caresses his back as she leans in to whisper into his ear. His eyes are glued to me, completely distracted from Celeste. A new surge of nausea rolls over me, and I break our eye contact.

Celeste looks out across the crowd before settling on someone in the group. I follow her gaze to Darian.

Darian stares back at Celeste with lowered eyebrows and rolls his eyes, breaking their eye contact. His face is emotionless as he throws his head back to guzzle down whatever is left in his flask, and he disappears off toward his room. Sadness flickers in Celeste's polished features as she watches him leave—a split second of longing and yearning. It vanishes so quickly, I almost wonder if I imagined it.

I stiffen as I recall the day I walked into his room. The letters and what little I saw scrawled on the bottom of each one.

'Love, Celeste.'

I have to force my mouth closed. *Does Cole know? And is that why Darian hates Cole so much?*

Archie and I take a seat across from Cole and Celeste.

Celeste beams as we settle into our seats. "Kat! We were wondering where you were."

I'm tempted to tell her only my friends call me Kat. "Ahh, yes. Sorry, I was practicing stitching with Marge."

"Not a worry! Listen, I was just telling Cole how I would love to steal you for tomorrow."

Cole whips his head in her direction, as if smacked out of his stupor. "If I may, Celeste, we desperately need Kat here at the outpost."

He's lying.

His fingers thrum against the wooden table, fidgeting with a noisy speed. I don't provide much value to the outpost—as a soldier or a healer. He must feel awfully obligated to save me from any such one-on-one times with his betrothed.

Celeste waves a hand. "Nonsense! I'm sure Marge wouldn't mind. Katerina deserves a break—I've heard she's not only been apprenticing with Marge but also training with your squad? Besides, I would enjoy her company to Windmere."

"Windmere? Why would we go there?" I arch an eyebrow. The thought of being separated from Daeja stealing my breath.

Celeste turns her radiant smile on me. "To go dress shopping, of course!"

"Dress shopping? What do I need a new dress for?"

Archie whines disappointedly. "Aww man, I want to go!"

"Sorry, ladies only!" Celeste laughs, sneaking a glance at Cole. "We are throwing a small dinner celebration for our betrothal."

Gods, she's so smitten. My mind jumps to them together: kissing, touching, tangled in the sheets. I have to stop myself before I vomit or blurt out the truth of our situation.

Instead, I fight for an excuse. "That's alright. I have a dress here I can wear."

"You can save that. I want to take you out for a new one! You don't even have to worry about spending a dime. It'll be my treat." She places her hand over Cole's, who subtly flinches at her touch.

"You know, I could always switch places with you. I would look incredible in a dress." Archie waggles his eyebrows.

It drags a chuckle out of me.

"I'll fetch you in the morning, and we will make our way there together," Celeste announces, saying it in a way that cuts off any more of my refusals. She's making this incredibly difficult to get out of.

I lock into her blue, doe eyes. "How are we supposed to walk to Windmere and back in a day?"

"No, we wouldn't walk, silly girl!" Celeste laughs. "We're going to take the carriage."

My eyes round. Only the wealthy had carriages and horses. Horses were tasty meals for dragons, so if you owned one, it meant you had the means necessary to keep them guarded. I should have known by the elegant sweep of her dress, the rich colors adorning the layers. She looks so…out of place in this rugged, dusty, monotone place of a camp. Gems dripping from her earrings scatter prisms of light across the room every time she moves her head. Gold bands encircle her fingers, but no engagement ring—Cole's mother's ring is missing.

I flick my gaze to Cole, and he's already staring at me.

I push up to my feet. "Great. I'll meet you in the morning then. I'm pretty tired, so I'm going to turn in early."

Celeste and Archie both groan in detest.

Archie pulls at my sleeve, pleading. "But you just got here!"

I offer him an encouraging smile. "I'll see you tomorrow!"

Tomorrow, I'll have to put on my best show yet, pretending to be Cole's sister.

Pretending to be someone I'm not.

THIRTY FOUR

TEA & PASTRIES

Each time I close my eyes and drift to sleep, my dreams are wrapped in fire. Cole, Darian, and Celeste flash behind my eyes. I fight against my drowsiness, sitting up and eventually slipping out toward the forest to see Daeja. The thought of being in another town without her settles like a stone in my gut.

"Hi," she chuffs in greeting and snakes her way over to me. She stretches forward, inching closer until we are nose to nose, her scales startlingly cool against my skin. *"You're stressed."*

There's no hiding from her. She's in my head, my heart, and every fiber of my soul. As if we're the same being.

She turns away from me and walks over to a tree. The wood groans and snaps as she rips the small tree from the ground. She swings her head back toward me with the tree in her mouth, nearly the full length of her.

I duck before I'm sideswiped. *"What are you doing?"*

Her lip pulls up to reveal a glimmer of her daggered teeth clenched around the wooden trunk. ***"You know what we haven't played in a while?"***

I snicker, thinking of the first night I met her, and how I threatened her with a stick. Which then turned into an unintended game of fetch. *"Daeja, I can't play."*

"And why not?"

"Because I can't pick up that tree on my own, even if I tried!" I laugh and pat her cheek.

If dragons could chuckle—I'm sure she would be. ***"Fine."***

She flings the tree off toward the lake. I flinch as it crashes into the water, swallowed down to its depths. Daeja runs her black tongue over her teeth repeatedly.

She jolts back as her eyes narrow, whipping her head back and forth. ***"Something is in my teeth."***

"Let me see."

She lowers her head for me and curls her lips to bare her teeth. If anyone else saw us, they might be frightened for me. Likely petrified. But I hook a thumb under her upper lip and examine her serrated teeth. I pluck a splinter the size of my finger out from her gums and toss it off into a bush.

"I have to go to Windmere in the morning. It's a town northeast of here, and I should be back by nightfall. I'll come see you as soon as I'm back. I need you to stay here by the lake while I'm gone."

Her billowed breath warms my face, a clear sign of her disappointment. But she must sense the shift of worry in me because she pushes her head into my chest. ***"I'll be fine. I do that every day, anyhow. And if you need me, I'll only be a flight away."***

I smile, resting my head on hers for a few seconds more, before we say our goodbyes, and I head back to the outpost.

After I've cleared the stone wall surrounding the camp, I near my room and pause when I pick up the sound of a soft knock. Dashing to the shadows, I press myself up against the back wall of my room and wait, my heart thundering in my chest.

The knock sounds again, and I peek around the corner toward the sound. A dark silhouette of a woman stands at Darian's door, the long sweep of her gown melting into the ground.

Celeste.

She stands, hand still balled into an upheld fist, waiting for the door to open. A few more long seconds tick by, and she raps her knuckles against the wood a third time.

The door whips open. Darian's walnut brown hair is strewn about his head, and his loose shirt hangs off his strong shoulders. His eyes narrow to slits as he realizes who has been knocking on his door at such a late hour.

"The fuck do you want?" he growls.

Celeste responds in a much quieter whisper, so soft I can't pick it up. With the two of them distracted, I slink closer, edging over to the storage tent separating mine and Darian's rooms. Still crouched on the ground, I edge out an inch just to get a glimpse.

From this angle, I see both of their profiles. Celeste reaches out with a gloved hand, her features soft as she brushes Darian's arm.

Darian tilts his head back at Celeste, anger simmering deep within his soul. He rips his arm back. "Don't. Fucking. Touch me, Celeste."

She retracts her hand reluctantly, eyes wide and pleading. "Can't we at least talk?"

"You and I have absolutely nothing to talk about."

"You're…you're being an asshole," she murmurs.

I flinch, not expecting such a vulgar response from someone as proper as she is. Her voice edges on frustration and desperation.

His hand squeezes tight around his door frame. "Yeah, I know. After all this time, how is that a shocker to you?"

She holds his stare, her own jaw clenching and unclenching. "Can't you at least hear me out? I *love* you—"

His chest inflates, his posture straightening as he towers over her, his nose crinkling. His glare alone could burn a village to the ground. "Don't you fucking use that word on me."

I swallow, my breath nearly knocked out of my lungs by the severity of his tone. Feeling all too overwhelmed by the intensity of this private moment, I pull away from the corner and hide back behind the cover of the storage tent, staring out at the forest beyond the crumbling stone wall.

Darian's voice cuts through the silence. "Get the fuck out of here. Go. You're making this much harder than it needs to be."

The sound of the door slamming shut rings in my ears.

Finally, a knock sounds at my door in the morning, and I absent-mindedly fiddle with small pieces of lint on my dress as I go to open the door. Celeste stands in the early morning light, her dark hair swept back into gracious curtains of pins. Brilliant pearls drip from her ears, a soft blush sweeping across her cheeks. She smiles warmly at me, her cheeks wrinkling her gorgeous blue eyes.

Gods, couldn't she at least be unattractive? Or mean? I shove the thoughts away and the jealousy racing in with it.

"Good morning! Are you ready? We can stop for tea and pastries on the way into town," Celeste chimes.

"Oh…that sounds great." I force enthusiasm into my voice, as I scan her expression. Though, I find no hints of the despair she willingly showed Darian hours earlier.

She opens the crook of her arm, and I hesitantly link my arm with hers. She leads us away from camp, past the eastern outpost wall and into a clearing glittering with morning dew. In the sunlight, a white carriage gleaming with gold accents awaits us. Two majestic white horses hitched to the carriage reach down to nibble at the grass, their long tails flicking and ears swiveling to every noise. Perched atop the seat of the carriage is a gentleman dressed in formal black. He dips his head to us and jumps down to open the door. Inside the carriage are plush, velvety red seats adorned with golden buttons and trim. Even the windows arch in delicate golden swirls and curves.

Now I'm the one out of place.

Celeste allows me to enter first, and once both of us are sat, the gentleman shuts the door and returns to his post. The sound of the door closing reiterates my situation. We are alone. I'm not quite sure how far Windmere is from here by carriage. I'm hoping not too long, as I'm nervous I may inadvertently slip and give away my true heritage.

The carriage jerks forward to a roll. I watch the outpost's stone wall and buildings disappear into the distance.

Celeste finally breaks the silence, "So, Kat! Cole told me you joined the squad recently. How have you liked it so far?"

I was really hoping we could enjoy the silence.

"It's been…uhh…good." I nod awkwardly. "I've learned so much in the short amount of time I've been here."

"How marvelous! I imagine it's been quite the adjustment transitioning from civilian life to military life."

"It has. I'm still adjusting, but I don't miss civilian life." I glance out the window toward the forest. At least here in the King's military I didn't need to worry about where my next meal will come from. Although, it sure puts a strain on my relationship with Daeja.

"Oh? You don't?" Celeste tilts her head to the side, her earrings twinkling with the motion.

"Well…maybe I do a little bit. I miss my mother—" I stop. "I-I mean, I miss my family."

Her features soften, her lips pull into a frown. "I know. I am so sorry about your mother. I know how hard it was on Cole, too."

She leans forward and glances at my hands. I try not to flinch at the thought of her grabbing them. Thankfully, she has the sense not to.

"Thank you..." I whisper, averting my attention back to the window.

"You know, since you've been back he's really lightened up."

I toss her a side glance. "What do you mean?"

"He just seems so much more...alive?" She laughs and waves her hand as if to erase what she's just said. "I—I don't know what I'm saying."

"Alive how?"

"He just...I don't know. When I first met him he was so solemn. Like a shell of a person. I don't think I ever saw him smile. And now he seems different. I thought maybe he was just warming up to me, but I notice how different he is around you. It's like the sun came out between the clouds."

I bite my lip, trying not to let a smile creep in. Not that it matters. I'm not the one he's engaged to. And now that we're in this situation...I'm not sure if we can ever be together again.

"I can tell from the way he looks at you and the way he talks to you. How his eyes light up whenever you're around. He really loves you." She sighs. "And I guess I'm trying to say I'm glad you're here."

"Thank you, Celeste." But I'm not glad I'm here.

Or her.

A cold bitterness stings me like a wasp—this isn't who I want to be. Angry and resentful toward someone I don't even know, someone who hasn't given me any direct reason to not like her. Regardless of whatever complicated situation we are in, and regardless of my aching heart, she doesn't deserve my loathing.

At least, not yet.

The carriage heaves upwards and sends us both flying. We smash into each other, my nose ramming into her sternum as we collide. A splitting ache cracks in my nose, and the carriage comes to a screeching halt. We scramble up from the ground, each trying to help the other back to their seat. Blood drips from my nose, and I cup a hand to catch the drops before it can stain Celeste's perfectly golden dress.

"Oh my, are you alright?" Celeste whips out a handkerchief from a pocket hidden in the folds of her dress. She holds it to my nose, the blood spreading like ink across the white cloth.

"I'll be fine," I say nasally, blinking through the tingling pain. I take the cloth from her, wiping the spots of blood off my hand and holding the handkerchief back to my nose. "Just a little bump, I don't think it's broken."

"My sincerest apologies!" the driver calls through the door. "Are you both alright?"

"Finneas! What was that?" Celeste demands.

"I'm not certain. One moment." The ground thuds under his landing. His footsteps patter around the carriage as he investigates.

"Are you okay?" I ask Celeste, finally.

She nods, subconsciously tracing her fingers over her chest.

"Madam Celeste?" Finneas calls. "You might want to come take a look at this."

"Stay here," she commands and slips out of the carriage, shutting the door.

I shift closer to the window, peering out toward the back of the carriage. Both of them are bent over and examining one of the carriage's wheels. Behind the wheel is what looks like a dark, thick branch. Celeste grabs it, despite Finneas's discouraging mumbles, and holds it up in the light. The sunlight ridges the edges of the branch and the sharp prong at the end. I'm unsure if Celeste and Finneas recognize what it is, but I do. Because I've seen it on Daeja.

It's a horn. Maybe half the length of my forearm.

Celeste levels a look at Finneas who dips his head. She slips the horn into a hidden pocket in her dress. Finneas returns to his seat, and I shuffle back to mine.

Celeste smiles as she slides back onto the bench across from me. "My apologies! Looks like we hit a branch."

Liar.

Because that was no branch.

It was dragon contraband.

My gaze wanders to Celeste's dress every time she isn't paying attention. I scan for the curve of the horn against her dress, but it's well hidden within the creases and layers of the fabric. A lingering fear of what else she might be hiding under her dress buzzes in the back of my mind.

She chatters on about all the towns she's been to and how her favorite color is purple. We talk of flowers and the spring. Small chit chat, but I oblige her. I actually prefer it. These sorts of simple conversations I don't have to lie or think about.

When we enter the gates of Windmere, the townspeople watch the carriage roll by with excitement and awe. We finally stop in a town circle with colorful buildings crowding the perimeter. Finneas opens the door for us, and we spill out into the street. In the middle of the circle is a towering fountain carved from a rich marble, stark white with faint gray veins spidering the stone. The marble is carved into the silhouette of a man pointing a sword at the sky. Its height soars above all the other buildings, and water murmurs at its base.

Celeste follows my wondrous stare. "Beautiful, isn't it? It was made for the King."

"We never had such things in Padmoor," I admit, my eyes wandering every curve of the fountain. The cost alone to commission such a thing could have easily fed a small town for months.

Celeste glides past me and closer to the fountain, the train of her dress brushing the cobblestones until she stops a few paces ahead of me. Her head tilts back to stare up at the fountain. "They say he was born here. The town commissioned the fountain to honor the King and his sacrifices for our realm."

Like how he so generously sacrificed his own sister to be King? I make an active effort not to scoff. "His sacrifices?"

She nods, still staring at the statue. "Yes. His wife and daughter. His daughter was burned to death by two dragons. She was a toddler."

My sadness and shock zaps all the warmth from my face, my expression melts into a gasp. "That's…that's awful. What became of his wife?"

Celeste turns toward me. Her characteristically cheery demeanor transforms into a heavy stone-cold sadness. "She killed herself. She couldn't live with the pain of such a great loss. After the death of his daughter and wife, the King banished dragons, so no one else would have to carry a burden so great or face a pain of that magnitude ever again."

But Daeja could never. *Would* never.

The silence between Celeste and I is filled with the soft gurgling water from the fountain. I'm so close to asking Celeste why the King killed his sister. But then I remember the horn hidden somewhere in her dress. I'm not quite sure what side she's on.

Celeste physically shakes her head to rid herself of the sadness, like a dog shaking off excess water from its fur. She clasps my hand and tugs me gently away from the fountain. "Come. Let us treat ourselves to some tea."

As we walk toward the shops lining the streets, the townspeople we pass watch us intently. They look Celeste up and down, admiring her stunning gown with wide eyes and soft smiles. A child points at us, and his mother swats his hand down with a scolding mutter. Men dip their heads and tip hats toward us in respect.

I pin a sideways glance at Celeste. "Have you been here before?"

She shrugs. "A few times."

We pass a lonely, dusty alleyway with a man curled into a fetal position, his eyes closed. His ragged clothes rise and fall with his sleepy breath, his skin stained with dirt. Celeste pauses mid-step as she fishes out coins from her purse. When she opens the clutch I stare in amazement at her collection of gold and silver coins. With gloved fingers, she retrieves several golds and places them near the man's hands. She notices my gaped mouth, and I blush in embarrassment.

"It's not mine, truly. Everything I have is my father's," she explains.

I drag my gaze away from her purse to her face. "And who is your father?"

"Jurrock."

The name spins me. I've heard that name before. I remember the night I saw Cole at the inn in Blackfell—Darian had been trained by Jurrock. My father wrote about him, too—the one who gave the King a dragon egg. If Jurrock was her father, and Darian was trained by him…

Gods, the way she stared at Darian so longingly yesterday. The way he brushed her off, as if she were nothing but a piece of dust. Celeste was jaw-droppingly gorgeous. A beauty I simply couldn't compete with. And if Darian had so much as a sliver of desire for me, I couldn't imagine what he might have felt toward her. They must have been close if he spent so much time training with her father to become the best swordsman in the kingdom.

A lot of time together, if she was writing him so many letters. Especially considering she ended each one with *'Love, Celeste.'*

My heart thunders in my chest as I recall their encounter last night, Celeste saying she loves him, and Darian snapping at the confession.

I couldn't help but wonder to myself if Darian loved her, too. If he was even capable of comprehending such a meaningful emotion through his constant haze of contempt.

"He was the King's general," Celeste interrupts my thoughts.

I knew of his position, only because of my father's journal. But I clear my throat. "Was?"

We stroll further down the street and away from the alley.

Her gaze flickers away from me and to the shop windows we pass by. "Yes, was. He died."

"Oh. I'm so sorry to hear that, Celeste," I say, and I mean it. No matter who endures it, the loss of a parent is devastating. Something I still wouldn't wish on my worst enemy.

She dips her head. "Thank you. He left me with a lot of money…and I just don't feel right keeping it to myself. I don't feel I deserve it. I have more than enough for a comfortable life, and I know there are so many people in this kingdom scraping by."

"Is that why you feel obligated to get a dress for me?" I ask impulsively.

"No." She chuckles with a wink. "I have other reasons."

Cole. Of course it's because of Cole. She wants to impress or perhaps befriend me, so that she might get closer to Cole.

We stop at a shop front, and the shopkeeper welcomes us in, hugging Celeste and kissing each of her cheeks before introducing herself to me. The shopkeeper ushers us back to a private table, away from the wide windows facing the streets. She doesn't even bother to ask me or Celeste what we want. Moments later, she delivers several dishes piled high with sugar-dusted pastries, a tea kettle, and teacups.

Celeste has definitely been here more than a few times.

"You'll love the tea here. It's divine," Celeste says as she mixes sugar into her teacup with a silver spoon. She pours me a cup.

I've never had tea. It was one of those things we weren't able to afford, but I knew a lot of the wealthy ladies drank it. When I lift the cup to my lips to sip the hot tea I try to school my features. But my nose wrinkles as I swallow the first sip, giving me away. It tastes like…hot, dirty water with flowers in it.

She laughs. "You don't like tea, do you?"

I try to clear my throat. For the first time, I'm honest with her. "No."

She smiles and offers me a pastry instead. "How about pastries?"

"That I do, thank you." I grin and take a bite of the pastry. The sugary treat is easily the most delicious thing I've ever tasted.

Celeste tilts her head to the side, watching me. "Do you mind if I call you sister?"

A cough steals my breath at her abrupt question. Luckily, my mouth is full, granting me extra time to respond.

Her eyes widen before shifting down to her cup in embarrassment. "Sorry, sorry. Far too forward of me. Please forgive me. I just…I know how close you are to your brother. I didn't have that, and admittedly, I've always yearned for it."

I nod slowly and swallow the bite of pastry. "It's okay. I get it."

She peers up at me through her dark lashes. "You do?"

Now I'm fumbling for some sort of parallel to offer. I think of how close I used to be to my own brother before he died. Aside from your typical sibling bickering, I had always been close to my brother.

So I offer her a half-truth. "I'm not very close…to my sister. We've always been at odds with one another. I used to think she was jealous of how close I was to Cole and that was why she never liked me."

I wondered if Vivian knew her brother was engaged to someone else other than me. If I know her as well as I think, she's relieved at the fact. Not to mention if he's marrying into such a wealthy family, she'll revel in the opportunity for dress shopping, tea, and pastries.

Celeste sighs and looks at her hands. "I relate to that, too. Except I've always been the jealous one."

"What do you mean?" I ask as I attempt another sip of tea.

"Darian and Edith have always been so close. I've always been the outlier."

I swallow, nearly spewing the tea out of my mouth. "You're—you're Darian's sister?"

She meets my gaze with arched eyebrows. "You didn't know?"

I shake my head. "I know he has a sister in a coma?"

"Yes. Edith." She frowns. "Her and Darian were so close when she was awake. Inseparable, even. He had always been the prime big brother to her. I suppose I'm not too surprised he never mentioned me."

But how do I tell her Darian never mentioned Edith, either? Hadn't mentioned any of his family. Or really anything about himself. Ever. The only facts I knew about him were shared by other people.

Celeste goes on, "He hardly considers me his sister. Most of the time he excuses the term. I've given up on reminding him that being half-siblings shouldn't mean our relationship is any different than his and Edith's."

"Half-siblings?"

"Well, our father met my mother first. They were together for several years, and when they didn't work out, he moved on to Darian and Edith's mother. Our father died shortly after their mother did. They have no one now. No one but each other..." Celeste's eyes glaze over in memory. "My mother is still in Helmbrook. I've debated leaving home to live with her, as I haven't seen her since I was a little girl. I've always lived with my father. But ever since I learned of his death, I can't seem to bring myself to leave the only home I've ever known."

"How did he die?" I ask gently.

She blinks, looking down at her tea. "He died in battle."

"I'm very sorry, Celeste," I murmur.

She forces a grin, finally making eye contact with me. "Thank you. I'm looking forward to getting to know you and your family and to become a part of it. I adore Cole. And I love how tight-knit you all are. I've always wanted that."

She drinks the rest of her tea and sets the cup down into the dish with a clatter. She flashes me a brilliant smile. "Now, what do you say we try on some dresses?"

"How am I supposed to walk in this without tripping?" I ask Celeste as I twist around, motioning to the plume of fluffy layers fanning out around me.

She giggles. "Very, very carefully."

"Will I even be able to fit through a doorway?"

Now she really laughs, a full whole-hearted laugh that makes me smile. "Of course, silly! That's what double-doors were invented for."

I stare down at the fluffed dress, holding my hands out to the side to accentuate just how wide it is.

"Okay, okay. Fine. No ball gowns. How about you try this one instead?" She holds up another dress she's selected.

I gulp. It's a dazzling midnight blue dress edged in golds glimmering in the light streaking through the shop windows. Far too elegant for someone like me. I take the dress from her, staring down at the stitchwork. The quality of the fabric alone tells me it's something I could never afford. Nor would it be something I'm comfortable asking Celeste to purchase on my behalf.

"Stop it, I told you I would take you shopping. Quit looking at the price tag, and go try it on!" Celeste eagerly flicks a wrist at me and sits back in her chair, crossing her legs.

Huffing my resignation, I slink back to the dressing room again. I shimmy out of the weighted ball gown and slide on the blue dress, pulling the silky material over my hips and chest. The dressmaker helps tighten the corseted back for me and hands me some tall, daggered heels. I shake my head, knowing I won't be able to walk in them without tripping. She returns with a pair sporting a shorter heel. A *kitten* heel, she calls it.

My thoughts wander to Darian, before I yank them back.

After I slip the heels onto my feet, I finally dare a look at my reflection in a mirror.

It's everything I would have dreamed of as a little girl and more. The midnight blue corset cinches my waist, and a sweetheart neckline plunges down to accentuate the curve of my breasts. Flecks of gold dust the rich blue material, and when I spin, it glimmers like sparks of a fire. I leave the dressing room and stand in front of Celeste.

She clasps her hands together, mouth dropped open in sheer excitement. "Kat...it's...perfect. You are absolutely gorgeous."

She turns to the shopkeeper and hands her a heavy bag of coins.

My eyebrows knit in confusion. "What about you? You didn't even try anything on."

"I know. I actually already picked out my dress. But don't worry, I'll have you come to help me pick out the big, white one." She grins mischievously with a wink. "We've got to head to Skylark now, otherwise we'll be late."

"Skylark?"

"Yes, Skylark is our estate. It's big enough to host a ball. Carlisle will be leading the squad so we can borrow Cole for a few days."

My mouth goes dry at the thought of being separated from Daeja even longer. A few days? We don't have a few days. Not to mention, I've never been apart from Daeja for that long. *"Can you hear me from here?"*

"Yes, why?"

I debate requesting her to follow me to Skylark but decide against it. It would likely be even more risky for her to move. Especially into an area we aren't familiar with and especially since we can't rely on her vanishing skills. Without the forest, and without the cover of darkness, she would be nearly impossible to hide.

"Apparently, I'm not coming back tonight. And it may be a few days before I'm back—"

"I'll be okay," she assures me. **"I've been out here on my own, another day or two won't hurt."**

I scramble quickly for an excuse, turning to Celeste. "What about Marge? She'll wonder—"

Celeste holds up a finger to me. "Ahh, ahh. You don't need to worry. I have it all taken care of. She knows you'll be back. Archie, Cole, and Melaina are on their way in a separate carriage, so they'll meet us there."

"And your brother?" I can't tell if I'm asking because I'm hoping he won't be there…or if there's some small part of me hoping he will be.

She scoffs, her earrings shimmering with the shake of her head. "He won't bother to show. We'll be free of his contempt and bad manners, so don't you worry about him."

I nod, partly relieved. At least I would have Archie with us. "Did you say Melaina?"

"Yes, she's been a family friend for a while. I almost brought her with us today."

"How come you didn't?"

A grin spreads her delicate lips with a hint of mischief, a striking resemblance to her half-brother. "I have my reasons."

THIRTY FIVE

SKYLARK

The city of Windmere gives way to lush green trees and open flat land. Dragon's Back Ridge rises into the sky, harsh shadows etched into its rocky sides. It's the clearest view I've had of the mountains so far. By the time Celeste and I arrive at Skylark, it's late afternoon.

We pass through massive curved iron metal gates. Rich green gardens fan out to my left and right, vibrant with bursts of flowers and bushes. A web of paths snake between the greenery and around fountains sputtering water. When Finneas opens the carriage door and we exit, my gaze sweeps left and up. My breath catches on large marbled columns and the flower-lined windows of a sizable chateau.

"Thank you for spending your day with me," Celeste says and squeezes my hand.

We ascend the front steps together, my shoes clicking against the stone. A pair of double-doors arch upward above us in greeting. The thickness of the doors alone could stand the weight of a group of men. Maybe more than that. Perhaps even the weight of a dragon. It's the only thing I can think about with how illogically tall the doors are.

"Guess a ball gown *could* have squeezed through here," I murmur, eyes wide.

Celeste giggles and unlinks her arm from mine. "I have some urgent matters to attend to before the ball. But I'll see you for dinner tonight."

We enter through the front doors, and I'm not sure where to look next. The foyer opens up to a grand staircase splitting into two different directions at the second landing, each railing glittering in gold. Every wall is adorned in intricate patterned stonework, gleaming candelabras, and rich red curtains. The marble floors are covered with expansive, vibrant rugs.

Celeste dips her head and struts through one of the several arched doorways, disappearing down a hallway.

Could the 'urgent matters' have something to do with the dragon horn she has stashed in her dress?

A suited man leads me through the winding hallways of the house. We pass by enormous rooms large enough to house our entire squad, a library with shelves brimming with books, and a kitchen bustling with people prepping and cooking. We reach the northern part of the house, and he opens a door for me, gesturing me in.

Light filters through the windows, caressing long, thick, red curtains spilling onto the marbled floor. A bed opposite the window is fluffed with layers of thick blankets and multiple pillows. I don't think I've ever seen so many pillows. How many people did they think were going to sleep in this damn bed?

I smile at the gentleman. "Thank you."

He hangs up my dress in a large wardrobe with intricate columns of brass before he leaves. I peer out the window, noticing the gardens I saw earlier. In a way, it reminds me of home and the forest. Just a little less…wild.

I sit on the bed, jumping up and down a few times, marveling at how plush the mattress and blankets are. I sink onto my back and stare at the ceiling.

"Daeja? Can you still hear me from here?"

"Yes, doing just fine, before you ask."

I snicker, *"Thank you for confirming. I've never seen a place like this…I wish you were here. I'm willing to bet they have more chicken than you could ever ask for."*

She snorts. **"Speaking of food…how much trouble will I be in if I eat a two legger?"**

"Daeja…" I scold as I shoot up to my forearms. *"We don't eat two leggers, remember? If you're that hungry—"*

"I didn't. Just curious, is all."

But I know better. She wouldn't be asking unless she had a reason to. *"Why? Have you seen anyone lurking about?"*

"The one who kissed you."

I stare out at the window. If she meant Cole, she would

have referred to him as the Red One, as she always did. My heart skips a beat. There's no telling what Darian was capable of. I've only seen him in combat with humans, but I don't doubt he could be vicious against a dragon.

"Daeja, if he sees you, I want you to fly as fast as you can—"

"How many times do I have to tell you I'm not leaving without you?"

"Then you come to me, and I will meet you. And we will go north together. But stay out of sight—"

"I know. I know. He didn't see me last night. I was across the lake, hidden by the trees. But I could smell him."

"What was he doing?"

"I don't know. I couldn't tell. It almost looked like he was carrying something. But I left before he could spot me."

My eyes narrow. What would Darian be doing stalking around the lake at night?

"Did you see him after I left you?"

"Yes."

Which meant he must have gone right after Celeste knocked on his door and he told her to leave.

As if the extra distance between Daeja and I wasn't already reason enough to feel uneasy. Tension strains every muscle in my body, like the string of a bow pulled tight.

Studying the room, an idea sparks me. Given Celeste's father was the previous military general, I suspected there was more than just dragon horns hiding in this massive estate. He had to at least have a map of sorts. Or, at least, I had to try and look for one.

"I'll check in with you later tonight. I'm going to try and look for a map here."

"Be careful. Stay out of sight. If they see you, I want you to run as fast as your two little legs will carry you…"

I laugh at her half-hearted mock.

"Just remember. Even if you're trapped, we don't eat two leggers."

"Thank you for clearing up my confusion."

An hour later, and I've brushed through my hair and slipped on the midnight blue gown Celeste picked out for me earlier today. I stare at myself in the ornate gold mirror perched on the bathroom counter for a long time. This was what I wished for all those years ago: balls, fancy dresses, the finest wines, friends, and handsome men.

Men…my mind slips to Cole, even as I dig my heels into the ground to keep from going there. But thinking of him is as natural as breathing. Despite my every effort to shut my heart off from him, I can't seem to take back what he took of me. I shouldn't be thinking about him. He's engaged. And even worse, *engaged* to a woman who has been nothing but kind to me, contrary to her impossible brother. An impossible brother that won't even show up for his *'half'* sister's engagement dinner party.

I'd bet even if he came to such a ball, he wouldn't bother to dress up. I can imagine him strolling into the ballroom, his brown hair stupidly bedraggled, muddied boots leaving debris with each step, still dressed in casual black fighting leathers. My thoughts tumble to what he might look like outside of the rugged wear he sports at the outpost.

What he looks like when he isn't wearing anything at all. Naked and sweating.

I audibly gasp at the thought and smack myself. *Stop thinking about Darian.*

Clearly, I need a lesson or two on self-discipline. I convince myself it's only a need leading me to think of him. A desire of my flesh, a dull roaring fire I try to keep locked up. I can't give in to such a thing again. And I won't give him the satisfaction of thinking about him...no matter how skilled he may be in bed. And no matter the sheer intensity of the emotions he summons within me.

But there's a part of me which wonders why my mind travels to him. I tell myself it's the thought that, no matter how awful I feel about sleeping with him, there's someone out there that's done worse. That *is* worse. One with no remorse—and at least I have that. Darian isn't up every night with guilt and shame clawing at his insides like a trapped animal begging to be freed. My stomach roils in guilt from the reminder of what I've done. Despite Cole's betrayal, did it make me any worse that I flipped so quickly into Darian's bed?

I blow out a breath before I walk out of my room. A soft lull of music drifts down the winding hallways, calling me forward like invisible fingers. I follow the sound, down several corridors, and through a massive arched doorway spanning high above my head.

I walk out onto a platform, and a set of stairs dips off into the room on my left. The room opens up to a wide expanse of marbled floors. Beams and columns stretch across overhead, intersecting and stretching into diamonds patterning the ceiling. Brilliant bursts of light flicker from ornate crystal chandeliers hung from the ceiling. A dull roar of multiple conversations lulls underneath the music. People crowd near a long table lined with dinnerware and crystal glasses shimmering with liquid. Off to the right, a man plays at a large ornate piano. I suddenly feel so out of place—perhaps coming here was a mistake. I should've tried searching for the map first. But any temptation to turn and run before someone sees me disappears.

Because it's too late.

Cole spots me. Completely withdrawn from whatever conversation he was in with another man. Captivated, his gaze devours every inch of me, his mouth parted in awe. The man has to repeat whatever he said to Cole, and I break our eye contact at Celeste's laugh ringing out amongst a group. A sigh of relief escapes me when I recognize Archie and Melaina gathered with her. I gather my skirts and inch down the stairs. For a split second, I imagine missing a step and tumbling all the way down to the bottom. Miraculously, I make it to the main floor without tripping.

Celeste glows as she approaches me. "Kat! You look exquisite."

I smile. "Thank you, you look lovely, as well."

She hugs me and hands me a glass of red wine. "I was about to come fetch you. I forgot to tell you where we would have dinner. I'm glad to see you found it!"

Archie gawks at me as I hug him in greeting. He's dressed

in formal wear, colored in rich plums with his sandy blonde hair swept back from his face.

I squeeze his shoulder. "And look at you! You look handsome."

His cheeks redden at my compliment. I exchange greetings with Melaina, who is wrapped in orange creams accentuating her bust. Her black hair is pinned back, a shimmer of color on her eyelids.

"How is your room? Are you comfortable?" Celeste asks me.

"Oh, definitely. It's a generous room, thank you. And a wonderful view of the gardens."

"I'm glad to hear it! Mel actually has a funny story about those gardens." Celeste smiles with a glint.

Melaina shakes her head, blushing. "Absolutely not."

"It's a good one, and she would get a kick out of it!" Celeste whines.

"Then you tell it, Cece."

Celeste takes the bait as Melaina shakes her head and begins to cover her face with her hand. "When Mel first came here, we used to play in the gardens all the time. You know, tea parties and what not. And one day she turned to me and asked, 'Do you believe in angels?' and I had to, of course. Who doesn't believe in angels? She then asked if I had ever seen a *gardening* angel here," Celeste sputters with a laugh.

"What's so funny about that? Are you saying angels can't have hobbies and indulge in gardening?" Archie asks.

We all burst into a fit of giggles.

"What?" he prompts again as he looks wildly from woman to woman.

I smile at Archie. "I think she had mistaken gardening angels for guardian angels."

Archie nods his head in understanding as it clicks. Melaina jabs a quick elbow at a snickering Celeste who tries not to crumple.

I glance back and forth between the two women. "So you two grew up together?"

"Unfortunately. Friends since we were…what? Ten you say?" Melaina looks to Celeste for confirmation.

Celeste crinkles her nose with unbound affection, warmth tugging at her smile. "Something like that. But I don't know if I would use the word 'unfortunately.' I'm glad we did."

"How did you two meet?" Archie asks.

"Our fathers were good friends. Her father was second in command to mine. They spent a lot of time together, so in turn we also spent a lot of time together," Celeste answers.

"And now I can't seem to get rid of you." Melaina glares playfully at Celeste.

Celeste bumps her with her hip.

"Anyway, is your brother going to be here?" Melaina glances around.

"Why? Still interested?" Celeste teases.

Archie shifts uncomfortably, and my stomach drops.

A faint blush creeps to Melaina's cheeks as she whips her head toward Celeste and swats her arm. "Absolutely not!"

"I know how much of a sucker you are for men with a lot of muscles." Celeste winks. "You don't have to fool me."

"You are just as obnoxious as your brother, you know?" Melaina scowls.

"Ahh! Someone's calling me!" Archie points off toward the bar cart, where no one stands. "I—I gotta go. I'll catch you all later!"

The crowd shifts as he disappears from our view, and an elbow collides with my side. The wine sloshes out of my glass, part of it spilling onto the front of my dress. Celeste gasps and several sets of eyes turn to me. My skin burns in mortification, the red wine splashed against my skin like a splatter of blood.

Celeste jerks her hand, her own glass of wine spilling out onto the front of her dress. Where mine only causes the fabric to darken a shade, the red wine stains her beautifully bright yellow dress.

"Ahh, clumsy me," she says with a laugh, brushing the fabric haphazardly with a hand.

A smile creeps to my lips—no one is around her to jostle her.

The man who bumped into me apologizes profusely, roping in servers to help clean the mess. I wipe the wine from my chest with a cloth supplied by a server.

A light bell chimes from somewhere, and everyone stops their conversations and takes a seat at the table. I follow suit a half-second behind, unfamiliar with such wealthy customs. Celeste takes a seat next to Cole and motions for me to sit in front of them.

I scan the room for Archie, hopeful for him to come and take one of the empty seats next to me. Disappointment pulls my lips into a frown when I don't spot him, but I take my seat anyhow.

"Wow, Kat…you look absolutely…" Cole stammers now that I have nowhere to hide. His eyes roam my face, my hair, my dress.

"Ravishing, isn't she?" Celeste coos. "I think blue is her color."

I smile at Celeste, not wanting to look Cole in the eyes. "I owe it to Celeste. She hand picked it."

Our clamor dies as the sound of the music abruptly stops. Everyone around me turns their attention to the pianist. A man dressed in midnight blue whispers to the musician, pats the pianist's shoulder, and turns toward us.

Darian.

I glance down to my own dress, and my toes curl. My midnight blue dress, trimmed with gold, nearly matches Darian's attire. I steal a side glance at Celeste who smiles at me.

"I didn't realize he was coming tonight?" I whisper through the silence, hoping for some sort of explanation from Celeste.

"Neither did I," Cole confirms.

Darian stalks toward us, the soft curve of his lips pulling up into a smirk when he sees me.

What is he doing here?

THIRTY SIX

GOOD MANNERS AND SUBTLETIES

An awkward silence settles around us as Darian sits in the seat next to me. After a few seconds, everyone makes a concerted effort to continue conversations until our meals are presented. Darian's shoulder brushes mine, and I try to edge away from the contact.

"So, Darian…" Celeste begins, picking at the food on her plate with a fork. "Have you been wine-ing and dining any women lately?"

Darian leans back and rests his arm on the back of my chair, allowing his knees to fall open. One of them knocks into my own, and I pull my knee away as I take a sip of my wine.

Darian smirks, eyes trained on Celeste. "I'm more of a sucking and fucking kind of guy."

I sputter, choking on the wine in my mouth. My face heats red, from both the embarrassment and the strain in my throat from coughing.

Cole glares at Darian. "I'm sorry, you do realize you just said that out loud?"

"Darian!" Celeste scolds.

Cole steals a concerned look at me as I attempt to pull a solid breath into my lungs. Darian has the audacity to look amused at the stir he caused.

Darian leans over to me, softly patting my back with a wicked grin as he whispers, "I'm sorry, are you choking?"

It prompts the memory of his hand wrapped around my neck when he nearly caught Daeja all those nights ago. How quickly his grip on my throat changed from choking to touching. Caressing. Teasing. Fingering. His naked body pressed against mine, his skin melting into me. Every wicked ounce of pleasure he tore from my body, ever so easily.

I suck in a breath and drive my heel into Darian's foot. A grunt escapes his lips, and he retreats back into his own personal space. Pushing up to my feet, I excuse myself, and leave the grand dining room. My heels click against the marble as I scurry down a hallway. The pianist's melody resumes to a slower, softer tune. I pause, leaning against a wall and coughing, still trying to settle the strain in my throat. Rubbing circles against my temple with a hand, I squeeze my eyes shut to force out the flashing memories of my night with Darian.

Footsteps sound behind me, pulling me out of my wavering focus. Glancing over my shoulder, I'm not surprised Darian's strutting my way. I spin toward him, my dress floating and sweeping the ground as I turn. He pauses a few steps away from me and leans one shoulder against the wall. As if we both casually decided to meet out here, away from wandering eyes and perked ears.

I smack him on the chest with the back of my hand. "Knock it off."

He has the audacity to look surprised. "Knock what off?"

"Stop looking at me like that! Or they're going to know."

He lowers his gaze, his eyes darkening.

"Yes, like that! Knock it off!" I hiss.

"What are they going to know?"

I glare at him. "That we slept together, you buffoon."

His eyebrows shoot up, mocking me. "What?"

I grab a fistful of his shirt, pulling him down to me. I clap my hand over his mouth, shushing him. "If you don't keep it down, I'm going to—"

He smiles against my hand, his words muffled by my skin. "You're going to *what?*" At my pause, he prompts me again with a whisper. "Or you're going to do what, kitten? Divulge me, preferably in great detail. Maybe start where we left off last with you screaming on your hands and knees, trembling as I—"

I push him away from me. "You're such a dick."

That gorgeous glint of his wicked smile slices into his cheeks as he snickers. "Is that why you like to put your hands on me?"

What did Cole tell me before? Drunks, terrorists, toddlers, and he's all three? Especially landing in that damn second category right now. I push past Darian and walk back to the dining room.

Cole jumps to his feet upon my arrival, his chair screeching against the floor. "Are you alright?"

"I'm fine," I reply curtly, taking a seat. As I shift into my chair, someone clears their throat. My gaze sweeps over to the sound, and Archie walks in with a swagger to his step, holding a plate stacked full with…*oh.*

Oh, no.

My cheeks flush in second-hand embarrassment as I watch it unfold before me. Archie slides into the seat next to Melaina, casually leans back, and grabs one of the many black shells stacked onto his plate. Snapping open the shell, he pops a piece of meaty flesh into his mouth.

Melaina begins, "Are…those…"

Archie glances at her sideways with a nonchalant grin. "Mussels? Oh, yeah, a *lot* of them. We used to eat them in Helmbrook all the time."

Melaina quirks an eyebrow up in bewilderment. My face falls into my hand as I recall the conversation Celeste and Melaina had earlier, before Archie excused himself.

Celeste meant Melaina was a sucker for muscles, not mussels, Archie.

"Want one?" Archie offers Melaina.

She shakes her head.

A strained chuckle comes from Celeste as she catches onto the clear misinterpretation. "How did you get all of those?"

Archie tilts his chin up. "I made a special request with the cooks."

The music swells, and Cole jolts to his feet again, his amber gaze darting to me. He holds out an open hand across the table, eyes begging me. "Kat, would you dance with me?"

"We were going to do dances after dessert, but I suppose this time is as good as any. You two go!" Celeste encourages us with a brush of her wrist toward the dance floor. "I'll join you later."

My palms itch with a nervous sweat. I can't seem to figure out a way to decline him without making things even more awkward. I swallow hard before taking his hand and rising. Our hands break apart, and I meet him at the end of the table, my body rigid with the many sets of eyes now watching us.

"What the hell are you doing?" I hiss once we are out of earshot.

He leads me out to the dance floor, bowing before me and offering his hand to me. He mutters under his breath, "Dancing."

I rest my hand in his, before he wraps his fingers around mine. He pulls me into him and swings the both of us off into a dance. I haven't afforded myself much time to admire him. But this close and with nowhere else to look...

He's devastatingly handsome. The breath-caught-in-your throat kind of beautiful. My heart swoons and crumples all in one swift beat. While a darkness still seeps from his eye sockets, his red locks are swept elegantly back away from his face, accentuating the curves of his cheeks and sharp nose. His beard is neatly trimmed to fit every angle of his strong jaw. Forest green fabric flatters every ridge and valley of his body. It fits him so perfectly; as a man of his brawn and height, it has to be custom tailored. Considering he's engaged to such a wealthy aristocrat—the daughter of the King's previous military general—it doesn't surprise me. Perhaps when they marry, this is how he will always look. Prestigious, dressed in the finest fabrics and living in the most ornate estate. It was more than I could have ever offered him, and it hits me as hard as if I were slapped. My heart aches at the hopelessness of any reconciliation or future with him.

He spins me into him, my back pressed against his chest, and his arms wrapped around me as he sways us. His whisper brushes my ear, "This was the only way I could think of to get some alone time with you, without intruding on your personal space."

"Oh, and this isn't personal space?"

He twirls me out of his grasp, finishing the spin to position me face to face with him. His hand falls to my waist, the other clasping my gloved hand gently. The curve of his hand meets mine, so perfectly as if we were etched from the same block. Where I dip, he bends into me.

He peers down at me through a pained expression, his lashes dark against the warm glow of his eyes. His lips are tight, a tension in the set of his jaw. And yet, the way he sways me around the floor is done in such loose elegance, with such confidence and expertise, I'm wondering when he's had the chance to practice. This wasn't our first time dancing together. It's a skill that catches me by surprise with each sway and step.

"I know I wronged you. I let my fear of losing you again overpower what was right, and for that I am so, so sorry, Kat. I never wanted to hurt you, I just wanted to find a solution before I told you. I thought as soon as I told you I'm engaged, you'd turn tail and run. You'd either die on the journey to the Dragon Lands, or you'd stay there. And I'd never see you again. I'd lose you all over again, for a third time. But you deserve the truth, no matter what it costs me. Even if it broke my heart. You left before you gave me the chance to explain—"

"Maybe I don't need an explanation," I snap. "You're engaged. And we slept together. That's it. There's no further explanation needed."

He bites into his lip, trying to conceal his misery as he shakes his head. "But it's not that simple."

Maybe I wanted it to be. Simple means it won't hurt. There won't be these dizzying questions of where my heart lies, this mind-numbing pain I'm struggling to keep at bay, or my self-doubt fogging over every thought. I allow my gaze to wander over to the table, and I am instantly snared in Darian's gaze. He lifts his flask to me with a wink and takes a swig.

I clear my throat, turning my attention back to Cole. "It is that simple. Celeste is absolutely smitten over you. I had to spend the entire damn day with her pretending I was your *sister*. Pretending I didn't want to be the one you're engaged to."

Cole breathes, "You were supposed to be…"

I'm starting to get angry at how pitifully sad he looks. I don't have it in me to carry his misery alongside my own agony. The pain *he* caused me. Doesn't he realize this hurts me, too? I mask the sadness dwelling within me with anger. It's just easier this way.

I break our eye contact and settle my gaze on anything but Cole. "Well, I'm not. And that's something neither of us can change. I'll take Daeja north in the next few days on my own, and I'll be one less thing for you to worry about. You can live out the rest of your life married into a wealthy family. Your father and sisters will never have to worry about finances. You can climb the ranks of the military until you're a general yourself."

He blinks tears away, his hand at my waist gripping me tighter. "Please don't. Can't you see this is killing me? Don't go where I can't follow you, just give me some time to figure a way out of—"

A shadow falls across Cole's face, and someone taps my shoulder. Cole lifts his chin and glares. With that reaction, I already know who it is.

"Mind if I cut in?" Darian's voice is that delicious whisper of velvet.

"We do mind. We're in the middle of something," Cole growls.

"Actually, I don't mind," I blurt, weighing that in this moment, I'd prefer Darian's agitating flirtations over Cole's frustrating excuses.

Cole's shoulders sag. If anything, I can always count on him to respect my wishes, even if he doesn't agree with them. He steps back from me and gives my hand to Darian. When he walks back to the table, I catch a shimmer of defeat and longing in his amber eyes, before he masks it with indifference as he turns to Celeste.

Darian pulls me taut against him, my breath escaping my lips in an audible whoosh, and ripping my attention back to him.

I tilt my chin up. "Are you going to behave yourself?"

He smiles and begins to twirl us into the melody of the night. "Never."

His hand clasps mine with such tenderness. It's odd to pair such a soft description with him. For a moment, he looks elegant in the way his hair floats with each sway of his steps, leading me across the floor with a detached grace.

"Who knew you'd be a better dance partner than sparring partner?" he murmurs.

"Wow, Darian. Is that a hint of a compliment? You could use some work but…"

He snickers. "Don't go expecting them of me."

"I've learned to not have any expectations of you."

"Good. People are disappointing. I'm glad to see you're finally learning."

A delicate gold trims the midnight blue of his coat with more gold accenting the rest of his attire. Celeste was very strategic in what I wore tonight, considering how coordinated our garments are. Perhaps she even manipulated me into this dress by having me try on such egregious options first.

Where Cole is tightly pressed and formal, Darian is the opposite. The sleeves of his coat are rolled part way up his forearms, exposing scarred olive skin. His collar is wide open, plunging low to reveal his collarbone and the dip between his chest muscles. I'm willing to bet he did it on purpose.

I arch an eyebrow. "Did one of your buttons break? How embarrassing."

"I thought you might like it." He winks.

"How considerate, you're thinking of what I like now?"

"I think about you a lot more than you'd probably like to know," he purrs.

Gods, and paired with that lethal smile of his. Part of me wants to smack it off him, so the other part of me isn't so tempted to kiss him right here. Right now.

What is wrong with me? When and how have I lost this much self-control?

I roll my eyes hard enough I might give myself a headache if I do it again. "Why are we dancing?"

The reflections in his eyes swirl like stars in a night sky. The glimmer from the chandeliers flash around us as we spin again and again.

"Because it pisses big red off," he says with a grin. "That, and I wouldn't pass up the opportunity to dance with the most brilliant woman here. Although, her choice of dress is questionable."

I snort. "And what's wrong with my dress?"

"Well…" He drops to a hushed whisper, "I'm hoping if I tell you I don't like it, you'll take it off."

I grit my teeth to block a shiver from passing through my spine. If I push him away hard enough, maybe he'll stop tempting every damn fantasy I have of him that keeps flashing in my mind.

"Fuck you," I say in exasperation and look away.

He pulls me closer into him as the music eases and dips me achingly slow. My neck stretches down and opens for him as my head tips back to stare at the ceiling. Vulnerable. If he so much as kissed me, it'd be over. It'd destroy every last bit of my self-control, if he only dared. His breath heats my neck.

"I hope you always keep your word," he whispers huskily.

Before I can react, he draws me back up to stand. My head swims in dizzying circles, and I dash off the dance floor before my desires get the best of me.

Cole watches me stride across the room from where he stands with Celeste. He gets sidetracked when she laces her fingers into his. With her other hand, she cups his jaw and draws his face to hers.

The softness of her touch, the implied intimacy of it, underlines the reality of our situation—she's free to be herself and doesn't have to hide her affections. The way she looks at him is the same way *I* want to look at him.

But he turns out of her grasp and instead focuses on me.

I could burst into flames or tears, but instead, I beeline straight for the cart lined with bottles of liquor.

"You're upset, I can feel it—"

"I'm fine." The words waver in my mind as much as they might have if they were spoken from my lips.

"I'm happy to dispose of anyone who's making you feel this way. Just saying."

"We have rules, remember?"

"Rules can be bent."

I pause at the bar-cart, bracing my weight against the lip of the counter. I stare at the bottles and snatch the closest one. Pulling a spare glass stored on a bottom shelf, I uncork the bottle and pour a knuckle's worth of liquor into the glass. With a shaky breath, I throw the drink back and swallow.

But the burn isn't enough to drown out the pain roaring inside me. When I tip the bottle up for more into my glass, only a drip escapes. With a frustrated grunt, I grab another bottle. Empty. Another one. Also empty. I shuffle through all of the shelves but find nothing.

I spin, surveying the grand room for a server to request something strong. But my gaze catches on one thing. Darian's flask has somehow been left unattended at the dinner table. His attire tonight didn't sport a way to clip it into his belt as his outfits at the camp do. Upon further observation, Darian is nowhere to be seen. I race for the flask, swipe it from the table, and cut out of the dining room. Uncorking the flask, I tip the cold metal to my lips and take a small sip, the liquor like a liquid fire sliding down my throat. I round the corner into the hallway I walked earlier tonight, and nearly collide with Darian.

He catches me by the shoulders before I can fall. Taking a step back from me, his gaze darts to the flask in my hands. *His* flask. His green eyes flick up to me. "What are you doing with that?"

"Trying to drown my sorrows," I blurt. "Bar-cart was out of liquor. I'm sure you won't mind sharing."

There's no amusement, malice, or coldness in his eyes. Just a blankness. "That's not a good way to drown your sorrows."

"Oh? And how would you know?"

"I know," he mumbles.

I snort and roll my eyes as I pull the flask to my lips again.

"Don't, Katerina," he warns.

It's the first time I've ever heard him use my name. A sound so foreign on his tongue, it makes me pause. It almost reminds me of my mother, only using my full name in instances where I did something needing scolding.

The little liquor I consumed before I ran into him already dulls the jagged pain piercing me with every breath, like broken glass lining my chest. With each passing second, it becomes a little easier to breathe. A little easier to exist. Eager for more, I flip the flask back and guzzle down more.

"For once, woman, would you fucking listen to me?" Darian snarls and lunges, seizing my wrist in one hand and tearing the flask from my grasp.

"Gods, you picked the wrong time to be so noble," I hiss. "And don't you dare say *I know.*" I try to imitate the pitch of his voice. I stalk off before he can respond, finding the only way away from Darian is back into the dining room. As I consider running up the steps to return to my room, Archie waves me over from the dinner table. When I approach and slide into the seat next to him, he holds one fork in each hand.

I blink. "Archie, what are you doing?"

He stabs with one fork and eats off the other, rinse and repeat. "Eating. Want some?"

"No thanks. Why are you eating with two forks?"

He stops mid-chew. "Are…you not supposed to use both?"

I laugh, maybe a little too hard and a little too loud. The scene of it all is hilarious. Not to mention, my poise is melting away each second longer the liquor settles into my blood. "No, silly. They have one for different parts of the meal."

We both laugh again in unison—his is a little embarrassed. I've got to admit, his assumption was logical. Those of us who didn't grow up in wealthy communities wouldn't have a clue. The only reason I know is because I watched how Celeste ate at dinner and mirrored her movements.

"What happened to all the mussels?" I ask.

"Well I uhh…I shared them with the rest of the table. Couldn't eat them all myself. Mussels…sort of make me sick."

"Why did you get all of them, then?"

His gaze travels over to the dance floor where Melaina is spun by Darian. They are locked in an intense stare, lips moving in inaudible words. I wonder if he unapologetically teases her the way he does me.

"Ahh," I whisper and glance back at a blushing Archie. "Why don't you go talk to her?"

"Ha! She would never be interested in me."

"You don't know that. You have to try! Tell her how you really feel."

He grimaces and shakes his head furiously.

"Okay, fine. You don't have to immediately tell her how you feel…but start small. Maybe try to ask her to dance?" My lips slow as if they have a mind of their own. Each blink blurs my vision at the edge. "The worsttt she can say is noo."

Am I slurring? And here I am giving relationship advice to someone else. Me, of all people. It's laughable.

Bile rises in my throat, and I hurry to my feet. "I gotta go, Arch. Excuse me."

I slink off, trying to walk a straight line and not trip over my own feet as I ascend the staircase out of the great dining hall. Each step of the way I'm trying to convince myself I'm fine. But I can't deny the overpowering dizziness washing over me. The blinding light of the ballroom's chandeliers fades away to the dark stretching hallway lit by flickering candelabras. My staggered steps throw me sideways into a wall, and I lean against it as if my legs will give out at any given moment. I shove off the wall and take a few more steps, commanding myself to make it back to my room before I collapse.

The hallway sways back and forth, churning my stomach. Clapping my hand over my mouth, I bite my tongue to distract myself from the heat traveling up my throat. I squeeze my eyes shut for a split-second, trying not to vomit. The effort of it all causes me to swing too far right, and I tumble into a hall table. Disoriented, I attempt to grab onto something to help me up, but instead scatter candles and picture frames on the table in my wake.

Finally, I find my footing and rise to my feet. I reposition the candles and picture frames, knocking over more as I do so. Luckily, nothing is broken from what I can tell. Bracing my hand against the wall for extra support, I walk farther away from the music. The endless hallways twist and turn, and I find myself lost.

My eyes keep dragging closed, prompting me to rest.

One of the rooms I pass by has a comfortable looking settee. The dark room is illuminated only by the moonlight spilling in through tall windows. Breathy, I stumble over to the settee and collapse. My feet pulse from the heels I've been wearing all night. I peel the shoes off and start rubbing at the balls of my feet, glancing around the room. My vision swims and twirls with each movement of my head. It takes a few seconds for my eyes to finally focus. A gasp escapes my lips, a shiver racing down my neck. A large skull encased in glass sits on the high tops of bookshelves lining the walls. And not just any skull.

A dragon skull.

Around the room is more contraband: horns, claws, a giant scale, an egg. Despite my body groaning in protest, I pull myself off the settee and stumble past the bookshelves to a desk. If Jurrock were to have any sort of map, it has to be here. I just know it.

I brace my weight onto the desk, my breath sawing in and out of my chest at the amount of effort it took to get here. My head hangs down, my vision swimming circles. I fight through my daze, pulling open drawers and skimming its contents with shaky fingers.

Someone clears their throat from the door.

I snap my attention up to the sound. Standing in the door frame, his silhouette black against the glow of the candle-lit hallway, is Darian.

"You're not supposed to be in here."

THIRTY SEVEN

DRAGONS AND DANGEROUS MEN

I freeze, as if I stay still enough, I may fade into the shadows. But Darian takes a step forward into the room, thawing whatever had me stuck to the spot I'm in near the desk. I backpedal until I hit one of the windowed walls behind me, and he charges toward me. Racing around the farthest side of the desk from him, I dash for the exit, knocking over books and knick knacks on the bookshelves in my staggered gait.

He hisses right behind me, "Stop!"

I get to the settee first, snagging one of my heels and spinning to him, knowing I can't outrun him and readying myself for a fight. Perhaps I should've considered the original heels the shopkeeper picked out for me—they would've been far sharper.

Darian pauses, watching me as if I were a caged wild animal. "*Why* are you in here?"

I take a few steps back from him and trip over the edge of the settee's clawed feet, falling back onto my ass. If I weren't so drunk, I may even be embarrassed.

He closes in on me. "Stop trying to run from me. You're going to hurt yourself—"

Still sitting on the ground, I chuck my shoe at him, pathetically missing his head by a few inches. Not sure if I should blame my intoxication or poor skills in throwing.

His gaze follows the heel's path over his shoulder with a laugh. "You missed."

I snag the other one off the ground and throw it at him, this time hitting him square in the jaw while he's distracted.

He turns a glare on me and lunges again.

I scramble backwards on my hands and feet for the door. But my movements are too sluggish, too inaccurate.

"Wait! Godsdammit, you impossible woman," Darian hisses.

My sweaty hands slip right off the polished floor, and I slam back onto the ground, my head cracking against the marbled tile. Black spots explode in my vision, my breath ripped from my lungs, followed by a screaming pain in my skull.

Darian drops down to a knee beside me as he holds out a hand. "Fuck. Are you alright?"

I glance at his hand, then back at him. There's two of him, then three, and then one. My dizzying, pounding head steals all of my sense of urgency. I shouldn't trust him...but the way the moonlight shines in his eyes. How shadows drag across the angles of his jaw and nose…I don't want to admit it. But in this light he is…*gorgeous.*

"Let me help you up," he whispers.

I see no way out of it, can't think much around the wicked sharp throbbing in my head, so I reach for his hand. He closes his strong, calloused fingers over mine, and pulls me up off my back to my feet. Leaning a little too hard into him for support, I fall into his arms, before I'm trying to right myself back into my own stance.

Our eyes link.

The light of this room is far too intimate. He clears his throat, and I take my hand out of his.

"You're really drunk, aren't you?" He snorts, grabbing my forearm to steady me when I start to lean again. "I told you not to drink all of that."

"No, I'm fineee," I lie and try to school my features.

"Can you even walk?"

I try to playfully smack his arm and miss. Terribly. I jolt forward, and he catches me once more.

"I'm just really…really dizzy," I finally admit. The more time that passes, the worse it seems to get.

With a sigh, he sweeps me off my feet and up into his arms. My breath catches in my throat, my cheeks flushing at the tenderness of it. Averting my gaze away from his face, I brush a thumb over the midnight blue of his jacket.

He looks ahead as he walks us out of the room and down the hallway. "Do you know where your room is?"

My laugh comes out squeaky. "No. Do you?"

He grumbles in response, "I suppose we'll walk around the castle until you can confirm which room yours is then."

"What if…I can't?" I grin up at him.

He raises an eyebrow at me, already recognizing what I'm implying, before looking back at the path ahead. "I don't do sleepovers."

"Who said anything about a sleepover?"

He clears his throat, still not looking at me. "I also don't fuck drunk women. Not my thing."

I sag head against his chest, his heartbeat murmuring against my ear. Every glance away from him ties my stomach into knots, the hallway flashing by at a nauseating speed. Instead, I train my eyes on him, admiring the elegant and precise edges of his cheekbones, his jaw, and scarred neck.

"You're staring," he calls me out and flicks his gaze down to me. When our eyes connect for a moment, a hint of a smile winks at his lips before it disappears.

He darts his attention away from me, a forced irritation rumbling in his chest. "What?"

The words fall out of my mouth before I can stop them. "I love it when you smile like that."

He whips another look at me, his mouth parted. "You—" He shakes his head and is back to scanning the hallway. "You're drunk."

"There's something else I've been meaning to tell you."

"Now's not the time for revealing all your deepest, darkest secrets, kitten."

"Well, I need to tell you this one anyway…I'm sorry."

He flinches, squinting down at me. "What? Sorry for what?"

"I'm sorry for using your sister against you at the battle of Blackfell. I manipulated you. That was wrong of me, and I'm truly sorry. I'll never…"

The ceiling above us threatens to collapse as it spins tilted circles. The pounding in my head roars over the sound of my throbbing heart, and my stomach tenses. I squeeze my eyes shut to give my brain a break, to escape the spinning and swirling before I vomit.

It's dark. Peaceful.

"I'll never…do that…again," I whisper, fading into the darkness beckoning me forward like an old friend.

"Don't close your eyes," Darian commands.

But it's too late.

"Hey, stop! Kitten! Open your eyes!" His voice sounds miles away. "*Fuck!* Katerina!"

The last thing I remember is the warmth of him against me.

Fire races across the floor. Or am I looking up at the ceiling? There's no wooden beams here to criss-cross above me, but the sound of wood still creaks and groans…or is that noise coming from me?

I turn to my side. The room swims and spins as my stomach drops.

Flames dance in a fireplace across the room, scattering shadows across the marbled floor. I cringe—the fire melds and transforms into the grimaces of all the people I failed to save. They stare back at me, haunting me. Holding a hand up to block my face, I turn away with a cry. An ominous whisper grows louder, ringing over and over in my ears:

Secrets never die, they're just buried in a grave.

Secrets never die, they're just buried in a grave.

Secrets never die, they're just buried in a grave.

"Shhhh," someone hushes across the room. A dark silhouette slinks out from the darkness, a trail of shadows in its wake.

Darian steps into the light, surveying me with arched eyebrows. He follows my fixed stare to the hearth, strides over to it, and extinguishes the fire. My eyes are still glued to the hearth, waiting for it to reignite and consume me.

Darian slowly sits on the bed next to me, his midnight coat from earlier is gone, leaving him in a loose shirt. With reluctance, he strokes my hair to calm me. The movement so gentle. His lingering gaze is tender and delicate. I'm not sure what is real and what isn't.

Then there's three of him. Their eyes fading back and forth between an otherworldly white and forest green as horns sprout from their heads. They all shush me as I slip back into the darkness.

Screams ricochet around me as I clench my hands tight to my ears. I'm screaming back, but they don't stop. The oranges, yellows, and whites of a wicked flame merge into a blur of red. Molten drops of crimson fire morph into something more sinister.

Blood.

My mother appears in front of me, but her eyes are blank—a whiteness clouding her irises and pupils. She reaches out a hand toward me, and I run away, but everywhere I turn, she's there. Blood drips from the corners of her eyes, racing down her cheeks until she melts into a puddle of blood and bone. Spinning away from her, I find the little girl, her hand still clenching her doll. The next direction I turn to, my brother calls from the depths of a river, his blank eyes ghostly white near the water's surface.

Stop it! I beg.

My mother's words echo, clear as if they were a bell. High-pitched, frequent, ringing and ringing.

In death blood is shed, but from blood there is life.

In death blood is shed, but from blood there is life.

In death blood is shed, but from blood there is life.

The rebel I killed all those nights ago appears, a gaping wound in his chest where I pierced him with his own sword. He lunges for me, and I barely dodge him.

Leave me alone! I scream.

I search for Daeja, panic-stricken. I don't know where she is. The rebel chases after me, grabs hold of my forearm, and tears me to the ground. I crawl away from him, but he seizes me by the ankle and drags me back to him as I scream.

An arm wraps around me, tight, and I squirm against it.

Don't take me, please don't take me.

But then I'm rocked, back and forth. A soft hum brushes my ear, a whispered breath against my neck. The hums drive the screams away, and everything evaporates. Like snow melting from the sun.

"You're okay. I'm right here, and I'm not leaving."

The pain equivalent to an ice pick slamming in my head, repeatedly, greets me when I wake in the morning. My whole body is wrung from its strength, even opening my eyes is a strain. Golden light washes into the room, shining directly into my face and blinding me.

Where…am I?

I sit up quickly. A little too quickly. The room spins around me and triggers a wave of nausea. I pull my knees up to my chest and rest my forehead against them until the dizziness subsides. Glancing up when I feel safe enough to do so, I find luxurious blue sheets and duvets wrap me in layers. The footboard of the bed is wrought iron twisting up high into brilliant curved pillars.

Last night's events all swim back to me slowly, though, most of it comes in blurry pieces. The dancing, Archie and mussels, Celeste and Cole—the last thing I remember is Darian carrying me out of the office I stumbled into.

Wait…is this *his* bed?

Ripping the sheets off my legs, I find myself still in the gown from the night before. My attention then darts over to my hand holding the blankets open, and the sleeve covering my forearm.

Wait…my dress didn't have sleeves. And the midnight blue, gold trimmed material was dazzlingly familiar. I survey the coat I'm wearing and confirm it's Darian's.

My mind races trying to recall everything that happened. The way he watched and taunted me. The way he spun me in circles on the dancefloor, chandelier lights flashing around us.

I glance over to the right side of the bed to find it untouched—still folded neatly up to the layers of cushioned pillows. Peeking over the edge of the bed, I find a throw blanket pooled on the ground with a spare pillow. My gaze travels across the marbled floor and up to the fireplace, stirring the distant memory of my nightmares and the fire crackling in the ornate stone hearth.

Across the room from me is a span of large skinny windows framing rolling hills and Dragon's Back Ridge. Another set of windows arch above them in a dome of skylights. A velvety blue settee lined in gold faces the windows. As if someone would sit there and stare out at the breathtaking expanse beyond.

Leaned up against the farthest left window is an easel with a painting and a cup with tattered paintbrushes underneath it. Swaths of black clash into bursts of blues and purples on the canvas, white freckled across the dark in varying sizes and depths.

A night sky.

I slip out of the bed for a closer look, the marbled floors cold under my bare feet. As I draw near, the brilliant details come into focus. A mountain's silhouette is hinted at the bottom of the painting. It's the view of Dragon's Back Ridge from these same windows. The sky is mottled in brilliant dark hues, stars glittering against the shadows. The only imperfection is a spot at the top. A shooting star is smudged across the top of the canvas, but a furious swipe of black muddies the brilliance of it. As if someone tried to instantly blot it out.

On the ground and resting against the wall is a large cloth draped over some sort of frame. I pluck the cloth and pull it away a few inches to see what it covers. A gold curled frame shimmers in the light. Peeling the cloth off the rest of the way, I let it fall to the ground in ripples. The painting is massive, and I have to take a few steps back to fully study it.

A woman with long, brown waves sits in a luxurious, burgundy silk dress, with matching gloves reaching up her arms. Sitting on her lap is a little girl with golden brown ringlets, her sparkling blue eyes round with innocence. Bows are tied into her hair, matching her light pink frilly dress. A teddy bear is tucked into her arm with similar bows tied onto its ears.

Standing behind them both is a young boy dressed in dark

formal attire. My heart skips a beat at the swipe of long, brown hair and those forest green eyes. Except, they are void of the malice and hardness I've come to know. A soft hint of a grin pulls at his boyish lips.

But what makes me shiver is the woman—his mother. Where there should be pupils and irises, is an expanse of ghostly white. It's oddly chilling compared to the intricate details of the rest of the subjects. It makes her look…haunting. Inhuman.

I stare for a little while, before an uneasiness creeps up on me, as if I'm looking at something I shouldn't be. Quickly, I pull the cloth back over the painting.

My stomach growls in a gnawing hunger. I find my shoes near the bed, slide them on, and drape Darian's jacket on the settee. Much to my relief, and despite not knowing the layout of the palace and my current location, I make it back to my room without garnering any attention.

I change out of my dress from the night before and into the modest dress I wore to Windmere with Celeste. Dragging a brush through my hair, I splash water on my face and head back out of my room. Winding through the hallways, I find the hall table I drunkenly crashed into last night. I adjust a picture I left upside down, and continue toward the great dining hall.

Archie bounds toward me once I join the rest of the group gathered in the dining hall, his eyes bright.

He hugs me from the side, his arm looped around my neck. "Good morning, sunshine! You'll never guess what happened after you left."

"After I left?"

"Yeah! I went and talked to Melaina. I told her how I felt." Archie bites his bottom lip. "We uh…we kissed."

"Archie!" I swat his arm playfully and hiss, "You shouldn't kiss and tell, you scoundrel, you!"

He blushes and ducks his head. A smile spreads on my lips as I squeeze his shoulder. I scan the rest of the room and catch sight of Darian off at the breakfast buffet table, piling fruit and pastries onto a tray. He turns to walk toward me. When he sees me, he grins and slows, motioning toward the tray in his hand.

I excuse myself from Archie, grab a glass of water and a pastry, before taking a seat at the table across from Darian.

"Wow…" I start, taking a bite of the pastry I grabbed. I survey the heaping amounts of fruit, cheese, bread, and pastries piled on his tray. "Quite the appetite you have there, huh?"

He blinks up at me and smiles that devilishly handsome smile of his. "Guess you could say enough for two people. I intended on eating it in my room, but there was a change of plans."

A shiver snakes down my back at the thought of it all, had I stayed put. Darian, bringing me breakfast in bed. In *his* bed. Where there were paintings and sweeping views of Dragon's Back Ridge. It was all so…personal?

A shuffle of feet approaches us from the corner of the room. A guard holds out an envelope for Darian, bowing his head. "Mr. Raventhorn."

Darian rips open the red wax seal and scans through it. I'm so tempted to snag it from him, wondering what on earth he could be getting correspondence for. Especially if all of his previous letters were addressed from Celeste.

His jaw tenses, the color draining from his face. He quickly folds the letter and stands with a suddenness that makes me flinch. Without a word, he turns and strides out of the room, his tray of food untouched. I watch him go as Celeste sits next to me.

"What a terrible waste," Celeste murmurs and motions to Darian's tray.

"Will he…not be coming back?"

"I'm not sure. Sometimes he's gone for days. Sometimes weeks or months. It all depends." She takes a delicate bite of berries with a fork.

I finally tear my gaze away from the door where Darian disappeared and back at her. "Depends on what?"

She shrugs. "I'm not sure. He never says, and I'm not the one he tends to share information with."

I grab some grapes off his tray as Melaina sits across from us, and Celeste's eyes narrow in on her.

"Sooo…" Celeste starts casually, a hint of suspicion in her tone. "You had quite the night last night, huh?"

A blush blooms on Melaina's cheeks. "I don't know what you're talking about."

"You don't have to fool me. I know you were with Darian last night."

I stiffen, hoping Celeste doesn't notice.

"I was not." Melaina glares with an arched eyebrow.

"I saw you two dancing after dinner. And I heard someone in his room last night. And I know you two—"

"Stop it. It wasn't me. I may have gotten a little carried away last night, but it wasn't with Darian," Melaina bites back before Celeste can finish.

Celeste's eyes widen as she leans forward, and I follow suit.

"I kissed Archie," Melaina whispers.

"What?" Celeste exclaims.

Melaina shushes her, before stealing a glance over at Archie who's already watching us. He smiles and waves before he turns his attention back to Cole.

Celeste raises an eyebrow. "Who was with Darian then?"

Melaina scoffs. "How should I know?"

"You know what? Good for you," Celeste says finally and leans back approvingly.

I grin at Melaina. "I think he really likes you."

"Sounds like we need to return back to camp early. Carlisle sent word there's been some suspicious activity near the lake," Cole says behind us.

I whip to him, our eyes meeting. Daeja. I got so drunk last night, I hadn't checked in with her, and my heart races to a gallop.

"Daeja? Are you okay? Cole is saying there has been activity near the lake and I thought—"

"I haven't been practicing flying, if that's what you're asking. So don't bother scolding me."

"Have you seen anyone?"

"Not since I heard from you last. It's been relatively quiet here since you've been gone."

"I'm so sorry I didn't check in with you last night, I'll be there tonight to see you—"

"You better bring me extra chicken. I expect a whole carriage full."

Celeste pouts and says something about a short visit. Cole assures her we can come back once we secure any threats. Melaina watches the back and forth between Cole and Celeste, and Archie stands right behind Melaina, his palms perched onto her chair casually.

Cole pulls my chair out from the table. "I'm sorry we must leave earlier than intended. But thank you for hosting such a wonderful evening."

As I stand and move for my room, Cole snatches my forearm. My gaze falls to where his fingers wrap around me, then back up at him. Everyone else's eyes fall onto us.

Cole pauses, his mouth parted, yet nothing comes out. He clears his throat, changing his mind about whatever he was going to say. "We need to leave quickly. Meet me outside at the carriage."

Once I get back out to the carriage, Archie, Cole, and Melaina are there waiting. Celeste watches us go from the front doors, disappointment painted on her delicate features.

My jaw flexes as Archie slides in next to Melaina, and Cole takes a seat next to me. The bench isn't quite long enough to accommodate Cole's large physique and me, without our thighs brushing. His hands rest on his thighs, dangerously close to mine. Movement sparks through his fingers, the veins under his skin dancing with each nervous drum against his leg.

As we jerk to a roll, the movement of the carriage shimmies our bodies together. My knees bump into Cole's, despite trying to tense my legs from doing so. Thankfully, Archie fills the silence with conversation of Helmbrook and his family. I stare out the window, daydreaming of flying through the trees on Daeja's back, away from here and to the Dragon Lands. While I missed my chance of getting a map in Windmere, I decide I'm done waiting for the perfect opportunity to go to the Dragon Lands. I'll do so without a map.

We only need to get to the next day.

THIRTY EIGHT

ONE. LAST. THING.

By the time we arrive back at camp, we all split. Cole is whisked off with Carlisle to discuss what he's missed, and I go to the healer's quadrant. As I enter, it's the first time I notice how much I missed being here. How familiar the smell of mint and lavender have become. How comforting it is that the light filters through the windows, spotlighting cascading swirls of dust.

Marge is surprised by my return, and sends me out to forage for mushrooms. I have to control my pace as I walk toward the forest, each stride closer to Daeja picks up in speed. Anything to get me to her faster. When I finally break through the tree line and spot her shadowy silhouette, a part of me relaxes. Struggling to maintain my composure, I break into a sprint, fighting every second keeping me apart from her.

My cheeks warm into a genuine smile. *"I couldn't bring you a carriage of chicken but—"*

She barrels into me, and I fall backwards to the ground. Her warm snout nuzzles into my neck, her strong tongue nearly licking the skin off my cheek.

"I've missed you." Her voice is soft and low, like the sound of the water against the shore. The three words have a noose around my heart, clenching and pulling and hurting. Wrapping my arms around her muzzle, I lean my head into hers as I scratch her favorite spot under chin, and she melts into a pleased rumble.

"I've missed you too."

"When we get to the Dragon Lands, will we always be together?"

My throat constricts, my chest tight. Had she asked me months ago, my answer would've been something entirely different. In the past, I imagined I'd drop her off at the border as easily as if I were trading something at the market. Trading her for a life of freedom where all I had to worry about was myself.

But now?

Now she feels as familiar to me as my own two hands. I can't imagine a life without her. In a world where I have absolutely no idea what the hell I'm doing—with her it all makes sense. Everything makes sense when she is next to me. And that is all I need. Whether or not we go down together or burn the world to ashes, all that matters is we are together.

Together has become my favorite place to be.

"Yes. Always," I answer her finally.

After dinner, I go off to my own room. I lay on my back staring up at the night sky through the gaps in the roof's tattered ceiling, watching the twinkle of the stars. Footsteps outside my room fade to silence as the early evening hours pass by.

"Are you ready?" I call to Daeja.

"Ready as ever."

I pack extra clothes, some food, and a water flask into the satchel my mother gave me all those months ago. I gather my sword and scrawl a new note for Archie and Marge, leaving the folded letters on my desk. I pause, mulling over one last task, before deciding out of respect to our previous relationship, Cole deserves one, too.

Cole,

There will always be a part of me that loves you, even if sometimes I don't want to. I'm sorry I had to go. But I hope you understand. I will always want the best for you, and I will never stop wanting you to be happy.

Love, Kat

Tears slip from my eyes, spattering against the paper. I still couldn't write the words *'I forgive you.'* Perhaps someday, I can. But today that is not that day. I am still far too broken, too hurt.

I slip out of my door and scan the camp one last time, partly to say goodbye to the place I called home for the last several months, and partly to ensure no one else is around. With a soft sigh, I leave. As I pass the crumbling wall encircling the outpost, a whisper stops my tracks.

"Wait."

I turn, slow. Each breath a staggering weight in my chest.

Cole stands rigid, a torrent of sadness drowning his features. "Don't leave. Not yet."

I don't say anything—I'm stuck.

He takes a few cautious steps toward me. "I know you don't want to hear it. I know I've hurt you. I'll beg for your forgiveness and mercy before I beg it of any god. But, please...just give me this one last chance to tell you how sorry I am, before you go. And then, you can go—" His voice wavers, tears glistening in his eyes. "I...I will let you go."

I nod, tightness constricting my throat.

The way he fidgets, he's dying to touch me. But he restrains himself. My emotions swirl around me, threatening to pull me under into a whirlpool of despair at the extent of how damaged we are.

He sighs, his shoulders sagging in relief that I'm giving him this last chance. "I'm not in love with her, Kat. Not like I am with you. I didn't agree to it because I loved her."

"Then why did you?" I whisper.

"Gods...I killed myself every day for not fighting for you when you told me to leave you alone back in Padmoor. I wanted to respect your wishes, even if I didn't want to let you go so easily. But I did. And it was the hardest thing I've ever had to do. Nothing makes sense when you're not next to me—it feels like a life left wasted. When you broke things off with me to take your mother to Stoneshire for the blue flame, my father was injured at work. He was forging a sword, and the sparks exploded into his eyes—blinding him."

I gasp.

He nods and takes another step closer. "He had to sell what little weapons we had left in the shop, but it wasn't enough. We only had enough to sustain the eight of us for maybe a few weeks. I was trapped and desperate for a way to support us, so the girls wouldn't starve. And then word of the draft came. Willard told me you were still in town and that you never left for Stoneshire. I went to your house, scared you'd be angry I wasn't honoring your wish to leave you alone. But I went anyway. I saw a flicker of movement near the window after I knocked on your door, but you never answered. I took it as your sign that you didn't care to talk to me. So I left and took the opportunity to join the King's army. The military pays well, and if I could work my way up in the ranks, I could send money back to him and my sisters."

My gaze settles on my boots. It wasn't me not answering his knock—it must've been my mother. And it must have been the day I fell asleep at the river, just as I told his sister Vivian back in Padmoor.

"And then you met Celeste," I finish quietly.

"No. I trained for a few weeks at a different outpost. But every day I regretted not staying to fight for you. So I left."

My eyes widen, searching his. "What? What do you mean you left?"

"I came back for you. I went back to Padmoor. I couldn't live a life without you anymore." He pulls out his mother's ring from his pocket, his thumb brushing over its gleaming metal. His voice wavers as he stares down at the ring. "And then my worst nightmare came true. You were gone. I dug through the ashes of your home, desperate to not find you. I asked around Padmoor, and everyone told me the same thing. I even asked Willard, practically begging him to say it wasn't true, desperate there had been some mistake. But he confirmed it—you and your mother had died in the fire. And I felt my heart shatter at that very moment. It broke something in me. Ever since then, I've struggled with who and what I am. I should've stayed with you, I should've fought harder because in my mind, maybe I could've saved you. That guilt never ceases to haunt me. I returned back home, and when my father learned I deserted my position in the King's military he—" He shakes his head, biting into his lip to keep tears from spilling.

A half-hearted laugh shakes his shoulders. "I have to stop saying that, but it's a habit. He's not even my father."

"What?"

He glances up at me. "When he found out I dishonorably left the military, he admitted I'm not even his real son. When he wed my mother, she was already pregnant, and had sworn him to father me. To raise me as his own. But I was such a disgrace in his eyes, he couldn't possibly be associated with me. Not to mention the repercussions if he housed such a treasonous bastard. He told me to never return, and that I could never see my sisters again."

"Cole...I'm...I'm so sorry," I murmur. My own heart aches,

knowing how much his sisters mean to him. And then for them to be ripped away from him, in a single moment, completely outside of his control. Ripped away as if they were torn from him by the currents of a river.

Ripped away, *all because of me.*

He continues, "I didn't know where to go. I tried to go back to my original squad, knowing they'd execute me for desertion. I didn't have you, and I didn't have my family, so they'd at least put me out of my misery. My original squad sent me to Arterias for a trial. I had two options: execution, or I could serve out the rest of my life as captain of the most northern squad. This outpost is where they send those they can afford as collateral. They know we'll be the first ones to die in rebel attacks. But I wouldn't get paid for it—which meant my family would die if I couldn't send them something."

He takes a shaky, heavy breath. As if this has been weighing on him for months. "And then I was offered a proposal. If I married Celeste, I would be wed into a wealthy family. I'd have a handsome dowry, and I could send that money back to my family. My life sentence would be lifted so I could be with her."

"How is that possible? How could they just lift the sentence so easily?"

"Apparently, since her father was Jurrock, they still have the favor of the King. But Kat—*I don't love her.* I've never touched her or kissed her. I've never felt about her like I do you. If I had known you were still alive…" He grabs my hand in his, pleading for me to listen to him. "I would *never* have agreed to it. I just wanted to take care of my family, can't you see that? I would take a lifetime of poverty and pain with you, than riches and prestige without you. I doubted your ability to work through the hard things, thinking if I told you I was engaged without a solution, you'd leave. But you weren't the weak one—I was. The fact is, you are so much stronger than I think. Than you think. You are single-handedly the strongest person I know. And I'm not saying that because I'm madly in love with you. Or because you're my friend. But because it's true."

He retrieves something tucked into his jacket and presents it to me. "Here...I want you to have this."

I take it slowly with a blink and pull open the scroll. A map. At a loss for words, I tuck it shakily into my satchel.

"And this." He pulls out another item and holds it out to me. A dark brown...journal.

My father's journal.

I dart my gaze up to him. "You kept it? All-all this time? Why?"

A sad smile blooms on his face. "Because I know how much it means to you. But I didn't want you to have to worry about the risk of me keeping it for you."

My voice cracks. "Cole—"

"Wait. One...last...thing. I promise," he whispers. He takes my hand and flips my palm open, places his mother's ring in the center, and closes my fingers around it.

His throat bobs as he twirls and tucks a stray hair behind my ear, dragging his finger underneath my jaw and locking my gaze with his own. "It doesn't matter what you think of me or how you feel about me now. Because for me, it's *always* been *you*. And it always will be you. I am fearfully yours, my love. Wonderfully in love with every piece of you, broken and whole. Regardless of whether you love me or not. Something might have changed in you, but you never changed in me."

My lips tremble at the delicacy of his words, my throat constricting. Tears blur my vision, and my heart swells and breaks all at once. Little does he know how much has changed in me. Part of me doesn't deserve his words—not when I fell so easily into someone else's bed and without giving him any chance to explain himself. Gods, the secrecy of what I've done alone is suffocating. I'm digging for the right words to say and for the right moment. The realization slams into me—this must've been what it felt like for him, keeping his betrothal to Celeste a secret.

"Cole, wait. There's something you should know—"

An alarm bell slices through the somber night from the outpost. Both of us whirl toward the sound. A glow of a torchlight leaks from the outpost, growing brighter by the second.

Someone cries out in the distance, "Captain! Somebody get the captain!"

Cole drags his gaze back to me, brushing a tear off my cheek.

He nods, a soft smile lifting his face. "Go."

THIRTY NINE

BLOOD OF POWER

But I don't go—I can't move. Cole disappears off into the outpost, and I watch him go with an overwhelming sense of longing crushing every breath from my lungs.

Gods damn it all. I can't help it—*I love him.* Even if I try not to. Even though it destroys every piece of me and would be so much easier if I could turn it off.

As I'm about to turn back toward the forest to meet Daeja, I catch a flicker of movement outside the northern part of the outpost. A group of three men march toward the camp, one of which pulls a woman by rope fastened around her wrists. She stumbles and lands face first onto the ground. Rather than waiting for her to get to her feet, her captor drags her along the ground.

One of the other men halts her captor and nudges the woman's side with a boot. "Get up!"

But she doesn't. She says something muffled by the distance between us, and the men flinch. The man demanding her to get up unclips a whip on his belt and rips it down her back.

I flinch.

Even from this distance, her cry echoes within my ears. The wicked snap of the whip draws me back to the night two prisoners were hanged from the outlook tower—their pleas a hushed whisper until it swells to a roar inside my head. The snapping of their necks resurface each time the man lashes her. Every sinister crack breaks something in me. Piece by piece. Every one of her agonizing cries ripples inside my head.

The third man of the group snatches her hair and rips her off the ground, pulling her to her feet. The four of them disappear off into camp.

Perhaps it's stupid—but I can't think past the opportunity to save her. Not when I failed to act all those weeks ago when two other prisoners were executed, and I stood idly by.

Before I can think better of it, I head back into camp as I slip Cole's mother's ring onto my finger and tuck the map and journal back into my satchel.

"Daeja, I have to do something first."

Everyone gathers in the middle of camp. Torchlight casts wicked shadows across the throng as I push through to get closer to the center. Everyone stills. The crowd falls silent as Darian pulls the battered woman, restrained by rope, into the center of the squad. The only sounds to cut through the silence are the flickering torches and heavy breathing from the woman. She rakes her gaze around the group, her lips pulled back in a feral snarl.

Horror settles in me at the rivers of crimson blood trickling down her face. I can't imagine what other wounds she has outside of the visible ones on her face. Considering I witnessed her whipping, the amount of pain lacing every inch of her skin must have been excruciating.

Darian scans the crowd. "We must send word to the King. We have captured a rebel!"

The squad erupts into triumphant cheers. We've never caught a live rebel before. They've either died in combat or killed themselves. No doubt to avoid the King's torture to glean critical information.

"Give her to me," Cole booms.

The squad falls silent again, all the attention turns toward Cole as he shoulders through the crowd.

Darian hesitates for a fleeting moment. "No. I'll be the one to deliver her to the King."

"I command you to," Cole rumbles, ripping the rope from Darian.

Darian snatches Cole's wrist, flicking a glance down at Cole's fist, then back up at him.

Cole's eyes darken as he growls, "Need I remind you of your place here?"

"As I've told you before, I don't take orders from lowly bastards," Darian spits.

Carlisle slinks through the crowd and stops beside me, his hand gripping the hilt of his sword. The movement draws Cole's attention in our direction. His anger falters when his eyes connect with mine.

Cole tears his wrist out of Darian's grasp and takes a step toward my direction, the rebel woman in tow. "Take her."

Carlisle strides forward to retrieve the rope as the woman flings like a caught fish, fighting with every step.

Cole shakes his head at Carlisle. "No. Kat, take her."

As our gaze locks in on each other, we have an unspoken understanding—I'll free the rebel woman. She'll lead the way to the Dragon Lands, eliminating any risks of rebels attacking Daeja and me.

"If we don't clean and stitch her up, she may either bleed out or die of infection," Cole explains aloud.

Darian's gaze travels over to me, his fisted hands relaxing. His attention darts back to the rebel woman, but he doesn't move when I take the rope from Cole.

Cole tosses a glare at Darian over his shoulder. "Darian, you and I will take a group to assess our perimeters to make sure there are no others lingering around. Archie, go with Kat and assist in any way you can. Carlisle, find Marge and station a few guards outside of the healer's quadrant."

We all break off into our assigned groups. Archie unsheathes a dagger as he approaches me, pointing it at the woman in warning. She stops thrashing against the rope momentarily but still digs her heels into the ground as I lead her back to the healer's quadrant. Once we get to there, I give Archie the rope. Squinting through the darkness, I dig through shelves with the bottles and vials, trying to figure out what to use when Marge walks into the room holding a candlestick.

"Sit!" Marge commands the woman.

The rebel glares at Marge and jolts for the door, taking Archie with her. Slingshotting forward, I dive for the rope and join Archie and the woman on the floor as she fights to escape. After a few scrambling moments on the floor, Archie regains his grip on the rope, tugging the woman until she slows.

Marge gathers materials while we wrestle with the rebel. She then crouches near the woman, her voice harsh. "Are you going to cooperate? Or are we going to have to just let you die?"

The woman peers up at Marge with a burning hatred.

Marge asks again, "Do you speak?"

Nothing.

Marge holds out a vial to her, and the woman's eyes dart to the scars lacing her hands. The woman smacks the vial out of Marge's grasp. The vial flies across the room and shatters on the ground. Archie and I both flinch.

"Spoiled!" the woman hisses and recoils.

"Listen, girl. You either let us help you, or you will bleed out by morning. What's it going to be?" Marge growls.

The woman glares at Marge, and Marge holds her gaze.

After an uncomfortable stretch of silence, Marge relents with a sigh and hobbles back to her bottles and vials, plucking a new one and handing it to me. "Maybe you'll have better luck. Rebels won't trust Spoileds."

The rebel woman watches Marge hand me the medicine, and her narrowed eyes widen, if only slightly. She stops fighting against her binds.

Marge exits the healer's quadrant, and a sadness sinks into my chest to think that it may be the last time I ever see her.

"What's a Spoiled?" Archie inquires.

I feign confusion and shrug. "Maybe she thinks this medicine is spoiled?"

We both turn our attention to the rebel. In the candlelight, a wildness shadows her eyes, her hair matted with blood. The flickering light catches a shimmer of an image engraved into her necklace. It's subtle, but I'd know it anywhere—the insignia of an A with a dragon perched on top of it.

"Archie," I murmur as I slowly grab the rope from him.

He watches me suspiciously. "What are you doing?"

"Do you trust me?"

"Of course I do."

"Then I need you to leave," I breathe.

"Are you out of your mind! I'm not leaving you alone with her!"

"Remember when I had to trust you not to kill me when you threw that dagger?"

He narrows his eyes, clearly not wanting to follow my lead.

I rest my hand over his, hooking his gaze with my own. "Now I need you to trust me. I need you to leave. You can stand guard at the door, but do not come in unless I call for you."

"I'm not leaving you."

"You're not leaving me." My voice wavers. Because little does he know, I'm leaving *him*. I shut down any lingering sadness with determination. "Stand outside the door, Archie. *Now.*"

The authority in my voice shakes him enough to release the rope to me.

He leaves reluctantly, pausing half-way out the door. "I'm right here if you need me, Kat! Right here. And don't get any ideas, lady! You so much as threaten her, and I'll knife you!"

Once the door shuts, I retrieve the dagger from my side. The rebel woman explodes into a hissing, flailing tornado.

"Shh, shh!" I try to whisper as I saw my blade through the rope. "Hold...still!"

The blade slices part of her skin with how much she wiggles. But the rope pops off her wrists, and she falls back from the newly found freedom.

Her mouth drops open before holding her trembling hands to her face, as if she doesn't quite believe what I've done. "Why... why did you do that?"

"Fire incarnate. Flame in flesh. Blood of power," I whisper, so softly I'm hoping she heard me.

She shakes her head, dropping her hands and looking at me. "Who the hell are you?"

"It doesn't matter." I grab a clean rag and inch forward to her. "Will you let me help you?"

Her gaze flicks back and forth between the materials in my hands and my face. "I don't really have a choice, do I?"

"You do have a choice."

"Then let me die. If the King gets his hands on me...my fate will be much crueler than bleeding out. Or suffering from infection."

"I know. And that's why I'm not going to let him. The King isn't going to get his hands on you."

She narrows her eyes at me. "What makes you say that? Why would you risk helping me?"

"Because I have a dragon."

She coughs at the information, and I use the moment to close the gap between us and offer her the rag. She hesitantly takes it and wipes the blood off her face before pressing it to the wound in her forehead.

I continue, "You would be the last of my worries. We can help each other get to the Dragon Lands." I hand her the vial Marge gave me earlier.

She takes it from me, eyeing the glass suspiciously. "Is this actually safe? How do I know to trust you?"

"You don't. Sometimes, you just have to take a chance."

She tilts the vial up and down, staring at the liquid for a long moment. With a shaky breath, she uncorks it, sniffs it, and throws the liquid back into her mouth. She swallows, and her body relaxes muscle by muscle.

"Thank you," she sighs, her eyes falling closed.

I work on cleaning and stitching the wound on her forehead. While I admit I'm not nearly as proficient as Marge is, I stitch her skin closed, at least. "Sorry, the scar might not be as pretty as if Marge were to—"

A thunderous roar sparks to life somewhere outside, and we both startle. An alarm rings out over the outpost in warning.

"They've come for me," the rebel woman whispers.

FORTY

REBELS

I don't have to ask her to know who.

Rebels.

"Then let's get you to them." I link my arm with hers and help lift her to her feet.

We burst out of the healer's quadrant into chaos. Archie is nowhere to be found, nor the soldiers who were assigned to stand guard outside of the healer's quadrant. Cries and screams mix with the roar of metal on metal. Flashes of silver glimmer in the night, soldiers dash by us as they race toward the thickening mob near the northern part of the outpost. My heart skips to a gallop, my skin unbearably hot as I scan the throng. All I can think about is the terrifying possibility of someone I know dying.

I lead the rebel woman toward the western part of camp

toward the wall, ducking under the cover of tents and tables as we make our way there.

"If you're near the outpost, Daeja, retreat closer to the lake. We are being attacked!"

"What! And where are you?"

"Making my way…" I glance at the rebel woman. Drops of blood trail in her wake with each limp. I pull her tighter into my side, trying to tug her into a faster pace. *"I'm moving a little slow—"*

"Doesn't surprise me. I'm coming to get you."

"No! Don't you dare—"

"I'm much faster than your two little legs," she snorts.

"Technically, right now, I have four."

"Huh?"

The woman stumbles forward, and I catch her before she can fall. Her breath is heavy, despite the noisy chaos swimming around us.

She glances over to me. "You have to let me go. Leave me. I'm slowing you down—"

"No. If I leave you, you'll die." I tug her again.

"Why do you feel the need to save me? You don't even know me."

"It doesn't matter—"

"Listen, you stubborn girl." She rips her arm out of mine. "We can't afford for you to die. Leave me. I'll tell the rest of them to fall back. You can meet us north near the river."

I scan the cloud of bodies surging in battle. My heart sinks as I pick out Cole's flame red hair against the darkness. He swings against another rebel armed with a club. Surveying the rest of the throng, I recognize Melaina struggling against two men.

We are *severely* outnumbered.

I nod, a shaky breath escaping my lips. Taking my dagger out of my thigh sheath, I place it into her hands. "Okay. Take this. Just in case."

She meets my panicked stare with a dip of her head and hobbles off, edging dangerously close to the thick of the battle.

A rapid thunder of footsteps tears my attention away from her. A man rushes from the shadows and charges me with a double-sided spear. He swings the spear, and I duck and slide, narrowly avoiding a slice to my leg. I've never practiced fighting outside of hand-to-hand combat, archery, and a sword. And I'm terrible at all of them. I'm not quite sure how to work with this.

Fuck.

He swings again, wicked fast, before I can unsheathe my sword. I fall back, barely in time to dodge his next attack. Catching myself on the ground with one hand behind me, my other is extended in front of me as if it'll stop him from delivering the killing blow.

An eclipsing shadow looms over from behind him followed by an earth quaking growl. Daeja's daggered teeth glint in the moonlight mere seconds before she snaps forward and snatches the man's shoulder into her mouth. She tears him back away from me, her cat-like eyes slanted in fierce determination. The screaming man writhes in her grasp and frantically stabs the tip of his spear into her outstretched wing. Daeja's roar rips out across the night.

She clamps down harder on him with a sickening crunch, and the man falls limp in her mouth like a doll. She flings him off into the night.

"Daeja!" I cry and jolt forward for her.

The spear pierces the thin webbing of her wing, ripping through the membrane and poking out the other side. I stop myself from removing it, knowing that doing so in a human could mean bleeding out. For dragons, I'm not sure.

"Can you move it?"

She glances at the spear, flexes her wing, and cringes with a high-pitched shriek.

I brush a tender stroke up and down the ridge of her nose to comfort her. The spears has to come out if we need to fly. Eyeing the dark sea of the battle, I guide her back toward the healer's quadrant. She tucks her wings into her side with a cry and squeezes her shoulders through the door frame. I hold out a hand to pause Daeja from entering further.

Marge freezes in her furious gathering of bottles tucked in the locked cabinet. She spins, positioning her staff in a defensive stance. When she realizes it's me, she relaxes. Slightly. Because her gaze shifts to Daeja behind me, her mouth drops open in a silent gasp.

Panic creeps into my voice. "Marge, please. I need your help—she's injured."

Marge abandons her stash of bottles, clears the space between us, and reaches a shaky hand out to touch the spear lodged in Daeja's wing. Daeja growls and snaps at the air near Marge's hand. In the same second, Marge swings her staff and smacks Daeja on the head.

I shift in front of Daeja, arms outstretched, and ready to block any further blows. "You will not do that again," I warn.

Daeja shakes behind me, clearing her head from the shock more than the actual blow. If anyone were to attack a dragon and not flinch, it would be Marge.

She stares past me at Daeja. "I need you to trust me, if I'm going to help you."

I glance back at Daeja, who stares back at Marge. Daeja's pupils flicker back and forth between slits and rounds, her upper lip twitching.

"Katerina, the green bottle over on the counter." Marge still won't take her eyes off Daeja.

Hesitantly, I slip past her, grab the bottle, and return.

"You'll need to pull that spear out quickly. It doesn't seem to be laced. As soon as you remove it, pour half the bottle on her wound," Marge coaches.

Taking a deep breath, I do as she instructs, ripping the spear out of Daeja's wing first. Daeja roars, her long tail sweeping across the room and smashing into the beds. I move quickly, pouring the green swirling liquid onto Daeja's wound as she hisses through gritted teeth.

I pull her head into my chest and scratch under her chin. *"All done…it's all done."*

Marge taps me with her staff. "You both need to get out of here before someone sees you. They'll kill you both."

I look away from Daeja and toward her. "Come with us."

She shakes her head. "No. It was foolish of me to ask you to take me there. You go."

"I'm not leaving you. Have you seen what's going on outside? You're in danger here."

Marge snorts, "I can defend myself."

"Hate to break it to you, Marge, but your razor-sharp tongue isn't going to save your ass from a rebel."

She slams her staff into the ground. With one hand, she clutches the staff's neck, and the other she twists the head, pulling the two pieces apart. The light shines on a metal blade as she unsheathes it.

My mouth falls open. "What the fuck—"

"Watch your mouth, woman." She glares, lowering the blade and pointing its sharp angled tip at me.

I clap my hand over my mouth. "You mean to tell me you've been hiding that this whole time?"

"I didn't know we were attune to sharing all of our secrets." She flicks a look at Daeja, then back at me.

"I thought you were crazy when you asked me to give you your staff when those rebels attacked last time."

She tilts her head to the side as she lowers the blade to her side. "Is this where you admit I have a lot more sense than you seem to think?"

"No."

"Well, you should." She sheathes the blade back into the staff.

"I thought you wanted to go to the Dragon Lands? This may be your only chance."

She considers me for a moment. "I'll just slow you down."

"No, you won't." I grab her and pull her out the door with me.

The sound of the battle roars back to life again as we leave the healer's quadrant behind. The three of us slink toward the trees. But Marge is right.

She isn't fast enough.

"I need you to get on her back," I whisper and pull Marge to Daeja.

Daeja narrows her eyes at the proposal. ***How about she gets on your back instead?***

"You might not like her or know her, but I do. And I need your help. Please."

Daeja blows out a breath and lowers her body to the ground. ***"Fine."***

"I can't," Marge says. It's the first time I've ever noticed a hint of fear in her voice.

"Yes, you can." I help Marge up over Daeja's neck, my weak arms straining under her weight as I lift her up and over. At least this way she will be safer off the ground and on a dragon. And faster.

We slip into the trees and edge closer north, my hand pressed against Daeja's shoulder, and my other wrapped around my sword's hilt. My attention is locked into the chaotic surge of the battle, each warring side advancing and retreating like an ominous tide. They are much farther north now, pushing back between the trees of the forest. The rebels have managed to cut the squad off from camp, forcing them back north step by step. Bodies are left slumped on the ground in the wake, a clear trail of how much land the rebels have gained on them.

A shine of red hair ripples in the sea of black before it disappears again, snatching my heart and holding it in a choke-hold. Cole's voice echoes in my mind as a soft trickle until the dam breaks, and I'm flooded with his rugged voice, drowning out everything else.

You are single-handedly the strongest person I know...

Wonderfully in love with every piece of you, broken and whole...

Because for me, it's always been you...

And it always will be you...

I am fearfully yours, my love...

I love you, Katerina Blackwind...

I freeze mid-step, locked in on the spot where Cole vanished into the throng. Waiting for him to get up, everything slows. Each second ticking by parallels my thundering pulse.

Promise you'll stay with me...

Promise you won't leave without me...

I drag my attention up to Daeja, and she turns her head to me, her white glowing eyes meeting mine. She blinks in under-standing. My gaze is drawn toward my hand resting on her shoulder. The cold, metal ring wrapped around my finger—Cole's mother's ring he gifted me, with the full intention of letting me go.

My own voice echoes in my ears, the words I uttered to Cole all those nights ago. *I promise.*

I explode into a run toward the battle.

I can't leave Cole. I can't leave any of them. Not Archie, not Melaina...not Darian.

Not like this.

"I just have to warn them," I murmur to Daeja as I race away. *"If the rebels push them any further north, they'll trap them at the river. And they'll all die."*

"Katerina!" Marge shouts after me.

"Tell her I'll be back," I murmur to Daeja.

Daeja snorts, ***"I'm not sure she'll understand me."***

"Just keep her with you, don't let her out of your sight."

"You're putting me on babysitting duty?"

"One of these days, I'll owe you a whole farm of chickens."

"Now you're talking."

My feet pound against the ground as I push my legs as fast as they'll go. Trees zip by me as I leap and stride over shadows, sticks, bushes, and rocks.

Cole's voice whispers back into every edge of my mind.

Single-handedly...

I run along the edge of the tree line until it thins out near a wicked dark river. Affording myself short glances toward the battle, I search for Cole's flash of red hair amongst the shadows.

...the strongest person...

Relief floods me when I finally spot Cole at the front of the squad. I cut into the battle, gunning straight for him. Sucking in a breath, I duck, spin, and slide out the way of stray swings and weapons as I dash for him.

...I know.

Cole swings in a series of attacks against a rebel, his red hair whipping with him in each strike. He knocks the rebel's weapon out of their hand before they turn tail and run.

"Cole!" I'm almost out of breath a few strides away from him. "They're going to trap you! You have to fall back!"

Cole turns to me, blood spattered on his face. I realize in horror I'm not sure if it's his or someone else's. His face is strained, broad chest heaving up and down in effort.

When he realizes I'm sprinting toward him, in a war he can't stop from raging around us, his relief to see me melts to fear. "What are you doing here? Get out of here, Kat!"

A rebel rushes in behind Cole with a raised axe. My heart drops as I realize I've distracted him, leaving him vulnerable. With a grunt, I slingshot forward, closing the gap between us and colliding into Cole's waist, tearing him down. The rebel's downward swing of his axe barely grazes my side, his blade slicing through my shirt and whispering an inch from my skin.

Cole and I crash into the ground, and the rebel rears back again for his next attack.

"Kat!" Cole cries. Tugging me into his chest, he spins over top of me, rolling the both of us out of the way as the rebel swings again. Cole pushes up to his forearms, bracing himself over me, his nose brushing mine and eyes swimming in my panicked gaze.

His attention darts away to the right where my sword is on the ground. He snatches it.

But he isn't quick enough.

Cole's body lurches forward, his forehead bumping against mine when the rebel's axe connects with his body. Every bit of air in his lungs saws out in a single breath. Gritting his teeth, he musters every ounce of his strength and slashes my sword out against the rebel's legs, severing them.

The rebel screams and collapses to the ground.

But it doesn't matter.

None of it matters.

My hand shakily grazes down Cole's side to confirm. An axe is lodged into his armor. When I pull my hand back to hold his face, to force him to look at me, I smear his cheek with fresh blood. My hand layered in thick crimson.

The gravity of the situation steals every pulse of my heart, every breath in my body.

He.

Can't.

Die.

"Cole. Cole! Look at me. Cole, look at me!" I cry.

He drags his warm honey eyes to mine, his head tipping up and down in a slow nod. A visible tremor shakes up and down his arms. "I'm okay," he wheezes.

Getting up off my back, I pull him into my arms, cradling him. With trembling hands, I gently assess where the axe is. The vile blade is jammed deep into his armor where his ribs are. My panic overflows when I realize how much blood there is. I can't even tell where it's all coming from. My hands soaked in the warmth of it.

Tears spill from my eyes, my voice a cracked whisper, "Remember that night you didn't want me to leave your room? How you made me promise not to leave you? I need you to promise me now, Cole. Promise me you won't leave."

He still struggles to pull in a breath, his eyes fluttering as he braces a hand on the axe's handle. But a smile cracks his lips, and he laughs.

Of all fucking things, he laughs. "You're not getting rid of me that easy, Kat."

"Just fucking promise me!"

He looks up at me and nods. "I promise."

His face contorts as he tries to remove the axe.

"Stop it!" I cry and snatch his wrist.

"This breastplate is from the King…" he wheezes. "It's stronger than normal armor."

My words tremble in hysteria. "Oh, fuck the King!"

But he rips the axe free from his armor and tosses it to the side, leaving a deep, angry gash tearing through the metal.

"You fucking idiot!" I rip my cloak off and shove as much of it as I can into his wound to slow the bleeding. Forcing all my strength through my compressions to slow the flow of blood, I beg every god and deity to save him. Willing him to live. My gaze catches on the two rings around my fingers. The dark ring tattooing my finger from when I met Daeja and the metal of Cole's mother's ring.

"I'm still here." Daeja's voice caresses my mind, calming my terror.

Cole finally catches his breath and starts to sit up. His hand grips my shoulder, forcing me to listen to him. "It's okay, it's okay, it's not my blood, Kat. I don't know whose it is, but it's not mine. I'm o-kay!"

The horror eases enough for me to survey around us at the chaos of the battle. As if in slow motion, I recognize everyone around me. Melaina. Gavin. Nolan. Archie. Darian.

Darian takes on three men, and at his back is Carlisle who fights two others. I stiffen as one of the rebels strikes Carlisle. In one moment, Carlisle's fighting back, and the other he slumps to the ground.

Dead.

Now there's five on Darian—and my heart stutters at the impending danger. Archie and Melaina roar to his defense, swinging swords and screaming.

I tear my gaze away to Cole and snatch his arm, demanding he listen to me. "You have to tell the squad to fall back. We are outnumbered, and they'll trap you against the river."

Cole hesitates.

"Trust me!" I scream over the fight.

Cole relents and yells out across the battle, "Fall back! Fall back! Fall back! "

Everyone pauses, confused, but then they turn and run north toward the river. I turn my attention toward Daeja, the pull of our bond directing my gaze toward her shadowy silhouette hidden near the tree line.

I spent so long terrified of flames and fallacies, but it transformed into something bigger in this moment—something deeper than any level of consciousness I could comprehend.

I am no longer afraid.

The only thing I am afraid of now, in this very moment, is the people I love dying. And not doing everything in my power to prevent it.

I tilt my head down, eyes connecting with Daeja despite the vast distance separating the two of us.

"Daeja, now!"

A thunderous roar rips out across the battlefield, and the night flares to life as a jet of fire bursts from Daeja's jaws. She shakes her head back and forth vigorously as she releases a torrent of flame, igniting everything it touches, and digging a hard line of dragonfire between us and the rebels. It's only mere seconds before the heat of the fire constricts the air around us.

I hold up a hand to temporarily block out the blinding light. When I dare a peek, a wall of flame separates us from the rebel silhouettes. The shadowy figures fade as the fire thickens and intensifies. My jaw slackens as I watch, my hand lowering from my face. Chants whisper in the back of my mind.

Fire incarnate.

Flame in flesh.

Blood of power.

The flames follow the direction of my hand—the more I

lower it, the more it bows to my will. I reach out, inching forward until I'm a hair's breadth away. The wicked red-orange flames slither and slide, calling to some innate part of me.

I raise my hand up.

The flames stretch and lick into the night sky above us, stretching like claws. Nothing but flame and power. It's terrifying, and in an odd way…*beautiful.*

The light in the shadows.

Cole tugs at my arm. "We have to go! Everyone across the river!"

The flames flare and spread, reminding me of the way water splits and rivers into pools, veins of power off the source, until a dam bursts.

I turn away from the fire, and together with Cole, I race for the river. Smoke fills my lungs and catapults me into a fit of coughs, and I stumble. My legs slow. My muscles scream, my head swimming and mouth drying. Cole helps steady me as I fumble through the river's cold water foaming around my legs.

My vision sways, my mind dizzying at an alarming speed.

"Daeja? Where's Marge?"

"She's safe."

I collapse into the river, but Cole catches me before I can dip completely underneath. An icy cold spreads over my body.

Something isn't right.

Cole lifts me out of the water and into his arms, clearing the last few feet of the water's edge. Once we get to the other side, my vision blacks out as another coughing attack steals my breath.

"Kat?" Cole lowers me to the ground, his face draining of color as he pulls his hand back from my side. It's soaked in blood.

My blood.

Whatever adrenaline was masking my pain vanishes in an instant, and a burst of agony ruptures in the side of my ribs.

Daeja's roar rings out around me before everything settles into a deafening silence.

The last thing I see is the reflection of the flames in Cole's eyes, and a star dusted sky over his head.

Such beautiful, beautiful stars.

FORTY ONE

YOUR SIDE

I swim back to my consciousness, breath by ragged breath. A cough rips me out of my sleep, and I sit up to cover my mouth, blood spattering my hand.

A woman hands me a glass of water. "Here, drink."

Wheezing, I take the glass and sip. My throat burns, as if I swallowed fire and it singed every nerve spanning my throat and mouth. As the fog of my sleep wears off, I realize the woman is the same rebel I set free. Except now, her skin is clear of blood and dirt. Her long black hair sweeps over the crusted gash I sewed up on her forehead.

Handing her back the glass, I scan the room around me. I'm in a bed, surrounded by rows of other empty beds.

But this isn't the healer's quadrant.

In fact, I don't recognize where I am. And I don't see anyone else in here other than the rebel woman.

My heart picks up its pace as I try to piece together where I am. And why I don't remember where I am. I fumble at my sides for a dagger, a sword, anything.

The words cascade out of my mouth. "Where am I? Why can't I remember? Who are you? Where are my friends? Where is my dragon? "

"You're okay. You're safe," the rebel woman whispers. She holds out a hand to calm me. "Your dragon is being tended to. I can take you to her, if you wish."

"Daeja?" I check.

A heavy sigh of relief blasts my mind. ***"You're okay! How are you feeling? You almost died—"***

"I...think I'm okay? Where are you?"

"Outside and safe, don't you worry about me. Let's focus on you."

I inch forward with a wince. *"I'm coming to see you."*

"The two leggers say you've been critically injured. Stay. I'm not leaving you. I'm just glad you're alive."

I turn my attention to the rebel woman. "And what of Cole? The captain with the red hair."

"He's talking with our leader, Sethan, who just came in from the north."

I breathe a sigh of relief. "Archie and Marge? The man with us when I cut you free, and the Spoiled?"

"They are both fine. He sustained minor cuts and bruises. But fine."

A smile warms my face, and I cover my mouth again as another cough sneaks up my throat. More blood specks my palm.

"You had a lot of smoke inhalation. Fire like that isn't good to breathe in. And you were wounded in battle…it's nothing short of a miracle you survived. You should rest," the woman says and tries to gently push me back down.

I brace against her touch, adamant I won't go back down. A deep ache sputters in my side at the flex, and glancing down, I find my torso is wrapped in thick bandages.

I glance back up at the woman. "Listen…"

"Tawny."

"Tawny," I mirror and hold out my hand. "Katerina."

But rather than shaking my hand, she takes it to reluctantly pull me to my feet and steadies me. She cups my elbows with her hands, allowing me to brace against her.

"Thanks," I whisper, grabbing her arms and grimacing at the way my muscles scream against the confines of my skin.

She dips her head in response.

My hands shake as I grip her biceps tighter, my body weak and threatening to collapse at any moment. "Why haven't you killed me yet? Am I a hostage? I thought rebels didn't take prisoners?"

"And aren't Arterians supposed to turn in captured rebels to their King?" Tawny counters.

I nod slowly, looking up at her. "Fair…point."

"You showed me mercy and tried to set me free, even if it risked your own life. That would have been considered high treason."

The thought of it makes me laugh. As if I didn't just spend the last several months smuggling a dragon hatchling across the realm. "And that's why you haven't killed me yet? Out of obligation?"

She chuckles, leading me to the door, linking her arm through mine to keep me upright. "I wouldn't try to kill a dragon rider. Besides…you're on our side now."

I blink into the blinding light as we walk out of the room. "Your side?"

Shielding my eyes from the bright sunlight until my eyes adjust, I lower my hand. Water babbles somewhere nearby. Rows of buildings sprawl out around us, and fluffy white clouds scatter on a picturesque blue sky overhead. There's something about the air here—it's cold and fresh. Jagged green pine trees line the distant horizon, but Dragon's Back Ridge is nowhere to be seen.

"Sethan will want to speak to you. They're in here," Tawny says.

We cut left down a cobblestone path to a building towering above the rest. She swings open the wooden door and ushers me in. Several groups of people line the walls, but in the center, Cole stands talking with a man who matches his height, their eyes locked while they talk.

The other man's short gray hair is stark against his tanned, chocolate skin. He has an elegance and grace to him, combined with a hidden lethality in the way he holds his posture. The leader— *Sethan*—has his arms crossed and jaw set, his shoulders pinned back. His eyebrows furrow at something Cole says.

Everyone in the room turns their attention to Tawny and I as the door closes.

Cole's expression deflates to a mix of relief and gratitude. Dark bruises mottle his face, and cuts slice his cheeks. Cole's fingers flicker nervously at the side of his leg before he curls them into fists to stop them. He clears the rest of the distance between us and embraces me.

"You're awake," he breathes as if it's something he held onto for so long.

"Is everyone okay? Did everyone make it?" I ask, my own voice is hoarse in my ears.

His face falls. "We…lost quite a few men and women."

My heart sinks, and I'm not sure I'm ready to hear who.

But I don't even get to ask because the door swings open again, followed by a horrified gasp. Melaina enters, a hand covering her gaping mouth.

"Father…?" her voice quivers, tears lining her dark brown eyes.

Sethan's hard features soften, a grin spreading across his face. "Hi, Melbell."

Melaina shoves past us and collides into Sethan, wrapping her arms around him tightly as she cries. Sethan rubs a scarred hand up and down her back.

I glance around. Clearly, Cole is as shocked as I am, judging by his expression.

"I thought you were dead? Wh-what are you doing here?" Melaina whimpers.

Sethan brushes a strand of black hair out of Melaina's face. "I could ask you the same thing, darling."

Cole clears his throat. "Listen. As I said, if you don't let us leave, they'll come looking for us. There's no way the King will let a full squad disappear in a night and not investigate it. And then they'll come here. They'll find you, and there will be a war."

Melaina backs away from her father, allowing him to respond.

"We can't risk them coming to the Dragon Lands," Tawny says to Sethan from beside me.

I swivel back and forth between Tawny and Cole.

The Dragon Lands.

We made it to the Dragon Lands? How long had I been out?

"Days," Daeja answers, overhearing my inner thoughts.

Sethan glowers at Cole. "I've already told you my proposal."

Cole stares back. "And I've told you, that's not negotiable. You know it as well as I do."

Sethan breaks his heated staring match with Cole and rakes his attention across the room to settle on me. "Then let her decide."

I flinch, then look over my shoulder to confirm no one else is behind me, before turning back to him. "Me? Why me? What is your proposal?"

Sethan flicks his gaze up to the corner of the room. "You may leave, but we keep him."

I turn to follow his stare, and the men and women crowding the corner scatter. My breath catches. Held between four rebels, his mouth gagged, and rope binding his feet and arms is Darian.

Blood soaks his hair and drips down, spattering onto the ground. Lacerations mar his olive skin. Dark, hollows blanket his eyes, and one of his swollen cheeks is bruised purple. When our eyes meet, I blink back in surprise. He looks…different.

Defeated.

Tired.

Worn.

He's a shell of the raging amusement, anger, and mischief I have come to know. Horror washes over me at the thought that perhaps his injuries weren't all inflicted by just the battle at the outpost.

If I had been out for days...

What the hell would rebels want with Darian?

"Why do you have him bound? Let him free!" I demand, whipping a heated scowl at Sethan.

Sethan scoffs, crossing his arms back over his chest. "We won't be letting the prince of Arterias free without negotiations."

My heart skips, the blood draining from my cheeks. I shake my head as if it'll clear the words, and I'll actually hear what he said. But the words sink, and I turn back to Darian, scanning his face.

"*What?*" I whisper. Unsure if anyone will answer me and make sense of it all.

But Darian's eyes narrow, tilting his chin up, the corner of his mouth perks up in a sly smile.

AFTERWORD

I sincerely appreciate reviews!
Feel free to tag me in any reviews/posts that are 4 or 5 stars.
My DMs are always open, if you have any questions or simply
want to share if you enjoyed it! I personally respond to each one.
:)

You can use the hashtag #offlamesandfallacies for any social
media reviews. OFAF is also on goodreads, storygraph, and
romance.io.

Please make sure to visit my website at **courtneywhims.com** and
sign up for my newsletter to get updates surrounding the release
of book two, giveaways, beta and ARC signups, as well as bonus
chapters! You can also follow me on Instagram or TikTok, my
handle is **@courtneywhims**

Thank you for reading and
giving my debut novel a chance!

COURTNEY WHIMS

Courtney Whims is a self-published independent author. *Of Flames and Fallacies* is her debut novel, and the first in the Arterian series. Courtney has hand-drawn and designed all of the artwork you see in this book; from the cover, chapter headers, interior design, and map. She lives in Los Angeles, California with her husband, toddler, black lab (who inspired Daeja), and cat.

For updates on book two, news, bonus content, and events, sign up for her newsletter here:
courtneywhims.com

ACKNOWLEDGMENTS

ONE FAILS, ALL FAIL.

Or in this case, if one succeeds, all succeed.
When I started brainstorming titles for this
book, I looked up acronyms to make sure I
wasn't choosing something inappropriate. Then
I stumbled upon this saying and it really made
me think. It took so many people to get this
book produced to what you are reading today.

First and foremost, thank you to you. The reader. Without you…
well…guess I would have been writing to myself. My biggest wish
for this book is that something resonates with you.

It took 35 days to write the first draft of this book between my
days (and nights) with a one year old, who has given me so much
perspective on life. I dedicate this to her, and to my supportive
and encouraging husband. Adam, you've given me the time to
write this story, even when it's hard to find, and inspired me to
write. TIMFPTB! I am endlessly thankful for you! ♥

A special shout out to Réka for being my PA. You've been so
supportive since day one and I'll always cherish you! Thank you
to all of my incredible beta readers: Georgia, Kaitlyn, Alyssa,
Maggie, Rini, Alex, Holly, Jocelyn, and Réka. Thank you to my
editors Kay and Sarah for taking OFAF to the next level! Thank
you Brit over at the Author Experience, you were absolutely
phenomenal in polishing this in the TWO WEEKS before
Christmas! To my ARC readers, your encouraging words have
meant so much to me. There were many times I struggled with
whether or not I was making the right decision in releasing this
book. Thank you for taking a chance on my debut!

I'm especially grateful for all of my lovely family and friends
for cheering me on, even when I wrestled with self-doubt and
imposter syndrome. My street team who has been so lovely in
rallying behind launching my debut. And those that have been
with me from the start: Alyssa, Alex, Jocelyn, Réka, Kate, Ashley,
Brittany, Sarah, Katie, Brianna, Rose, and Rikka.

Shout out to A.N. Caudle, Cortney L. Winn, Rachel Schneider, and M.A. Frick who have become my author friends. Thank you for always answering my many debut indie author questions and always encouraging me.

Queen Rebecca Yarros, not sure if you'll ever read this, but I also have to shout you out. You flew so I could walk. Had I not read Fourth Wing and Iron Flame, I likely would have never written this series.

Lastly, thank you to God–I am nothing without you.